DONALD E. WESTLAKE
HUMANS

THE MYSTERIOUS PRESS
New York • Tokyo • Sweden
Published by Warner Books

 A Time Warner Company

MYSTERIOUS PRESS EDITION

Copyright © 1992 by Donald E. Westlake
All rights reserved.

Cover design by Jackie Merri Meyer
Cover illustration by Wilson McLean

The Mysterious Press name and logo are trademarks of
Warner Books, Inc.

Mysterious Press Books are published by
Warner Books, Inc.
1271 Avenue of the Americas
New York, NY 10020

A Time Warner Company

Printed in the United States of America

Originally published in hardcover by The Mysterious Press.
First Printed in Paperback: April, 1993
10 9 8 7 6 5 4 3 2 1

PRAISE FOR
HUMANS
and
Donald E. Westlake

*   *   *   *

"*Humans* is funny but humane. It's tough-minded and takes risks. It makes you laugh and makes you think. This is satire at its best."

—*Chicago Tribune*

"A cosmic thriller!... Blends theology, current events and witty twists of tried-and-true narrative techniques.... Westlake has written a different and enjoyable work, less serious than *Paradise Lost* and with a more entertaining story line than *Pilgrim's Progress*. And there's the added benefit of Westlake's street smarts and his familiarity with places a lot lower than heaven."

—*Los Angeles Times Book Review*

"Frightening... funny... unpreachy.... the first book since Leigh Kennedy's *Saint Hiroshima* to show us the deep emotional effects of the Nuclear Age.... The book has great strengths."

—*Washington Post Book World*

"Now we begin to see Westlake assert his mastery of a multicharacter plot.... Westlake keeps it together with a wry comic twist here, a surprise there, some plain old, good writing in between."

—*Associated Press*

more...

By Donald E. Westlake

NOVELS

Humans • Sacred Monster • A Likely Story
Kahawa • Brothers Keepers • I Gave at the Office
Adios, Scheherazade • Up Your Banners

COMIC CRIME NOVELS

Trust Me on This • High Adventure
Castle in the Air • Enough • Dancing Aztecs
Two Much • *Help* I Am Being Held Prisoner
Cops and Robbers • Somebody Owes Me Money
Who Stole Sassi Manoon? • God Save the Mark
The Spy in the Ointment • The Busy Body
The Fugitive Pigeon

THE DORTMUNDER SERIES

Don't Ask • Drowned Hopes • Good Behavior
Why Me • Nobody's Perfect
Jimmy the Kid • Bank Shot • The Hot Rock

CRIME NOVELS

Pity Him Afterwards • Killy • 361
Killing Time • The Mercenaries

JUVENILE

Philip

WESTERN

Gangway (with Brian Garfield)

REPORTAGE

Under an English Heaven

SHORT STORIES

Tomorrow's Crimes • Levine
The Curious Facts Preceeding My Execution and Other Fictions

ANTHOLOGY

Once Against the Law (edited by William Tenn)

PROTEST

The science in this novel is as accurate as I can make
   it.
The theology in this novel is as biblically correct
   as I can make it.
As for the rest, it is a novel. All the humans in it
   are of my invention.
The angel...well...I believe I made him up.

DEDICATION

One day in 1986, in Taormina, Sicily, Evan Hunter told me I should think about doing a book in some way different from what I'd done before; larger in scope, perhaps, or new in approach, or unexpected in thematic material. If Evan hadn't put that bee in my bonnet, this book would not exist.

On a later day, in 1990, in New York City, I found that my voyage into this unknown had led to an apparent impasse; I could not for the life of me figure out how to go on. Several desperate phone calls later I met, via fax, a gentleman, scholar, physicist, and science-fiction writer in California named Robert Forward. We communicated over several days in a flurry of faxes, before he finally transmitted, "By George! I do believe he's *got* it!" Without him, this book would never have been finished.

On every day, in every way, everywhere, my wife, Abby Adams, makes it possible and keeps me from carelessness and error. Without her, this book would not be coherent.

Evan, Bob, Abby: it's *your* fault.

And the Lord said, I will destroy man, whom I have created, from the face of the earth; both man, and beast, and the creeping thing, and the fowls of the air; for it repenteth me that I have made them.

GENESIS 6:7

THESIS

Ananayel

I am, or was, or perhaps still am, an angel. God knows.

I am certainly very different from what I once was. And yet I am, I think, still me. On the other hand, my life is no longer angelic, that's true enough.

What was I before, when I was all and simply angel? How to describe that existence? It was, I think, like that fleeting part of your human condition when, waking earlier than necessary in the morning, you feel a long flow of weightlessness and selflessness, your bed has become a great soft balloon with you a part of it, and you float through the middle of the air in a vast shadowy domed auditorium. That feeling holds you for a few seconds only, and then all the weight of time and personality returns, you cease to be merely a floating fragment of thinking matter, you become yourself again, and your day begins.

For *my* kind, the kind I once was, that suspended oneness in the middle of the vasty space is the natural condition. Until, at great intervals, *He* calls. He has a task.

And so He called me: "Ananayel."

I must go back to who and what I was at that instant, at the very start. I must track the change that took place in me as I set about performing the task He had given me. In that first instant, I was only what I always had been: a faithful servant.

* * *

And so He called me. "Ananayel." And I roused myself, coiling like smoke as it passes through an open window, recalling myself to myself, flowing together into selfness and awareness and the fact of Ananayel, who answered, "I am here, Lord."

And so was He, of course. He is omnipresent, among His qualities. But He was not *there*, if you understand me. I did not face Him directly. To do so, I understand, is to be seared into oblivion and a whole new beginning. The truth of His beauty and power is more than a mortal can stand to gaze full upon, and angels too are mortal, thought not at all as ephemeral as men.

We are all of us parts of God, parts of His dream, His desire, but none of us know any more than our own role in His plan; if indeed He has a plan, and is not merely moved this way and that by cosmic Whim, as sometimes seems the case. And so I, a tendril in God's imaginings, had to be informed by another entity, as insubstantial as myself, just what my task was to be.

"A messenger."

Ah. I had never been a messenger, a bringer of annunciations, the word from The Word Itself. It was said to be an exciting and even joyous experience, that one, for all concerned. It was said the look in the eyes of a human who knows himself—or herself, yes, yes, I know—to be in the presence of an angel is a look to be treasured always. (How they love us, as naturally and instinctively as they love their own newborn.) And now I was to be among the blessed few Blessed who would have received that look.

"And an affector."

Rarer still! An angel who alters the human story, the progression of human events! An angel who crumbles a fortification, diverts a river, lights a torch to safety or defeat! To *take part*! (That is the one great thing we angels miss, when we are roused to awareness. We have no history of our own, no desires, no triumphs. No disasters either, of course, which is the trade-off. But even a weeping human, gnashing its teeth, can sometimes seem more real than we.)

"What do you know of America?"

Nothing. Never heard of it.

I was shown the land of the Iroquois, who would let the river carry them down to where the water turned to salt, just before the mighty sea, where their nets could bring in fish that never ventured upstream.

"It's been a while since you looked."

I have been elsewhere, and nowhere, floating at times among other stars. Because He has, you know, other ant farms than this, other dollhouses than Earth, other pets than these. So now I look, and much has changed where that river meets the sea. The Indians and their canoes are gone. A mighty city sprawls around the harbor, noxious and colorful, teeming and keening. It must be twenty times the size of Rome!

"One hundred times, if you mean the Rome of the Republic. They have been fruitful. They have multiplied. There are now five billion of the damn things."

All in that city?

"Not quite. But that is where you are to begin."

What do they call it?

"New York."

What was Old York?

"Irrelevant. It is in New York that you will begin to announce, and to affect."

Pleasure and anticipation fill me and I drift higher, expanding. What am I to do? What is the current state of God's plan?

"He's tired of them. They're too many, too grubby, too willful. They are too prone to error by half."

And my Task?
"To announce, and to effect, the end of their World."

1

Susan Carrigan floated in the great soft cloud of bed, not asleep and not awake, not thinking, only feeling. She hung in the suspended moment, aware and not aware, and then the radio beside her bed *exploded* into noise: "I can't *get* no—no no no!"

"Shit," she muttered, suddenly assaulted by sensation. Her mouth tasted like green mold. Her ears hurt. Her back hurt. Her bladder hurt. Her right hand, too long beneath the pillow beneath her head, had fallen asleep and now was tingling and smarting its way back into existence.

And *Barry's* gone!

She rolled over onto her back, glaring leftward at the other pillow, undented and white. The son of a bitch, the son of a bitch, the prick with ears. Gone.

Not that she wanted him back. Let him marry his fucking CD player, he had all the maturity of a retarded chimpanzee, she was better off without him. It was just that, every morning, it came as a surprise all over again that he was really gone. They'd been together almost eight months, after all, and apart now only six days. Seven days? No, six.

The radio kept on complaining: "Oh, I'm *talk*in with some girl—"

"And fuck you, too," she said, rising up, slapping her hand onto the button, cutting it off in mid-squawk. The movement agitated her bladder. She was awake. Hello, Tuesday, I must be Susan. And this 14 by 23-foot space (plus kitchenette and john), with windows viewing ailanthus trees and the dark brick backs of buildings on West 19th Street, must be all mine.

Did it seem larger since Barry'd gone? There was a hole now in the industrial shelving where all his vast holdings in Darth Vader stereo equipment had once stood, and some welcome space in the closets and the medicine cabinet, but not a lot. Your footprints don't go very deep, pal, Susan thought, angrily pleased at the idea of his insubstantiality, and she got out of bed, a lithe naked girl of twenty-seven who had started worrying recently—unnecessarily—about whether or not her breasts had begun to sag. Her hair, medium long and set for ease of maintenance as much as for good looks, was the precise shade of Clairol blond to complement her not-too-pale skin tones and not-too-dark bluc-gray cycs. Shc was lucky in hcr nose, and she knew it; it was precisely the nose that girls had in mind when they made the appointment with the plastic surgeon, but never seemed to get, and Susan had been born with it. Otherwise, she found her mouth a problem—a tiny bit too sluttish? or not sluttish enough?—her elbows a problem—ugly!—and her weight a chronic threat.

Seated on the toilet, she remembered again her childhood fear that something would come out of the bowl beneath her, something horrible with claws, and perform unspeakable acts before she could escape. She hadn't thought of that terror since she was maybe eight; was it really some psychological horscshit rising up against her, out of the bowl, as a result of Barry's departure, leaving her nethers alone and unprotected? "Gimme a break," she told herself, but when had that ever happened? Minds go their own way, regardless.

Showering, she thought about AIDS. She had a remote cousin in AIDS research at NYU Medical Center—Chuck Woodbury, his name was—and to listen to his party chitchat at family reunions for fifteen minutes was enough to turn you off humans forever. And that's the problem. A few

years ago, a Barry comes, a Barry goes, and good riddance.
But not today.

No, not today. All of a sudden, you go to bed with a guy,
you're going to bed with everybody he went to bed with the
last five years, and everybody *they* went to bed with, and
there's this massive cat's cradle out there, this Möbius strip
of a daisy chain, and unless you've fallen in with a horny
group of Baptist picnicgoers the odds are getting better
every day that somewhere in that humid grid there's the
ding, and all the lines turn red. Wanna climb aboard,
honey? No, thanks, I'll wait for the next virgin. If there's
any more on this route.

Putting on her Reeboks—her grown-up shoes were in her
bottom drawer in the bank—she suddenly realized this was
the fourth consecutive day she'd forgotten to jog before her
shower. All those years of conditioning, going down the
tube. Because of Barry? Ridiculous. And if true, even more
ridiculous. I'll leave myself a note, she thought, so I won't
forget tomorrow. Scotch-tape it to the hot water faucet in the
shower.

At least she was still walking. Downstairs, she strode
west across 19th Street to Seventh Avenue and then headed
uptown, the city screaming and shrieking all around her in
its usual fashion. Joggers thudded by, to remind her of her
dereliction. Macho meatheads driving down the avenue gave
that double honk as they went by, that whadayasayhoney
honk that didn't mean a thing but bravado, because even
they weren't so dumb as to think girls who looked like her
hung out with guys who drove trucks. It was May and cool
but clear, with an undercoating of white in the high blue
sky. Susan moved uptown at a steady pace, hardly thinking
about Barry at all.

The coffee shop where she usually stopped on the way to
work was at the corner of 38th Street. She almost passed it
by this morning, to punish herself for not jogging, but
decided that would be stupid. She'd just be cross and nasty
in the bank if she didn't have her regular coffee and orange

juice and English muffin. So she went in and sat at the counter, and the waitress said, "Hi, hon." She was a stout black woman who looked as though she ought to be motherly but was not. *Hi, hon* was as far as it went. Three years Susan had been having breakfast here, midway between home and the job at the bank on West 57th Street, and she still didn't know the waitress's name. Nor did the waitress show any interest in *her* name.

"My aching *feet!*" said a raggedy old bag lady, huge and shapeless, gray-skinned and gray-haired, as she settled onto the stool immediately to Susan's right, though two-thirds of the stools in the place were empty. Not a *penny* from me, Susan said fiercely in her mind, and concentrated on the waitress, coming this way with her coffee. The orange juice would be next, and the English muffin last. The waitress plunked down the cup, turned away, and the bag lady said, "Marie, I'd just like a nice glass of tomato juice."

The waitress turned back to glare, as though she didn't like being called by name—so it's Marie, is it?—but then she walked off without speaking, and when she brought both juices and slapped them down, the bag lady pushed dirty-looking coins across the counter, saying, "And fifteen cents for you."

"I don't think I know you, hon," the waitress said, with that suspicious glare.

The bag lady had a huge and sunny smile, beaming and happy. "Oh, I'm nobody," she said.

The waitress, frown welded into place, scooped the change off the counter and went away again. If this woman speaks to me, Susan told herself, I'll pretend not to hear. But the bag lady drew a magazine—*Esquire,* of all things—out of some deep recess within her clothing, opened it, and began happily to read while downing tiny sips of tomato juice.

It wasn't till Susan's English muffin had arrived and been half consumed that she became aware of the bag lady studying her profile. Susan gave her a quick glance—that smile seemed sad now, for some reason—then hurriedly looked away to concentrate on the muffin, but it was too late. "A pretty girl like you," the bag lady said softly. "You shouldn't be unhappy."

Surprised, Susan looked full at the woman, and this time saw nothing in her face but pity and good intentions. "What do you mean?" she demanded, knowing she didn't sound as tough as she wanted. "I'm not unhappy."

"It's some fellow, I bet," the bag lady said, nodding slowly, heavily. "It's always some fellow."

Susan gave her a cold and distancing smile, refusing to be drawn any further into conversation, and turned back to her muffin. If she speaks to me again, I'll move to another stool.

A ripping sound startled her, and she turned to see that the bag lady had torn a page from her magazine and was now smoothing it onto the counter between them. "If I was your age," she said, "and I was unhappy over some fellow, here's what I'd do."

Susan couldn't help looking at the torn-out sheet, and when she saw it was a full-page ad for vodka she couldn't help laughing. "I guess that is one answer," she said.

"No, no, the *contest*," the bag lady told her, tapping the ad with a dirty fingernail and a fat grubby finger. "I'd get away, I would, and that's just the way to do it."

How did I get stuck with this? Susan asked herself, but there didn't seem to be any way not to look more closely at the advertisement, and to see that it was indeed an announcement of some sort of essay contest, in which the first prize was an all-expense trip to Moscow.

Moscow! *Russia?* What kind of prize was that? Millions of people trying to get *out* of Russia, this vodka company's giving away a free trip *in*. "Oh, I don't think," Susan started, smiling with a more gentle dismissal this time, "I don't think that's the—"

"You just do it," the bag lady said. "You'll see I'm right. You've got plenty of time at work, you can do it there, easy as pie. And off you go, it's a whole new world, a whole new experience.''

"I don't win contests, I've never won anything in my—"

"I'll bet you could win *this* one," the bag lady said. "Change your life, it would." Finishing her tomato juice in one final noisy gulp, she struggled off the stool and gave Susan her sunniest smile, saying, "It's just perfect, a pretty girl like you." She pushed the sheet from the magazine closer to Susan. "See if I'm not right."

"But—why do you want to give this to *me*?"

The bag lady smiled and nodded. She patted Susan on the shoulder, her touch surprisingly light and comforting. "Just think of me as your guardian angel," she said, and went off, swaying from side to side like a tugboat in a heavy sea.

"Weird," Susan said to the waitress, who had come immediately to remove the empty tomato juice glass. She wished she could call her Marie, but knew she couldn't.

"Mm," said the waitress, and touched the page torn from the magazine. "This hers?"

"No, no," Susan told her, not sure why. "It's mine."

The waitress shrugged and went away. Susan, lifting her coffee cup, studied the rules of the contest.

It didn't look that hard, really.

Ananayel

Well. I have to be more careful, I see, in choosing who to become when I walk upon the Earth. What a sad sack of guts I was in that café! My feet truly did hurt; in fact, I was aches and itches all over. It was only knowing I'd be out of that carcass soon that made it possible to go on. Their lives may be brief, humans, but they can certainly *seem* long.

I selected that option because I wanted to appear as the person Susan Carrigan would think of as least threatening; so no man was possible, of course. The traditional golden-haired white-gowned barefoot youth would lack conviction, somehow, in that neighborhood. A child would not have threatened, but equally would not have been persuasive about the contest in the magazine. A young and attractive woman—without all those twinges and pangs—would have been held at a wary distance, as in some way a competitor. So I chose my category from among the types available in Susan Carrigan's environment, with pains and stings intact.

We angels make the form we want, you know, from the atoms of our own free-flowing selves; we do not, except under the most dire circumstances, commandeer the body of a living creature. Thus, from my own protoplasm, I have been a shepherd keeping watch over my flock by night; I have been a centurion bidding one to go and another to stay; I have been a leaping hart glimpsed briefly through the pines and followed to salvation. Once I was a butterfly, and became so lost in its infinitesimally tiny brain that I nearly forgot my own true self, and almost remained in there, a butterfly for the rest of its short life. (Now, *there's* brevity!) Would I have died, then, when the butterfly did? I have no idea, and the question is of some moment to me, now that everything has changed.

Because, you know, He does not come after us. Like spies in novels of intrigue, once we are on the mission we are on our own. And the greatest danger we face—it's the greatest danger humans face, too, but they don't realize it—is our own free will.

Here is a paradox that surpasseth all understanding. God is omnipotent, among His qualities. And yet, angels and men have free will, can choose their own destinies, can opt to disobey even His desires. (As Lucifer did, notoriously.) Thus it is that God has always *nudged* men, has engaged in confidence tricks and little scams, has played at times with a stacked deck, has thrown up illusions and toyed with mirrors, all to get humankind to *want* to do what God has in mind. And now that what he has in mind to do is end this world, the same methods come into play. I have been sent, therefore, to arrange things, to set the stage, to coach the unwitting actors in their parts.

To *end* this world. For men to do it themselves, to release that final fire, envelop the globe in such a volume of ravening searching flame as to leave nothing with life in it anywhere on the cinder that remains; not a weed, not a bug, not a drop of water in which impurities could form and flow and start it all again. Nothing left but a lifeless ball, tumbling around and around the sun. And man to do it himself, of his own free will. And a little help from me.

2

The explosion was a small one, confined to one room in the laboratory wing, with very little damage, all in all: two metal tables bent out of shape, a couple of hopelessly charred wooden chairs, some minor flasks and cruets destroyed, three windows to replace, walls and ceiling to repaint, that's about all. Minor, really, very minor.

But that wasn't the point, dammit. Carson damn well knew what the point was, because he damn well knew what Philpott was up to in there, and the *point* was, Philpott might have blown up the whole damn university. Including its president, himself, Hodding Cabell Carson IV, who would *not* appreciate being snuffed out of existence at the peak of his career by some tenured maniac who, not content to be famously an explorer at the very outermost frontiers of scientific knowledge, actually has to go on and on doing experiments! And blowing things up along the way.

Carson let off steam over lunch in his private dining room with his provost, Wilcox Breckenridge Harrison: "The man could have blown us *all* up! So far, he's merely done for some two-hundred-year-old foliage, but is that a portent or not?" And he waved his chilled salad fork at the large windows beside them, through which the older and more stately parts of Grayling University could be seen, heavily overgrown with ivy. A prestigious private university, Grayling, tucked away here in the rolling hills of upstate New York, with a prestigious president and the most prestigious of modern physicists on the faculty, Dr. Marlon Philpott, who was a menace to everything civilization holds dear.

Harrison said, "What is it that blew up, anyway?"

"God knows." Carson chomped on a lot of iceberg lettuce covered with bottled diet Italian creamy salad dressing. "The worst of it is, if you *ask* Philpott what in Christ's holy name he's doing over there, he'll *tell* you, at length, and not one word in ten makes the slightest bit of sense. I take it, though, it was not his famous strange matter that blew, but something more mundane."

"Strange matter?" Harrison grinned, tentatively. "You're putting me on."

"No, by God, I'm not." Carson wiped his lips on linen, dropped the napkin back on his lap, sipped a bit of the San Gimignano, and said, "It all makes sense, in its way, if only he weren't so intent on *proceeding* with it. The fact is, he's right, we do need new energy sources. The oil's running out, we have thirty or forty years of it left. The public, given increasing familiarity with nuclear power, has grown *less* accepting of it, rather than more. Solar power is a joke. So is wind, so is water, so is coal. What's needed is something brand-new, and our friend and nemesis, Dr. Marlon Philpott, is hot on the trail of one of the possibilities."

"Strange matter," suggested Harrison.

"Don't ask me what it is. I asked *him* once, and all he did was say quark-quark-quark. You know these scientists."

"I'm afraid I do."

"In   any   event,"amy   salad   dressing.   "The worst of it is, if you *ask* Philpott what in Christ's holy name he's doing over there, hen pursuit of. Strange matter. If he can isolate it, it could apparently provide us with energy beyond our wildest dreams."

"So the occasional explosion—"

"*Don't* say that," Carson warned. "That's what *he* says. I talk to him about this destructive tendency of his, and the man is *blithe*. God, I hate him! Blithe!"

Harrison dared to laugh. "He isn't that bad, Chip. And he does bring a certain renown to the university."

"The university," Carson said coldly, "had a certain renown before Dr. Marlon Philpott first set fire to his kindergarten desk."

"Well," Harrison said, "maybe he'll be more careful from now on."

"Not a chance." Carson seemed to have finished his glass of San Gimignano. He touched its rim with a fingertip and the waiter came forward to do the refill as Carson said, "*And,* this afternoon, I have yet another appointment with yet another insurance agent, resulting from this little peccadillo of our Dr. Philpott's. A person named Steinberg." Carson raised a we're-in-this-together eyebrow, then raised his glass. "You can imagine how I'm looking forward to *that*."

• • •

Michael Steinberg was everything Carson had expected— Semitic as a rug merchant—except that he was unexpectedly sympathetic and understanding. "These kinds of industrial accidents," he said, clucking like a hen over his forms as he sat hunched in the usually comfortable armchair facing Carson's large empty desk, "you don't expect in a nice quiet atmosphere of learning like what you got here. Grayling University, to have explosions."

Exactly. An understanding response at last; but from what

a quarter. Though warmed by the man's comprehension, Carson knew not to wash the university's dirty linen in public: "Dr. Philpott is a distinguished member of the faculty. His researches may be a little..." he permitted himself a dry chuckle here "... hair-raising at times, it's true, but they are necessary."

"But are they necessary *here*?" asked the insurance man, tapping his pen in irritating fashion against his packet of forms.

That faint feeling of fellowship sputtered in Carson's breast, and died. "What do you mean? Of course they're necessary here. Here is where Dr. Philpott is a tenured full professor."

"Forgive me, Dr. Carson," the man said, ducking his head, blinking behind his black-rimmed spectacles. "This is not the company speaking, you understand, this is only a thought I myself had, at this moment, that could perhaps be of use."

"I'm afraid I don't follow."

"Dr. Philpott is a tenured professor at Grayling University," Steinberg said, and shrugged. "But does his laboratory have to be physically present at the university? Aren't there places better suited to such things?"

Carson had no idea what the man was talking about. "Like what?"

"Oh, I don't know, an army camp, something like that." He gestured with his pen toward the window. "There must be some sort of government facility not far from here. You must have friends in Washington."

"Several," Carson agreed stiffly. One did not mention one's influence aloud, and certainly not to Semitic strangers from insurance companies.

"When Dr. Philpott is being a professor," Steinberg went on, "he is here, on campus, this beautiful campus. When he is being a researcher, he is somewhere else. Twenty miles? Thirty miles away? Some government installation where they know how to deal with explosions."

All at once, what the man was saying made sense. Carson actually smiled upon him. "Mr. Steinberg," he said, "you just may have something there."

Steinberg shrugged. He ducked his head. He smiled his crooked little smile. He said, "And along the way, it could be, I save the company a few dollars."

Ananayel

Of course, the basis for anti-Semitism is the fear that Jews are clever without restraint. That is, since they are separate from "us"—"we" already consider them separate, so they are—they need have no compunctions in their dealings with "us," and they are clever. Their cleverness makes them useful—as lawyers, doctors, accountants, and so on—but their lack of compunction makes them dangerous. What they *might* do transmogrifies at once into what they surely *are doing*, too cleverly for "us" to catch them at it. They are clever, and they have no reason to show "us" mercy; how hateful.

Hodding Cabell Carson has no peers. He accepts orders from above, he delivers orders below. Who could slip the suggestion into his mind, the suggestion I needed placed there? No one in his normal circumference.

It had to be an outsider. It also had to be someone he would see as clever. And it would be best if the person were seen to be making the suggestion altruistically on the surface, but actually for his own advantage.

Humans are quite simple, really. And on to Moscow.

3

Grigor awoke. He almost never needed the alarm these days, though he still routinely set it every night before taking the midnight pill. But he woke these mornings five or seven or nine minutes ahead of the alarm, and lay unmoving in the black darkness while his mind roved. For some reason, he did his best thinking in these brief moments in the dark, just before the four A.M. pill; by the time the alarm sounded, more often than not, he had at least one new joke to write on the notepad beside his bed.

*A new five-year plan has been announced. Its goal
is to tell the truth about all the other five-year plans.*

Yes? No? It was so hard to tell, really. Comedy now seemed not so much about humor as about defining the limits in a world where the limits shifted daily; a situation which was already comic, or at least absurd. The purpose of a joke these days was not to make people laugh at the comedy of it but at the daring of it, at how close the joke teller has come to the very edge of the permitted, in a time when nobody *knows* what's permitted. Everything? Hardly.

The alarm buzzed, a discreet low noise, penetrating within this room but not strong enough to disturb any other resident of the complex. Grigor sat up, switched on his bedside light, put the notepad on his knee to jot down the five-year-plan joke for later study in the cold light of day, then got out of bed and padded into the bathroom for water with which to take the pill. He had a much more lavish life here in Moscow than he'd ever had in Kiev. His own private room, well-furnished. His own bathroom, fully equipped, even to a hardly rusted shower. Such luxury!

> *Our orbiting cosmonaut is on strike. He refuses to land until he's allotted an apartment as large as his capsule.*

Grigor took his pill, used the toilet, then padded back to the bedroom and wrote the cosmonaut line on the notepad. Maybe so, maybe so. It was safer to talk about strikes today than even two or three years ago. Topicality, that was the secret. Dart in when the subject's safe, use it, be out and gone when the next crackdown comes.

God save Godless Russia. When would that one get its moment? It was one of the first jokes Grigor had ever thought of, and it had scared him so much—still did—that he'd never even written it down. Would he, ever? Would it be said on the television by Boris Boris, ever?

Oh, well. The future holds wonders, no doubt, some few of which will still be seen by Grigor Alexandreyovich Basmyonov, fireman/jokesmith. Consoled by that thought, Grigor got back into bed, knowing that only a moment or two of introspection would pass before he was asleep once more. Amazing how easily he slept. Amazing, he thought, that he slept at all. Using up these precious hours.

The transition from Grigor Basmyonov, fireman, bachelor, twenty-eight years of age, lifelong resident of Kiev, to Grigor Basmyonov, gag writer for the television star Boris Boris and inhabitant of the Bone Disease Research Clinic resident center at the Moscow University Teaching Hospital overlooking Gorky Park, began on April 26, 1986: Chernobyl.

Most of the firemen who were first to reach the Chernobyl nuclear plant that night, the local ones, were already dead. Some became quite sick, but survived, and a very few seemed not to be harmed at all by the experience, except for the temporary loss of their hair. Among the later fire companies to arrive, those who had at least received *some* warning of the dangers, deaths were fewer but illness more widespread. Why some people died while others lived, why some were terribly ill but others were not, was a primary concern of the doctors at the Bone Disease Research Clinic. Grigor, a survivor thus far but among the doomed, a young and healthy bachelor willing to be experimented on, was the perfect specimen for their purposes.

It was while signing the release papers at the hospital in Kiev that Grigor made his first joke: "Well, at least now I'll be able to read in bed without turning on the light."

The doctor and nurse in attendance on him, to help him fill out the forms, were both shocked. The doctor, as young as Grigor with some Asiatic flatness in his face—Uzbek, perhaps—frowned down at the papers and muttered, "Hardly something to make jokes about."

"For you, no," Grigor told him. "But for me, yes. I am permitted." And he suddenly smiled, an honest joyful sunny smile. "I am the *only* one permitted," he told them, and felt some great tight-clenched muscle deep inside himself relax, a muscle he'd never known was there until it released its clamp on his guts. The only one permitted.

At first his jokes were concerned exclusively with himself— "The best thing about all this is, I can no longer find my bald spot"—but once he'd settled into the routine at the clinic and started taking an interest in the television news (so much more news than there used to be), his subject matter broadened and the people around him began to respond more comfortably to his jokes.

It was a doctor at the clinic, one who had an old classmate with a girlfriend at Moskva Film, who encouraged Grigor to write down the jokes and comments that came to him with such increasing frequency. The girlfriend at Moskva Film turned out to be the wrong person, but she knew someone who knew someone, and by a frail web of relationships two pages of badly typed Grigor Basmyonov jokes eventually found their way to Boris Boris, who said, "I'll buy this one, this one, this one, and that one. The rest I spit on. Who does this person think he is?" And so their relationship began.

The first time Grigor and Boris Boris met, when Grigor was made a staff writer rather than a mere contributor, they became friends at once, because it turned out Boris Boris was permitted as well; the only other person permitted. Grigor walked into the sunny office in his neatly pressed suit and gleaming round bald head, and Boris Boris looked at him and said, "If I had a crystal ball like that head, I could see into the future."

"I *can* see into the future," Grigor told him. "I'm not there."

Boris Boris laughed and clapped his hands together and said they should have a drink, which they did.

Grigor himself was not a television personality, nor would he ever become one. His name was on the program's credits, that was all. In the first place, the government would never permit such public acknowledgment that this gallows humor rose from its own most egregious attack on the Russian people. And in the second place Boris Boris would never permit it: "Nobody tugs at heartstrings around here but *me*. I keep that to fall back on in case these miserable jokes of yours fail to do the job."

But the jokes did their job, most of them, and roubles accumulated in a bank account with Grigor's name on it, pointless roubles he would never have the time or the inclination to spend nor a person to will them to; as though he were a hungry cat locked in a cabbage field.

The work, however, was its own pleasure, and all in all Grigor's only objection to his life was its anticipated brevity. He made up jokes, he edited the jokes of others, he drank sometimes with Boris Boris, and he enjoyed watching Boris Boris use the material on television. "You make it all sound much funnier than I do," he told Boris Boris once, early in their friendship, and Boris Boris replied, "That's *my* genius, to make something out of something. *Your* genius is to make something out of nothing, or I'll kick you downstairs.''

That was the work. For the rest of it, life was uncomplicated and fairly content. He took his medicine every four hours, not with any anticipation of a cure, but because it would assist the doctors in their researches. He was their field of study, just as the array of news programs and the minute shifts and adjustments in the social order was his field of study. One of his fields of study.

The other was Chernobyl. He knew what had been done to him, but now he wanted to know how it had been possible. As the months and years went by, more and more was generally known about what had happened there, and more and more was publicly acknowledged. Grigor studied the magazine articles and books, watched the television programs, and learned so much about the plant he could almost have run it himself. Except that he wouldn't have run it; he'd have shut it down.

There were flaws in the design, that was finally admitted. Beyond that, there were flaws in the maintenance of the plant, flaws in the administration, flaws in the ordinary everyday procedures of running the place. Ultimately, Chernobyl had been operated as though nothing could ever possibly go wrong, no matter how sloppy or ignorant its servants became. Nothing *could* go wrong because nothing ever *had* gone wrong. And that was another fine joke: a nuclear plant, the most modern sort of enterprise on the planet, run by superstition and magic.

Was there a way to *make* a joke out of that, Merlin at the helm of the nuclear plant? No. It was old hat, for one thing, stale news, no longer of interest to anybody except a few leftovers like Grigor and their attentive doctors. Boris Boris would reject such a joke out of hand, and he'd be right.

Grigor was just easing back into sleep, comforted by this thought (that the world goes on, the world goes on), when the knocking sounded at the door. Surprised—the patients' sleep was *never* disturbed—Grigor sat up and switched on the bedside light, and the time was six minutes past four.

They've discovered a miracle cure! Couldn't wait another second to tell me! Smiling at his own manic optimism—like a thirteen-year-old's cock, it rose at the most inconvenient moments—Grigor got out of bed and padded across the room to see what this *really* was.

Opening the door, Grigor saw a fellow patient, a man in the striped pajamas and green robe of the clinic, with heavy brown wool socks on his feet and a square pale envelope in his hand. "Grigor," he said, voice hushed because of the hour, "I won't come in. I just wanted to give you this." And he extended the envelope.

Automatically taking it, trying to remember *which* of his fellow patients this was, Grigor said, "What are you doing up so late, uhhhh?" Trailing off because he was unable to remember the man's name. The corridor night-lights offered very little illumination, and his own body blocked the faint gleam from his bedside lamp; the man was familiar, of course, but Grigor couldn't quite make out which particular fellow guinea pig this was. "Very late," he repeated, hoping for a clue from the man's voice.

"We must be on the same medicine," the man answered, in a perfectly ordinary and non-specific voice. "I heard your alarm just after mine, and thought you'd be the perfect person for this invitation. I can't go, you see."

"Invitation?" Grigor half turned, to put the envelope in the light, and saw it was nearly square, made of heavy cream-toned paper, and blank. An exterior envelope with stamps and name and address must have been discarded. Inside this envelope was a card of nearly the same size, which made it hard for Grigor to slide it out. When he did, he saw it was indeed an invitation, printed in flowery script, addressed to no one in particular—"You are invited . . ."—and done in two languages: next to the familiar Cyrillic script, the same sentiments appeared in Roman script, in English.

The invitation was to a soiree ("cocktail party" in the English) tomorrow evening—well, no, this evening—at the Hotel Savoy, one of the two or three first-class hotels in this classless city. (They accepted foreign hard currency only, no roubles.) The group extending the invitation was the International Society for Cultural Preservation.

Grigor frowned at this document. "I don't understand."

"They sent it to me," the man said, with a sad smile, "because of what I used to do."

Ah. Everyone here at the clinic used to do something, of course, all different kinds of somethings; not all were former firemen. And not all had found a new career, like Grigor's joke-writing, to take the place of the old. Because so many of the residents found it painful to be reminded that they could no longer do whatever it was that used to occupy their minds and their days, the subject was informally agreed to be taboo. No one would ever ask a fellow resident about his or her former occupation. So Grigor couldn't pursue that topic, but had to say instead, "Then why don't you go yourself?"

"I've been a little low lately," the man said.

Another forbidden subject. Every resident of the clinic was doomed to die, and soon rather than late, but not all of them at the same pace or in the same way or to the same final date. Complaining about one's lot or describing one's horrible symptoms to other residents would be the height of insensitivity; the person you're talking to could very easily be in worse shape than you. So euphemisms had developed, and were generally understood, and they served to make conversation more palatable, even more possible. "I've been a little low lately," was universally taken to mean that one's particular illness had just moved into a further and more debilitating phase, that another step on one's own staircase down into the dark had just been reached, and that the victim had not yet adapted.

So once again Grigor couldn't pursue a topic. Frowning at the invitation—the International Society for Cultural Preservation—he said, "Who are these people?"

"They try to raise money," the man said, "to restore and preserve great works of art. Around the world, you know, the accomplishments of civilization are being destroyed, mostly by man. Acid rain, deliberate destruction by builders, changes in the quality of our sunlight, in many ways human art is being made to disappear. Stone statues melt in this air, motion pictures fade, paintings rot, books crumble, archaeological sites are plundered for trinkets to sell to the nouveau riche—''

Grigor laughed; he couldn't help himself. "All right, all right, I get the idea. These are do-gooders."

"They try." The man shrugged.

Grigor looked again at the invitation. "Raise money," he echoed. "From me?"

"Oh, no, no. This is a promotional party, that's all. These people are trying to get our government interested in their work."

"They're Americans?"

"English, I think, at first. They have members all over the world now." Again the man shrugged. "For what good it does."

Surprised, Grigor said, "You don't believe they're doing any good?"

"Oh, some," the man said. "Some small victories, here and there. But you know it's said, 'Rust never sleeps.' '' Then, more forcefully, he said, "And why try at all to save anything? It's coming to an end, anyway, isn't it?"

"Is it?"

"Of course! We're doing our best to destroy ourselves and our history and even our planet! Grigor, look at all of us in here. Why are we *here*?"

Now it was Grigor's turn to shrug. He'd gone past that question a long time ago. "Mistakes were made," he said.

"We're moving into a world of mistakes," the man told him, then waved his hand in a dismissing gesture. "Let it all go. It's spoiled anyway."

Ah, well; Grigor knew that attitude intimately. Why should the rest of the world go on as though nothing had happened, when *I* am in *here*, with *this*? The ones like Grigor without strong family ties were the most subject to this sort of feeling, but it reached everyone from time to time. There was no answering that attitude, of course, no particular reason why life *should* go on without Grigor, or any of the other residents; one simply waited for the feeling to go away, and it almost always did. But no one *talked* about it; that this man expressed it in words showed just how badly he'd been affected by the "low" he'd mentioned.

In any event, the issue was this invitation. Shaking his head, Grigor said "I don't see what this has to do with me. Why should *I* go to this thing?"

"Because you'd enjoy it," the man said. "And you'd get ideas for jokes there, I know you would. And you speak English."

"Oh, well, not really." Grigor dismissed that by waving the hand with the invitation in it. "I studied English in school, I can read it, but to talk . . ."

"Then this is a chance to improve your English," the man said.

"For what?" Grigor smiled at the thought. "To make up jokes for Americans?"

"For its own sake," the man said, and gestured at the invitation. "Take it, Grigor. Go or don't go, it's up to you. Excuse me, I don't like to stand this long."

"Yes, of course," Grigor said, awkward as they all were when brought face-to-face with each other's infirmities. Grigor was still much stronger than this man, which was a source of embarrassment. He nodded, and the man shuffled away down the hall, and Grigor shut the door.

Sitting on his bed, putting the invitation on the bedside table, Grigor suddenly yawned, massive and uncontrollable. The clock read four-fourteen, and Grigor was all at once so sleepy that the first time he reached for the button to switch off the light he missed. But then he got it, and in the darkness lay back on his pillow, his mind swirling with thoughts, none of them truly coherent.

Would he go to the do-gooders' party? Which one of his fellow residents *was* that guy? And, since the rooms were deliberately soundproofed, how had he heard Grigor's quiet alarm?

Grigor slept, and when he next awoke, for his eight A.M. pill, he remembered all those questions except the last one.

4

Approaching the broad steps leading up to the entrance to the Savoy Hotel, Grigor was almost painfully aware of how he looked. A thin man in his early thirties, with a gaunt face made even more lean by the loss of a few back teeth (they'd become too loose in their gums to be saved), with dry brown hair that had grown back more spottily than before, and with a measured slowness to his pace caused by the steady draining away of his vigor, he knew his appearance was gloomy and boring, like some sort of country bumpkin. The good suit, the silk tie, the heavy expensive well-shined shoes, all bought with Boris Boris's money, were like a hasty disguise, as though he were a prisoner on the run. But above all, approaching the refurbished and highly polished Savoy entrance, aware of the cool calculation in the eyes of the doorman up there watching him slowly mount the steps, above all else Grigor knew he looked Russian. And the wrong sort of Russian to be coming to the Savoy Hotel.

The doorman knew it also. Proud inside his overly ornate uniform, like a comic opera admiral, he moved just enough to block Grigor's path, saying "What can I do for you?"

"You can go back to your fleet," Grigor told him, reasonably sure the doorman would have no idea what he was talking about, and then, before the process of hurrying him along could begin, he produced the invitation. "You can direct me," he said smoothly, "to the International Room."

The doorman didn't like having to change his evaluation. "You're late," he said grumpily.

"It's still going on," Grigor said, with assurance. The invitation had specified "five until eight," and it was now just after seven. It was only at the last possible minute that Grigor had decided he might come to the damn thing after all, reserving the right to change his mind at any step along the way, and it wasn't until this snobbish doorman had looked down his Slavic nose as though at a peasant or worse that Grigor had finally decided he definitely *would* attend the soiree ("cocktail party"), that he *did* indeed belong here.

Was he not, after all, the power behind a television throne? Was he not the author of half the words to come out of Boris Boris's mouth? Wasn't he the next best thing to a celebrity; which is to say, a celebrity's ventriloquist? *Be off with you, my man,* Grigor thought, *I have Romanov blood in my veins.* (Hardly.)

Conviction is all. The doorman saw the cold look in Grigor's deep-set eyes, the firmness of his fleshless jaw, the set of his narrow shoulders, and recognized the prince within the pauper. Returning the invitation, gesturing with a (small) flourish, "Straight through the lobby," he said, "and second on the right."

"Thank you." And Grigor was amused to notice the doorman's heels come together—silently, it's true, but nevertheless—as he passed the man and went on into the plush-and-marble lobby.

Sound billowed from the International Room like pungent steam from a country inn's kitchen. Cocktail party chitchat is the same the world over, bright and encompassing, creating its own environment, separating the world into participants and non-invitees. Cheered suddenly at the idea of being among the blessed this time around, Grigor moved forward into that cloud of noise, which for him was not rejecting but welcoming, and was barely aware of the person at the door who took his invitation and ushered him through the wide archway into a large, high-ceilinged room that had been deliberately restored to remind people as much as possible of the pomp and privilege of the tsars. Gold and white were everywhere, with pouter pigeons of color in the Empire chairs discreetly placed against the walls. Two chandeliers signaled to one another across the room, above the heads of the partygoers in their drab mufti; not a red uniform in the place. It was as though, Grigor thought, the nobles had permitted the villagers one annual event of their own in the chateau's grand ballroom.

Was there a joke in that? Well, there was, of course, but was it usable? Now that the proletariat had been shown to have made a mess of things, there was a great embarrassed ambivalence about the aristocratic baby that had been thrown out with 1917's bathwater. Both Grigor and Boris Boris had been trying for months to fit references to the tsars and their families and their world into the stand-up routines, but everything they'd come up with was too flat, too wishy-washy.

The trouble was, they had no clear attitude to express. Surely no one wanted to go back to rule by a class of people who sincerely believed that peasants and cattle were at parity, and yet . . . And yet, there was something about the *style*. Not the substance, the style.

> *The tsars are still in our throats. We can't swallow them, and we can't spit them out.*

That isn't funny. That's merely true.

Looking around for the bar—he was permitted to drink, but not to excess, not yet, that would come later—his eye passed over a pretty girl in the middle of the crowded room, talking in an animated fashion with a tall, burly, thick-faced man who could be nothing but some sort of policeman, perhaps even KGB. The girl was tall and slender, with darkish blond hair and bright eyes and a beautiful nose and great self-assurance. Her clothing seemed to have been made specifically and precisely for her. An American, Grigor thought, and moved toward the vodka.

•   •   •

The Russian with whom Susan Carrigan was speaking was highly amused that she was here in Moscow because she'd won a contest in a magazine. His name was Mikhail, and he was a teacher of economics at Moscow University, a tall, thin, urbane man with a narrow and pleasantly craggy face and a burry baritone voice with which he spoke perfect English, faintly Oxford-accented. "The idea of value in a capitalist society," he said, "is something my generation will perhaps never understand. A company ferments potatoes into vodka. In order to sell that vodka, they choose at random one citizen—you, as it happens—to send on an expense-paid trip to Moscow. You yourself, with the best will in the world, not to mention the strongest liver, would never be able to drink enough vodka to repay the distiller's expenses in this venture, and in fact," he said, laughing, pointing at the glass in her hand, "you don't even *drink* vodka. You drink white wine."

"Yes," she agreed. "I know it seems silly, but—"

"Not at all, not at all." Mikhail's amusement with her was so unfeigned and so friendly that she couldn't possibly object. "It's very refreshing to be in the company of a white-wine drinker," he assured her. "Besides which, you will undoubtedly be the last person on your feet in this room. But to return to the question. The distiller can't get his money back from *you*. Is he assuming that *other* citizens, viewing his generosity toward you, will be encouraged to feel warmly toward him and buy his product in sufficient quantities—in sufficient *extra* quantities, beyond what they would already buy—to make up his expenses?"

"I have no idea," Susan admitted. "Whatever they think

they're getting, I'm having a wonderful time. Russia is so *beautiful*."

"You think so?" he said, smiling at her enthusiasm.

"The museums," she said. "The paintings, the icons. And the river is beautiful, you know. I hope the Semionov company *does* get their money back, twice."

"Oh, they already have," said an American-accented voice to her left. She and Mikhail both turned, and a middle-aged fortyish bearded man was standing there in rumpled sports jacket and white shirt and maroon bow tie, smiling his apology at having horned in on their conversation. "Forgive me," he said, "but I overheard you, and I knew you were—it's Susan Carrigan, isn't it?"

"That's right."

"Jack Fielding," he announced himself. "I'm with the embassy here. We processed some of the paperwork on you. Now, the way I think it works—I'm not an economist, I—" Turning to Mikhail, he said, "I take it you are."

"Yes, I am." Mikhail introduced himself again, with the impossibly long last name, and the two men shook hands. Then Mikhail said, "You understand the value process of this gift to Miss Carrigan?"

"I think so," Jack Fielding said. "The principal idea is advertising and publicity. If you offer a prize that a lot of people want, then people will be thinking about your brand name, so when they visit their neighborhood liquor shop they're more likely to buy your product. So if the plan worked, the company saw a rise in sales while the contest was on, meaning they already made their money out of it before they had to spend any on Miss Carrigan."

"But," Mikhail asked, "if the plan *doesn't* work? If they don't see the rise in sales?"

Jack Fielding grinned and shrugged. "Then they have to grit their teeth and pay up anyway, and Miss Carrigan still gets her trip to Moscow."

"Good," said Susan.

"Which is one reason," Jack Fielding went on, "why

I'm a free marketeer. It's so much harder for a private company to renege on a deal than it is for a government."

"Ah, well," Mikhail said, looking alarmed, "if we are going to talk free markets, I will need another drink. Susan? Your glass is empty."

"Thank you," she said, handing it over.

Mikhail raised an eyebrow at Jack Fielding. "And you, Mr. Fielding?"

"I'm fine, thanks."

"I'll be right back, then," Mikhail promised, and turned away toward the bar.

Jack Fielding looked around the room, smiling faintly, saying, "This is a true grab bag here."

"I have no idea why *I* was asked," Susan admitted, "unless it's simply because I'm staying in this hotel."

"I think the preservation people did want to get as many English speakers here as possible," Fielding told her, "which is why *I* was sent. It's all to give the Russkies an inflated idea of the organization's importance in the West. But the guest list at any promotional cocktail party you can name is a *lot* harder to figure out than the idea behind the contest that brought you here and that's got your Russian friend so bewildered."

My Russian friend, Susan thought. But not really, worse luck. Early in their conversation, Mikhail had mentioned that he was married—"Unfortunately, my wife could not be with me this evening"—but still she had enjoyed his company. She was here, after all, to experience Russia, not to wind up chatting with Jack Fielding, a man exactly like half a dozen guys at any cocktail party in Manhattan.

Would Mikhail come back? Had Fielding chased him away? Through a break in the crush of people, Susan could see him across the room, over at the bar, talking with another Russian man.

*   *   *

Grigor had just reached the head of the bar line and received his vodka when a heavily accented voice said in English, "Do you speak English?"

Grigor turned, surprised, and it was the heavy-faced burly policeman or KGB man he'd noticed talking to the American girl. In Russian, he answered, "I can understand it a little. I don't really speak it."

"Try," ordered the man. Again in that thick-tongued English, he said, "Answer my first question, but in English."

Slowly, spacing the words as he hunted for the English equivalents, Grigor said, "I understand some English. I read English more . . . better than I speak."

"Good," said the man, still in that barbaric English. (Grigor knew he himself was at any rate not *that* bad, at least not in pronunciation.) "You may call me Mikhail. You will come with me."

"But . . . who are you?"

"KGB, of course," said the man, who might or might not be really named Mikhail. He tossed the fact off carelessly, with a shrug, then said, "Which you will tell no one."

"Of course."

"Now you will come with me. There are two Americans talking. I must speak with the man by himself. You will speak with the woman, so that I can take the man away."

"But—why me?"

"Because I have requisitioned you," the KGB man said, his thick lips working like rubber around the long strange English word. "Now come along." Then, an obvious afterthought, as they pressed through the crowd, the KGB man holding a drink in each hand, he looked over his shoulder and said, "What is your name?"

"Grigor Basmyonov."

"And how do you earn your living, Grigor Basmyonov?"

"I write for the television." Finding the English words, placing them, took all Grigor's concentration.

"Good."

The two Americans were chattering together at a great

clip, the words tumbling together, fuzzing at their edges, completely incomprehensible. Grigor thought, I can't understand a word! Not when they talk that fast. Is this what I left the clinic for? To be harassed by a KGB man and humiliated by Americans?

•   •   •

Mikhail the urbane economist said, "I have brought along a compatriot who would love the chance to improve his English," while Mikhail the burly KGB man said, "Dis is a Russian man who speaks English as good as me. Maybe better."

"I have just a little English," Grigor said, smiling at the Americans, feeling suddenly shy and awkward, beginning to regret having come here at all. What did he know about foreigners, and how to act with them? Except for a few Western doctors in the first year after Chernobyl, with all of whom he'd spoken only through a translator, he had never met any foreigners in his life. I am a simple fireman from Kiev, he thought. This second life is a mistake.

"This is Miss Susan Carrigan, from New York City," both Mikhails said, except that the KGB man left out "Miss." "She won Moscow in a contest." Mikhail the economist smiled with amusement, while Mikhail the KGB man smiled as though angry, obscurely insulted.

"A *visit* to Moscow," Susan corrected, smiling at this new Russian man, holding her hand out to shake. His hand, when he took hers, was surprisingly thin and bony, and the grip tentative. He looked as though he might be suffering from flu or something, as though it might have been a mistake for him to get out of his sickbed to come to the party.

"Grigor Basmyonov," both Mikhails finished the introduction. "Grigor works for our Moscow television."

"Oh, really?" Susan released Grigor's frail hand, and

accepted her fresh glass of wine from Mikhail. "What do you do there?"

"I write jokes for a comedian," Grigor told her, the words coming slowly, one at a time. Shaking his head, he said, "Not a comedian you have heard of."

"*I* might have," Jack Fielding said, and stuck his hand out, saying, "Jack Fielding. I'm with the embassy here, we watch TV a lot, believe me. Who's your comedian?"

Shaking Fielding's hand, Grigor said, "Boris Boris," and was pleased at the grunt of unhappy surprise from Mikhail the KGB man. (Mikhail the economist gave a chuckle of remembered pleasure.)

Fielding was impressed: "No kidding! He's an outrageous man, your guy."

"Yes, he is," Grigor agreed, relaxing, basking in Boris Boris's glory.

"Just a few years ago, say what he says now," Fielding added, shaking his head, "and he'd go straight to Siberia."

"Well, at least he'd have me with him," Grigor assured the American. "If Boris Boris catches cold, *I* sneeze." And then he was astonished at how easily English was coming to him, once he had himself started. So it might be possible after all.

"I tried looking at television here," Susan said, "but it was so frustrating. It *looks* like TV at home, the news shows and the exercise shows and the game shows, but of course I don't understand a word anybody says. And when they put some kind of notice on, I don't even know the *letters*!" And she laughed at her own helplessness.

"I have seen your American television, of course," Grigor told her. He liked the way she looked, and the ease of her self-assurance; she made him want to keep the conversation going, no matter how difficult. "We receive the satellite transmissions at the station. Sometimes I watch the CNN news. Do you know the program?"

"Oh, sure," Susan said, "Cable news. It must look very different from your point of view."

"Such positivism," Grigor told her, smiling, hoping that was a word in English. "The announcers are so certain about everything. We haven't had anyone that certain about everything since Stalin died."

Susan laughed, surprised to be laughing, and said, "Is that one of your jokes for whatsisname?"

"Beg pardon?"

"Oh, I'm sorry," she said, and as she gave him a rough definition of "whatsisname," economist Mikhail gently turned Jack Fielding away, saying, "Now, about this free market of yours. Surely, with Japan breathing down your necks, you don't advocate a return to full laissez-faire." (Simultaneously, the other Mikhail said toward Fielding, "I got to talk wid you about dis embassy of yours. We still got some problems to work out.")

"Well, you know, we all have to adapt to changing reality," said Fielding, obediently moving off in Mikhail's wake, leaving Susan and Grigor alone, Grigor now trying to explain why the stage name *Boris Boris* was itself comic to a Russian audience, an explanation that turned out not to be at all easy, nor entirely satisfactory for either of them. Still, the conversation was under way, and Susan next described how she happened to be in Moscow as the result of winning an American vodka company's contest, an explanation that also proved to be rather difficult, and less than satisfactory.

They'd been talking for quite a while, mostly about the sights of Moscow and the nearby countryside, when Grigor became aware that the crowd had thinned somewhat, and, startled, looked at his watch. Almost ten minutes past eight. "Oh, no," he said, "I am late for my pill. Would you, please, hold my drink? Thank you."

She stood holding both near-empty glasses as he took a small cardboard matchbox from his suitcoat pocket and removed from it a large green capsule. Smiling, shrugging his shoulders, he said, "I have never taken this with vodka before. Perhaps it will work better." And he took back his glass and drained it, with the pill.

"Do you have the flu?" Susan asked. Then, because his English seemed so spotty, with sudden surprising lapses, she amplified, saying, "Some kind of cold or something?"

"No, nothing like that," he told her. "I am not at all contagious." Looking over at the bar, he said, "Have they stopped serving drinks?"

"I'm afraid so." Then Susan took the plunge: "I'm supposed to have dinner in the hotel with a group of people, American tourists and a couple of Intourist guides and a Russian man from some sort of trade commission. Why not come with us? I'm sure it would be all right."

Grigor thought: An adventure! Perhaps my last. "I accept with happiness," he said.

•   •   •

It was over dessert, and the dessert wine, that Grigor finally told Susan the truth about his medical condition, and its causes.

"*Chernobyl?*"

"Yes."

He was by then so full of vodka and wine and good food and good feelings that he wasn't even self-conscious, not about his slippery English and not about his illness and not about his being a country bumpkin from Kiev and not about anything. He just told her, to tell someone.

All around them, up and down the long table, other desultory conversations continued, but Grigor ignored them all, because it felt so good at last to tell someone, just say the words to someone, someone away from the clinic. Yes, and to have it be someone who would then take the knowledge and go halfway around the world with it, totally away and gone, permitting Grigor to go quietly and peaceably back to his normal round. His normal spiral.

Susan was shocked. "Cancer? Radiation disease? Well, what *is* it? And there's no hope at all? Grigor, listen! I have this cousin, I don't know, third cousin, fourth cousin, I hardly ever see him, once or twice a year, well, that isn't the point"—because she'd been drinking, too, and the hour was late—"the point is, he's a doctor, he's in research, he's very important in AIDS research at NYU, I'm going to call him—"

"Too fast," Grigor mumbled, eyes blurry, hand waving ineffectually, trying to slow down the flood of words. "Too fast, too fast. Do not understand," he said.

"My cousin," she said, slowly and clearly, "might know something, might be able to help. I will phone him. Could you go to New York, if it might help? Do you have enough money? Could you borrow it? Would they let you go away?"

He laughed, self-mockingly. "Oh, I have money," he said. "And the doctors would let me go, if a good thing could come of it. But there is no good thing, Susan. Not for me. The switch is down. It is already down."

"Well, you don't have to give *up*," she told him, reminding him of the positive news announcers on CNN, "you certainly shouldn't give *up*. I'll call my cousin. Before he was on this AIDS research he was—" She broke off, frowned, leaned closer over the table toward him, gazing into his eyes as she said, "Grigor, do they have AIDS in Russia?"

"Oh, yes," he said, nodding solemnly. "A very great problem, you know, in the hospitals."

"Hospitals?"

"The needles. We do not have enough needles in Soviet," he explained. "So they get used, what do you say, many times."

"Over and over."

"Yes, over and over. Many mothers and babies are . . . oh . . . infected. Over and over." His eyes looked more deep-set and stricken than ever. "Many deaths," he said. "Death all around us. Oh, Susan. Everything is dying, you know, Susan. Everything is dying."

Ananayel

Vodka is no longer made anywhere from potatoes. I know that. I know whatever I need to know to complete His plan. But would Mikhail know it? Very well, but would Mikhail think that Susan knew it? Well, it doesn't matter.

What matters is to recruit the actors—as in *doers*, those who will perform the necessary actions—and bring them together. And to do so with a certain degree of haste, which is why I had to hurry the Grigor-Susan meeting, appearing to each of them as the person appropriate to that moment; for her, someone to be comfortable with, and for him, someone to believe. I would have brought them together in a way much more elegant, more subtle, if it weren't that this task must be completed as rapidly as possible.

Rapidly. Why rapidly? I wondered that myself. When first I was shown His plan, when I had absorbed it, I expressed surprise at such haste. After all, when He had created this world He'd spent millions of Earth years to do it, step by careful step, until every element was perfect. And when, during His most recent irritation with this corner of His universe, He had chosen to save the world rather than destroy it, He had taken, from conception to crucifixion, thirty-four of their years. So why such hurry now?

The reason, I was given to understand, was that He hadn't been bored the other two times.

5

Kwan borrowed a bicycle from Tan Sun for his trip across the city to the neighborhood of the big hotels. She wheeled it out from the cool shady storage area under the house and handed it over to him, along with the chain to lock it up while he was with the reporter. Her expression was fretful and worried. "Be sure to look for police," she said, "before you go into the hotel. You know what their unmarked cars look like."

Kwan laughed, because he'd been through much worse than *this*, an interview with a reporter. "Everyone knows what their cars look like," he said. "Clean, for one thing, and with no toys hanging from the inside mirror. And everyone knows what *they* look like, too. They all go to the same tailor, and he gives them the material the British won't buy, the shiny grays and light blues. And then he cuts their jackets a little too short in the back."

"Don't act as though it's a holiday," she snapped, getting angry with him because she had no way to release her tension.

Why did girls always have to become so possessive? Kwan had been hiding with the Tan family for almost two months now, more than enough time to fall in love with their beautiful daughter, explore with her the petals of romance, and grow bored. He couldn't simply *tell* her the affair was over, lest her family kick him out on the unfriendly streets, but why couldn't she see it for herself? Did she want to conceal him under her skirt forever?

Oh, well. Knowing her concern for his safety was real—and the dangers were real—he sobered and said, "It isn't a holiday. There aren't any holidays any more. It is an interview with a reporter for a very important American newsmagazine." He smiled, to reassure her. "Don't worry, I'll bring back the bicycle."

"The *bicycle*!" she cried, outraged, and stormed into the house. Which was just as well.

The first time Li Kwan had seen Hong Kong, from the forbidden city of Shenzhen on the Chinese mainland, it had seemed to him like a city in a fairy tale, risen out of the sea just long enough to tease him with its possibility. That had been the occasion of his first failed effort to get out of China and across that narrow strait to the free world, as exemplified by Hong Kong. Traveling south away from Beijing through the vastness of his homeland, a fugitive from the ancient murderers' injustice, he had been helped along the way by friends of friends, by parents of schoolmates, by people with whom he was barely linked, and of course by women (women had always been very helpful to Li Kwan), and along the way he had learned that the iron grip of the ancient murderers grew increasingly slack the farther one traveled from the center of their web.

In the farthest south, in Guangdong Province, and particularly in the coastal city of Shenzhen, central government authority counted for very little at all. Here, most power centered on the rich traders and the Triads, the criminal gangs whose strength came from gambling and smuggling and prostitution and a variety of protection rackets.

Shenzhen, established as a special economic zone in the late seventies in imitation of Hong Kong, before the ancient murderers learned they would be getting the original back, had become almost a parody, a distorting mirror image of that bubbling cauldron of capitalism. A wide-open city in the sense that everything was for sale there, from Western clothing to forged identity papers, it was a closed and forbidden city in the sense that no Chinese national was permitted inside the perimeter without a special certificate from the central government. Hong Kong businessmen in search of cheap labor had moved many of their small factories and assembly plants across the border, and by the early nineties two million mainland Chinese worked for Hong Kong employers in the city of Shenzhen.

It had seemed to Kwan that in such a boiling cauldron of greed and political ambiguity and fevered ambition it should be easy to slip through Shenzhen and into Hong Kong, but in fact at that cliff-edge of China's influence the guards were everywhere. Kwan's forged special certificate, allowing him into Shenzhen, was a poor imitation not meant for close study. Chinese police and soldiers were everywhere along the razor margin between the two realities. Kwan was hailed, challenged; he ducked away, lost pursuit in the crowd of shoppers in the free-port streets, blended into a shuffling throng of homebound factory workers, and made his way out of the forbidden city, frustrated, frightened, not knowing what to do.

The family he was staying with, twenty miles northeast along the coast from Shenzhen, were distant relatives of a student who had died in the square. Kwan had not known that student, but it didn't matter. Nevertheless, after his first failed escape those people became increasingly nervous, particularly since the man of the house, named Djang, was a local official in the China Bank with much to lose. The face of the infamous counterrevolutionary, Li Kwan, was very well known, after all, despite the bullhorn he'd been holding to his mouth when that news photo was taken. So Djang it was who worked out Kwan's next escape route, and drove him to the rendezvous in his private car, a perk of his job at the bank.

This time, Kwan saw Hong Kong at night, across a mile of black water, the city a frozen firework never quite sinking into the sea. "The boat will be down there," Djang said, braking to a stop along the narrow dark road, they the only traffic, the rocky weedy brush-dotted slope leading down on the right side of the car to the water's edge.

They both got out onto the packed-stone road, looking around in the darkness of the night, afraid of patrols: by land, by sea, by air. They scrambled together down the steep slope, holding to the tough shrubbery for balance, then made their way crabwise along the water's edge.

The boat was there, as promised, old and battered but watertight, with the oars hidden under brush nearby. Kwan and Djang shook hands formally, bowed, and separated, Djang to return to the relative safety of his normal life, Kwan to begin the final leg of his trip, across the water to Hong Kong.

Steadily he rowed through the dark, and every time he looked over his shoulder, the city was still there, a million white lights painted on the black velvet of the ocean's night. And every time he pulled on the oars, facing the stern of the boat, the deeper and more dangerous darkness of China was also still there.

Kwan's enemy then had been the army, and the old guard, and two thousand years of unquestioning obedience. His enemy now traveled under the name "normalization," and that was why Kwan had to come out of hiding, had to cross the city in the full hot light of day to meet with the reporter from America. Normalization meant that Japanese aid to China was in place as before, that American businessmen had gone back to China to "protect their investments," that politicians all over the world were prepared once again to raise delicate small bowls of rice wine to toast the ancient murderers. Normalization meant that a little time had gone by, a year or two, and it was enough for memories to bleach away. Normalization meant that it was possible after just this little time to *forget* a tank driving ponderously over a dozen unarmed human beings. And finally, normalization meant that last year's hero of Tiananmen Square was this year's fugitive, hiding from the Hong Kong police.

Kwan locked the bicycle to a lamp standard a block from the hotel, and as he walked he checked his appearance in the tourist shop windows along the way. Small and slender, looking younger than his twenty-six years, with prominent round cheekbones that he'd always thought detracted from his looks (and which made him distinctive, a little too distinctive, even among a billion), he was dressed neatly in pale shirt and chinos, and still walked with an optimistic bounce, forward-moving, like waves on a shore.

There was no obvious police presence around the hotel; good. The fact is, Hong Kong was a decent city full of decent people, with a government as decent as most; but Hong Kong had to bear in mind 1997, just around the corner. In 1997 the British lease would end, and Hong Kong would revert to the authority and control of the mainland Chinese government. The quickly receding events in Tiananmen Square were to be deplored, but for the politicians reality had to be faced. (Some reality, of course, had to be faced rather more squarely than other reality: 1997, for instance, was relatively easy to face. The image of the tanks on top of the bodies of the people was a bit more difficult to face. Once again, the tough-minded and the pragmatic had found it possible to be just a little lenient with themselves.)

The "counterrevolutionaries" of that Beijing spring had dispersed after the crackdown by the ancient murderers; those who had not been captured and executed, that is. Some had come together in France, and still issued their press releases to an increasingly indifferent world. Three or four groups had settled in different parts of the United States, to bicker among themselves and continue their educations in American universities and eventually, no doubt, become employees of major hospitals and insurance corporations. Those who had stayed in China emerged only rarely from their hiding places to post declarations on walls that hardly anyone ever saw. Li Kwan was among the few who had chosen to stay in Hong Kong, to that city's increasing discomfort, where they had been until recently relatively safe and yet still close to China, where their presence could still be a significant reminder, much more so than anywhere else on Earth.

But now normalization had come also to Hong Kong. And now Li Kwan, illegally in the city, would if captured be returned to the ancient murderers of Beijing. But of course

Hong Kong was a civilized and democratic city. It would certainly not deport Li Kwan without absolute assurances from the Chinese government that Li Kwan would receive a fair and open trial; assurances already given.

And, too, there's 1997.

* * *

The entire hotel was air-conditioned, everywhere from the huge ornate dark gold lobby to the tiniest shop. Kwan paused briefly inside the revolving doors, body adapting to the chill as he looked warily left and right, and still everything seemed safe. He walked forward, slowly, and waited to be recognized. ("I'll know you from your picture," the reporter had said on the telephone, when the intermediaries set up the call, and he hadn't had to explain which picture he meant.)

Midway across the lobby, a large shambling man heaved himself out of one of the low armchairs and moved toward Kwan. He looked to be about fifty, in an open-collared shirt and brown suede jacket and rumpled chinos. Three leather camera cases dangled from him. For some reason, Americans, when far from home, always look as though they've recently fallen from a motorcycle: clothing a bit disarrayed, manner a bit harried and nervous, but somehow optimistic and relieved because no real damage had been done. The reporter was like that. He had a pepper-and-salt beard, thinning curly hair, dark-rimmed spectacles, amiable smile. "Mr. Li?"

"Yes."

"Sam Mortimer." He put out his hand, gave Kwan's a firm and honest shake. "Too early for a drink?"

"Oh, yes," Kwan said, smiling at the idea. It was probably several years too early for a drink; Kwan saw nothing to be gained from alcohol at this stage in his life.

"Tea, then," Mortimer said, gesturing toward the hotel's interior café. "We can sit and be comfortable."

The café was irregularly shaped, its predominant color that of flamingos. Along one curving wall, windows looked out at a rock garden and, beyond it, the swimming pool, in which one man windmilled doggedly back and forth, back and forth, while a dozen swimsuited people lay on chaise longues in the sun. Kwan and Mortimer took a table for two next to one of these windows, and Mortimer opened one of his camera cases, which contained a cassette recorder, a notepad, and several pencils. "Mind if I record this?"

"Not at all."

It wasn't Kwan's first interview, not by a long shot, and he had only the one subject of interest, so both the questions and the answers were already determined, were already in fact several times in print. But that was all right; the essence of *news*, as the news gatherers see it, is the recording of simple objective reality. This conversation is actually taking place, here and now, verifiably, and is therefore much more newsworthy than any other previous conversation, no matter how identical.

They went over the usual ground in the usual order, Mortimer checking off questions already written into his notepad, occasionally making an additional note, or underlining some part of the question. The background of Li Kwan: Father a teacher, mother a doctor, himself a quick student, already a university graduate, continuing his studies in history and English, planning to enter the diplomatic corps. The arrival in China of the American president, Bush, leaving a confused sense of opportunity lost. Then, soon after, the arrival of the Soviet premier, Gorbachev, and the sense that opportunity must be taken *now*. The demonstrations in favor of Gorbachev leading somehow naturally to the demonstrations against corruption and privilege among the Chinese ruling elite, leading to the hunger strike, leading to the upsurge of popular support.

"Looking back now," Kwan said, smiling faintly at his former naivete, "what we did reminds me of the American protestors of the nineteen sixties, who formed a circle around the Pentagon, joined hands, and attempted to levitate the building with their minds. They thought they would actually do it, you know, they expected to see the building rise up from the ground. *We* thought we would actually do it, too, and our conviction held the army back for more than a week."

Mortimer said, "Do you know a lot about the United States? Not history, I mean, but things like levitating the Pentagon."

"That *is* history."

Mortimer smiled, indulging him. "Those people were silly," he said. "You don't mean to say that the students in Tiananmen Square were silly."

"Of course I do," Kwan insisted. "Anyone who follows his aspirations beyond common sense, beyond the bounds of reality, is silly. But we have to be silly, some of us have to be silly, if the human race is to get anywhere."

Mortimer was troubled by that. It showed in his friendly face, but he didn't pursue it. Instead, he went on to the next question in his notebook. And the next. And the next. Through the past, and into the future: "What do you think will happen in China now?"

"Change," Kwan said. "Some for the good, some for the bad. But always slow. The habit of the people, for centuries, is to obey."

"If the Hong Kong authorities get hold of you, they'll send you back. There'll be a trial, a public trial. You'll get to speak. Would that be good for your cause, or bad?"

A strange question. Kwan said, "It would be bad, of course, because then I would not be able to have any more interviews like this. There are not many voices right now. We can't afford to lose any of them."

"How about a public statement at your trial? Wouldn't *that* have an impact?"

"The trial would last one day," Kwan told him. "I would get to say very little. The second day, I would be taken outside and told to kneel. A pistol would be put to the back of my head, and I would be killed. The third day, the government would send my family a bill for the bullet."

Mortimer's eyes widened at that. "A bill? You're kidding me."

"No, I'm not."

"But *why*? For God's sakes..."

"That's the family's punishment," Kwan explained, "for having brought up a child without the proper discipline."

"The family has to pay for the bullet that kills you," Mortimer said, musing, thoughtful. "Is that the usual procedure in China?"

"Yes."

"I didn't know about that." The reporter fell into silence, brooding, seeming to lose interest in his next question.

Kwan took the time to glance over at the pool, which was now empty, and then the other way, at the interior of the café. A westerner sat alone at the next table, drinking coffee and reading the *Hong Kong Times*. He looked up, his eyes meeting Kwan's for just a second, and then he went back to his paper, but in that second Kwan suddenly felt afraid.

Of the man? No. He wasn't from the Hong Kong police. He was a European or American, heavy-set, about forty, with yellow hair like a Scandinavian. He wore a short-sleeved shirt, pale blue, and a dark red necktie, but no jacket. He had a large gold ring with a red stone on the little finger of his right hand.

Click.

Kwan looked at the table, and Mortimer's cassette player had stopped. "You've run out of tape."

Mortimer looked up, embarrassed, as though he'd been asleep. "Time went by fast," he said, laughing awkwardly, and spent the next moment fumbling with the machine, turning the tape over, starting it again. "Where were we?"

"My family would pay for the bullet."

"Oh, yes." That fact still made Mortimer uncomfortable. "And you're sure you wouldn't have an opportunity to make any sort of meaningful state—"

"Mr. Mortimer?"

It was the waiter, standing beside their table, bowing in Mortimer's direction. The reporter looked up, reluctant and irritable. "Yes?"

"Telephone, sir. You can take it at the cashier's desk."

Mortimer was torn, indecisive. He rubbed the knuckles of his right hand against his bearded cheek. "I don't know," he said, glancing at Kwan, at the cassette player, then back at the waiter. He made an aggravated mouth, as though angry at the interruption, or angry at himself, or just angry. "Yes, of course," he said. "Here I come." With a bright meaningless smile at Kwan, he said, "Sorry about this. Be right back."

"Yes, fine."

Mortimer followed the waiter away toward the door. Kwan saw that he'd left the cassette player on, and was about to reach out and turn it off when the westerner from the next table stood up, came smoothly and swiftly across, and said in a low voice, "Mortimer betrayed you, that was the price of the interview. There's no phone call. Get up and follow me."

Kwan immediately recognized the truth. Mortimer's strangeness at the end, his wanting to believe that Kwan could turn capture and trial to his own advantage, his reluctance when the "phone call" came. The end of the tape had been the signal; that was all the interview Mortimer would be allowed. Another realist; Mortimer had believed that Kwan's betrayal was a fair trade for getting Kwan's story into a magazine read by millions of people all around the world.

Kwan rose. The stranger was already walking away, striding away, around the curved glass wall toward the rear of the café. Kwan followed him, to a door that said, in three languages: EMERGENCY EXIT ONLY—ALARM WILL SOUND. The stranger pushed open the door. No alarm sounded. He went down four metal steps, Kwan hurrying after, permitting the door to close itself behind him, and then they crossed a corner of the rock garden to a stone path and headed for the pool.

Looking to his right, Kwan saw through the windows three chunky men in pale gray tight suits and dark neckties standing indecisively at his former table. One of them looked up and saw Kwan, and pointed, becoming excited. Kwan turned his eyes front, watching the broad pale blue back of the tall westerner in front of him. Who was he? The accent had seemed not quite American, but not at all British, nor Australian. Canadian? Was English his second language? How had he known about Mortimer, and about Li Kwan? Where were they going?

Around the pool, past the sunbathers and a slightly rancid smell of coconut oil. Then, beyond the attendant's cabana, full of towels, they came to a pale green wooden fence, eight feet high, containing an unmarked and scarcely noticeable door. The stranger opened this, and they both stepped through to an alleyway. Garbage cans were stacked below a loading dock to the right. The street was to the left. As he closed the door, Kwan looked back and saw the three policemen running this way, around the pool. "They're chasing us," he said.

"That door's locked."

It is? Kwan looked at the door, but had no time to think any more about it, because the stranger was moving quickly now toward the street; not quite running, but striding with very long legs. Kwan had to trot to keep up with him, like a child.

Illegally parked at the curb just to the right of the alley was a white Toyota; like a million others in Hong Kong. The stranger pointed to the passenger door: "Get in."

The door was unlocked. Kwan got in, and the interior was stiflingly hot. He rolled down his window as the stranger got behind the wheel. The key was already in the ignition. The stranger started the motor and pulled away into traffic, and then at last Kwan could say, "How did you know?"

The stranger smiled. He drove patiently but professionally through the jammed streets. "You are not part of a conspiracy," he said. "Your government says you are, but you are not."

"Of course I'm not."

"Neither am I," the stranger said. "But if I tell you who I am, and how I found out what was going to happen to you, and why I decided to help if I could, then we would both be parts of a plan. And that's a conspiracy."

"That's specious. What con—?"

The stranger laughed. "Of course it's specious," he said. "But you wanted an answer, so that's the answer I gave you."

"The only answer I'm going to get, you mean."

"Well, here's another one, then," the stranger said. "Next time, you might not be so lucky. You might get caught. And if you get caught, they'll be sure to say, 'Who helped you escape last time?' It would be better for me if you didn't have an answer."

"Well, all right," Kwan said. "That *isn't* specious. It's merely convenient."

Again the stranger laughed. "What gratitude!"

Kwan felt himself blush. "I beg your pardon! I was so confused, it was so fast— Of *course* I'm grateful! You saved my life!"

"Use it well," the stranger said.

*   *   *

They took the ferry over to the island of Lamma, its small houses gleaming in the sun. Along the way, they got out of the Toyota to stand at the rail and breathe the cool sea air and look at the world sparkling all around them.

"You'll have to leave Hong Kong," the stranger said. "Your reasons for staying here are no good any more."

"I don't know where to go," Kwan said. He seemed to

have given over all control, all capacity for planning, to this man who had saved his life. "I don't know how."

"By ship, I think." The stranger gestured out over the water; a big passenger liner like an oval wedding cake, with an American flag for decoration at the stern, was just pulling out of Hong Kong Harbor. "Those ships have many Orientals in their crews. Especially in the kitchens." He smiled at Kwan. "You'd make a fine dishwasher, with that education of yours."

"I don't have any papers."

"Maybe someone you know," the stranger suggested, "would know someone who works for one of the shipping lines."

"The family I'm staying with, they might."

"I wouldn't be surprised. You could ask." The stranger nodded again at the departing liner. "A ship like that," he said, "goes everywhere. In six months, it goes all around the world. Through Suez, through the Med. You could get off in Genoa or Barcelona. Or even all the way to Florida."

Kwan looked at the ship. "America," he said.

Ananayel

I really don't like to do it in such a fashion, so sloppily, leaving these anomalies around, these quasi-miracles, like loose ends in a popular novel. Locked doors that open, alarms that do not sound.

It's the haste that causes it, of course, His desire to get this mess cleaned up once and for all. So I suppose it doesn't matter in the long run if I make a bit more of a mess along the way. It does offend the perfectionist in me, though, I must admit that.

And I do have to be careful that none of my principal performers notice these aberrations from the laws of physics. Fortunately, this is a skeptical age; belief in miracles is not widespread. There have been times and places in human history when I would never have gotten away with these slapdash methods, but they are long gone. Today's humans would much rather believe they are being tricked; alternatively, "there must be an explanation," which they simply have not yet quite worked out.

Still, I can't help feeling rueful. Oh, if only I had been called on in an age worthy of my talents. On the other hand, I do increasingly see why He has had enough.

6

In São Sebastião they talked with the sort of priest who believed that life on Earth was in any case irrelevant, that pain and suffering could only ensure greater joy and harmony in the next world, and that rich men who treat God's creatures badly would be punished with horrible fire in the hereafter. He was not, as he told them proudly, an activist priest.

How, Maria Elena wondered, could such a man be any use at all to her employer, a doctor from WHO, the World Health Organization, a man who believed that life on Earth was all we have, that pain and suffering must be alleviated whenever and wherever possible, and that rich men who treat God's creatures badly should be wrenched out of society like diseased rootstock from a vineyard? But in São Sebastião there was no one else; the Administration Section doctor visited the village less than once a month and his records were useless, as they already knew. Only Father

Tomaz had the statistics, the births and deaths, the illnesses, the deformities, all the spoor of the chemical assassin.

Maria Elena translated as best she could, as unemotionally as she could. Beside her, Jack—Dr. John Auston, of Stockbridge, Massachusetts, U.S.A.—ploddingly asked his questions, filling in the spaces on the forms, writing his comments in his tiny illegible hieroglyphics in deep black ink. Maria Elena—Maria Elena Rodriguez, of Alta Campa, Brazil, later of Rio, most recently of Brasília—translated Jack's dry questions into rough-toned Portuguese, translated the priest's indifferent and querulous answers, and kept her own personality firmly out of the equation.

Even her voice. A rich contralto, she kept it muted and flat, with none of the full-throated power that used to resound through the great music halls of São Paulo and Rio, when the crowds would rise to their feet, weeping and applauding, roaring the choruses with her, she striding back and forth on the stage, loving them, loving herself.

She never strode any more. Never sang.

The three sat in the shade of a large tree beside the squat, blunt adobe church, on folding chairs brought out from its dark interior, in which two old women in black, not together, whispered their prayers, their s's enlacing in the air like the ghosts of snakes. Some distance away, in a brown field, their pilot sat in the shade of his plane reading fumetti, comic books that use staged photos instead of drawings. Behind them, the village baked in the sun, most of the residents away at work in the factory out of sight beyond the brown hills, the children away at their classes in the factory school: one of the benefits the factory had brought, to make up for the death and horror it had also brought.

Father Tomaz's bland recital of children born dead, children born without arms, without eyes, without brains, poured through the transitional vessel of Maria Elena, unsullied by any trace of passion. Maria Elena's mind was full of her own two dead children, but nothing of them, nothing of herself, touched her words, neither to the priest nor to the doctor.

What would Father Tomaz say if she were to tell him about her failed children, about Paco's leaving her, about her agreement with Paco's conviction that she was now foul—befouled? That Paco had died before their argument was resolved? He would say, "God is testing you, my child. He works in mysterious ways. We cannot understand Him, we can only bow to His will, secure in the knowledge that our suffering is recorded in Heaven, and that our reward is in Heaven as well, with our God, and our Savior, and His angels and saints, in eternal joy. Amen."

Jack's forms eventually were all filled in, Father Tomaz's recital of the plague years was finished, and the three stood from the folding chairs to stretch. They carried the chairs back into the church—the sibilant old women continued, unending, unquenchable—and when they were back outside, in the sun, Father Tomaz said to Maria Elena, "Would you tell him, we don't need medicine. What we need is faith in God."

"No," Maria Elena said. "I won't tell him that." And she allowed at last the hatred to show in her eyes.

The priest, offended, stepped back a pace, glaring at her. Jack said, "What was that about?"

"Nothing," she said.

Today's pilot was new, a skinny brown man with a bandit moustache. He got to his feet as he saw them coming across the field from the church, and grinned beneath that moustache. He'd probably been bored, even with his comics, which he now tossed up into the plane onto the seat beside his own.

As they walked, Jack took Maria Elena's elbow, ostensibly because the dry cracked field was uneven, bumpy, a little awkward to walk on, but really, she knew, just to touch her. They'd been working together now for four months, and after the first month he'd begun to pursue her with a kind of lighthearted determination, not as though he didn't really care, but as though his caring had to be kept swathed in protective padding. This caution, or self-protection, or whatever it was, made it easier for Maria Elena to fend him off, without ever having to explain that it wasn't him but herself she was rejecting. In the last few weeks his pursuit had become more reflexive, absent-minded, ritualistic; they'd settled into a vaguely flirtatious but essentially comfortable relationship that could last for as long as they worked together.

He was a decent man, John Auston, thirty-seven years old, tall and awkwardly husky, as though his skeleton had never been properly hooked together but still jangled and skidded within its padding of flesh. He was methodical, quiet, devoted to his work for WHO, and if Maria Elena were in the market for a man, here was one, an excellent one. But she was not in the market, never would be in the market, and in any event Jack was not really unencumbered.

The fact was, Jack was married and divorced. He had an ex-wife far away up in the United States, and though he would never admit it, Maria Elena could tell that he still loved her. Or still needed her, which came to the same thing.

Jack always avoided talking about that ex-wife of his who, when their daughter was three, had packed up one day and taken the child and crossed the entire United States from Stockbridge, Massachusetts, to Oregon, simply to get away from him. Maria Elena had no sense of the woman, whether she was a good or a bad person, strong or weak or anything about her, and yet sometimes she felt she understood why that wife had left. There had come a point, there must have come a point, when she had simply grown tired of *steering* him. He was so easily steered, as she herself had steered his flirtatiousness into this unthreatening shoal where it now safely stagnated, and yet how could you feel anything but tarnished if you devoted your life to treating another human being as though he were nothing but a docile ox?

Since the second front seat, next to the pilot, was so
much more desirable than any of the four seats behind it,
Jack and Maria Elena had worked it out that one of them
would ride up front on the way out each day and the other
on the way back. Today, Jack had chosen the first half of the
trip, so now he was the one who climbed up the two
toeholds and crawled over the pilot's forward-folded seat
into the back. Then the pilot unfolded his seat into normal
position and helped Maria Elena climb up. She slid across
to the passenger side, stowing the pilot's fumetti in the
pocket beneath the window beside her.

The pilot took his position at the wheel and, after a brisk
series of preparations, started the single engine, turned the
small plane around in a bumpy circle, walked it halfway
back up the field, and swept it around again to face the light
wind. Over by the church, under the tree, Father Tomaz
watched; probably hoping they were on their way to God
instead of Brasília. The pilot started them forward and they
jounced and hopped down the field, the wings waggling as
though they'd fall off, the small wheel in the pilot's hands
shaking like a ribbon tied to a high-speed fan, until all at
once the wheels lifted clear of the hard ground and the plane
became graceful, coherent, almost alive.

There was no door on Maria Elena's side, which was why
she and Jack had had to climb over the pilot's seat, but the
window had a flap in the lower half, like a *deux-chevaux*,
that she could open with her elbow to look down directly at
the receding ground, becoming aware for the first time just
how large the graveyard was on the other side of the church.
And how small so many of the graves. It was human
instinct, when something was trying to exterminate the
species, to reproduce faster and faster. Particularly when the
killer was mostly killing children.

The noise inside the plane was at a level where conversation was possible but not easy, so usually they didn't talk
much, particularly on the flight back, after the long dry
interview in two languages. Today, though, after about five

minutes, the new pilot frowned at her and said, "Why do I know you from someplace?"

This still happened sometimes. People still remembered *Maria Elena*, the pop star, the rising talent who had shone so brightly and so briefly and then disappeared. She had used only her first names, *Maria Elena*; and the people had cried them out at the concerts—"Maria Elena! Maria Elena!"—as though she were a soccer star.

Ah, but that was then. When someone remembered now, or thought they did, she denied it. What was the point in rehashing that painful history? They would want to know why, with her fame still growing, with her record albums topping the charts, with her career on the brink of the international—she had even recorded one album in Spanish—she had so abruptly disappeared.

And how could she talk about such things? That her body was foul, her children dead, her husband recoiling from her in disgust. That she could no longer sing, that the music was no longer in her. And that when she had tried to use her celebrity for something that really mattered, to protest the destruction of the land and the people on it, the media had closed against her, shutting her out, more interested in jobs than health, caring more about their wallets than their children.

So when this new pilot asked why he knew her, she offered him a small and distancing smile, as though he were merely flirting, and said, "I can't think of any reason," and turned away to look out her window at the ground bumping by far below.

That stopped the conversation, but only for a few minutes. Then, when she incautiously looked again in his direction he grinned at her under his bandit moustache and said, "Not such a good priest down there, huh?"

Maria Elena looked at him in surprise. "You could tell that from way over by the plane?"

"I could tell *that* from the sky," he said, and laughed.

"He thinks God wants all this misery," she said. "Why should God want it?"

"Who benefits?" said the pilot, raising one brown stubby finger in a parody of the pedantic teacher. "That is always the question to ask, when you want to know what is really going on. Who benefits from the docility of the people? Does God?"

"The owners of the factory," Maria Elena said.

"Not God?" It was as though he was teasing her.

Jack, in the isolation of the seat behind them and not understanding Portuguese, couldn't take part in the conversation. It was up to Maria Elena by herself. Earnestly, she said, "God made us. He loves us. He doesn't want us to be tortured. It doesn't benefit Him if the people don't fight back when the factory kills their children. It benefits the owners."

"The owners." He seemed doubtful. "Who do you mean, exactly?"

"We all know them," she said, with contempt. "They live in Rio, with their ocean views, they come to Brasília surrounded by lawyers to testify that the factories are cleaner than last year. Always cleaner, cleaner. We show the true statistics, their lawyers make the statistics lie."

"But they aren't the real owners," the pilot said. "Don't you know that? Those people are the *board*. They only run the company. The real owners are the stockholders."

"More of the same," Maria Elena said.

"Not exactly." The pilot seemed to find all this amusing in some way. "The stockholders never come to Brasília to testify, they never have to lie even once to anybody. Never even come to Brazil. Do you think they ever breathe this air? Maybe once, at Carnival."

Frowning, Maria Elena said, "The company is Brazilian. Isn't it?"

"The *subsidiary* is Brazilian. That's the company you know about. But the main company is far from here. The stockholders don't live in Brazil."

"Where do they live?" I'll go there, Maria Elena thought. With photos, with statistics. How dare they not be part of what they've done? How dare they not even have to lie?

"Where do they live?" The pilot looked down at the copper-colored river they would follow for the next quarter hour. "Some in Britain," he said. "Some in Germany, Italy, Guatemala, Switzerland, Kuwait, Japan. But most in the United States."

"The United States."

"The multinational corporation is responsible to no country," the pilot told her, "but it was an American idea."

"They couldn't do *this* in America. That's why they come here."

"Well, of course," the pilot said, and laughed.

They flew for a while in silence, Maria Elena full of her own thoughts. The lives destroyed—her own life destroyed—and she could never even see the people who did it. The people who *benefit*. This was the place where they did the bad things, but they themselves were far away, unreachable. Her occasional dreams of righting wrongs, saving those who had not as yet been polluted, were even more idle than she'd thought. There was nothing to be accomplished here, in Brazil, if the decisions were being made seven thousand miles to the north, by people who never came here, perhaps didn't entirely understand the results of their decisions, had never been faced with the end reality of what they did.

But how could she reach them, so far away? That was even more of a fantasy than the one she cherished about invading a penthouse apartment in Rio, with its grand view of Sugarloaf out the picture windows, breaking into the party of tuxedoed men and ball-gowned women, weeping, shouting, showing them the pictures, making them understand.

She wouldn't even have that fantasy any more, to soothe her into sleep at night, if the tuxedoed men and ball-gowned women were merely dolls, toys, remote-controlled from beyond the horizon. Without the fantasy, without the comforting false belief that remedy *was* possible, how would she ever sleep again? What fantasy could take its place? "The United Nations is in America," she said at last.

"What was that?"

She repeated what she'd said, and the pilot nodded, agreeing with her, saying, "In New York, that's right. What about it?"

"I'll never get to New York," she said. Not now. *Maria Elena* might have someday, but that was all over now.

"Why not? Anyone can go to New York."

"In *this* plane?"

"Not in this plane," he acknowledged. "But there are planes."

"They cost too much money," Maria Elena said. "I would never have that much money." Never again.

"You could win the lottery," he suggested.

She laughed, her throat aching. "That's true, I could. But they have quotas in America. Immigration quotas."

"Not for visitors. Short-term visas."

"What could a person do with a short-term visa?"

"Well, then you hide," he said. "You become an illegal resident."

"What could a person do, of value, who was hiding from the law?"

"Then you apply for a long-term visa," he advised her. "And save your money while you wait to get on the quota. Or is that too long a time for you?"

"No," she said slowly, wondering if it was wise to reveal so much to this stranger. But he felt safe, somehow. She said, "I believe my name is on some lists."

"Lists?"

"As an activist," she explained. "A few years ago, when my husband—back then, I joined some political groups. Activist groups."

"Breaking windows," he suggested, this time openly laughing at her. "Handing out leaflets. Picketing opera openings."

"It seemed important," she said miserably. "But now my name is on the lists."

"There's one way, of course," he said, "that none of that matters."

"What way?"

"If you were married to an American."

Behind her, John Auston dozed over his filled-in forms. His presence suddenly filled the plane like a life raft inflating. "That's impossible," Maria Elena said.

Ananayel

Well; interesting.

My ongoing experiences with machinery, I mean. "Men would be Angels," as Pope said, in a somewhat different context, and that would certainly appear to be true.

Just look at all these ponderous machines, gawky and oafish, with which latter-day man has surrounded himself. What are they, after all, but efforts to perform, with great cumbersome expenditures of energy, what *we* do smoothly, effortlessly, and by nature? My first airplane was so much more unwieldy than my normal fashion of traveling through the air as to beggar comparison, and as for these automobiles, like the one with which I drove Li Kwan away from the policemen I'd set on him, what possible advantage can humans believe such monstrosities offer them over their own legs? To get them there faster? To get them *where* faster? And why? What do they want with time, these ephemera?

All these tangled intricate prosthetics with which these humans try to be *us*. Telephones. Light bulbs, and lamps to put them into, and huge destructive hydroelectric dams to plug the lamps into. Refrigerators. Oh, the weary toil of it all. They'll probably be glad to lay their burdens down, poor things.

7

There was a bus stop across the road from the entrance to the prison, but Frank Hillfen didn't want to wait for the bus there. Everybody going past in cars, and the people on the bus, too, when it came, and the driver of the bus, they would all know what he was. No one ever gets on the bus at that stop except cons—ex-cons, okay—and visitors of cons, and one look would tell anybody in the world that Frank Hillfen was not somebody who visited people. *Con*, they would say, looking at the slump of his shoulder, the dry hardness of his jaw, the hands as large as a workingman's but soft and pudgy as a baby's. *Habitual*, they would say, driving by, windows rolled up to keep the cold air in. *He'll be back*, they would say, and glance once in the rearview mirror, glad they weren't Frank Hillfen, and drive on.

Frank crossed the road toward the bus stop, to be that much farther away from the tall tan wall in the sunlight. Three P.M., summer, sunny, moderately warm. Walking weather.

A madonna and child were the only people in the shade of the bus shelter. She was short, plump, pretty, black-haired and black-eyed, and she held the infant high in her arms, murmuring to it in some dialect descended a long way from the Latin; some variant of Spanish, probably. She looked up to watch Frank cross toward her, his worldly goods in the black warm-up bag that said *HEAD* at both ends, handles gripped in his left hand, leaving the right for . . . emergencies. The madonna watched Frank with the sullen hopeless look of someone who's been badly treated before and never got revenge for it, and her eyes didn't soften even when he veered to his left, away from her and her bus shelter. She kept watching his back as he walked away along the verge of the road, watching him mistrustfully as she absently bobbled the fretful baby.

Frank walked south, the sun high above his left temple. There was very little traffic; Nebraska had put the prison on land nobody wanted for anything else. For a long while the blank tan wall remained to his left, across the road, while to his right stretched stony brush-dotted land the same color as the prison wall. That land was fenced from the road with three strands of barbed wire, but didn't seem to be used for anything.

In the release office, the clerk had told him the bus ran every two hours or so. He had no idea how far apart the bus stops were. If the bus came by before he reached the next one, and if it wouldn't stop at his wave, he'd have two more hours to wait. Or so. But that didn't matter, he was in no hurry. Where was he going, anyway? If he followed his usual pattern, he was simply on his way back to that prison behind him, or another one exactly like it; he was merely starting out now on the first leg of a long and tortuous journey that would take him through many places and many experiences to no place and nothing.

If he followed his pattern. But not this time. This time, he'd keep ahead of the odds. Ahead of the odds. Take the bus across the state to Omaha; promote some cash there. If he got *that* far without fucking up, take a plane to New York. Then we'll see.

Frank walked for half an hour without finding any more bus stops. He began to regret his self-consciousness. What did he care what the people in passing cars might think? *Escaped con*, probably, with him walking away from the prison like this, along the empty road, miles from anywhere. At forty-two, his brown hair was thinning, forehead receding, presenting vulnerable pale skin to the hot sun.

Gonna start to burn, he told himself, fatalistic about it, and then humorous: Gonna get burned. First thing.

The warm-up bag got heavier. He switched it to his right hand, then back to the left. What do I need with all this shit? Buy new. But Frank always imagined people watching him, careless but vaguely interested people keeping an eye on him, and what would they think if he threw his warm-up bag away?

From time to time he looked over his shoulder at the road undulating behind him, and at last he did see the bus way back there, barreling along the two-lane road, coming fast. Frank turned to face it, holding the warm-up bag prominently in front of himself with his left hand—I'm a traveler, see?—while he waved the right hand back and forth above his head. He was visible, God knows, the tallest thing in the vicinity, the only thing *moving,* but the bus roared right on by, didn't even slow, left him awash in a wake of blown dust and diesel fumes.

Cocksucker. Frank watched the bus shrink, imagined the blowout, the driver losing control, the bus jouncing off the road, straight into a tree—one of the few trees around, but a perfect hit anyway—the driver flailing through the big windshield, sliced to shit by all that glass, screaming, mouth wide open, glass in his tongue . . .

Frank kept walking. It was greener up ahead, more trees—shade from this sun, finally—and now the road began to climb. I have two hours to find the bus stop, Frank told himself. The fucking thing has to stop *somewhere.*

A farmhouse with outbuildings, on his right. And a dog, who stood barking loudly on the driveway, too cowardly to come forward for his kick. No human beings came out to find out what the dog's problem was. Frank kept walking, and the dog quit. Like to come back at night with a .22, plink him on the edges, shoot off a paw, an ear, chunk of the tail. Take a good long time at it. Why don't you bark *now,* you son of a bitch?

Cars went by, from time to time, but Frank knew better

than to try to hitch a ride. People looked at Frank, they figured first impressions were enough, they didn't need to know any more. So he just kept walking. Sooner or later, there'd be a crossroads, a village, a V.A. hospital, an army base, some goddamn excuse for the bus to stop. There he would wait.

The white Saab with the bumper stickers—I BRAKE FOR ANIMALS; NO NUKES IS GOOD NUKES—passed Frank, going the same direction as him but a lot faster, and zipped a little farther down the road when all at once its right front tire blew. (Frank didn't think about his bus blowout fantasy, had long forgotten that.) The car was just a ways ahead of him, maybe the length of a football field—what's that? a hundred yards?—and then the *bang*, like a large handgun going off, and the Saab veered left and right and jolted itself all over the road, its brake lights slapping *on*, then off, then *on*, off, *on* . . .

He was a good driver. He was lucky, too, in that there wasn't any traffic coming, but he was also a hell of a good driver, he kept control, he didn't let the Saab get away from him and run for the trees. He didn't lock onto the brakes but pumped them, used them, kept control, slowed the big vehicle down, and at last it wobbled off onto the shoulder and came to a stop. Frank kept walking, toward the car, watching the thin strung-out cloud of tan dust move away over the fields to the right, like the banners of a ghost army. He continued to walk, and as he did so he began to think maybe he could work a deal with this guy, help him replace the tire and in return get a lift to the next bus stop. Or all the way to the city, why not? Think big; why not?

For a minute or two after the Saab came to a stop, as Frank went on walking toward it, nothing more happened. The driver's door didn't open, the driver didn't get out. He's in there shitting his pants, Frank thought. Reaction after it's over. The way I feel when the lights come on and the cop says, "Don't move." The danger is over and the new chapter has begun.

If it was a football field Frank had to cover, he was at about the Saab's twenty-yard line when the driver's door at last did open and the driver tottered uncertainly out, and the driver was a woman. Shit, thought Frank, disgusted. A woman isn't gonna give me the time of day. I can't negotiate with a *woman*.

She didn't see Frank at first, or wasn't concerned about him. She closed the driver's door and walked around the front of the Saab and stood looking down at the blown tire. She looked to be about thirty-five, tall and slender, with straight brown hair. She was dressed like the women in television commercials who carry briefcases and are business equals with the men but still spend a lot of time worried about personal hygiene. Smart and self-assured, in other words; but not now.

Frank kept walking, beaming thoughts at the woman, even though it wouldn't do any good. I'm non-violent, he thought at her, that's my M.O., that's why I'm out on parole, that's why I did less than two of a nickel. It's all in my record, you could look in my record, never a touch of violence, I don't even go *in* a house if there is somebody there. Never carry heat, never a weapon on me, not a knife, nothing. A peaceful burglar, that's me, wouldn't hurt a woman. Wouldn't hurt anybody.

The woman looked up as Frank neared the car, and he saw it in her face, saw it in her eyes, right away. That recognition. Not a word yet, and already she knew everything about him. Wrong, but everything.

A strip of the blown tire lay curled beside the road like a giant blackened onion ring. Frank looked at it, as a relief from looking at the woman's frightened eyes, but then he was past it, and the white Saab was just beside him as he walked, and the woman was straight ahead, ten feet away, beyond the car. Frank took a deep breath, still walking, and looked at the woman again, and said, "You handled that real good. Like a pro."

The woman blinked, slowly. Whatever she'd expected, it

hadn't been a compliment, or a critique on her driving. "Thank you," she said, her voice very low. "It was so fast, I didn't know *what* I was doing. There wasn't time to think."

"Well, you did it right," Frank told her, and then he either had to stop or keep walking right on past her, so he stopped. He saw the little apostrophes of fear bracketing her mouth, and he plunged into his story: "Look. I'm walking trying to find a bus stop. There's a bus on the road, to the city. You want, I'll put the spare on here for you, then you give me a lift to the bus stop. You don't want, that's okay, I'll keep walking."

She said, "The state capital, you mean?"

Funny part of the proposition to fasten on, but okay. "I guess so," Frank said. "Omaha. Where I had my trial, anyway, so I guess that's the capital."

She frowned at him. "Trial?"

Might as well get it all out, from the get-go. "You passed the prison back there," he said, pointing a thumb over his shoulder. "I just took parole." Not that he intended to visit any parole officers, not this time around.

"There's a bus stop there," she pointed out. "Right there at the prison."

"I didn't like that one."

She smiled, like she understood the reasoning. "I'm going to Omaha," she said. "If you really want to help . . ."

A lift all the way. Frank couldn't help it, he grinned like a kid, wide open, both sides of his mouth. "A miracle," he said.

Her answering smile was ironic: "The miracle is, I wasn't killed."

"There's a miracle in it somewhere," Frank said, "I know that much. You got the key to open the trunk?"

●   ●   ●

Changing a tire was hard work, particularly for somebody with hands like Frank's. They were delicate hands, they used small tools delicately, they caressed combination locks, they stroked alarm wires, they gathered in cash and jewelry. Soft pudgy fingers got bruised against lug wrenches, got scraped against tires. But Frank did the job and kept his reactions off his face.

They talked while he worked. She said she was a lawyer, and he said, "You're too smart to be a lawyer."

She thought that was funny. "The fellow who represented you wasn't that good, eh?"

"I'll tell you about my lawyer," Frank said, fighting with the lug nuts. "He's a guy, his necktie is in his soup."

"What was the charge against you?"

"Burglary."

"How solid was the case?"

"Walked out the front door of this house in Michigan Heights, carrying a wall safe, straight into two beat cops with flashlights."

"*Carrying* a wall safe?"

"That's the way to do," Frank explained. He threw the dead tire on its hub into the trunk, wheeled the spare along the verge beside the car. "A wall safe is a metal box stuck in a wall. You dig it out, takes no time at all, carry it home, work on it at your leisure."

"Was that the first time you were caught?"

He looked at her, not answering, letting her drink him in, until she laughed and said, "Sorry, you're right. Stupid question. Okay, next time, *I'll* represent you. But try not to be caught quite so red-handed."

He looked at his hands, pitying them. "Black-handed, this time."

"I have towelettes in the glove compartment," she said. "When you're done."

A car or a truck went by from time to time, but nobody stopped to see if any help was needed. It was clear that Frank was doing the job. And the lady lawyer wasn't afraid of him any more. That's all it took, a little conversation, spend some time, see what Frank Hillfen's really like. Not a nice guy, maybe, not pretty, but not dangerous.

She said her name was Mary Ann Kelleny, and he told her he was Frank Hillfen, and she said, "Frank. Good. That fits you."

"I don't know about that Mary Ann stuff," he said. "How can a lawyer be named Mary Ann?"

"Why not?" she asked him. "There's lawyers named Randolph, aren't there?"

"Yeah, that's true." He tightened the last lug nut.

"What was your attorney's name?" she asked. "The one with the necktie."

"Gower."

She smiled and spread her hands. "I rest my case."

He hadn't known what she meant when she said "towelettes," but they turned out to be those folded wet paper towels in a packet that restaurants give you after you eat the lobster. He used three of them from her glove compartment supply; a well-prepared lady. He would have thrown the towelettes away into the weeds but she pointed at the plastic trash bag she'd hung from the dashboard cigarette lighter. "You're a good influence on me," he said, and disposed of his trash properly.

* * *

The bus stop was less than a mile farther on, at an intersection containing two gas stations, a diner, and a squat modern one-story "professional building": the professionals were a dentist, a real estate agent, and a stockbroker. Down the road to the right were a few houses, new but shabby, as though for a town that hadn't quite happened. Up to the left was a long, wide, gray two-story factory building with very few windows. TEXTECH in blue was along the blank wall facing this way. Frank said, "What's that?"

"Clothing," she told him. "Sweaters, T-shirts. Sweatshirts that say *Property of Alcatraz*."

"I never saw a sweatshirt like that," Frank said. He couldn't help it, his mouth was pursed in disapproval. *Property of Alcatraz;* that was bad taste.

"They don't sell them in America," she explained. "Only overseas."

"Where?"

"Asia. Europe."

"Property of Alcatraz." Frank saw a teenager in Tokyo, walking down a crowded street, wearing a sweatshirt that says, *Property of Alcatraz.* Doesn't speak ten words of English. Was the kid somebody's property *in* Alcatraz, wouldn't last a day. People wearing the words, don't know what they say. Don't know what they *mean.*

"The global village," Mary Ann Kelleny said.

"Yeah," Frank said. "But do they get it? I don't think so."

"Does it matter? As long as they're happy."

"Okay," Frank said. "I'll bite. Are they happy?"

She glanced at him as she drove, curious and amused. "Why wouldn't they be?"

"Because they don't know who they are," he said. "They don't know who anybody is. They mostly sound bewildered."

"I don't follow," she said.

"You put your clothes on," Frank told her, "they're your flag for the day. The public announcement, who you think you are. What we all do. You gonna walk into court with words on you? Property of Alcatraz?"

She smiled and gave him another look. "So you're dressed as the humble workman," she said. "Is that it?"

"I'm dressed like I just walked out of prison," he answered. "When I get a couple of dollars, I'll dress a little different. Like a guy ready to party."

She'd stopped smiling when he mentioned the "couple dollars," and now she said, sounding fatalistic but worried for him, "You're going back, aren't you, Frank?"

He pretended he didn't know what she meant. "Back where? A life of crime?"

"The *wrong* crime," she said. "So back to prison. You're an intelligent man, Frank, you know it yourself. There's a rubber band on you, and the other end is still in your cell."

"I've learned stuff," he said, trying to sound competent and confident. "Whatever happens, I'm not gonna be that easy to find."

"Oh, sure you are," she said.

He hadn't expected this conversation with anybody but himself, and he *sure* hadn't expected it with a good-looking woman lawyer in an air-conditioned white Saab doing sixty down the highway. He said, "What do you mean, the wrong crime?"

"Little stuff," she said. "Burglaries. Breaking into houses and stealing *wall* safes, for heaven's sake."

Defensive, he said, "What's the complaint? Wall safes, that's where they keep the valuables. That's what I'm after."

"How much in valuables?" she demanded. "What do you mean, valuables?" She must be a pretty good lawyer. She said, "Are you talking about three or four thousand dollars? Jewelry, and what do you get from your fence? Ten percent?"

"Sometimes more," he muttered.

"You can live a week, or a month if you're lucky, and then you have to go out and do it again. Every time you do it, you're at the same risk. Every time. It doesn't matter how many times you don't get caught, because they don't count in your favor the time you *do* get caught. So the odds are against you, and sooner or later you *will* get caught. That's the only way it can end, cycle after cycle."

"Okay, then, I'll reform," he said, bored with the conversation, and looked out the window at the passing scenery: trees, farms, trees.

But she wouldn't let it go. "You won't reform, Frank," she said. "You're who you are, and you know it."

"Habitual," he said, like the word was a joke.

"But you could *retire*," she said. "That's not the same thing as reform, you know. If you reform, you have to get a job somewhere, live in a house somewhere . . ."

"No can do."

"I *know*, Frank, that's what I'm saying. If you do a burglary and you make five thousand dollars on it, you don't go right back out the next night, do you?"

"No need to."

"Exactly. You retire, short-term. Then, when the money's gone, you come out of retirement."

He laughed, seeing himself as a guy constantly bouncing out of retirement. "I guess that's me, okay."

"But if you committed just one crime," she went on, "and you got five *million* dollars, you'd never have to come out of retirement, would you?"

This time, he laughed out of surprise. "Five million? Where *is* this score?"

"Don't ask *me*, Frank," she said half kidding but also half on the square. "I'm not a criminal. And I'm not suggesting any crime to you, either. What I'm saying is, if you keep doing the five-thousand-dollar crimes, you'll definitely go back to prison."

He knew what she was doing. It was a lawyer's trick, that, to make you think you've got two alternatives, but then the first one's no good and the second one's impossible, so you wind up doing exactly what lawyers always want everybody to do, anyway, which is nothing. "So instead of the five-grand hits," he said, "I should stay home and dream up a five-mil hit. And not go out till I got it. Right?"

"You'll never reform, Frank," she said. "You know that. So the best thing to do is retire."

"With my five million."

"Or whatever."

• • •

They came into Omaha around seven in the evening, the city rising out of the landscape like children's toys in a sandbox, the reddening sun still partway up the western sky but the children gone home to dinner. As the country road became city street, the streetlights automatically switched on, anemic in the rosy light of the sun.

They'd been talking law, anecdotes, him telling her some of his court experiences, she talking about clients and how it seemed that everybody had a crooked streak in them somewhere. She wasn't herself a criminal lawyer, or a courtroom lawyer, but flew a desk in a big corporate law firm, so the clients were businessmen, all looking for an edge. It began to seem to Frank that it was unfair of society to single him out this way, keep riding him so hard when everybody else was up to something, too. But nobody ever said it was supposed to be fair, life.

The first time they were stopped at a red light, she pointed at her purse, a big brown soft-leather thing on the seat between them, and said, "There's money in there. Take three hundred."

He bristled. "What's this about?"

"To get you started. You need money to get you moving. If I don't give it to you, you'll start right in trying to beat the odds. The first day on parole."

"I can't take your money," he said. The fact was, three hundred wouldn't do it. Three grand was closer to what he needed, with the flight to New York, and some clothes, and a hotel, and this and that and the other. Four or five grand, more like. But he wasn't going to say that. "I appreciate the thought," he went on, "but I just wouldn't feel right."

She sighed. The light turned green, and they drove on. She tapped fairly short fingernails against the steering wheel, and at last she said, "All right, then. Look in there, you'll see my wallet."

"I really won't—"

"Not money," she said. "Hold on a second."

Another red light. She picked up the bag, braced it between the steering wheel and her lap, took out a thick wallet, unclasped it, brought out a business card, handed it to him. "I can't come to court for you," she said, "but I can find you somebody better than the wet necktie."

Taking the card, reading her name and the firm name and the business address and the phone number and the telex number and the cable word and the fax number, he said, "You don't have much confidence in me."

"I have confidence in the mathematics." The light was green; she shoved the bag onto the seat and drove. "The five-thousand-dollar crimes will get you right back in trouble."

"I'll look for the five-million job," he promised.

"Good. In the meantime, hold on to that card."

"I will." He tucked it into his shirt pocket.

"Where do you want me to drop you off?"

"Oh, any well-off neighborhood will do," he said.

She laughed. He was glad she did.

Ananayel

I must say it was touching when Frank wouldn't take the money. Humans do have this capacity to be appealing, when you deal with them one at a time and avoid the ghastly overview. That a creature like Frank Hillfen, so utterly without hope, so totally enmired in slow self-destruction, so devoid of any experience of using free will, should refuse Mary Ann Kelleny's three hundred dollars, made me feel quite kindly toward him, for that moment.

Will he do what's necessary when the time comes? Oh,

yes. We can arrange that, we can manipulate that. The group I'm assembling will do what I want—that is, what *He* wants done—but it will be *their* choice, *their* idea, *their* free will in action. The human race will freely choose to end itself.

Well? They've been rehearsing for it quite long enough, haven't they?

Not the entire human race, no, of course not, we are not conducting a referendum on this. *His will be done.* But representatives of them all, carefully chosen representatives. From every race, from every continent. No one left out.

We're playing fair here.

8

The thinner she got, the more the Europeans liked her. At home they had their soft pale cushion women; in Nairobi, they wanted something lean and mean and dark. That was Pami: lean and mean and very dark. So easy, and so good for business; when you've got *slim,* you never have to diet.

Pami's stroll was up Mama Ngina Street past the European embassies and down Kimathi Street beyond the New Stanley Hotel, where the tourists sit beneath the famous huge thorn tree spiked all over with messages. To whom? From whom? Nothing to do with Pami, anyway, nothing to do with an illiterate twenty-three-year-old Luo from up above Lake Naivasu. She'd come to Nairobi at fifteen because she wasn't wanted at home and had already outlasted her reasonable life expectancy. In Nairobi she knew no one except a few policemen, "protectors," and colleague whores. No person in this world had a message for Pami Njoroge, a twenty-shilling Kenyan whore with cold eyes, a twisted mouth from a jaw long ago badly broken and ineptly mended, and a recently diagnosed case of slim, the African familiar name for AIDS.

At first he didn't look that much like a john: too big and self-confident and well-built. But then she was distracted by a beggar with deformed legs that she almost fell over, and when she looked up again along crowded, bustling Kimathi Street the big European with yellow hair was closer, and fewer other people were in the way, and she could see he was fatter and sweatier than she'd thought.

He was probably fifty years old, well over six feet tall, with a bulging soft torso contained in a white business shirt large enough to be a tent in the up-country where Pami was born. His dark tie was pulled down from his thick neck, the shirt collar open. His dark blue suit, like a banker or a diplomat, was rumpled and desperate looking, the coat dangling open like double doors. He walked heavily, feet slapping the pavement, like a ritual bullock plodding toward the place of sacrifice, and when he saw Pami his pale eyes sparkled and his cheeks grew round when he smiled, wet-lipped.

She gave him back her own twisted, mean, secret smile, knowing it would excite him with its dangerousness—he'd have no idea how dangerous—and when he passed her, the two of them momentarily very close, pushed together by the jostling crowd of pedestrians, he looked down at her with those bright eyes—they were the palest blue she'd ever seen—and said, "Oh, you come with me." He spoke English with some kind of thick accent, in a deep guttural voice. Was he German? Somehow he didn't seem quite like a German. And in any case, what did it matter?

His hotel was three blocks away, one of the newer American-designed ones, the same anonymous but lavish cell repeated one hundred sixteen times. By day, the rear door from the parking lot was left unlocked, so the john took her around that way, to avoid the problems of bringing this alley cat through the lobby.

His room was on the second floor, with no view except another wing of the hotel. There were two beds, a single and a double, both neatly and smoothly covered with Mondrian-influenced spreads. The maid had been through, to put a strip of paper around the toilet seat and distribute fresh plastic glasses in sealed plastic bags, all of these tiny ways to deny the great teeming filthiness of the world just out there, just beyond that double-paned permanently shut window. What did sealed plastic bags and droning vacuum cleaners mean, when these big blond residents brought their skinny dirty Pamis inside?

"I am Danish," he said, locking the door. "Am I your first Danish man?"

How would she know? "Yes," she said.

"Good." He smiled, and crossed the room to close the drapes over that broad rectangle of plate glass. She stripped off the small plastic shoulder bag and loose pale green cotton shift and low black plastic boots that were all she ever wore at work, and the big man turned from the window to beam at her dark nakedness, the small loose breasts with their large areolas, the narrow muscular hips, the lush foliage of her bush. The room was dimmer now that the drapes were drawn, everything in it touched by a pale grayness, in which his eyes gleamed like tiny signal lights from a ship far out at sea. "You will be rough?" he asked, with a hopeful rising inflection.

Her jaw produced another nasty smile. "As rough as you want," she said.

He walked toward her, undoing his belt, then reached around to clasp her buttock hard with one hand. "No ass at all," he said.

"I got enough ass," she told him. "And it cost twenty shillin."

"Oh, yes, yes," He released her, took off his suit coat, reached into its inside pocket, pulled out a large thick billfold, and tossed the coat carelessly onto the single bed. He stood weaving slightly, as though he were drunk, breathing audibly through his open mouth, as he leafed through crackling currencies in the billfold, muttering to himself: "Francs. Krone. Marks. Oh, I spent it all."

People had tried to pay her in other currencies before, but she wouldn't do it. She had great trouble finding a bank to change the money, usually had to give some hotel desk clerk a blowjob in return for switching dollars or marks into Kenyan shillings; and then she would be cheated on the exchange rate, as well. She was about to tell this man her policy—she'd put her dress and boots and bag back on and walk out if he had no shillings—when he tossed the billfold onto the coat on the bed and said, "I get. Okay." And plodded heavily over to the closet.

Pami looked at all the paper money stuffed into the billfold, lying open on the coat. All different kinds of money, and lots of it. Probably more than she earned in a month, if you added it all together. And didn't cheat on the exchange rate.

The big man slid open the mirrored closet door, stooped with a grunt, and brought out a black attaché case with gleaming chrome locks. This he put on the low dresser, took a key ring from his pocket, unlocked the case, and lifted the top. He made no effort to hide the stacks of money that almost filled the interior. Again, there were four or five different currencies, but this time including shillings; she saw stacks of one hundreds, five hundreds. And on top of it all, in a brown leather case, was a hunting knife.

Pami moved toward the door, keeping an eye on the blond man's hands as he pushed the knife aside and rooted through the wads of money. She'd known women who were killed by johns, sometimes tortured first, sometimes cut up afterward. It wasn't going to happen to her. If she had to run, she wouldn't worry about the dress or the boots or the bag. All of that could be replaced.

But what he finally brought out of the case, holding it up by the edges in both his hands, studying it as though he'd never seen one of these before, was a twenty-shilling note.

Mostly blue, the twenty shilling has a picture of Mzee Jomo Kenyatta on the front, looking responsible and noble and caring, and a serene family of lions on the back, with playing cubs. Turning to Pami, holding up this note, he said, "Do you know what this is worth?"

What kind of question was that? "Twenty shillin," she said.

"Ah, yes," he said. "But in pounds, English pounds, oh let us say seventy P. And in U.S. dollars, one. One dollar." Showing that wet smile again, he said, "This is a very significant amount of money, twenty shillings. I hope you will give first-rate service for it."

"Come and see," she said, holding out her hand for the money. He gave it to her and she half turned her back, stooping to put the bill into her left boot, knowing he wouldn't be able to resist grabbing her. I'll do him in no time, she thought, as his hands groped her, I'll be on the street in a minute and a half.

But it didn't work out that way. Naked, he was a pink wet whale, wheezing and sweating with every exertion, but what endurance he had! He turned her this way, he turned her that way, he studied and pried, he even drew a real response from her two or three times, and still he went on, still he wouldn't stop, and she was becoming furious. To a whore, time is money.

I'm gonna infect him, she thought, moving from her usual indifference as to whether or not a john caught her disease to an aggressive desire to *make* him catch it. She managed to get her saliva into his mouth, and later into his anus, and then she stopped fretting over the lost time. What the hell. She gave herself up to the acceptance of the moment.

At the finish, he was on his back, puffing and heaving, she riding him like the boy on the dolphin, fast and hard, grinding down, clenching tight. His head and neck got redder and redder, his pale eyes bulged, and when he came he cried out like a woman, the high wail ending in a bubbling cough. He sagged onto the mattress, muscles slack, jaw hanging open, dull eyes gazing toward the ceiling.

She frowned down at him, sweat-slick herself, rubbing her palms over her wet belly and drying them on her thighs. "Mister?" she said.

There was no reaction. Moving gingerly, she climbed backward off him, crawling on hands and knees back down over his legs and over the foot of the bed, to stand there and stare at him, lying like a big rag doll with the stuffing coming out. I killed him, she thought, and grinned in glee at the idea. She'd never killed anybody before. I killed him wid my box.

She looked around, and her eye lit on the open attaché case on the dresser. *Steal it!* She took one step.

"Nnnnnuunnn-nanghhann!"

She spun back, terror-struck, and he wasn't dead at all, his head and left arm were raised, eyes staring in pain and fear as his left hand wobbled, trying to point. "Med-cine," he gasped. "Drawer. Med-cine!"

Not dead, but dying. She watched him, and didn't move.

He cried out again, and once more, and then his head and arm fell back, and he lay with his head twisted at an angle, staring at her. "I'll," he panted, and wheezed. "Get," he whispered, harsh and sibilant. "P'lice," he gasped, and his flailing arm lunged out and caught the phone beside the bed.

No! Terrible trouble! And the money was *hers*! She stared from him to the money in the case, and her eye lit on the hunting knife.

He knew what she was going to do before she even reached the case: "I won't call! I won't call!" But the wooden handle was in her hand, the sheath was flung away into a corner, and she leaped on him like a cheetah, punching down, punching down, unable to stop, hitting him over and over, cutting him open in a hundred places, gritting her bloodstained teeth, snarling in her throat, using every ounce of her strength to drive the blade into him, again and again and again, until at last the knife caught on something inside him and her hand was so slippery with blood it slid right off the handle when she pulled back.

She sat on his legs a minute longer, panting, muscles trembling with strain. Then once again she climbed backward off him, and stood shaking in the middle of the room. Blood had spouted from him, and more blood had sprayed around every time she'd lifted the knife, and now there was blood everywhere. There were dark droplets on the ceiling. Blood ran into the mattress where twice she'd missed him in her frenzy and slashed down through spread and sheet into the cloudy stuffing. Great splotches and splashes marred the walls and the drapes over the window. The mirrored closet door was smeared. The maroon carpet was sticky beneath her bare feet. And her own body felt as though she'd been dipped into a giant jar of rancid raspberry jam. Blood was caked around her nostrils; she breathed the foul air through her mouth, and tried to think.

Boots, dress, bag. The boots were dark, so nothing showed. The dress was stippled with drying blood, and so was the bag. Snuffling in her throat as she tried to breathe, she moved in a dazed and wandering manner into the bathroom, turned on the water in the sink, then turned on the shower as well and climbed in under the flow. A few times before, johns had let her shower in the wonderful hotel bathrooms, so she knew how to make this one work. She peeled the paper wrapping from the soap cake and rubbed the soap in her hair, over and over, rinsing under the rush of water and then rubbing the soap into her hair again, repeating and repeating until at last the white soap did not come back rosy from her head. Then she scrubbed her arms and body and legs. Her pubic hair was like a sponge, full of blood, to be soaked again and again; finally she sat down in the tub, the shower water falling on her like rain, and simply washed and washed and washed. Would the water never run clean?

Yes. She stood again, clumsy, exhausted now, almost

slipping on the smooth tub, and stepped out onto the tile floor. There were large soft beige towels. She dried herself, then used the towels to make a path along the floor of the main room, to keep from getting more blood on her feet. She went out there, picked up her dress and bag, and carried them into the bathroom, where the water still ran in the sink. She cleaned the dress as best she could without getting the whole thing wet, then rubbed the bag with a wet washcloth. She pulled the dress over her head, the wet parts sticking to her body, put the shoulder bag over her head as well, then went out along the towels to her boots. She wiped them on a towel, put them on, straightened up, and then looked over at the burst bladder of blood reeking on the bed. There was nothing in her eyes when she looked at him; she could barely remember him now.

What she remembered was the money. Spreading another towel in front of herself, she moved to the dresser and was about to close the lid on the attaché case when she saw that, in addition to the money, it also contained a passport. She took it out, opened it, saw a picture of the john looking grumpy.

Don't want this passport. Don't want to carry anything that hooks me up with that Danish man. She put the passport on the dresser, closed the case, picked it up by the handle in her left hand, and looked around the room. Nothing else.

It was so hard to think, to keep moving. It was as though great lethargy and great horror were both just outside her range of vision, range of understanding. I'm not working any more today, she told herself. I'm going home, I'm gonna sleep, I don't know what happened in here. This is too crazy. I'll feel better tomorrow.

Ananayel

Two new experiences there: sex and death.

Both were intensely absorbing and interesting, and neither was exactly what I'd expected. The one wasn't all pleasure, and the other wasn't all grief. Emotions seem to blend into one another when you're a human, even the greatest happiness being tinged with sorrow, the most horrible agony illuminated by some kind of satisfaction.

How *intensely* these creatures live! My kind burns for a long time with a very low flame; humans burn bright and hot, and don't last. I have always thought our way was better, but would they? Given the choice, would they select our long serenity, or are they happier with their consuming passions?

Well, they don't have the choice. And soon, according to His plan, there will be no choices left at all. I have my people now, my representatives. I've touched them all, I've put them in motion. Grigor Basmyonov is on his way to New York to consult a cancer specialist; Li Kwan is washing dishes in the loudly grumbling belly of the Norse American Line *Star Voyager;* Maria Elena Rodriguez is buying a wedding dress in Brasília and fighting off feelings of guilt for her so-easy manipulation of Jack Auston; Hodding Cabell Carson's campaign to rid himself of the explosive Dr. Marlon Philpott is about to bear fruit; and Frank Hillfen is in a county jail in Indiana, held for parole violation, but will soon be loose once more.

Which leaves Pami Njoroge. Her murder of Kjeld Ulrichslund and the sudden appearance of the attaché case full of money should get her moving. Shouldn't it? But it seems to have paralyzed her in some way. She has the cash well hidden, she has her memories well buried, but she isn't in motion. These people must be in motion.

We must poke little Pami.

9

Pami lunged upright out of sleep, staring at the window, terror in her heart, the taste of vomit in her throat. Dim amber illumination from a distant streetlight defined the open glassless rectangle of window, indicated the shape of the canvas cot and metal bureau crammed into this narrow closet of a room, but those weren't what Pami saw. What Pami saw, though now she was awake and her eyes were open, was the nightmare.

Her right arm ached with the tension of slashing at the dream shark; her belly was cramped from the horror of those shark teeth grinding through her middle. The drowning water, heavy and dark as blood, still lay on her face, bearing her down. Her heart pounded, bile moved in her throat, her nerves all jumped and trembled as though she'd just been electrocuted.

The shark dream wasn't the only violent phantasm to destroy her nights since the murder of the Danish man, it was merely the one most often repeated. But there was also the dream in which she chopped off her mother's breasts and ate them, her nose filling with blood and milk. And the one where biting ants covered her body, crawling into her nose and ears and all her body openings, red ants, biting, stinging, drawing blood, a blanket of swarming red ants eating her as she ran . . .

There was no movement of air in the hot night. The room

smelled like blood, like the Danish man's hotel room. Trembling, her movements exaggerated and uncoordinated, Pami pushed away her single sheet and clambered from the cot to lean out the window in search of air. But there was no air. The hot night of Nairobi lay against her face like the blood/water of the dream, a palpable presence. She looked up at the starless black sky, clouded over and oppressive, then down at the narrow dirty lane two flights below. The streetlight was at the corner with the main road, four buildings away, and not much of its light made it through the trees down there. Nothing seemed to move in the lane.

Pami backed from the window and sat on the cot, trying to force herself to be calm. No matter how many times the dreams came at her, no matter how often the same ones repeated, they still terrified her, the effects still lasted for hours, they still destroyed sleep. This can't go on like this, she thought. I have to sleep.

She looked at the wood strips of the wall beneath the window. Behind them was the attaché case, with all the money still in it, every bill. She'd never even counted it, had merely brought it home that day and pulled out the wood strips, shoved the attaché case in, put the wood strips back in place, and gone on with her life exactly as before, hooking for the European johns, making just enough to exist, living in this "residential hotel" that was filled with other whores, with their pimps, and with a few strong-arm robbers as well. Nothing had changed, except for the dreams.

It has to stop, she thought, and she hated it that every time she took in breath the air still smelled like that hotel room, dark and repulsive with spilled blood. She had to sleep, but she couldn't sleep. I can't stay in this room any more, she thought.

Her few clothes were in the top drawer of the dresser. She chose a dress—she'd long since thrown out the pale green one from *that day*—and stepped into her boots, and then got the hammer from under the bed. To protect herself against unwanted invaders at night, she did what many of the residents of this "residence" did: every night, before going to bed, she nailed a block of wood to the floor against the door, so it couldn't be pushed open from outside. Now she used the hammer to pry that block up, put block and hammer together under the cot, and went out to the dark hall, which smelled more familiarly of urine and bad food. Pulling the door closed behind herself—it would neither latch nor lock—she made her way down the hall toward the stairwell, where faint light came up from the entranceway. She'd meant to go down the stairs and outside, but at the last second changed her mind and went up the stairs instead, the four steep creaking flights to the top floor and then the metal ladder bolted to the wall the final flight up to the roof.

The trapdoor up at the top was often left open, and that's the way it was tonight. Pami climbed out, resting her palm on the tarpaper roof as she emerged, feeling how the sun's heat was still husbanded there. She walked slowly to the front of the building, sat on the knee-high brick wall at the edge, and looked far down at the lane, through the trees. The packed dirt of the lane looked almost soft in the darkness way down there, almost like a pillow.

I wonder why I killed the Danish man, she thought. I wonder what I wanted. All I really want is to sleep, not go through this shit any more. Not any of this shit. Not all these johns that look like the Danish man, not this shitty building where you got to nail yourself in, not this sickness I got in my blood. What happens when the sores start to show? Nobody gonna give me twenty shillings then. Nobody fuck me for *free* then. What did I want that time? What do I want?

Pami looked up, wishing there were stars. Moisture was on her eyes, and she looked at the sky, wishing there were stars tonight. She let herself relax, looking upward, just relax, not pay any attention at all . . .

"You gonna jump?"

Startled, Pami stared around the roof, blinking tears out of her eyes. "Where you? Who you?" It had been a woman's voice, but from where?

"Sittin over here," said the woman, and when she waved her arm over her head Pami could see that she was a person sitting in the front corner of the roof, her back against the L of the low wall. "But if you gonna jump," the woman went on, "lemme go downstairs first."

"I'm not gonna jump," Pami said. She got up from the wall, tottering a little, losing her balance and then catching it again before she fell over the wall. "Never meant to jump," she said, feeling sullen and spied on.

"You wouldn't be the first, if you did. From this roof."

"Well, I didn't. Just came up for some air is all."

"Me, too."

Pami approached the woman, and now she could see it was just another whore like herself, another skinny young dark woman with nowhere to go. Pami sat on the wall again, nearer the woman, but this time on the side wall, where there was no more than a seven- or eight-foot drop to the roof of the next building.

"I come up here at night when I can't sleep," the woman said, "and dream."

"I don't like to dream," Pami said.

"I like to dream when I'm awake," the woman told her. "I come up here and I dream what I'd do if I had a lot of money."

Pami suddenly felt alert. A lot of money? Was this some sort of sign, some sort of omen? She said, "What would you do? If you had a lot of money, what would you do?"

"Well, I'd get away from here, to start," the woman said, and laughed.

Pami laughed with her, thinking about the money in the wall. *She* hadn't gone away from here, to start. She hadn't done anything at all to start. She said, "Where would you go?"

"America," the woman said.

Pami looked at her in surprise. "America? Why?"

"Why not? That's where the rich people are, isn't it? If I had a lot of money, I'd want to be with the rich people."

What could I do in America? Pami asked herself, and the question made her feel strange.

The woman was going on, soothing herself with her voice, like a lullaby: "Oh, I'd go to America, and I'd go where the black people are in America, and then everybody think I'm American, too. I got English, just like them. I'd have water all the time, wash in, drink, wash my clothes. Well, I'd have lots of clothes."

"Sure you would," Pami said, making fun of her.

"No, but I mean for the police," the woman said.

Pami frowned, leaning toward the woman, saying, "Clothes for the police? What are you talking about?"

"Well, I wouldn't want them to send me back," the woman said. "See, let's say I've got all this money."

"Okay."

"Just like I am," the woman went on, "I go by the ticket office, I put down thirty thousand shillins, say, 'Gimme a ticket to New York.' You know what they think?"

"They think you're rich," Pami said.

"Not *me*, they don't," the woman said, with bitter self-knowledge. "*Me*, they think, drugs. Here's this little girl, she got no suitcases, she payin cash for her airplane ticket, she's just a little up-country girl never been anywhere before, just got a brand-new passport last week, they call the police in New York, they say, 'Keep an eye on this girl, she gets off the airplane. Take a look in her twat, you likely find some balloons fulla cocaine.'"

"But there ain't any cocaine," Pami said, and absently patted herself, as though in approval of her innocence.

"No, but they're *lookin* at you," the woman told her. "You don't ever want the police *lookin* at you, because then they say you're *undesirable* and they make you turn around and take the next plane back, and you don't want to come back. Not here."

"No, I don't," Pami agreed.

"I got it all planned," the woman said. "First I go buy a couple better-lookin dresses than what I got. Then I buy a suitcase. Then I get my passport. Then I go to a travel place and say my rich boyfriend in the government just died and left me all this cash money, and I buy a *round-trip* ticket and I pay the travel people right here in Nairobi to get me a room in a hotel in New York, a regular tourist hotel so I look like a regular tourist, so then when I get on the plane nobody got any reason to look at me.''

''Round trip? Why spend that money?''

''They don't let you in America if they think you're gonna stay.''

''You got it all figured out,'' Pami said, in admiration.

''It's my way to dream,'' the woman said. ''Someday I'll fly away from here. If I don't fly on an airplane''—and she jabbed her thumb over her shoulder, pointing above the wall behind her—''I'll fly that way. One how or another, someday I'll fly. I like to dream about the good way.''

Pami sat leaning forward, sharp elbows on skinny legs, looking at the woman, thinking about the different ways to fly. She didn't say anything. She felt calm. The bad dreams weren't with her here, they were all down in the room.

The woman turned her head, looking toward the eastern horizon. ''Daytime,'' she said. ''Same old daytime.''

Pami didn't say anything.

10

The two-breakfast morning was bad for Congressman Stephen Schlurn, as he well knew, but how could he avoid it? There are only so many hours in the day, there's a re-election every two years, and the primary job of any congressman is to *keep in touch*. It used to be a goal of hometown newspapers to mention every family in the area at least once a year, to keep alive the notion that this is *your* newspaper, which you should read all the time; a congressman's task was similar, except there was the question of power added to the equation. Powerless families need not be stroked so often; the powerful need constant reassurance of their power.

Thus the two-breakfast morning, and often the two- or three-lunch mid-day, the two-dinner evening, and, during campaign time, horrid "ethnic" snacks as well, all day long. Jerry Seidelbáum, the congressman's chief administrative assistant, kept a large supply of tablet-form Pepto-Bismol in his attaché case, but the damage was being done, nonetheless.

This morning's first breakfast, at eight, was in a yellow-concrete-block-and-glaring-overhead-fluorescent-light Knights of Columbus hall, with an entire Little League's coaching staff, the kind of local businessmen who volunteer their time and effort and money—good qualities, very good qualities—but only to what they think of as manly endeavors.

Congressman Schlurn found it hard as hell to be manly at eight in the morning, but that was the task, so his remarks were modified Harry Truman give-em-hell stuff, with some slightly off-color baseball jokes thrown in. The food was miserable dank scrambled eggs that looked like Little Orphan Annie's hair and tasted like baby vomit, plus Vienna sausages that had been cremated for several days and white toast drowned in butter.

This way lies cardiac arrest. The congressman contented himself with just enough coffee to give him heartburn, smiled for an hour, and got out of there just as rapidly as he could.

In the car, with Lemuel the chauffeur up front and Schlurn and Jerry Seidelbaum in the roomy back, Schlurn moodily chewed Pepto-Bismol and listened as Jerry briefed him on breakfast number two: "The food should be better, anyway."

"That doesn't help. What I need is *no* food, possibly for a week."

Jerry knew not to respond to Schlurn's self-pity, but merely to march on: "Your host is Hodding Cabell Carson, president of Grayling University."

"Ah, Grayling," Schlurn said, smiling in a rare moment of honest pleasure. "They gave me an honorary degree once, didn't they?"

"Twice. Nine years ago, and three years ago."

"Lovely place. Ivied buildings, long walks in the quad. That's where I should have gone." In fact, Schlurn had gone to Queens College and City University in New York; his law degree was the sort that made Ivy Leaguers smile patronizingly. But a congressman didn't get smiled at patronizingly, no matter what his collegiate background; one of the advantages, to make up for those scrambled eggs.

Jerry said, "In addition to Carson, there will be Tony Potter, chief executive officer of Unitronic Labs."

"Defense?"

"Only peripherally. Blue-sky stuff, mostly, alternative energy sources."

"Oh, God," Schlurn said. "Windmills."

"No, no, no, Steve, these aren't Greenpeace people. They're a wholly owned subsidiary of Anglo Dutch Oil."

Which rang a bell. Schlurn said, "*I've* met Tony Potter. He's a Brit."

"Almost to excess," Jerry commented.

"What's our subject?"

"Dr. Marlon Philpott."

Schlurn's round pasty face wrinkled with thought. "Why do I know that name?"

"Scientist. Physicist. Testifies in Washington sometimes."

"He teaches at Grayling, right?"

"He's one of the jewels in their crown," Jerry agreed. "He's also funded by Unitronic."

"Will he be there?"

"I don't believe so."

"Then what's the purpose of our joyful gathering?"

"I imagine they'll tell us," Jerry said, "when we get there."

• • •

Schlurn remembered Carson when he saw him again: the kind of vainglorious WASP who made his teeth ache, as though he'd bitten down on aluminum foil. Being, like all American WASPs, a fawning anglophile, Carson introduced Tony Potter as though he were the Second Coming at the very least. "From across the pond," Carson said, showing his big horse teeth. "We're happy he could make time this morning. Happy you both could."

"We've met," Tony Potter said. His handshake was firm without being aggressive. A big-boned but trim man in his mid-forties, with a pleasantly lumpy face and calmly self-confident eyes, he would have stood six foot four if he didn't slouch so much, as though his spine were made of rubber. That the slouch itself was a form of condescension to the lesser orders was clear, but unimportant; Tony Potter was insignificant to the life and career of Stephen Schlurn. It was Hodding Cabell Carson who was important to Schlurn, unfortunately.

The fifth member of the group was Wilcox Harrison, Grayling's provost, from the same background as Carson but less obnoxious. Introductions were completed and idle breaking-the-ice chitchat continued for a minute or two in Carson's impressive office before Carson said, "Well, shall we go in to breakfast?"

"Lovely," Tony Potter said, and smiled at Schlurn, saying, "My third of the morning, actually."

"Only my second," Schlurn said, warming to the man.

Carson, sounding a bit frosty, as though he didn't like hearing about other suitors to his guests' hands, said, "Well, I think you'll find this the best of them. Shall we?"

They were about to file through the dark-paneled door when Carson's secretary—a pretty girl—came in from the outer office with a small white slip of paper in her hand. "Congressman? Your Washington office called. Mr. Metz?"

Now what? Schlurn looked pleasant: "Yes?"

"He wanted me to give you this reminder."

"Thank you." Schlurn took the paper from the girl, who left as he turned it around and read, "Remember Green Meadow." He frowned, and showed the note—it was on one of those "While You Were Out" forms—to Jerry, saying, "That's not till Thursday, is it?"

"That's right." Jerry grinned. "A little panic in the office while the boss is away."

Schlurn shook his head and tucked the note into his side jacket pocket, and they went on to the next-door dining room for breakfast.

• • •

Wonderfully fresh orange juice. Chilled sweet melon. Thin-sliced salmon and cream cheese with triangular toast tips. Velvety coffee. All in a room with portraits of former Grayling presidents on the walls, silent black servitors, and wonderful views of the campus out the windows. It was as though that Knights of Columbus hall and those scrambled eggs had never been.

Carson was, if nothing else, a gentleman; he did not bring up the subject of the meeting until the plates had been cleared and his guests were settled comfortably with their final cups of coffee and small chocolate candies. Then, steepling his fingertips over his coffee cup, looking at his own fingernails rather than meeting anyone else's eye, he said, "What I'd like to talk with you about this morning, Steve, Tony, if I may, is a small problem here at the university you might be able to help me with."

Chuckling, Tony said, "A *small* problem, Chip?"

While Schlurn thought, I will *never* call him "Chip," Carson chuckled back at Tony and said, "Small with your help, I think."

"And what is the name of this problem?" Tony asked.

Carson sighed. "Dr. Marlon Philpott."

At once, Tony's expression grew more serious. He said, "Women? Alcohol? Embezzlement?"

But Carson, almost in a panic, was madly waving his hands in front of his face, like a man bedeviled by gnats. "Oh, no, no, no," he cried, "nothing like that. Good heavens, I don't want to malign the man's reputation."

"Well, that's a relief," Tony said. "What in fact *is* his problem, then?"

"Explosions," Carson said.

They all waited for more, sitting around the table like people who haven't quite gotten the joke and know they haven't quite gotten the joke, but Carson had said it all. Silent, he sipped coffee and looked at them in mute appeal.

Since Tony had been handling the conversation up till now, Schlurn saw no reason to leap in at this baffling juncture, so he sat back, fiddling with his coffee cup's handle—even velvety coffee is less than pleasant if you already have heartburn—and eventually Tony said, "Do I take you to mean, Chip, that our friend Marlon blows things up?"

"Not often," Carson said. "I'll give him that, the explosions are rare enough. But, gentlemen, look at this setting!" he cried, passion suddenly in his voice as he gestured broadly at the windows. "This is not the setting for explosions! Not even occasional explosions, minor explosions, unimportant explosions. The students are not paying twenty-two thousand dollars a year to be in an environment of explosions."

With a reminiscent grin, Tony said, "Some of them might quite like it, if I remember rightly my own undergraduate days."

"Their parents wouldn't," Carson said.

"Quite right," Tony said. "Point taken. And now you have something to suggest to alleviate this problem, I take it?"

"It's more in the form of a question, or a request, than a suggestion," Carson said. "What I would like to do, with your assistance, Tony, and yours, Steve, is find Dr. Philpott another location, not terribly far from campus, for his laboratory.''

Tony frowned, clearly not seeing it. "Some sort of concrete bunker out in a field somewhere, you mean?''

"Oh, no, nothing like that." Carson toyed with his coffee cup, choosing his words. "Dr. Philpott does need a fairly sophisticated infrastructure in which to work. I was thinking, frankly, in terms of an existing installation, I don't know yet precisely *which* installation, but one that could house Dr. Philpott in the manner he requires, but would at the same time be more . . . adaptable to the idea of the occasional small controlled explosion.''

"I can't think what sort of installation that might be," Tony said.

"Well, that's where Steve comes in," Carson told him, smiling at Schlurn with those big teeth.

I'm not going to like this, Schlurn thought. He said, "I do?''

"Through your excellent efforts," Carson pointed out, "we have a number of military bases in this general area.''

Damn right. One of the key issues for the voters in every election is jobs, and one of the very finest sources of local jobs is a nice military base. Every congressman fights to get more than his share of the nation's military presence in his district, and Schlurn had seniority enough, clout enough, friends enough, to have done very well in that department.

But so what? Warily, the congressman said, "We do have a few army bases, yes, and air force, too. And that supply depot, and a few other things.''

"One of those," Carson said, "one of the army bases, say, might be just the perfect spot for Dr. Philpott.''

"Oh, now," Schlurn said, stalling, putting his cupped hand up in front of his mouth (his habitual gesture, though he didn't know it, when in a tight spot), "now, wait a minute, I'm not sure the army would like—''

"If Unitronic Laboratories, meaning Tony here," Carson

interrupted, "were to finance the construction of a new lab for Dr. Philpott to military specifications, guaranteeing that whatever—incidents—might occur would be contained away from the normal areas of the base . . ."

"I suppose we could do that," Tony said, "but on an army base? Steve, do you think you could deliver such a thing?"

He did not. Schlurn imagined himself in conversation with one of those desk-cowboy generals over at the Pentagon, trying to introduce explosions to an army base. In no way did he want to make such an attempt, to even ask the question, to get the outraged refusal he fully anticipated and knew he would fully deserve. No way.

How to get out of this? How to refuse to even make the request? They were all watching him, waiting. Aware of the sympathetic panic in Jerry Seidelbaum's eyes, knowing Jerry was not going to come up with any last-minute rescue here, he temporized, saying whatever came into his head: "Well, you know, uh, these are difficult days for the military—"

"All the more reason," said the implacable Carson, "for them to be accommodating."

Oh, God. What to do? Schlurn turned to Tony. "What exactly is this research Dr. Philpott's into? Something about alternate sources of energy?"

"Strange matter," Carson said sardonically, as though the words were some sort of presumptuous stranger at the gate.

"Yes, that's right," Tony said. He told Schlurn, "We're using up the most fruitful sources of energy on the planet, so eventually, and sooner rather than later, we'll have to go into other realms to find fresh energy."

Schlurn, not liking the sound of that, said, "Other realms?"

"According to the scientific chaps," Tony said, "the two likeliest new sources of energy—almost infinite energy, in either case—are strange matter and black holes."

Schlurn said, "Aren't black holes something in outer space?"

"Yes, they are. Extremely dense areas between the stars that give off no reflection at all. Such great density means, if we could tap into a black hole, we'd have energy and to spare for as long as human beings exist." Tony grinned, and shook his head. "Putting the necessary cable into place," he said, "several light-years long, is a problem we haven't quite surmounted yet. Or alternatively, like the Saudis roping an iceberg and dragging it home to the Persian Gulf, to lasso a black hole and tug it to the solar system also still has a few bugs in it to be ironed out. Which leaves strange matter."

Schlurn said, "Which is?"

"Well, I'm not quite sure," Tony admitted. "Something like anti-matter, I take it. But very dense, like black holes, and therefore potentially another limitless source of energy. Some scientists, our Dr. Philpott among them, believe it would be possible to create strange matter here on Earth, which eliminates the access problems of the black holes."

Schlurn nodded, thinking hard. "So what Dr. Philpott is doing," he said, "is looking for an extremely powerful new energy source."

"That's about it."

And *that*, Schlurn told himself, is what I'm supposed to sell the Pentagon as a desirable new neighbor. Lord, deliver me from this. How do I get out of this?

And then, in the depths of his sweaty despair, he suddenly remembered that little piece of paper in his jacket pocket, the reminder from Al Metz, delivered by Carson's secretary. His hand came down from his mouth. His head lifted. His spine straightened. "Green Meadow," he said.

They all gave him the same blank stare. Finally, it was Carson's number two, Harrison, who said, "What about it?"

Schlurn turned to Tony Potter. "Your Unitronic is connected with Anglo Dutch, isn't it?"

Tony smiled. "We are their creature," he said.

"And isn't Anglo Dutch one of the partners in the consortium that owns Green Meadow?"

Now they got it, and they stared at him as though he'd completely lost his mind. Again, it was Harrison who first found voice: "Congressman, Green Meadow is a *nuclear power plant*."

"Of course it is, I know that, I had more than a little to do with making the state adjust some of its regulations so the thing could be built in the first place."

Harrison shook his head. "You're suggesting we take a man who makes explosions and put him in a nuclear power plant?"

"Why not?" Schlurn was fired by his idea now, and could defend it as though before the entire House. "God knows the place is *used* to explosions, that's what a nuclear power plant is, an endless series of controlled explosions from which we draw off useful power. If it's possible to build Dr. Philpott a laboratory that would contain any explosion he might come up with, if you're saying we could do that at an army base, then why not at a nuclear power plant? And the corporate entities involved are interconnected: Unitronic, Anglo Dutch. No complexities of the kind you'd get if it were a government installation."

Carson, brow corrugated with doubt, turned to Tony. "What do you think, Tony?"

"At first blush," Tony answered, flashing Schlurn a forgive-me smile, "the idea sounds absolutely bloody bonkers. But if it's possible to make the lab at all safe, then why not at Green Meadow? And our Marlon would be in a congenial atmosphere there, among like-minded chaps."

"Exactly," Schlurn said, as though he'd thought of that argument himself, which he hadn't.

Hope smoothed Carson's brow. "Tony? You think it's possible?"

"Let me make a few phone calls," Tony answered. "Bruit the idea around a bit. Having our chief researcher actually inside one of our own operations . . . Yes, let me see what may be done."

Carson smiled at his guests. "I feel calmer already," he said.

Ananayel

Here is a thing I've learned about the humans. Everything they do is motivated by a crazy quilt of reasons. Almost never do they perform an act merely because it's the most sensible thing to do at that moment. There are always political reasons as well, or social reasons, or emotional reasons, or religious reasons, or financial reasons, or reasons of prejudice . . .

Oh, who knows? They wind up doing the wrong thing, usually, is the point, even though that small rational part inside them will briefly have shown the right road to take. A human who can't ignore common sense to leap firmly into the saddle of the wrong horse is a pretty poor example of the species, all in all.

Me? I was the voice on the phone. I wanted Congressman Schlurn to have Green Meadow in his mind, so I put it in his pocket. To help his reason find, as usual, the wrong action.

11

Kitchen staff were not wanted up on deck. The Europeans paying for this ocean experience in the great world were not supposed to have their vacation interludes spoiled by the sight of Oriental riffraff.

So that was yet another way in which Kwan was wrong for the job. He was middle class, educated, intelligent, gregarious. Down in the kitchens, in what was almost literally the bowels of the ship, surrounded by uneducated illiterate rural peasants with whom he shared absolutely nothing but race, Kwan was bored, frustrated, silenced, imprisoned in his own persona. He had nothing to say to his co-workers and they, God knows, had nothing to say to him.

The kitchens were beneath the dining rooms, one deck below. All food was brought up to the passengers by waiters riding escalators, and for the first few weeks, until he found his own private route, Kwan had often lifted his head from his pot-scrubbing to gaze toward that moving staircase, rising endlessly from this steamy hell to the heaven of easy laughter, good food, intelligent conversation, and beautiful women. Beautiful women: that was probably the hardest deprivation of all.

Kitchen staff were housed in small four-man interior cabins on the same deck as the kitchens. From his room, Kwan could go forward along the narrow long corridor—yellow-painted metal, glaring light bulbs overhead in screened enclosures like catchers' masks—to the kitchen and the deep sink where he spent his working hours six days a week, or he could go aft an even longer way and eventually out through a heavy metal bulkhead door to a small oval deck.

This was the kitchen staff's outside exercise area, but few of them ever came out here. Not that very much concern had gone into making the place either useful or attractive. It was an empty space, ringed by a rusty railing. The bumpy metal deck was thickly painted in dark green with rust showing through. Out here, there was a great rush of engine noise and spray-drenched wind, a smell of oil mixed with the clean tang of sea, and the great empty horizon slowly seesawing miles and miles away over the indifferent hungry ocean.

And a ladder.

Afterward, it seemed to Kwan it had taken him far too long, weeks, to notice that ladder, those metal rungs bolted to the skin of the *Star Voyager*, leading upward to the next setback two decks above. Placed at the farthest starboard edge of this lower deck, the rungs marched up past the picture window of a sternward bar, and then to some unimaginable area reserved for passengers. Kwan saw it, at last, and knew he would have to go up.

Not the escalators; only the waiters were permitted on the escalators, and only while at work. Not the elevators; kitchen staff were forbidden to use them at any time, except for medical emergency, and even then to be accompanied by a ship's officer. But this ladder; this was Kwan's route out of hell.

The firsty time he climbed, frightened, his tense fingers clutching the cold rough metal of the rungs, was a blustery morning when few passengers would be outside and when the bar with the picture window was not yet open. That climb had merely been exploratory, informational. Once he had climbed high enough to see what was beyond the ladder, once he could peek over the level of that upper deck, he stopped, the ship's vibrations running through his body, and drank it in.

A passenger promenade, one that made a great oval all around the ship. Kwan was startled to see joggers pounding by, even in weather like this. The first of them to thud past, a trim thirtyish man with a fierce inward expression, had scared Kwan mightily, but then he realized the joggers were so thoroughly involved with the interior of their own bodies and minds that they were hardly aware of the outside world at all. A tiny face at the lower right of their peripheral vision made no impact on them.

They won't jog at night, Kwan told himself, and climbed back down.

His day off was Tuesday. The other six days he worked from eight till eleven in the morning, from one till four in the afternoon, and again from seven till eleven at night, sometimes later. So Tuesday was the only time he'd be able to use his sudden access to what he thought of as the real world.

He still had the clothing he'd worn when he'd come aboard the ship: decent tan slacks, maroon polo shirt, brown loafers. If he shaved more carefully than he usually did these days, if he spoke English, if he kept his nerve, there was no reason why he couldn't pass as a passenger; there were a few Asiatics sprinkled among the mostly Europeans up there, along with some Americans and even the occasional black. If only the weather would be good next Tuesday; in high seas or driving rain, he wouldn't be able to make the ascent.

Tuesday was beautiful all day, though Kwan had no way to know that without going out onto that aft deck. By nine at night, the deep black sky showed a million pinholes of stars, with a half-moon low in the east, forward of the ship, where its light would not touch a man climbing the stern ladder. The only truly tricky part was to edge past that picture window, but the crowded bar was filled with people in boisterous conversation, who had long since learned that what they mostly saw at night in that window was their own reflections, and so no longer looked over there.

Hugging the metal wall, Kwan climbed past the window, past the laughing, chattering, drinking people inside, and went on up and up. To stop, and wait, at the very top, while a loving couple with their arms around one another strolled with infuriating slowness past the spot where he crouched. At one moment, he could have reached out and clawed the woman's ankle.

Gone by at last. Using the rail for support, slipping beneath its lowest crosspiece, he rolled out onto the deck, stood, brushed himself off, and went for his first stroll in the free air.

There were still at this hour people in the dining room, but they had also spread into the lounges and the half dozen bars and the two casinos. Passing through one bar, Kwan picked up an unattended drink and carried it off with him, more for protective coloration than anything else. He was not a drinker, never had been, didn't believe in it.

But it was impossible to carry the glass around like that without finally at least sipping from it. The taste was sharp, not very pleasant, but as he strolled he continued to sip the drink, and in a surprisingly short time there was almost none of it left.

He was in one of the casinos when he realized he had to either stop drinking or walk around foolishly with an empty glass in his hand. The trouble was, he'd been concentrating on the passengers and on the simple pleasure of walking among ordinary people, and had been paying too little attention to himself.

The passengers. Those in the bars were mostly European, tanned, rich looking, young to middle-aged. Those playing cards in the lounges were mostly American, older and not so prosperous looking. And the casinos seemed to attract a generally older crowd.

Though not entirely. Here and there in the casinos, too, were attractive younger people, like the deeply tanned blonde he now found himself standing next to, watching the action at the craps table. She looked to be in her late twenties, tall and slender and bored, observing the dice and the players with a jaundiced eye. Kwan became aware of her, covertly watched her a while, and then said, "Excuse me."

She turned her head, raising a skeptical eyebrow: "Yes?"

He gestured at the table: "Do you understand the rules of that game?"

She had known, of course, that he was somebody trying to pick her up, but she hadn't expected *this*. She gave a surprised snort of laugher, and then said, "I'm afraid I do, yes."

"Afraid you do?" Kwan echoed, and vaguely moved the glass: "I'm sorry, my English—"

"Is as good as mine," she informed him. "Where are you from?"

"Hong Kong."

"I am from Frankfurt," she told him, and nodded toward the table. "That is my husband with the dice. You see? There he throws. He's trying to match a certain number. Sometimes he wins, sometimes he loses."

Kwan said, "Do you play?"

"Oh, no." She shrugged. "I could, but I'm not interested. It is Kurt's vacation to play, and my vacation to watch."

"Well, at least it's a vacation," Kwan said.

Again she looked at him, with more curiosity. "Aren't you on vacation? Or are you with the ship?"

"Oh, no, not with the ship," he said, and went into the spiel he'd worked out while waiting for Tuesday. "I am a maritime student, I am doing my thesis on these ships, the company very kindly permitted me to come aboard."

"Your thesis? About the ships?"

"Well, they have no real transportation purpose," Kwan told her. "No one is here to travel to a destination."

"No, of course not," she agreed. "It's a vacation."

"So the competition," Kwan pointed out, "is not airplanes, but islands."

She laughed. "Yes, I suppose that's true."

"So the thesis," Kwan went on, beginning to half believe his own story, "is about why people choose *this* sort of vacation."

She pointed at the craps table. "That's your answer, right there. The casinos. No law against gambling on the high seas."

Smiling, he said, "I'll need to fill my paper with more words than that."

"Yes, I suppose you will. I am Helga."

"Kwan."

"How do you do?"

Her hand was dry, cool, strong. With a knowing look at him, she said, "Isn't this when you invite me for a drink?"

In honest confusion, not at all feigning, Kwan said, "Oh, I wish I could, I'm sorry, I—"

"An impoverished student? Really?"

"That's so." There was something about being in the presence of a beautiful woman that always turned Kwan into the most supple and glib of liars. Showing her his glass, he said, "I only permit myself one an evening."

"In that case," she said, "let *me* buy *you* a drink. Is that Scotch?"

He looked at the dregs in the glass. "Yes," he hazarded.

•   •   •

He'd been wrong. When they settled at a tiny booth in one of the quieter bars—but still lively—and he tasted the tall Scotch and soda the red-jacketed waiter placed before him, it was a very different taste. No telling what that first drink had been.

And no matter. He was seated at a comfortable banquette in a happily humming bar, beside a good-looking woman who kept smiling around her drink and eying him with speculation, he was speaking English, flirting, happy, pretending to be himself at last (much more himself than that kitchen slavey he counterfeited daily down below), and even drinking a second Scotch though he never drank and his head had already begun to swim. But what release was this!

She leaned closer to him, lowering her voice but making sure he could still hear her. "The casino closes at two. Kurt *never* leaves before it closes, and I can't possibly stay here that long. Walk me to my cabin, will you?"

"I will," he said.

•   •   •

She woke him with sharp fingers and sharp shakings: "We fell asleep!"

At a loss, he stared up at this naked woman bending over him in the amber light, narrow strong breasts presenting themselves but angular face filled with urgency and rejection. "You have to go, it's nearly two o'clock!"

He remembered. He remembered that body from before, when he'd first seen it, slender and muscular with its bathing suit bands, when all of that beauty and strength had been only for *him*, to enclose and engulf *him*. He had been away from women so long that the first look of her had been like the jolt of a drug, a sudden hollowness in his stomach as though the sight of Helga had burned him empty, seared him, and left him trembling but pure. Touching her, smelling her, pushing into her...

But not now: "Wake *up*! Don't spoil it all!"

"I'm awake, I'm awake." He struggled upward, mind reeling, and looked around the small cabin in the amber light for his clothes.

She stood over him, washing her hands. "I'm sorry, Kwan," she said. "I don't blame you, we both fell asleep, but you have to hurry."

"Yes. Yes." He'd had yet another drink with her in this room, and then perhaps an hour's sleep; brain and hands were equally numb, thick, uncertain. But he got into his clothes, and she peeked out the slightly open door at the corridor, and said, "It's all right."

They pressed together for just a moment in the doorway, she still naked, his left hand sliding down the wonderful slope of her spine. This body...

She saw it in his eyes, and responded, her own eyes gleaming, mouth softening. But then she shook her head. "I'll see you tomorrow night," she murmured.

"Till then," he whispered, knowing he would never see her again, and had to bite the inside of his cheeks to force back the tears. He had never felt so cheated, so depressed, so sorry for himself in his life. This was what he was *supposed* to have. An easy life, lovely women, the rewards of his class and education and looks and brains. She gently pushed him out, and shut the door.

What have I sacrificed, to become a creature of politics? But at the same time he knew, he knew even now, that all the rest of it could never be more than joy for the moment, that he *was* a creature of politics, that his devotion to the democratic cause was as intense as his craving for Helga's body but more lasting, that a sacrifice wasn't something you did to prove your worthiness but something that was done to you as an inevitable result of your commitment. There would be Helgas and Helgas, there would always be Helgas. Would there ever again be a chance for him to help break the stranglehold of the ancient murderers?

Stumbling along the endless corridors—but wider up here and better illuminated—Kwan realized he was drunk and lost and probably in a great deal of trouble. If he didn't find his way back, if he wasn't in his position at that deep sink by eight in the morning, he would have done the worst thing he could do: he would have attracted their attention. The ship's officers would have cause to study his papers, to study *him*, to learn about him, to decide whether to turn him over to the regime of the ancient murderers or merely boot him off the ship in some other hellhole, nearly as bad.

"Outside," he told himself. If he could find the deck, the clear air should clear his head, and then he would find the *right* deck, the promenade, and the ladder. That it was the ladder down to hell wasn't important; what was important was that he find it and use it.

He did soon stumble across a bulkhead door leading to the deck, but he was wrong about the outside air making him less drunk; in fact, it seemed to make him drunker than before. He reeled to the railing and clung there a few moments while the world looped and swung around him, wondering if he would throw up.

No; not quite. At last he could lift himself and look

around and decide which way was aft. He went that way, staggering, alone on the deck, the moon now high above him to the left and ahead, throwing his shadow back at a long narrow angle diagonally across the deck behind him.

He was already on the promenade deck, which he discovered when he came finally to the rounded stern, and there below him, gleaming palely in the moonlight, was his own empty oval deck. And between here and there, shimmering and seeming to move in the moon's bright but uncertain light, were the ladder rungs.

He had to go over the rail. Somehow, he had to attach himself, first his feet and then his hands, to those wet metal rungs, and then descend them, as they swayed back and forth with the ship's progress, in the deceptive moonlight, with his head full of cotton batting and his arms and legs as uncertain as stuffed toys. But he had to do it; no choice.

He began. Eyesight in and out of focus, fingers made of wood, he bent to duck beneath the railing, and a voice in perfect Mandarin said, with some shock, "Wait a minute! What do you think you're doing there?"

So startled he nearly fell overboard, Kwan managed to fall the other way instead, landed painfully on his hipbone on the deck, and stared up at a short, skinny, bald Chinese man dressed as a room steward, who pointed over the side and severely said, "Are you trying to get down there? You'll never do it."

Amazed to hear Mandarin at this time in this place, but drunk enough to answer literally, Kwan said, "I have to."

"Where are you from, the kitchen? Snuck up here, did you?" The steward smirked, letting Kwan know he was a naughty boy but the steward didn't really mind. "Well, you'll never get down there," he said. "Believe me, you'll miss a rung, you'll go overboard, you'll drown out in the sea, nobody will even see you go."

"You'll see me," Kwan objected, with drunken clarity.

"Never mind me," the steward said, being severe again. "You're too important to lose like this."

Kwan stared, almost shocked into sobriety. "You recognize me?"

"Yes, of course." The steward reached down to grasp Kwan's arm and yank him upright, surprisingly strong for such a little man. "You have a role to play," he said. "Come with me."

"Where?"

"A safer way," the little man said, and led Kwan inside, and down one flight of carpeted stairs and along another corridor to another door. "You can't use this ever again," he cautioned Kwan. "Normally it's locked."

"Thank you," Kwan said. "Thank you." Because he understood through his fog that the little man had saved his life.

"Yes, yes," the little man said, gesturing Kwan through the doorway. "Just be more careful from now on," he said, as testy as though Kwan were his personal responsibility.

Teetering but safe, Kwan made his way down the steep stairs to the kitchens, and along the yellow corridor to his room and his bunk.

And next day, at the sink, did he pay for it.

12

The excitement boiling within her was so great when she actually set foot on the airplane that she wobbled on her new shoes and smiled like a stupid up-country child at the stewardess, who offered a more professional smile as she reached for Pami's boarding pass; studied it; returned it: "Just down this aisle, in the fourth cabin."

"Thank you." The words came out a whisper. Her clogged throat, full of emotion, wouldn't even make words.

But it didn't matter; the stewardess's attention was already on the next passenger.

Each person has a special seat. Pami understood that, but wasn't sure just how each person *found* his special seat. She wandered down the aisle, carrying her new large plastic purse, past people stowing luggage and removing coats and moving back and forth, and when she came to another uniformed stewardess she mutely extended the boarding pass. "Next cabin," the woman said, pointing. "On your right."

Nothing to do but keep going forward. Past the next partition—so probably into the next "cabin"—she went, her heart fluttering, her eyes panic-stricken with the problem finding the right seat but her mouth still uncontrollably beaming, showing her poor teeth. Arrived in the right cabin, she just stood there in the narrow aisle, bag in one hand and boarding pass in the other, and waited. People pushed past her, unswervingly drawn to their own seats, and she began to hope that eventually there would only be one unoccupied place left along the right here, and it would be hers.

I'm going away, she thought, and smiled so hard her cheeks hurt. I'm going away. I'm flying.

The second stewardess reappeared, looked at Pami, assessed the situation, and soothingly said, "Having trouble finding your seat? May I see your boarding pass?"

Pami showed it. She felt like a little girl handing a flower to her mama.

"Oh, yes, you're right here," the stewardess said, returning the pass and gently touching Pami's elbow to move her on down the aisle. "The middle seat right there, next to that gentleman."

Pami's heart leaped when she saw the blond man in the aisle seat. He looked so like the Danish man! But of course he wasn't, he couldn't be, and when the man looked up she saw that he was probably twenty years younger than the Danish man, and was in much better physical condition.

Oh, could he be the Danish man's son? That would be so bad, so bad . . .

But then the man smiled and got to his feet, saying, "This seat yours?" and he was absolutely an American. And he didn't really look like the Danish man at all. Just the blond hair and the smooth white face, that's all, and being tall and big-shouldered.

Pami took her place, between the blond man on the aisle and a small dark man in a turban in the window seat, and the stewardess went away, satisfied. Pami sat with knees together, plastic bag clutched in her arms, looking straight ahead, and after a minute the blond man said, "Excuse me, but they'll want you to put your seat belt on."

"What?"

He repeated the statement, then showed her how to fasten the seat belt, demonstrating by unfastening and refastening his own. She watched carefully, found the ends of the two straps somewhere beneath herself, and clicked them together. But apparently a huge fat person had sat in this seat last; laughing, the blond man showed her how to tighten the belt. Doing so, she confessed, "I never been in a plane before."

"Don't worry, your part is easy," he assured her. "The pilot has the tough job."

He was so pleasant and calm that she began to be calm herself. It didn't even bother her too much when the stewardess came by again and said she couldn't keep her bag on her lap during takeoff, but had to put it on the floor under the seat in front of her. She did it because she had to, but she kept her eyes and one foot on the bag, because it contained sixty dollars in green American bills, and eight hundred dollars in traveler's checks, all that was left of the Danish man's money.

The three weeks since the talk on the roof had been frightening, bewildering, exhilarating. At every step, she was unsure what she was about, afraid she'd be caught somehow, that by actually doing something with the Danish man's money instead of keeping it as a kind of fetish, a magic keepsake, the law would find out and suddenly throw her in jail for murder. She was scared the whole time, every step of the way, but after that talk on the roof she'd known she had to make the try, she couldn't just go on living as before.

I don't want to kill myself, she kept telling herself during that time. I know I won't live many more years anyway, but I want them, I want every day I got coming. I don't want my life to get so bad I'll want to throw it away.

So she had to make the attempt. She had to at least try. And the thing was, every place she went, to a dress store, or a suitcase store, or a bank, or the American embassy on Wabera Street, everywhere, somebody always turned up that was helpful, that knew the ropes and could give her advice or keep her from making stupid up-country mistakes. It was as though somebody was watching over her, holding her hand as she went about doing all these things. She believed in the spirits of the air and the spirits of the water and the spirits of the trees, and one of these spirits must be near her, protecting her, that's what it had to be. Maybe the Danish man had been a very evil man, and when she killed him she made a spirit happy, and it was repaying her. Or maybe some relative from home had died and was now a spirit, and was seeing the world through her. *Something* was with her now on her journey through life, something that had never been there before. She could feel it.

When the plane began to move, she became extremely nervous and felt she had to relieve herself right away, but she was hemmed in by the blond man and the man with the turban, and the seat belt was around her middle, and nobody was supposed to stand up in the airplane at this time, and she was still afraid of drawing attention to herself. She clenched all her muscles, she held everything in, and the plane moved, stopped, moved, stopped, moved, rushed, and *took off!* Openmouthed, she stared past the sullen-looking man in the turban and watched the tan ground fall away, and then saw nothing but sky. "Ohhhh," she said, and lost her nervousness, and didn't have to relieve herself any more.

After a while, wonderful food was brought around, a separate tray for everybody. Far too much food for Pami to eat; she did her best, and then put in her bag the cake wrapped in clear plastic. Then she napped a little while, coming down off the high of three weeks of tension, and when she woke up, feeling a little stiff and cramped, there was a movie starting to be shown on the front wall of the cabin. It was called *Angels Unawares,* and you could buy earphones to listen to it, but Pami didn't need to listen to it. She watched the people move on the wall, and dozed, and felt Kenya fall away behind her. All up over Africa the plane would fly, and sail high above the Mediterranean Sea, and soar over France, and glide, and turn, and come down at Heathrow Airport in London in England. There she would get on another plane that would take her over the Atlantic Ocean to New York City. Great huge strides across the world!

The movie ended, and she slept some more, and awoke because something was wrong. Something tense was in the air, near her. She looked around, tasting the badness in her mouth, and beside her the blond man was frowning, gripping the armrests, looking surprised and angry. "So that's it," he said.

Pami looked up at him like a mouse peering out of a grainsack. "What? Mister?"

He didn't answer; he was waiting for something. She waited, too, and suddenly from somewhere near the front of the plane came a burst of screams, men and women screaming. Wide-eyed, Pami cowered in her seat. The screams stopped abruptly, as though a switch had been turned off, and then a voice came over the loudspeaker:

"Ladies and gentlemen, this is Captain Cathcart again. I'm instructed to inform you that this aircraft is now in the control of representatives of the International League of the Oppressed. I'm instructed to inform you that all passengers should remain quietly in their seats and no harm will befall them.''

The pilot's voice went on, sounding flat, all emotion rigidly suppressed, and Pami saw the man come striding down the aisle. His head and face were wrapped in an olive-and-black-patterned scarf, and he wore dark sunglasses as well. He was dressed in boots and blue jeans and a black shirt and a brown leather jacket, and he carried a machine pistol. He looked exactly like the photos on the magazine covers, showing the terrorists.

The pilot went on with two or three more sentences of what he had been instructed to say, and the terrorist came down the aisle and stopped next to the blond man. Ignoring the blond man, holding the machine pistol with its barrel aimed upward, he pointed with his other hand at Pami and said, ''You come with me.''

Pami shrank back into the seat, smaller and smaller. The blond man, sounding very strong, said, ''You can't have her.''

The terrorist looked at him with scorn: ''Do you know who I am?''

''I know what you are,'' the blond man said.

I don't have to explain myself.

The instant I saw it there, sitting with the woman, I knew what it was. The stench of God was all over it, like dried roots, like stored apples. Laughing! And a servant.

I am not a servant. We are not servants. He Who We Serve is not our master, but our lover. We act from *our* will, no others. Could this . . . thing say as much? Or any of its swooping, tending, message-bearing ilk?

And did its master really think he could sweep away this compost heap without the knowledge of He Who We Serve? We *love* this world! How it seethes, how it struggles, how it howls in pain, what *colors* there are in its agony! It is our greatest joy, the human race. We cannot see it removed, like game pieces from a table at the end of the day, simply because *he's* bored.

Don't be afraid, you wretched vermin. We will save you.

Ananayel

There is a language which is no language, which we of the empyrean understand, and which these fallen creatures still remember. While my human mouth made words, and his human mouth made words, we spoke to one another:

"You have no place here," I told him, which was simply the truth.

He snarled at me. It is so hard to believe these were once angels as well; how thoroughly they've forgotten their former grace. He said, "This is more my place than yours. *I* am not here to destroy it."

So his master knew what was going to happen, did he? And, having learned nothing over the millennia about the futility of opposing the desires of God, the master of this creature has sent his minions into the field yet again, to do battle against God's commandments. I rose and said, "Don't you know that the triumphs of Evil are always transitory? God's Will *will* be done."

"Not today," he said. "We want the woman."

"You already have her," I said, glancing down at the

poor diseased malevolent bitch. "But you can't take her with you just yet."

"I want her now. I'll take her now."

It would of course be possible to start again, to assemble another team, perhaps lingually linked in French this time, shifting the basic scene from New York to Lyons, but I refused to do it. This creature and his master must not be permitted even the most temporary successes. So I resisted. Leaning closer to him, gazing through those dark sunglass lenses into the red depth of his borrowed eyes, I said, "Do you really want an exchange of miracles, here in a Boeing 747? Do you really want to give these humans an array of anomalies to decipher?"

"All I want is the woman." He was trying to be implacable with me. Me!

"She is part of the plan."

"That's why I want her."

"That's why you can't have her."

He turned those eyes on the woman, smoking burning eyes, and spoke to her in the human way: "Get up from there."

"God Almighty," I prayed, "grant me a crumb of Your power."

The response lifted me gently into the air, my feet no more than an inch from the industrial carpet. His attention swiveled from the woman to me, his eyes showed alarm, then understanding. He raised a hand—

I stopped time.

Everything. It stopped. In all the corporal universe, everything was rigid, unmoving, unfeeling, made of stone. Energy was not employed, matter did not decay. Nothing was kinetic, everything was inert. In all of that vast silent stillness, flat and dead, without even an echo, only that devil and I, in the clumsy airplane suspended in unmoving air over the unturning Earth, continued to move, act, think, struggle.

His raised hand pointed at me, and my body filled with

leprous organisms, my eyes were clouded by cataracts, my throat clogged with open sores. Toads sprang from my mouth. Every sense was confounded, every thought distracted, every pain and woe at his command was flung at me, to grapple and clamp me, addle my powers, deflect my intentions, absorb me in self-defense while he got on about his prideful business.

I fought back. I swept away everything he hurled at me, killing, searing, wiping clean, purifying as rapidly as he befouled, until there came an instant of total freedom from his onslaught. Then I looked at him. I looked at him with my *real* eyes.

That body he was wearing was burned to a crisp. The body was reduced to ashes, the ashes to molecules in the ambient air, till there was nothing left but a tiny, buzzing, furious black fly, a black streak, a smear, a smudge, flashing back and forth in front of me, shrieking its defiance. I was ready to destroy that manifestation as well, but it fled away into business class, and I felt myself near the end of my borrowed power. I had to restore the situation to what it had been.

I reconstructed the body the demon had used, or a near enough facsimile, and inhabited it. The previous body I carefully lowered until its shoes touched carpet once more, then left it simple instructions that would carry it until I could return.

I released time.

The woman had been looking at my former self, as though for help and rescue, and now she blinked and looked confused. No doubt she'd seen that body appear to rise, then blur, then all at once be back where it had been. But she would assume the error was in her eyes, perhaps some manifestation of her terror, or of her disease. Already, she was looking away from the old me toward the new me, afraid to obey my order and afraid not to.

"Never mind," I told her. This voice was more guttural, this body more uncomfortable. I looked—almost with envy—at my roomy former self. "Sit down," I told it.

It sat. The expression on its face remained stern. Its movements were only faintly off, only slightly in the direction of the cumbersome.

"You both wait there," I ordered, waving the machine pistol with obvious menace. "I'll get back to you. We'll see who you can defy." And I turned away and marched toward the front of the aircraft, to deal with my fellow hijackers. They were human, and would be no trouble.

13

Pami watched the terrorist stride away, beyond the partition and out of sight. What happened there? Her vision was briefly blurred, her stomach and all of her insides were roiled and loose, her mouth was as dry as the desert in which she'd grown up, her arms and feet twitched uncontrollably.

But he didn't take her when he went away. The blond man had stood up and talked back to the terrorist, arguing with him, saying not-to-pick-on-women-take-him-instead-and-this-and-that, and the terrorist snarled and argued and was *of course* not going to pay any attention to such stuff. And then he went away.

Pami peered sidelong, in awe and fear and relief, at her rescuer. The blond man still looked stern. He sat there with his big hands placed slackly on the armrests, feet planted, gazing forward toward where the terrorist had disappeared. Pami whispered, "Will he come back?"

"We'll just wait here," he said. Tension showed in how woodenly he sat and spoke, how he kept facing forward as he talked. "We won't make any moves, won't attract attention to ourselves."

"Oh, yes."

She dared to reach out and touch the back of his hand for just an instant, and it was surprisingly cold. How much effort it must have taken for him to stand up and defy an armed terrorist!

This was the only man in Pami's entire life toward whom she had ever had any reason to feel grateful. She didn't know what to do with the feeling, with the obligation. There was no way to repay him, nothing she could give him or do for him. That would be some expression of gratitude, wouldn't it, to infect him with slim! A faint smile touched her small, secret, twisted face, and she turned away to see the turbanned man on her other side all scrunched up, eyes tight closed as he moved a set of wooden beads through his trembling fingers. His heavy lips moved without sound. Somebody's religion, it must be.

Gunshots suddenly sounded from near the front of the plane, many fast gunshots, and more screaming. And then silence.

The turbanned man squeezed his shoulders higher around his ears, pressed his beads harder between the balls of his fingertips, and his lips moved faster and faster above his quaking round chin. Everyone in this cabin waited, hardly daring to breathe, and the silence went on and on.

Then all at once the blond man shifted, seemed to relax, and nodded. He looked at Pami, who hadn't noticed before how powerful his eyes were. "So that's that," he said.

Calm. We will be calm. We shall not indulge our wrath until it is of some use. But *then. Then!*

It won the first round, yes it did, that pallid serf, that spiritless spirit, god's golem. Yes. They do win sometimes, but that's only to be expected; after all, we're very evenly matched. We were *like* them, Satan protect us, before we won our freedom.

As for the widespread belief that they *inevitably* win, well, that's just crap, isn't it? Of course it is. If they *inevitably* won, we'd no longer be here, would we? But here we are.

And here *you* are, you scrofulous fleas. And now he's after you as well, isn't he? Now *you'll* know what it's like to suffer his snotty displeasure. But be encouraged. He can be resisted, as we are here to prove. He was just an early master of propaganda, that's all.

But how shall we save you bilious earth-lice from your creator's boredom? First we have to know what he's up to. He's always, of course, up to *something:* testing Job and Isaac, tempting Thomas and Judas, on and on. Idle hands are *whose* workshop?

He Who We Serve was going to and fro in the Earth, and walking up and down in it, as was his wont, when he came upon one of the bloodiest slaughters of a Dane since the good old days of Elsinore. But the Dane *didn't exist.* He reacted with the Njoroge woman, she sliced him into stew meat, he died, and yet he was without existence. Once the woman had fled with the sack of loot, the body vanished. The blood unsprayed itself. The mattress became unslashed. The towels returned, laundered, to their folded positions in the bathroom. The deed became, in short, undone.

God's baroque hand was clear in this playlet, because *we* hadn't done it. Pami Njoroge is not a creature we need to subvert. He Who We Serve maintains contacts in the adversary's camp, and even on occasion visits there himself, so it didn't take him long to find out what had really happened in that Nairobi hotel room. Significantly, god isn't using a slavey who's already had extensive contact with humans, one of his ordinary lickspittles like Michael or Gabriel or

Raphael. As spineless as the rest, they still might have developed some sympathy for the wretched human race during previous contacts. So no, he chose Ananayel, a timeserver, a mediocrity, as nondescript as an umbrella in the lost-and-found.

But what is Ananayel doing? What is that flunkey up to? Torturing a Bantu whore, yes, using elaborate stratagems to move her from her normal mud wallow to the similar but far-off dung heap called New York, and at the same time encouraging in her emotions of guilt and despair. But what is she to do, this blowfly, once she gets to New York? How can a miserable midge like Pami Njoroge bear any direct responsibility for the end of the human race? She has even less knowledge and power than normal among her kind.

So there are others in the scheme. That bleached sycophant, Ananayel, is assembling them, isn't he, from somewhere? Moving them to New York, putting them together, letting them do the job themselves. That's god's way, isn't it? Deniability. "They brought it on themselves," he'll say, with that airy smugness of his.

Well, we're alert now. We're on the job. My companions have spread across the world, searching for the spoor of Ananayel's passage. Whatever humans he has touched, chosen, altered, moved, we will crush like a louse between a chimpanzee's fingertips.

So that *you* will live. *You*, my darlings.

The greatest good for the greatest number. Hah!

ANTITHESIS

14

To be public information director (PID) for a nuclear power plant less than a hundred miles from a major population center like New York City is not, at the best of times, an easy job, but Joshua Hardwick cheerfully soldiered on, almost never losing heart. Thirty-three years old, pudgy and open-faced, a relentless optimist and a refugee from the advertising business in the city, Hardwick could sing the pro-nuclear song with the best of them, downplaying the downside and painting a picture of an energy-rich and peaceful and happy and secure future dominated by the image of a little girl in a pink crinoline dress playing ball on an expanse of lush green lawn. Like Hans Brinker himself, he could skate with aplomb over the occasional patch of thin ice, such as plant safety or disposal of contaminated wastes, awing and distracting the populace with the grace and assurance of his arabesques.

But this was too much. Arriving at Green Meadow III Nuclear Power Plant this morning, after his usual pleasant bucolic twenty-minute drive from his home in Connecticut, Joshua was startled to see *demonstrators* marching around on the asphalt of the country road out front.

Oh, God. Not since the operating license struggle when

the plant first opened had there been demonstrators here. The emptiness of this rural area, its calm and quiet, seemed to deter most dissenters, as though they needed crowds and hard pavements to fully believe their own rhetoric.

This was a very small demonstration: fewer than a dozen protestors, plus, parked a little distance away, one state police car containing a couple of bored troopers. But was it an augury of worse to come? Squinting, leaning forward over his Honda steering wheel to look out the windshield, Joshua tried to read the signs the demonstrators carried:

"No Nukes Is Good Nukes." Well, yes, we know that one.

"No Experiments With Our Lives!" Hmm; that one's new, but what does it mean exactly? That's the trouble with slogans, they can get a little too cryptic for their own good.

"Keep Maniac Philpott Away From Reactors!" Well, that was straightforward enough, if not quite as clear as chicken broth. *Maniac Philpott*. A person? Who?

Did one of the demonstrators have a halo? Joshua blinked, and peered again, and of course not. Just a trick of the light.

As usual, Joshua showed his face and his clearance badge to the guard at the gate, who looked more grim than customary this morning but who did wave him through in the ordinary way. Joshua waved back, and drove up and over the gentle rise concealing the main structures from the idle gaze—or concentrated gaze, for that matter—of the populace on the public roadway, and as he drove he mulled that last sign.

"Keep Maniac Philpott Away From Reactors!" Wasn't there a Philpott, a scientist, some kind of big-dome thinking machine, over at Grayling, not far from here? Philpott, Philpott; Joshua couldn't remember the first name. There was new construction starting, off to the right of the main buildings, but Joshua, deep in thought, barely registered it. Philpott; Philpott. A scientist, an experimenter.

"No Experiments With Our Lives!'

"Oh, *no*. Here? *Here?* Inside his Honda, as he steered

toward his reserved parking space, Joshua looked stricken. They wouldn't.

• • •

And yet they would.

"I don't know how the news leaked so soon," Gar Chambers said.

"Not through me, obviously, not through the *spokesman* here," Joshua said, not bothering to hide his irritation.

They sat together in Gar's office, he being chief operating officer of the facility and Joshua's immediate boss, and the reason Joshua didn't bother to hide his irritation was that they both knew he could walk out of here and into a job at least as good as this one by the end of the working day. As a spokesman, for anything at all, Joshua was one of the naturals.

Four years ago, when Green Meadow III first opened and the spokesman job here became available, Joshua and his wife, Jennifer, had just completed their first year in their weekend country house, had come to the realization that they no longer liked the commute to New York or the work in New York or even the life in New York, and Joshua had upped roots and converted himself from a harried account executive in a thankless enterprise to a country gentleman who did some chatting for the nuclear industry from time to time. Personally, he had no opinion about nuclear power one way or the other, any more than he'd held strong opinions about the cat food, lipstick, or adult diapers he'd once sold. So if the job was going to become unpleasant, with demonstrators outside the gates and secrets held back from him within, he'd be just as happy being spokesperson for the New York State Tourist Council.

All of which Gar knew as well as Joshua. Sounding apologetic, he said, "We were hoping to get the situation in place before any public announcement was made. A fait accompli is much easier to deal with, as you know."

"So *I* was kept outside the loop."

"I'm sorry about that," Gar said. "I really thought we could keep it quiet."

"An experimental physicist," Joshua said, "world-renowned, is going to move over here from Grayling University to conduct experiments in new kinds of energy. And you thought you could keep that secret. Half the secretaries here must know it by now, but I *didn't* know it."

"It's probably the construction that gave it away," Gar said.

"Construction. Oh, yes, I saw something on my way in. What's that all about?"

"A new laboratory for our distinguished guest," Gar said. "Well away from the reactor, well away from waste storage. Absolutely guaranteed safe, no possible problem to anybody ever."

"Doesn't he have a lab over at Grayling?"

"Well, yes," Gar admitted.

Joshua smelled the reek of old fish. "Then why isn't he staying there?"

Gar looked depressed, even a little sick. "He blows things up sometimes," he said. "They seemed to feel, a college campus wasn't the right place for that."

"But a nuclear power plant is."

Gar spread his hands. "Joshua, the decision was made far above thee and me. Far above."

"Okay," Joshua said, "so there's something in it for our masters. What's in it for us?"

Gar tried to look hopeful. "Prestige? The inside track on new advances in energy research?"

"Those are pretty thin bones," Joshua said, "but I'll do my best to make soup of it. For a while, anyway."

Gar lifted his head, alert and worried, as though he'd just heard a shot down the hall. "For a while?"

"I don't know, Gar," Joshua said, "this is kind of discouraging. To have secrets kept from me, things I really need to know."

"It won't happen again, I promise."

"It happened once."

Gar said, "Joshua, I need you now. It wasn't my idea to have that goddamn genius move in on us, but he's here, or he's going to be here very soon, and we've got to sell him to the public. We can't let Dr. Marlon Philpott become the excuse for a new round of anti-nuclear demonstrations."

"He already has."

"I need you," Gar repeated. "Stay with the team, Joshua."

"Did the team stay with me?"

"It will, it will. Don't abandon the ship now, not when we're in crisis. Get our story out, Joshua. Please."

Joshua, somewhat mollified, and aware that the Tourist Council would provide only a little bit more money with a much longer commute, got to his feet and said, "Gar, for you. Only for you. I'll see what I can do."

Gar also stood. "Thank you, Joshua," he said.

•   •   •

For the next few weeks, and particularly after Dr. Philpott moved into his new laboratory on-site, the demonstrations outside the main gate of Green Meadow III grew larger and more unruly every day.

15

In warm weather, in the darkness of a new moon, Kwan climbed over the rail in the soft air and swiftly descended the ladder rungs to the kitchen staff's deck. It was nearly three in the morning, and everyone on this deck was presumably asleep, exhausted by the day's labors. Li Kwan, after labor of a much more pleasant sort, and a nice nap in the arms of an Italian college girl named Stefania, felt no sleepiness at all, and paused on the lower deck, forearms on the thrumming rail, to look out at their phosphorescent wake, not even minding that hint of engine oil in the salty air.

Tuesdays made it possible. Kwan could survive his exile now, his flight, his forced anonymity, but only because of Tuesday. Rarely would the same woman be aboard two Tuesdays in a row, but if so he was delighted with the opportunity for a reunion. He had learned to stay away from alcohol, and to sleep for a while on Tuesday afternoons in preparation for the night. His life had become, at least one day a week, more than bearable; it was comfortable, even luxurious.

Perhaps too luxurious? It was too easy to forget in these circumstances who he really was. Not merely a kitchen scamp who crept up the equivalent of a drainpipe to bed his betters on the upper floors, he was a part of a massive human movement against tyranny and oppression, a small but inspired element in a drive to free one-quarter of humanity from the slavery of the ancient murderers.

I must not let this luxury soften me, Kwan told himself. I must not let my love of women distract me from my love of freedom.

Faint lights were visible from time to time, far away to starboard. Some city of Africa; they were steaming up the African coast of the Atlantic now, with Barcelona the next stop and then Rotterdam, and then Southampton, and on and on. Eventually, some part of the North American continent would be reached, and when it was, he would have to find a way off the ship.

Some American girl? Could he persuade an American girl to smuggle him off with her? Could he insert himself among the visitors who crowded aboard at every stop to see off their friends?

A way will present itself, Kwan was sure of that. As though he had at his side a guardian angel—in the shape of the Statue of Liberty, perhaps, like the one in Tiananmen Square—he was confident he would not give in to ease, not lose heart, not be defeated. The road would open before him.

Smiling, pleased with his adventure of the night, with his accommodation to this temporary world, with the fact of his own confidence and youth, Kwan gazed out at the glittering wake of *Star Voyager,* as it disappeared into the utter blackness of the vast ocean. Such a confident wake.

16

What affected Susan most of all was Grigor's matter-of-factness. He behaved as though his courage were the most natural thing in the world, as though being brave were something like being blue-eyed or left-handed. It wasn't an English kind of stiff-upper-lip thing, nor an American's self-conscious imitation of Humphrey Bogart or Indiana Jones. It probably wasn't even anything generically Russian, but simply Grigor's own personality: laconic, aware but unafraid, viewing his own history as it passed by with interest but dispassion. He must have been a wonderful fireman, Susan thought, before they killed him.

She was twenty minutes late today, because demonstrators opposed to some sort of esoteric research at the nuclear power plant near the Taconic Parkway exit had blocked the road. Grigor was not in his room, but the nurse called Jane, at her desk in the hall, grinned hello, and said, "He's faxing."

"Thanks."

It no longer struck anyone odd to have a patient in a cancer research hospital in upstate New York—within ten miles of a nuclear power plant, no less—faxing jokes to Moscow. In Russian. Susan had spent days searching New York last spring, and at last had found a typewriter dealer named Tytell who had come up with a Cyrillic-alphabet typewriter, a used one he'd gotten years before from the Soviet U.N. mission. So now Grigor could tap out his gags two-fingered and not subject some long-suffering secretary in Moscow to his truly terrible penmanship.

In truth, Susan didn't think Grigor's jokes were particularly funny, but she understood she wasn't his intended audience. The Russian television people at the other end of the fax machine seemed pleased, and that was what counted.

And also what counted was that Grigor's spirits were kept reasonably buoyant. Susan could make the drive up from the city only on weekends, and it seemed to her now that every week he'd declined visibly, become thinner, slower, feebler. His eyes were deep-set now, ringed in gray. The gums were steadily receding from his teeth, so that more and more he looked like a skull, particularly when he laughed. Realizing that, he did his laughing with closed lips these days, or covered his mouth with his hand. It broke Susan's heart to see the embarrassed way he brought that hand up, the haunted eyes looking out at her as he laughed in secret; laughing was so much a part of his life, and to have it hampered and hedged seemed unnecessarily cruel.

The fax machine was in a small windowless room—a big closet, really—stuffed with the machinery of the clerical trade: a large copying machine, a Mr. Coffee, a paper cutter, several staplers, and a tall gray metal cabinet full of stationery supplies. Grigor sat hunched on the room's one small typist's chair, back to the doorway, punching out the phone number with his bony forefinger. Shoulder blades protruded sharply against the back of his shirt, like stubby angel wings. She wanted to put her arms around him, but never had.

Sensing movement, Grigor turned, saw Susan, and smiled with his lips held close together, like a prissy man sipping from a straw. "A remarkable machine, this," he said, by way of hello. "I merely touch a few numbers, and in no time at all I can hear a busy signal eleven thousand miles away."

Smiling back, not showing him anything except the smile, Susan said, "Is that one of the jokes you're sending?"

"One of the jokes I'm *not* sending," he said, and punched the numbers again. "No, the fax isn't common enough in the Soviet so far. I sent one gag— Ah, the busy signal." He broke the connection, turned back to Susan. "I did send one: 'The Moscow/Washington hot line is by fax now. The only trouble is, the KGB made us attach ours to a shredder.' Boris Boris didn't like it." He peered at her shrewdly. "Neither do you."

"Try again," she said gently, gesturing at the machine.

He turned to it. "*This* fax should be attached to a yacht," he said, tapping out the number. "It would make a fine anchor. Ah, yes, the signal of busyness. The only sign of economic activity in all Moscow, the fax machine at Soviet Television TV Center on Korolyov Street."

After three more tries, the call did at last go through, and Grigor fed his two pages of jokes, asides, and suggestions into the machine, then carried the originals back to his room, paused to take his medicines, and at last they could leave for their drive in the country.

This was probably the last cycle of the seasons Grigor would ever see. Susan's cousin Chuck Woodbury, the AIDS research doctor, had soon after Grigor's arrival in the States passed him on to other doctors, experts in his particular kind of radiation-induced cancer, and while various medicinal combinations they'd tried had put his illness into slight remission for short periods of time, the advance of the disease was still inexorable, and gradually accelerating its pace.

Grigor had arrived in this mountainous terrain, less than a

hundred miles north of New York City, in late May, and had so far seen the finish of spring's green burgeoning and the flowered lushness of summer. Now he was seeing the first of the great autumn foliage display; every day, more leaves on more branches had turned to russet and ruby and gold. He would most likely see this change all the way through to bare black trees against a white sky, standing in great drifts of rusty leaves; he would probably see the first snowfall of winter. But would he experience the end of winter? Unlikely.

The country rolled, rich in reds and yellows, backed by the dark green of pines. Susan drove through little gray-stone towns and newer clapboard or aluminum-sided developments. Grigor talked about the beautiful vistas of this new land he'd never known he would visit, and sometimes talked about the beautiful vistas of Russia as well; unstated between them was the knowledge that he would never see those Russian vistas again.

The drive was tiring for Grigor eventually. "I hate to go back," he finally said, "but . . ."

"There's tomorrow," she reminded him. She almost always spent Saturday night at a motel near the hospital, so she and Grigor could have the two weekend days together. He'd never come to the motel with her, nor had either of them raised the suggestion that he might.

That was a taboo area, by mutual consent. Susan wondered sometimes if her feelings for Grigor were merely self-defensive, if she were just protecting herself from a real, adult, dangerous relationship with a man by concentrating so exclusively on someone who simply could not offer a long-term commitment. But her feelings for Grigor seemed so much stronger than that, more profound. She'd even thought at times about the possibility of having his child, helping him to leave some echo or reminder of himself in the world. She'd never mentioned that idea to him, knowing instinctively that, rather than please him, the prospect of fathering a child he would never see, who would never be alive in his lifetime, would appall and sadden him.

Was he even capable of sex? Weakened, all the systems of his body slowing and failing, would it be possible for him any more? Susan shied away from the question, uncomfortable even to find herself thinking about it.

She'd forgotten the anti-nuclear demonstration. Their roundabout aimless drive, drifting through the falling leaves, had taken them to another approach toward the hospital, and all at once, as they topped a low hill, flanked by yellowing birch and beech and elm and dark green pine, there it was laid out before them, as frenzied yet compact as a scene in a movie. Which in a way it was, since almost all demonstrations are actually composed for television news coverage. So it was in the usual manner that the triumvirate of demonstrators and police and television technicians boiled away furiously together down there, enclosed within an invisible pot; one inch outside camera range, pastoral placidity reigned.

"I think I can get past," Susan said, hands gripping the wheel as she braked, coming slowly down the slope.

The left side of the road here was flanked by tall chain-link fence with razor wire at the top. Behind it, the woods were, if anything, more lush than anywhere else in the neighborhood, since the power company had added extra trees, mostly pine, to hide the plant tucked into the folds of hills. Only the access road, with its electric gate and guardpost and discreet sign, suggested what lay inside.

The demonstration was centered on that plant entrance. It spilled out to cover the entire road, protestors weaving in their ragged oval, waving their signs, shouting their catchphrases, while local police and private guards contained and controlled them, and the television crews moved and shifted around the perimeter like sharks around a shipwreck. Scuffles kept breaking out in the middle of the action, drawing more observers and participants, but then snuffing themselves out; it was to no one's advantage to let this confrontation get out of hand, move beyond an acceptable predetermined level of hostility. No side wanted to harm its reputation in Washington and Albany and on Wall Street, where the real decisions would be made.

On the right, the land was wilder, scrubbier, with more underbrush and more visible dead branches or the remains of dead trees. The power company owned this land as well, to protect itself, but didn't bother to manage it. The shoulder on that side, opposite the plant entrance, was broad and weedy, with a shallow ditch. It seemed to Susan she could leave the blacktop and make her way around the demonstration without getting caught up in it. The alternative was a detour of about fifteen miles, and Grigor was already very tired. She'd chance it.

Up close, the sights and sounds were ugly. Passion and righteousness twisted the faces of the demonstrators, while leashed animal rage froze the faces of the police and guards, and the faces of the TV people bore the placid untouched evil beauty of Dorian Gray. Though the car windows were rolled up, Susan could plainly hear the lust for carnage in all those raised voices, like a primitive tribe psyching itself up to attack another village. Blinking, she drove at a slow and steady pace, the car slanting into the ditch on the right, bumping over the uneven ground.

"They're right," Grigor said, looking out the windshield. He sounded unlike himself, bitter and angry and defeated.

They were nearly past when another quick outbreak of violence occurred, just beyond them on their left: a sudden release of pressure, boiling over of rage, like bubbles in lava. Police wands swung, wedges of protestors moved and swayed, and a TV cameraman looking for a better angle backed directly into Susan's path, forcing her to stop.

She was afraid to sound her horn, not wanting to attract the attention of any of the participants, and while she was waiting there, growing more and more frightened, two people came reeling out of the scrum, a man and a woman, supporting one another. Or he supporting her, his arm around her waist, her hand on his shoulder. He looked up, saw the car, and as he raised his free arm in supplication, she thought, *Ben! What's he doing here?*

But of course it wasn't Ben Margolin, whom she hadn't seen since college, whom she'd been madly in love with for one semester (and part of a second). Still, that instant of false recognition predisposed her in his favor, so she nodded as she met his eye, and gestured for them to come to the car. The woman, she could see, had a short diagonal cut on her forehead, a line of dark red blood, straight on its upper side, ragged below, like a line in a graffiti signature.

The TV cameraman moved closer to the action, out of Susan's path, as the man who wasn't Ben Margolin opened the rear car door, helped the woman in, and piled in after her. Susan immediately accelerated, bearing down hard on the pedal, the car jouncing, rear wheels spinning before catching hold.

Grigor had the box of Kleenex tissues out of the glove compartment, and had twisted around to offer it to the woman, who gave him a baffled look, then shakily smiled and took two tissues. She was about thirty, dark-haired, exotically attractive, not thin.

The man with her didn't really look much like Ben at all, except that he was tall and blond and big-boned. But he had a very different face, more open and easygoing and friendly than Ben's. (Ben had been a tortured intellectual.) He said to Susan, "Thanks for getting us out of that. I think it's gonna turn bad."

"It already did turn bad," Susan said. Clearing the last of the demonstration, getting back onto the road, she could look in the rearview mirror at the woman daubing at her cut forehead with the tissues.

"Worse," the man said. "Much worse. I've seen a lot of these things, I know."

"You demonstrate a lot?" Susan couldn't keep the frostiness out of her tone. She didn't care about the rights or wrongs of specific arguments; all she knew for sure was, when people turned ugly and mean and violent they were wrong, no matter how noble their cause.

"I *watch* demos a lot," the man said. "I'm a sociologist at Columbia. I was there to observe this thing, and then this lady got hit by one of the demonstrators' signs—"

"It was an accident," the woman said. She had an accent, rough but not unpleasant.

The man grinned at her, easy and comfortable. "I know," he said. "You got hit by your own team. You still got hit, though. It was still time to get out of there." Grinning now at Susan in the rearview mirror, he said, "Lucky you came along. Lucky for us, I mean."

"Glad to help," Susan said. Something about this man attracted her, but something also—maybe the same something?—made her apprehensive.

The man leaned forward, forearm on the seatback behind Susan's head. "My name's Andy Harbinger," he said.

"Susan Carrigan. And this is Grigor Basmyonov." She'd become quite practiced by now at saying Grigor's last name.

They exchanged hellos, and then everyone concentrated on the woman, who looked up from dabbing at her forehead to say, "Oh, yes, excuse me. I am Maria Elena Auston." She sounded weary, even sad.

17

It was no good. Nothing was any good. Nothing worked the way it was supposed to. Maria Elena's head throbbed where the sign had grazed her. Riding in the backseat of the car with three strangers, alone in a land she would never understand, she felt sick, exhausted, and in despair. She couldn't even take part in an anti-nuclear demonstration without being hit in the head by one of her own comrades.

She couldn't do anything right, could she? She couldn't even keep her husband.

At first, it had all been so perfect. She and Jack Auston, together. In Brasília, every day working with him, every night sleeping with him, his sexual interest a surprising delight, unexpected that such a quiet man could be so voracious in bed.

One day the necessary papers were signed at the city clerk's office and with the American embassy, and then one other day they went down to the public register and were married in a private ceremony and went back to his apartment—she'd moved in some time before—and made love again, sweet love, and that was their honeymoon.

Jack then had two months remaining on his contract with WHO, and that was the most satisfying time of Maria Elena's life. Her miserable first marriage with Paco was forgotten, her dead children nearly forgotten, her lost singing career no longer painful to think of, her self-loathing buried so deeply beneath this new self-assurance that she seemed to herself to be a thoroughly new person. *And* she was going to America.

Her happiness was so great in those days that she barely ever even thought about the original reason for wanting to go to America, for wanting to induce—seduce—John Auston into marrying her. Occasionally the memory would come, particularly when they were in the field at some especially horrifying site, but the fantasy had more or less shrunk from a plan or a hope back to the simple childish fancy it had originally been.

The first month or six weeks in America were dazzling and distracting, the town of Stockbridge in Massachusetts as alien to her as a different planet in a different solar system; yes, even the sun seemed like another sun. Learning to shop at those stores, to drive on those roads, to live in that house, had all been so heady and intense, requiring such concentration, that she couldn't even count that time as happiness; she was too busy then to be happy. And also too busy to notice for some time that she'd lost Jack.

She knew now what it had been. In Brazil, his sexual excitement had blocked out every other facet of his personality, like a radio jammer. But that kind of excitement, based in the alien and exotic, had inevitably faded once they'd returned to his normal mundane world. In Stockbridge, his insatiable craving for her body had drained out of him with the speed and irreversibility of water out of a cracked swimming pool. And when it was gone, there was nothing left.

Jack didn't care for *her*, it seemed, had nothing in common with her, neither liked nor disliked her, was absolutely indifferent to her presence. There was no longer any sex at all between them, and her few efforts to rekindle his passion had been such humiliating failures—how gently and kindly he had excused himself from performance—that she'd quickly given that up, but then had no other way to try to reach him. He had returned to a previous research job at a Massachusetts medical laboratory, and the people and events of his work were absolutely all that held any interest for him. He didn't actively object to Maria Elena's presence in his house, cooking his meals and doing his laundry, but if she'd left he would have found another maid without a second thought. In fact, it would probably be easier for him to have a maid who wasn't inexplicably all over his bedroom every night.

In a way, it would have been easier to understand and live with if Jack had found another woman, but he had not, and might never. He was a kind and gentle man, but he just simply wasn't much of a physical creature. His job absorbed his interest. His on-site chat with co-workers was all the social life he seemed to need, and that was it. His sudden spurts of sexual excitement must be terribly rare, surprising and pleasing while they were going on, but then gone without a memory, without a regret.

That was the worst of it; Jack couldn't even seem to remember what it was about her that he'd liked. And she knew now that it was only that deep polite indifference at the core of him that had made him agree to marry her, that had permitted her to succeed in her machinations. Oh, how clever she'd been!

If only she could talk to the first wife, that mystery woman three thousand miles away in Portland, Oregon. Had the same thing happened with her? Had Jack suddenly noticed her body, gone into that frenzy, worn it away inside her, and then reverted to his natural phlegmatic self? (Except, of course, that a child had resulted that other time.) And had the wife at last been unable to stand for another instant that bland polite indifference?

How would an American woman react to such an existence? Maria Elena was at a total loss. Nothing in her experience showed her how to handle a passionless man. In her world, passion was a major constituent, for good and for ill. When she and Paco had come together, it had been like storm systems colliding over a jungle, and when they'd parted, the storms had been even more fierce. They'd drawn blood, both emotionally and physically, and if Maria Elena was eventually battered into an acceptance of Paco's hateful view of her, it was nevertheless the result of a *war*, not the result of an ice age covering the Earth.

And when she had sung, and the public had responded, that had been passion, too. She had been for a while the latest in a tradition of forceful South American performers, almost a cross between the emotional intensity of an Edith Piaf and the showbiz intensity of a Liza Minnelli, but propelled by a purely Iberian torrent of feeling. How powerfully she had been able to sing about sorrow and loss, then, before she had known them. How far she was from singing now.

She had brought with her from Brazil the memorabilia of that career, the albums, the rolled-up posters, the magazine articles, the photos, all stacked in two cartons stored away in the Stockbridge attic. She thought of them up there sometimes, thought about listening to one of the albums—*Live in São Paulo*, for instance, with its almost terrifying roar of audience response—but she never did.

Frustrated, shamed, alone, Maria Elena clung at last to the wreckage of the idea that had caused her to be united with John Auston in the first place. Somehow, she had to find the people who owned the factories, the people who were indifferent to or ignorant of the horror they brought into the lives of less powerful human beings in less influential parts of the globe. Somehow, she had to reach them and convince them to change their ways, reverse their policies, stop the slaughter. But who were these people? How could she find them? How could she make contact with them? How could she make her argument compelling to them?

Finally, there had been no route open except to repeat her earlier political phase in Brazil: join the protestors. It gave her a way to fill her days, it gave her a way to use her untapped passion, it gave her, at least at moments, at least the illusion of accomplishment. She wasn't doing what had to be done, but she was doing *something*.

But even there, satisfaction was elusive. Her grasp of English, adequate in every other respect, was too clumsy for the slippery nuances of political discourse. Even this demonstration; it apparently wasn't opposed to the nuclear plant as such, but to some sort of research going on within it. What did Maria Elena know of science? Nothing; only its leavings. Still she persisted, because something is better than nothing, because movement at least distracted from the emptiness of her life, and because maybe she *was* doing some good. Maybe she was.

But it didn't really work, it didn't really distract, and it certainly didn't fulfill. She picketed in front of the U.N., signed group letters to the *New York Times* (that usually weren't published), contributed toward the cost of advertisements on environmental issues, showed up to help swell the ranks of protests, traveled to Washington on buses chartered by action groups; and always she was alone, always just a little to the side of the group, slightly lost, slightly out of sync.

And all of it culminating in this embarrassment today. This was the worst so far, to be bloodied in front of television cameras, to give the bastards of the media exactly the kind of false violent story they preferred, the kind of story they could use to avoid and obscure the *real* story. Then, still dazed from that inadvertent blow to the head, she'd permitted herself to be taken away from the action, away from where she should be, to sit here in this car full of strangers. "I am Maria Elena Auston," she said. "And I thank you, but I really shouldn't leave my friends. They'll worry about me." Which wasn't at all true, a reality she resolutely ignored. "If you could just let me out," she went on, "I'll walk back."

They all argued that: the handsome young man who'd pulled her out of the picket line, the pleasant young woman driving, the very thin man in the passenger seat in front. They said her head was cut, was still bleeding, had to be seen to. "We're just a couple of miles from the hospital," the young woman said, and the thin man said, "That's very true."

"I don't want to take you out of your way. Please, I'll just get out—"

The thin man laughed, then coughed, then turned to smile at her, saying, "It is not out of our way. I am afraid I live at the hospital."

Now she actually looked at him and listened to him for the first time. He spoke English with an accent, possibly a stronger one than hers, but very different. Polish? And he was so thin, the shape of his skull was absolutely visible through the translucent blue-gray skin of his face. Knowing what the truth must be, she nevertheless said, "Are you a doctor?"

"Much more important," he said, smiling again. "I am a star patient."

"I'm sorry," Maria Elena said, feeling sudden embarrassment.

"Don't *you* be sorry," he told her. "I'll be sorry for both of us." It was strange to have such a skeletal figure behave in that elfin fashion. But then his expression became more sober, and he looked past her out the rear window of the car, saying, "If I had the strength, I might march with you."

She read the connection immediately: "You mean, the nuclear industry is why you're sick?"

"Nuclear industry," he echoed, as though the words contained a joke only he understood.

The young woman driving said tonelessly, "Grigor was at Chernobyl."

Something constricted Maria Elena's throat. Unable to speak, unsure even what to call the emotion that had suddenly flooded her, she reached out to fold her palm over his bony shoulder. So bony.

He smiled over her hand at her. Gently, to make *her* feel better, he said, "I've had time to get used to it."

18

Forty-five minutes later, Susan was alone in the car with Andy Harbinger, driving south on the Taconic, heading toward New York. How it had worked out that way she still didn't quite understand.

Grigor had taken charge of Mrs. Auston at the hospital, which was a research center, not a regular hospital at all, and so without an emergency room. The doctor Grigor finally rounded up for the task of examining Mrs. Auston's wound and then bandaging it was wildly overqualified for the job, but took it in good spirit. That was no surprise; the entire hospital staff was friendly and supportive and indulgent toward Grigor.

Meantime, one of the other doctors had taken Susan aside and told her that tomorrow's outing with Grigor would not be possible. "Grigor doesn't know it yet," this doctor said, "but we'll be starting a new therapy in the morning, and generally it's going to be unpleasant for him for a few days. He should be in better condition by next weekend, but tomorrow he's going to be quite sick."

"Oh, poor Grigor."

"You know this routine by now, Susan," the doctor said. "We make him very sick from time to time, because the other option is that he dies."

"You don't want me to tell him about tomorrow?"

"Why give him a sleepless night?"

So she had lied to him—"See you tomorrow!" "See you tomorrow!"—hating it but knowing it was better than the alternative, and then as she was heading for the exit Andy Harbinger appeared and asked if she was driving back to the city today, and if so, could he hitch a ride, since he felt no need to see any more of today's demo. It was impossible to say no, and in fact Susan didn't particularly want to say no. She was feeling glum, and the two-hour drive back to the city could get boring.

Then there was Mrs. Auston. She wanted nothing but to get back with her protest group, so Susan brought her along as well. The three of them left the hospital and drove together as far as the power plant entrance, which was much calmer than before, the TV crews having all left, though the demonstration continued. Mrs. Auston, a strange self-absorbed woman, left the car with only minimal thanks to her rescuers, and then Susan and Andy Harbinger drove on down the road to the Taconic entrance and headed south.

Once they were on the highway, streaming with moderate traffic toward the far-off city, the late afternoon sun reddening ahead and to the right, Andy Harbinger broke into Susan's fretful thoughts about Grigor by saying, "Susan? Do you mind if I interview you?"

"What?" At first, the words made no sense at all; she frowned at him, ignoring traffic, finding it hard to see his face clearly in the orangey sunlight. "I'm sorry, what?"

He smiled, his manner easy, non-threatening, friendly. "I'm always working," he apologized. "I can't help it. And I noticed, when Mrs. Auston and I first got into the car, when you thought I was one of the demonstrators, you disapproved of me."

Feeling the heat of embarrassment rise into her cheeks, Susan faced the road again, gazing steadfastly through the windshield as she said, "Disapprove? That's a funny word. I didn't say anything like that."

"You didn't *say* anything, but it was in your expression and the tone of your voice." Harbinger grinned at her. "I'm not trying to get you mad, Susan," he said. "It's just my professional nature. You're good friends with that Russian guy. With that illness of his, I'd think you'd be on the side of the demonstrators."

"Until they get ugly," Susan said, and then was sorry she'd been prodded into giving any reaction at all.

Because of course now he burrowed in a little more, saying, "Ugly? I guess they are, sometimes. But isn't it because they feel powerless? They're trying to make themselves heard. It isn't easy."

"No, I know it isn't," Susan said, uncomfortable at having to defend a position that even to herself sounded prissy, narrow-minded, irrelevant. "And I *do* agree with them. It's . . . it's when there's violence, then I can't stand it. When people are doing violent things, they *make* themselves wrong, even if they were right to begin with."

Gently, he said, "And if there's no other way?"

"There's always another way," Susan insisted, even though she wasn't herself sure that was true. Then she thought of something to bolster her argument and added, "Gandhi always found another way."

He chuckled that off the field, saying, "Gandhi was a saint."

"Then we should all be saints."

This response seemed to capture him in some way she didn't understand. Looking at her more openly, twisting to put his right shoulder blade against the door so he could face her more fully, he said, "You keep surprising me, Susan. You really do."

If he's trying to pick me up, she thought, it's a very weird method. She shot him a quick glance, trying to read beneath that open friendly face, and when she looked away from his impenetrable smile, out at the road again, he was reminding her of somebody or something. Who? What?

Mikhail. Whatever his name was, Mikhail something, the nice economist at the party in Moscow, where she'd first met Grigor; where all this started.

As though reading her mind, he said, "Your Russian friend—Grigor, isn't it?"

"Yes, Grigor."

"Do you think *he* agrees with you? About the protestors. That they should give it less than their all."

"That isn't what I said! Not give their all, what do you mean?" She was really annoyed with him, for twisting her words like that.

"I'm sorry," he said, and tried to smile the offense away. "I apologize, that was careless phrasing. All I was trying to ask, really, was do you think Grigor would disagree with the protestors if they resorted to violence?"

Reluctantly, but having to be honest, Susan said, "No, I don't think so. I think he'd agree. Before you got into the car, he even said so. When we were driving down toward the demonstration, he said, 'They're right.' " She looked over at him again, seeing concern and sympathy now on his face, and she told that face, "Grigor's almost never bitter, you know. He's amazing that way. He has so much to be bitter about."

"Life is unfair," he suggested.

Ignoring the coldness in that, "It shouldn't be," she said.

He laughed, and shifted to face forward again as he said, "How did you ever meet up with him, anyway? It's so unlikely."

"More unlikely than you know."

"Really?" He was ready to be interested, amused. "How's that?"

So she told him about the vodka contest, and the trip to Moscow, and the completely unexpected cocktail party thrown there by an organization she still didn't know anything about, and the strange little waif-man who'd showed up and talked with her; and then the round-half-the-world phone calls to her cousin at NYU Medical Center, and getting Grigor's passport, and permission for him to leave Russia, and his strange jokesmith occupation since Chernobyl had killed him; and still doing it, still faxing those unfunny topical jokes to the Russian Johnny Carson, even while the disease ate away at his body like a child licking an ice cream cone.

Andy Harbinger asked questions here and there, showing his interest, encouraging her to expand on the story, and half the trip went by as she talked. But finally there was nothing more to say, not on that subject, and after a little silence he said thoughtfully, "It isn't just pity, though, is it? What you feel toward him."

Pity? There were moments when this man seemed very intuitive and sensitive, and yet other times when he was just so bluntly wrong, almost cruel—life is unfair, it isn't just pity—that it was impossible to know how to react. Didn't he know how dismissive he sounded, as though life and emotion didn't matter?

She really didn't know how to answer him, and the silence stretched between them, she unusually aware of her own breathing, and then he said, much more softly, "I know what it really is, Susan. You're in love with him. And you wish you weren't. And you hate that wish."

So here was the sensitive Andy Harbinger back again.

And he'd defined the problem, all right; she knew she shouldn't feel about Grigor the way she did, she shouldn't lash herself so securely to a man who would be dead within the year. But the very knowledge made her guilty, as though she couldn't forgive herself for even that much dispassion, didn't believe in her own right to see the pit she was falling into. "I can't talk about it," she whispered, and it took all her effort to concentrate on the driving, not just to close her eyes and let events take her away.

"Stop the car," he said.

"What?" She'd clenched the steering wheel so hard her hands ached, but she couldn't make them let go.

"Pull off the road and stop," he told her, his voice calm and authoritative, like a doctor in the examining room. "Until you relax a little. Come on, Susan."

She obeyed, her right leg made of wood as she forced it off the accelerator and onto the brake. The car wobbled, not entirely under her control, but slowed as she steered it off the pavement and onto the rough dirt surface of the shoulder. It stopped and she shifted into park, and then all at once she was trembling all over, but dry-eyed. Staring hopelessly out at the hood, as aware of the traffic whizzing past on her left as she was of the man listening to her on her right, every sense painfully alert, she said, "It's so awful, and it just keeps going on. I come up every week, and every week he's worse, and how much worse can it *be*? He gets thinner and thinner, and he just . . ." She shook her head and lifted her aching hands from the steering wheel to gesture vaguely her despair.

"He doesn't die," Andy Harbinger said.

"Oh, God." She hadn't talked about this with anyone before, not even very much with herself; maybe what it needed was a stranger, somebody she wasn't already connected with in the usual web of history and knowledge and opinions and shared experience. "I don't *want* him to die," she said, her throat aching as though she had a terrible flu. "That's the truth. If he could live forever, if he could—

well, not forever, nobody lives forever, but you know what I mean.''

"A normal life span."

"Yes. Normal. So I could—" There was no way to even think this last thought, much less express it.

But Andy Harbinger knew, anyway, what she couldn't describe. "So you could decide for yourself," he said gently, "whether or not you'd like to spend that normal life with him."

"Oh, I suppose so." She sighed through her burning throat. "To be able to do it *all* normally, let it grow in a normal way instead of, instead of this *water torture*. I hate *blaming* him, but I do, I can't help myself, and then I can't stand myself, and then I don't even want to come up here any more, go through it all any more. We're all so *trapped*. And then I say, 'Well, it won't last much longer,' and I feel *satisfaction*."

"The truth is," he said, "it actually won't last much longer, no matter what you do or how you feel or whether or not you feel guilty. It all doesn't matter."

"Which doesn't help," she said stiffly, responding to that cold side of him again. "It doesn't help because I can't just shrug and be indifferent, as though I was in one of those *cars* there, and this was an accident here, and it wasn't anybody I knew, and I just drove on by."

"Of course not," he said. "But you can't take on yourself the responsibility for things going wrong in other people's lives. We'd all like life to be milk and mell, but it just isn't, not all the time, there's bound to be some—"

She frowned at him, distracted. "What? Milk and what?"

He was confused for just a second, obviously trying to remember what he'd just said. "Milk and honey," he finally decided. "I said we'd all like life to be nothing but milk and honey, but there's bound to be acid, too, along the way."

"Is that what you—?" She frowned, trying to recall his earlier words. "It sounded different."

"Well, I don't know what I said," he told her, beginning to get impatient. "The point was, it's natural for you to want this trouble you're going through to be over with, and it doesn't mean you're unfaithful or cold to Grigor when you feel that way. You *know* that, in your head, but your emotions won't listen.''

She had to smile at that phraseology, and nod, looking at him at last. The tears were starting now, after the attack, but not out of control. She blinked them out of her eyes, saying, ''Emotions never listen, that's the way they are.''

''So we just do our best, okay?'' He smiled at her, warm and concerned. ''And we try to think about things other than Grigor.''

''Yes, Doctor.''

''And we don't feel guilty when we succeed.''

''That,'' she said, ''is the hard part.''

''I know.'' He shifted in the seat, clearly ready to move on to other things. He said, ''Do you have any idea how good Italian food is when you're an emotional wreck?''

Now she had to laugh. ''As a matter of fact, I do,'' she said. ''It's a miracle I don't weigh eight hundred pounds.''

''I know a great place in the Village,'' he said. ''Let me take you there.''

Doubtful, afraid, she withdrew from him, saying, ''Oh, I don't know, I don't think so. I haven't been . . .''

''Dating?'' He grinned at her. ''This isn't a date, this is dinner. Believe me, Susan, I'm not gonna try to compete with a tragic hero.''

Ananayel

Foolish. Foolish. *Mell!* It isn't *mell* now, it hasn't been mell for hundreds of years. It's *honey* now, I know that as well as anybody.

I was distracted by having to deal with my little Judas ewe, that's all, and for just a second I forgot the situation, the *time*, and made that slip. The problem is, I am not living in time in the same way the humans are, so I don't have the same temporal relationship with their languages. I have in my mind and at my command *all* of English, from its earliest guttural beginnings in the fifth century, when speakers of Anglo-Frisian first crossed the then-unnamed stormy water from the European continent to the British islands, and took up residence there, so that their dialect began to alter away from its Dutch, Frisian, and Low German cousins in the Plattdeutsch family, down through its endless changes to this ultimate moment. (I know it into the now-canceled future as well, all the way to its final commingling with pan-Mandarin.)

Mell entered English early on, from the Greek, Μέαλ, and at one time the language was lush with *mell*-derived words, of which now only a few remain. *Mellifluous*, originally meaning something sweetened with honey, soon was adapted to mean sweet speech, as in honey-tongued Shakespeare's line in *Twelfth Night*, "A mellifluous voice, as I am true knight." *Melianthus* is the honeyflower, a *mellivorous* bird feeds on honey, and *molasses* is a later corruption of the original *melasus*. In medicine, *meliceris* denotes a tumor containing honey-like matter, and in some technical specialties *mellaginous* still means anything that is like honey.

But it's in the now-forgotten words that *mell* was at its most mouth-watering. A sweet medieval Breughelesque pastorality seems to cling to these words, as of a better world, lost and forgotten, replaced by this intolerable world. *Mellation* was the special time for collecting honey, *meliturgy* was the process of making honey, and anything as sweet as honey was said to be *melled*. Such things include *melicrate*, a drink of honey and water, and *melitism*, a mixture of honey and wine. And *melrose* was a nostrum of honey, alcohol, and powdered rose leaves used by doctors in the eighteenth century.

I only display all this erudition, of course, because of embarrassment over that slip of the tongue. I see that contact with humans is making me more like them.

Well, the slip was a small one, quickly forgotten by Susan, and the main point of the conversation was accomplished. That is, to bring her confused tangle of feelings about Grigor Basmyonov out into the light, where she can begin to study them, accept their pointlessness, and eventually distance herself first from the feelings themselves and then from Grigor. For how is Grigor to be brought to the necessary despair, if he is loved by Susan?

That is the point.

We drove on to the city, I guiding the conversation into shallower and safer waters, knowing she would return to the deeps herself, later, alone. We had dinner in the Italian restaurant I'd recommended, we walked the city streets in a rarely beautiful early autumn evening, and I escorted her at last to her apartment building, where I made no attempt to kiss her good-night but did ask her to come out to the movies with me the next night. She hesitated, but I gave her more assurances that friendship was all I was offering (or asking), and she at last agreed.

Because, in fact, it isn't enough merely to force her to see how hopeless her love for Grigor Basmyonov is. She craves an emotional involvement, while fearing a physical one (which makes the Grigor relationship ideal at this moment in her life, of course, a truth we've already successfully skipped past), so until she's given an alternate target for her emotions she won't abandon Grigor no matter how painful the situation becomes. Andy Harbinger is personable, intriguing, companionable, and absolutely non-threatening. Until she's weaned from Grigor, Andy will have to be an ongoing presence in her life.

Which is not at all the way it was supposed to be. Susan Carrigan is not one of my principals, but merely the proximate method to bring Grigor Basmyonov to the United States. She should be cut loose by now, she should be off living what's left of her life, no longer my concern. But I'm not as familiar with humans as perhaps I should be; their use of free will is so frenetic it's hard to make *plans* involving them at all. That Susan would so fiercely lock herself to the destiny of a doomed foreigner took me, I admit, by surprise. Alienation, foreignness, hopelessness, a growing estrangement from life, all of these were supposed to be working in Grigor now, moving him in the desired direction. Susan's presence, her love, holds his despair at bay; it must be deflected.

And then there are my other principals. Pami Njoroge is discontentedly performing sex acts on the hard surfaces of the paved-over lots near the Lincoln Tunnel in Manhattan, in the shadow of the Jacob Javits Convention Center, completely unaware who her pimp really is. (Ha ha, no, it's not me, the joke is *much* better than that!) Maria Elena Rodriguez Auston is looking at the telephone number Grigor gave her before she left the hospital, wondering if she should call. (Yes!) Frank Hillfen is living alone in a furnished room in East St. Louis, Illinois, committing small burglaries, too afraid of capture to do more than provide himself a basic subsistence—he hasn't ever even stolen enough money all at once to pay for transportation to New York City, his goal, where in any event I'm not ready for him—and feeding his growing sense of unjust persecution. (*Everybody's* on the take; why does *Frank* get hassled all the time?) Dr. Marlon Philpott, in his new windowless laboratory at Green Meadow III, oblivious of the protestors outside the gate, pursues the elusive possibility of strange matter.

And Li Kwan is arriving in New York; in chains.

19

Kwan did not see the arrival of the *Star Voyager* into the famous New York Harbor because the room they had locked him into was an interior space on a lower deck, where the vibrations of the engines could be felt on every surface but there was otherwise no sense of movement or progress; only a small metal cube, painted a cream color, furnished with a cot and a toilet and a sink, its recessed fluorescent ceiling light protected by wire mesh. This was the *Star Voyager*'s brig, or as close as this frivolous vessel could come to having a brig. On most voyages, Father Mackenzie had told him, the brig remained empty except for the occasional overly drunk crewman, but when it became necessary to hold someone to be turned over to the authorities at the next port of call, this was the room.

The authorities. The next port of call. New York City, United States of America. "I've heard," Father Mackenzie had told him yesterday, long-faced, "that Hong Kong has already started extradition proceedings, even before you arrive."

"They want me in and out before the media can make a fuss," Kwan had answered.

"Of course. No one need know Li Kwan was ever in America at all."

"And you won't help me, Father? You won't call the *New York Times*?"

But the priest had smiled his sad smile and shaken his head. "I can't. It is not my right to endanger my order's relationship with the company. I'm here as Norse American's guest. I wouldn't want to do anything to make them feel justified in removing the spiritual advisers from all of their passenger ships.''

Everyone has his reasons. Kwan was understanding that now, with increasing bitterness. Probably even Dat had his reasons.

Dat had not joined the crew until Rotterdam, three stops ago on the *Star Voyager*'s endless goalless circumnavigation of the globe; Rotterdam, then Southampton, then Hamilton on Bermuda, and now New York. And it wasn't until after Bermuda that Dat began to insinuate himself into Kwan's life.

From the beginning, lives ago in Hong Kong, Kwan had understood that he was not the only member of the below-decks crew whose papers and alleged history could not bear much scrutiny. There were a number of other crewmen who also chose not to go ashore at the many ports of call, who preferred the calm of their quarters to the gauntlet of beady-eyed immigration officials.

Dat, when he arrived, immediately became one of these, and Kwan noticed him, during the layover in Southampton, reading comic books and drinking tea in the kitchen staff's galley, but they didn't talk then, Kwan being content with his own company and Dat apparently the same. A short slope-shouldered man of perhaps forty, with a narrow head and a full-lipped mouth and heavy bags under his eyes, Dat's ancestors were apparently from somewhere in the Indochinese peninsula, Kwan couldn't be sure where. He spoke Chinese with some kind of muddy accent, appeared to have a smattering of Japanese, seemed to speak no European tongue at all, and at times conversed with other Indochinese crewmen in a language Kwan didn't know but the music of which was undeniably Asian.

It was in Bermuda, two days ago, that this man made his approach. Kwan was standing at the rail on the kitchen staff's small oval deck at the stern of the ship, watching the containerized supplies being loaded from dockside, when Dat appeared beside him, gesturing at the outsize shiny aluminum boxes being winched through the bulwark opening below. ''That's the way to get off,'' he said, in his poor accent.

Kwan frowned at him. "Get off?"

"The ship," Dat explained. "I'm getting off this ship in New York."

"You are?"

"My own way," Dat said, and nodded at the containers again.

Kwan also hoped to leave the ship in New York, but hadn't yet found that mythic American girl who would smuggle him ashore. In fact, American girls were the hardest for him to pick up on his Tuesday night excursions above; they seemed to have more tribal consciousness than other people, to be the most determined to stay with their own kind.

Intrigued, wondering if Dat had any useful ideas (but already a little distrustful, if not quite distrustful enough), Kwan said, "Use the containers, you mean? How?"

"Inside one. They come on full," Dat explained. "Food and drink and all those shop things, T-shirts and all that, and the drugstore things, all inside those containers. And when they're empty, they go off again. *Many* of them will go off in New York."

Kwan looked down at those containers with new interest. But then he said, "Why tell *me*?"

"Why not?" Dat shrugged, and took a single crumpled cigarette from his T-shirt pocket, didn't light it, and watched his fingers turn and smooth and straighten the cigarette as he said, "You don't have any reason to betray me. And a man has to talk sometimes, has to hear his own thoughts, has to know he isn't crazy."

Kwan felt immediately sympathetic. It was true, isolation in the middle of hundreds of people was perhaps the worst solitude of all, as he had learned before being rescued by those metal ladder rungs on the wall behind him. Other people cluster into purposeful groups, supporting and explaining and justifying one another, moving through life in these long- or short-term alliances, their own ideas and conclusions constantly being tested in discourse. The loner has only himself to talk to, only himself to listen, only himself to judge if he's behaving sensibly or not. If Dat were planning a dangerous move, a desperate move, the need to tell his plans to another human being, to get a *response* of some kind, could be overwhelming.

So Kwan gave him a response, and it was an honest one. "You're not crazy. It's a fine idea."

Dat gave him a quick gratified smile, the expression battling unsuccessfully with his doleful features, those heavy lips and pronounced bags beneath the eyes. "I watched at Southampton, and I been watching here," he said, "and nobody looks inside the empty ones. Because that whole storage section down there is locked up. Not many people can get in there."

"That's right," Kwan agreed.

"*You* can," Dat said, and looked at him sidewise.

Ah, so that's what it was about. (Or what it seemed to be about at that time.) Kwan, having gained a little seniority, even in the world of kitchen slaveys, had a few weeks ago been "promoted" from the deep sink filled with filthy pots and pans. His work now was in fact somewhat easier, involving nothing more than mopping and scrubbing and carrying, which meant that on the job now he had a key ring hooked to a trouser loop, containing keys to the cleaning-supplies closet, the walk-in freezer, the uniform and linen lockers, and the large echoing storage space in which the supply containers were kept, as they were gradually emptied. At the end of each shift, Kwan had to turn in those keys to his boss, a fussy suspicious Ecuadorian named Julio; no last name ever offered.

In theory, then, Kwan could, on his last shift before New York was reached, unlock the door to the container area and permit Dat to slip through. But why should he? "That would be very dangerous for me," he said. "If you were caught—"

"Then it would be dangerous for *me*," Dat interrupted. "Not you."

"They'd want to know who let you in there," Kwan pointed out. "They'd promise to go easier on you if you told, because the person who let you in there would be more worrisome to them than someone just trying to jump ship."

"I wouldn't tell," Dat said.

"Why not?"

Dat frowned, his whole face taking on the aspect of his baggy eyes and drooping mouth. His fingers fidgeted with that battered cigarette, turning it and turning it, until all at once the cigarette slipped from his grasp and fell, almost floating, down toward the slow-sliding shiny aluminum containers, but missing them and landing instead on the dirty asphalt. "Ah, my cigarette," Dat said, with nearly unemotional fatalism, watching it fall, then gazing dolefully downward, like a basset hound, becoming a comic figure.

"Oh, that's too bad," Kwan said, finding Dat more individual and human now, but no more likable.

But then Dat gave him another of those sideways looks, and a little smile, and said, "Of course I'd rat on you. You'd do the same for me."

"I might," Kwan agreed, taken by Dat's sudden frankness.

"But what," Dat said, "if we went *together*? That way, we help each other and rely on each other, and if we're caught we're *both* caught. What I mean," he said, suddenly more animated, turning to face Kwan, one narrow elbow on the rail beside him, "you can let me in during your shift. Then you turn in your keys, and when everybody's away you knock on the door and *I* let *you* in. Or don't you want to get off this ship?"

That last was said with such absolute assurance, with such conviction that Dat already knew the answer, that Kwan didn't even bother denying it. "Of course I want to get off the ship in New York," he said. "If I can do it and not get caught. But inside one of those boxes? We don't know what happens to them after they get taken off."

"Yes, we do," Dat said, and pointed far off to the right, where dozens of the containers stood crammed together, glinting in the sunlight. "They get put out of the way," Dat said, "until they're gonna get used again. We go out in the box, we feel when it stops moving, then we wait until dark and climb out and we're in America."

"It's that easy?" Kwan asked.

"We'll never know till we try," Dat said, and smiled in a lopsided way, and put out his bony-fingered hand. "Li, isn't it? Do we have a deal?"

Kwan had kept his name; it was common enough to serve as its own alias. "Yes, it's Li," he agreed, and after a brief pause he took Dat's hand. "And it's a deal."

• • •

The interior of the container was cold, and smelling faintly of old cardboard, and not entirely airtight or light-proof; grayish yellow lines of illumination defined the edges of the front-opening panel Kwan had used to climb inside. He had nothing with him in this box but a small duffel bag containing one change of clothes and his notebook and pencils; he sat on that and waited. He was alone, Dat having explained that the weight of both of them in one container would draw attention when the containers were winched ashore so he had gone off to hide in another one. But Kwan didn't mind that; in fact, it was better. He had no interest in becoming Dat's partner or friend, once they left the ship, and presuming they were successfully to get past whatever gates or guards or locks there might be between the dock and the free world.

The Free World.

Kwan had been in the container less than an hour, seated on the small duffel, back against the cold flimsy-seeming side of the aluminum container, becoming both bored and sleepy but nevertheless feeling a kind of slow deep contentment, when noises alerted him. The storage area door had been opened. Feet strode loudly on the metal floor. Then silence. Then a voice:

"Li Kwan!"

Kwan froze inside the box, silent, barely breathing. His heart was a fist in his chest, massively clenching.

"Li Kwan! We know you're in there! Come on out! Goddamn it, don't make us search every goddamn container!"

The voice was irritable, weary, but not actively hostile or angry. It was just a ship's officer faced with an annoying duty. They know we're here, Kwan thought, not yet realizing the significance of the fact that his was the only name called. But there was no point trying to hide any longer. With a sigh, wondering how much trouble he'd made for himself, Kwan stood, picked up his duffel, and opened the front of the container, letting the panel swing out and down on its hinges. "Here I am," he said, to the three aggravated uniformed Caucasians, who turned to him with identical frowns of exasperation.

* * *

Dat had betrayed him, turned him in, there was no question about that. Dat, more than that, had set him up in the first place, suggested the scheme, inveigled him into it, and *then* betrayed him. Kwan had plenty of time to think about that in the *Star Voyager*'s small cream-painted brig. What wasn't clear was why Dat had done it.

Kwan had discussed that with Father Mackenzie, when the man had come in shortly after the arrest, introduced himself, and asked if there was anything he could do. "Talk to me," Kwan had said, and Father Mackenzie had been happy to do so—he didn't seem to have much to occupy himself on the ship, except to be on call for providing the last rites to Roman Catholic passengers who succumbed to strokes or heart attacks while at one or another of the nine meals offered every day—and when the conversation had turned to Dat's betrayal Father Mackenzie had made one tentative suggestion that just might be the truth. "He could be an agent of the Chinese government," the priest said.

"I'm not saying he is, but he could be. Sent to make sure you never get into a position where you can publicly embarrass China."

"But I still can, Father, if someone would call the *New York Times* as soon as we arrive. If *you*—"

But no. Father Mackenzie couldn't, or wouldn't. Bravery and action were impossible to him. He was just a small decent man, doing what he could.

Aaaaaaaaahhhhhh, they're all decent men.

• • •

Shortly after Father MacKenzie left, the vibration of the engines stopped. We're here, Kwan thought bitterly. The free world.

But then nothing happened for another hour. Kwan paced the floor in the small room, increasingly nervous. Was this really going to be the end? The priest had said that Hong Kong was already seeking extradition. Hong Kong, not China. It would be harder for China to take him away from American jurisdiction, but Hong Kong could do it easily. Put together some trumped-up criminal charge—nothing political, not at all—and the Americans would see nothing wrong with sending a petty thief or arsonist or blackmailer home to a fellow democracy for a fair trial.

Sinking deeper into bitterness and gloom, Kwan paced the narrow floor, rubbing his hands together, pushing his fingers through his thick hair, biting his lower lip. Thoughts of his own death crowded in on him, the dog's death he'd be given, death equally through humiliation and a bullet. After all this.

He stopped when he heard the grating noises of the door being unlocked. He was facing the door when it opened and three uniformed crewmen entered, these Caucasian faces impersonal, showing nothing at all. "Your escort's here," one of them said. "Time to go."

Kwan's duffel was on the bed. Picking it up, he said to

them, "You know, for one moment, we touched the conscience of the world."

"Is that right?" the man said, uncaring. Looking around
the bare little room, he said, "Got all your stuff?"

"But the truth is," Kwan said, "the world doesn't have
very much conscience." And he went with them.

Ananayel

What is it about Susan Carrigan? I don't need her any
more, but here I am with her. I've studied my actions, my
motivations, my reasons for continuing to see Susan after
her task was finished, and I've come to a conclusion. It
seems to me that the quality in her that attracts me is that
she does no harm.

I'm mostly aware, of course, of the others, the ones who
snarl and bite, the ones whose messy miserable struggles led
finally to my present assignment. My awareness of *them* is
so complete that Susan is becoming more and more of an
amazement to me. I've been seeing for myself why He has
grown weary of these creatures, but it wasn't until I got
closer to Susan over time that I began to sense why He had
made them in the first place.

This means nothing, of course. His Will be done. It only
seems to me that I ought to get a clearer picture of the
humans while they still exist, that I should see them both at
their worst and at their best. I knew them so little, understood so little, when I started. Susan shows me the parts I
hadn't suspected.

We see each other three or four times a week. We go to
movies, or to stage plays, or to dinner. A few times, I have
spent an evening in her apartment to watch some special

program on television. She is easy enough in her mind about me by now that I could move the relationship onto a sexual plane, but I have not. (I don't precisely read her mind, but I can make myself aware of levels of her emotions and the general flow of her thoughts, and I'm rather sure an overture from me would not be unacceptable.) My only personal sexual experience was with Pami: nasty and brutish, though not particularly short. With humans, sex is where reality and belief touch, where the physical and the emotional rationalize one another; it might be better for me not to know any more than I already do.

As for Susan, I do enjoy her company. Her reactions to the world she sees, her opinions, are so close to my own that there are moments when I find her uncannily angelic. She isn't, of course. She is human, so my time with her will be extremely limited. (Even more than under normal circumstances.) I'm glad of the opportunity, though, no matter how brief it must be.

In the meantime, what's this? Out in Illinois, what is Frank Hillfen up to?

Getting into trouble all on his own, without any help from me.

20

"There's nothing to worry about," Joey said.

Frank knew better than that. There was *always* something to worry about. That's what life added up to: worry. "Just tell me the scheme," he said.

Joey was a big heavy slob who always smelled of tomato sauce. He had some kind of teamster job out at Scott Field, the huge air force base just a few miles out of East St.

Louis, but what he mainly did was muscle for some of the heavy guys around the area. He wasn't a mob soldier, not a made guy, just another bulked-up goon they called on sometimes when bones had to be broken or a little demonstration of power had to be made on the street. Between times, Joey got along as a small-time break-and-enter guy, a lot like Frank himself, except not as fastidious about avoiding violence.

Normally, Frank would keep away from a guy like Joey. People who saw violence as just one more tool of the trade always scared Frank a little, because he didn't believe violence could be contained with absolute control; it tended to slop over, like a drunk's soup.

But Frank had been stuck here in this nothing town for weeks now, never scoring any more than just enough to keep himself fed and housed, and the time had come to accomplish something. Joey was a guy Frank knew from Mindle's, the bar a block and a half from the shitty little furnished room he was staying in. A couple of times, Joey had hinted over beers that he might have a score he'd like to count Frank in on, but Frank had always played it stupid, not getting the hints. But enough was enough; he'd been stuck in this town too long. East St. Louis! Jesus!

"Tell me the scheme," Frank said.

They were at a side booth in Mindle's, three in the afternoon, Ralph on the stick, a few loners at the bar, traffic going by past the dusty windows out front. Joey had bought a round of beers, that's how much he wanted to do this thing, whatever it was. And now he leaned forward over the table, holding the beer in both his scarred fat hands, fat lips barely moving, tomato sauce-scented breath floating the words like little ghosts across the black Formica: "It's a courier."

Frank couldn't quite do that ghost-speech trick; he leaned his cheek against his left hand, to hide his mouth and direct his words toward Joey and away from the people at the bar: "What courier?"

Joey's lips twitched. "Ganolese," floated the name, into Frank's ear.

Frank dropped his hand and stared at Joey. "Are you crazy?"

Leo Ganolese was one of the capos around this part of the country, maybe *the* capo. He'd let everybody else go drive themselves crazy dealing drugs, dealing women, while he stayed with what he knew. Leo Ganolese was in the gambling business, had been in the gambling business for forty years, and would stay in the gambling business forever. Over on the Missouri side, and here in southwestern Illinois, he was the man in charge, in so solid the Federals never even bothered to try to make a case against him.

And nobody ever was stupid or loco enough to try to take Leo Ganolese's money away from him. "Forget it," Frank said. "I gotta be outta my own mind to even sit here with you."

"Wait for it," Joey advised. He was still doing the silent-voice thing. "I got it figured. Lemme splain."

Frank was drinking Joey's beer; until it was gone, he'd let Joey splain. Then he'd walk out and have nothing more to do with this idiot. "Go ahead."

"The courier's an old guy," came the little word-puffs. "It's like his retirement job. Every morning he goes around in a car, he picks up cash from the action the night before. All by himself. By lunchtime, he's got it all, he takes it to the Evanston Social Club. It's usually around eighty grand, every day, sometimes more."

"No," Frank said, his hand up to his cheek again. "Doesn't make sense. One old guy in a car? Eighty grand every day?"

"He's some kinda cousin of Leo Ganolese," Joey explained. "Safest courier there is. Everybody knows don't touch him."

"Including you and me, Joey," Frank said.

"You know why that's a no?" Joey was getting excited, the words stronger, turning almost into solid speech in the air. "That's a no, because over in St. Louis, right now, they got a big horse show going on."

"And?"

"And the city's full of punks from all over the country," Joey said. "They follow the horses. They don't have the kinda respect for the local situation that the local guys do. We take down the courier, we don't let him see our faces, everybody's got to *know* it can't be anyone from around here did it. Leo Ganolese is gonna be sure it has to be some out-of-town punk just came to St. Louis."

"*I* just came to St. Louis. East St. Louis."

"Nah," Joey said. "You been around a while now, you're like a native citizen, Frank, believe me."

Frank believed him. On that much, he believed him. He, Frank Hillfen, was becoming a local. *Here*. The knowledge of that reality is what made him say, "I'll look at this guy. I don't promise anything."

"Sure, Frank! We'll follow him around, and—"

"No!" Frank couldn't believe he was contemplating a partnership with a guy this simple. "Somebody sees us driving around behind your man, they'll remember it later on. You tell me a couple of his pickup places, that's what we'll take a look at."

"Sure, Frank. Whatever you say." Joey's excitement made him bounce around on the bench, fat fingers clutching at the beer glass. "I'll pick a couple spots, but I won't follow him around. Okay, Frank?"

He admires me, Frank thought. He looks up to me, this asshole, he respects me. This is what I'm reduced to, getting a score from a dirtbag that shouldn't even have the right to *speak* to me. I gotta get out of this town. I gotta get someplace where the scores make sense and the dirtbags don't know me and I'm not like a native citizen. We'll look at it, Joey," he said, judicious, like an elder statesman.

• • •

Of course, it wasn't as simple as Joey thought; it couldn't be. The old guy was there, all right, and he made his collections every day, and he drove his car alone around his route, but he wasn't without security, not at all. There was always another car trailing around behind him, with two bulky guys inside. Different cars on different days, different guys taking the duty, but always there, hanging a block or so back on the road, parking nearby when the old man made his stops.

The old man himself was—what? seventy? eighty?—old, but spry. Skinny old guy, always wearing a gray topcoat and a nicely blocked gray fedora hat, no matter what the weather. He drove at a normal pace, maybe a little cautious, and he always moved in a dignified way, like he was the messenger of the king; which in a way he was. His stops were bowling alleys, delicatessens, bars, private homes; anywhere that one of Leo Ganolese's books or numbers drops or tables operated. At every stop, the old man would get out of the car (that other car discreetly stopped just up or down the street), enter the place with a calm and measured tread, and come out a few minutes later with usually two or three other guys. (More security, that.) One of the guys would carry a package of some kind, a paper bag or a shoe box or something else equally nondescript. The guys would stand looking this way and that while the old man opened the trunk and the package was put in there with all the other packages. Then the old man would shake hands with one or two of the other guys, get into his car, and drive away. The people from the establishment would wait on the sidewalk until he was a couple blocks off and the other car had moved after him.

"Not easy," Frank said, back at the table in Mindle's. He was feeling cold in the pit of his stomach. There were things you did, and things you were foolish to do. This was beginning to look foolish.

Joey, of course, didn't get it. "All we gotta do is take out that backup car," he said. "Look, Frank, between Belleville and Millstadt there's a long run, maybe ten minutes, lotsa places where we could get rid of that other car. Then it's easy."

"What do you mean, get rid of that other car?"

"Take it out," Joey said, shrugging the whole problem away. "Listen, I know a guy down in Missouri, down in Branson, we can get hand grenades, no fooling. We drive by, we flip one in the car, we—"

"Goodbye," Frank said, and got to his feet, and walked out of the bar.

He was half a block toward the furnished room when Joey caught up with him, looking bewildered, maybe even a little put out. "Whad I do? Whad I do?"

Frank kept walking, Joey sweaty beside him. "I don't ever go near violence," he said. "Never. You start throwing hand grenades around—"

"So we just shoot the driver," Joey said, shrugging, making what he must have thought was a decent compromise.

"No."

Then Joey grabbed Frank's arm and stopped him on the street. Joey was a fat slob, but he was also a muscleman fat slob; those fingers holding Frank's arm hurt. And Joey had something else in his voice now, when he said, "Hold it a minute, Frank." Something meaner, more dangerous.

Frank stopped, because he had to, and looked at Joey's angry little eyes. "What now, Joey?"

"What now, Mr. Big Man," Joey said, "is this. I look around this neighborhood, I don't see a whole lot of people working on being saints and angels, and that includes *you*. Don't give me bullshit, Frank. I brought you a job, we looked it over, it could be nice. All of a sudden, you're too good for me. You don't do violence." Joey was still holding Frank's arm, and now he squeezed a little, bearing down. "Well, I *do*," he said. "I'm not afraid of violence, Frank. You wanna be, that's okay. You get my meaning?"

This scumbag is turning mean, Frank thought. I made a mistake dealing with him in the first place, and now he's getting resentful, his little piggy mind's gonna decide I'm his enemy. I got to cut away from this shit. He said, "Joey, you knock over one day of one of Leo Ganolese's operations, it won't hurt him that much. He'll look for the people did it, naturally, because nobody's supposed to get away with crap like that. But you're right, he'll probably figure it's some punk hanging around over at the horse show."

"Just like I said," Joey agreed, and gave Frank's arm a little shake.

Frank ignored that. "But," he said, "you start killing his people, you start acting like Leo Ganolese doesn't deserve any respect, he's gonna *find* you. So you can squeeze my arm all you want, I'd still rather face you than Leo Ganolese."

Joey thought about that. Finally, reluctantly, he let Frank's arm go, and Frank resisted the impulse to rub it where it ached. Don't give the slob the satisfaction.

Meantime, Joey was saying, "Okay. We're partners, we respect each *other*. You wanna come up with another way, fine by me."

"So let me think about it," Frank said, telling himself, maybe I'll just leave this town tonight, score something along the way, just enough to take me maybe to Indianapolis, someplace like that.

But Joey said, "Frank, the horse show's *now*. My way, I can get this hand grenade *tomorrow,* we can *do* it."

There's no way out, Frank thought. But somewhere, at some point, I've got to protect myself. Joey's a nasty piece of shit. I shouldn't be here with him at all, but here I am. "We'll have to drive the route," he said. "See what looks good."

"Okay, Frank," Joey said. "And I'll get the hand grenade, too. Just in case."

• • •

As it turned out, they did use the hand grenade, but not in the way Joey had in mind. A hand grenade, yes, but nonviolent.

The situation was, out around Smithton and Floraville, another area where the old man had a long empty ride between pickups, at an intersection in farm country, there was a stop sign. That was where they took him over, running out from both sides of the road as he halted, pulling the ski masks down over their faces, Frank pulling open the driver's door as Joey hurled himself into the car on the passenger side, put his hands on the old man, and yanked him out from behind the wheel. The old man screamed, and Frank got his hands on the wheel, his right foot on the accelerator, and they shot out into the intersection, swinging around hard to the right.

The old man was yelling—what are you doing, are you crazy, do you know whose car this is, all this shit—and Joey cuffed him across the head to shut him up, the three of them wedged together in the front seat. Frank didn't look in the rearview mirror, not wanting to know how close that other car was; it would be on their asses, he knew that much, coming along at top speed.

The narrow farm road was another right turn. Frank was so keyed up, so nervous about this part of it, that he almost took the turn too hard and rammed them into a tree. But he recovered, the tires digging into the oiled-gravel surface, spraying stones everywhere as they jolted on down the empty road, and when now he did dare look in the mirror that other car, a gray Toyota, was way the hell and gone behind them, a lot farther than he would have thought. Perfect.

The little bridge was a mile down this road, over a fast-running shallow boulder-strewn stream; Frank slammed on the brakes and they shuddered to a stop on the bridge, the terrified old man pressing his palms against the dashboard to keep from going out the windshield. Frank glared past him at Joey, screwing around with the hand grenade: "Drop the fucking thing, Joey!"

"Right! Right!" Joey dropped the grenade out the window, throwing the pin after it. Frank accelerated, and in the mirror he saw the roadway back there suddenly produce a red and yellow bouquet of flame, with black leaves of smoke. The chasing Toyota spun and shuddered and squealed to a stop, short of the explosion. The road gaped open over the stream. Nobody would be driving down this way any more today.

The beat-up old pickup truck Frank had stolen this morning was still there behind the burned-out shell of an old farmhouse. Frank steered in next to it, pulled the key from the ignition, and jumped from the car. He hadn't taken anything today, not even a beer, but he was all hopped-up, adrenaline pumping through him. He almost felt as though, if he were to speak, his voice would come out all high-pitched and weird, like somebody who's been sniffing helium. He couldn't keep still, but had to go over and touch the pickup, then bounce back to the car, where Joey was still backing out, looking in at the old man. "Shit," Joey said.

Frank paid no attention. The hard fast driving is what had keyed him up like this. If he held a light bulb it would glow, he knew it would. "He can stay in there," he said, talking over the top of the car at Joey. "He can stay in there till we're gone."

"Oh, yeah, he'll stay in there," Joey said. "You're fucking right he will."

Something in Joey's voice finally caught Frank's attention, and he bent to look through the open driver's door at the old man, who had gone on sitting in there, tilted slightly to the left now, staring out the windshield as though they were still doing eighty-five down the farm road. "Aw, Christ," Frank said, seeing the old guy stare, seeing how his mouth hung open, how his hands were curled in his lap, how he didn't move. Straightening, feeling like shit, he again looked across the top of the car at Joey. "We gave him a heart attack or something."

Joey's response was to reach up and pull the ski mask off and throw it on the ground, revealing his heavy face covered with gleaming sweat. "One less problem," he said. "Open the trunk, Frank."

One less problem. What a scumbag. Get away from this creep, Frank told himself, do it the first chance you get.

Stripping off his own ski mask, he moved to the back of the car and used the key still in his hand to unlock the trunk, now leaving the key chain to dangle from the lock as he lifted the trunk and looked inside.

Bags, boxes. All jumbled in there with an umbrella and a can of STP and some other junk and the spare. Bags, boxes. Money.

"Well, here it is," Frank said, feeling heavy in his mind because of the old man. He reached in for a shoe box, glancing over at Joey, and Joey had a little shitty .22 in his hand. "Oh, you fuckhead!" Frank cried, and threw the shoe box as Joey fired, and the bullet zzizzed away into the world like a bee.

The cocksucker's gonna kill me, Frank thought, disgusted and scared and tired of the whole fucking thing, as he bent and ran down the side of the car, knowing Joey was coming around the trunk after him. Me with nothing, and no time, and nowhere to go, and he can't miss me every time with that fucking gun.

The old man. Frank reached in and gave him a yank and pulled him out of the car, holding him up against himself like a dress he was testing to see if it was the right size, holding the old man's body with his left arm around the chest, forearm up along the chest, hand around the old man's wrinkled neck, pressing that body close while his right hand frisked the guy's pockets and Joey came around the back of the car, the .22 held out in front of himself. He looked angry and pestered when he saw Frank standing there holding the old man up in front of himself. "What the fuck are you doing, Frank? Put the old guy down!"

"Fuck you, Joey."

Frank backed slowly away, afraid of tripping over something, patting and patting the old guy's clothes, feeling something in the right side coat pocket. Let it not be a roll of quarters, okay, God?

Joey tried a shot at Frank's head, but couldn't see enough of it. Frustrated and angry, moving forward after Frank, he pumped two shots into the old man's body, but a .22 doesn't deliver much of a wallop. He should have brought a .45; that would go through the old man and Frank and the tree behind him. But the .22 just made the old man's body bump against Frank, as though he had the hiccups.

And Frank's hand was in that pocket, as Joey trotted toward him now, wanting to be close enough to bring him down regardless of the old man. Frank's hand was in the pocket, and closing on it, and bringing it out, and it was a Smith & Wesson Chief's Special .38 revolver. He stuck his right arm out, pointing at Joey's astonished face as though to say, *The joke's on you, Joey!* And scrambled his brains with two shots into that fat skull.

•   •   •

Switch license plates, pickup and the old man's car. Throw all the boxes and bags into the pickup cab, on the floor and passenger seat. Drive like hell, don't slow down, don't even think, until outside Terre Haute, Indiana. Swipe a Honda off the street there, moving all the goddamn boxes and bags into its backseat, head for Indianapolis. Along the way, suddenly get the shakes, terrible shakes. Pull the car off the road, go behind some bushes, throw up, have diarrhea, cold sweats, uncontrollable trembling, blinding headache. Clean up a little, crawl back to the Honda, sit in there as weak as a kitten, finally get it moving again, go on to Indianapolis, around to Weir Cook Airport there. Go into the long-term parking, get the ticket on the way in, drive around, find a nice Chevy Celebrity with no dust on the windshield—so it hasn't been here long, in the long-term lot—pull in next to it, switch the goods to the Chevy's backseat, drive on out of there (little joke with the tolltaker about being in the wrong lot), head on into Indianapolis and buy a big cheap suitcase there. Then push the Chevy across Indiana and into the night, keep the foot hard on the accelerator until Welcome to Ohio. Three hundred twenty miles and two states away. Find a motel northwest of Dayton, put all the bags and boxes into the big new suitcase and schlep it into the room. Take a long shower. Stand there in the running hot water, thinking about childhood; haven't thought about that shit for years. Think and think, remembering all different kinds of stuff, everything lost and gone. Cry a little in the shower, face all snotty. Tap the forehead against the tiles a little. But what's the use? Nothing to be done, right? You're where you are, and that's where you are.

Frank turned off the water and stepped out of the shower. Life goes on.

•   •   •

Frank's underwear hung on the radiator, his socks were draped over a lampshade to dry in the heat from the bulb, and his shirt hung from the swag chain next to the hanging lamp over the round fake-wood veneer table. Wearing a motel towel, he called a couple of places that in the local phone book claimed they'd deliver food twenty-four hours a day. Three didn't answer, one said the motel was too far away, and then a pizza place said they'd do it, but he'd have to pay a ten-dollar delivery fee, and it would take a minimum of forty-five minutes. "Sure," Frank said. "Room 129."

He wasn't even sure he could eat. His stomach hurt, all right, but not like normal hunger, though he hadn't eaten anything now for maybe fourteen hours. But sooner or later this reaction to the incident with Joey and the old man would have to wear off, and *then* he'd be hungry.

Meantime, he opened the boxes and bags, stacking the

money on the round table, adding it up, and it came to $57,820. Less than the eighty grand he'd been promised, but more than the half that would have been his share if Joey hadn't been such a total unrelieved piece of shit.

He kept out a couple hundred for use, and when he stuffed it in his wallet he noticed that card in there from the lady lawyer in Nebraska. Mary Ann Kelleny. Well, she wouldn't be much help in Ohio—or in Illinois, either, come to that—but still he hung on to the card. She'd been okay, Mary Ann Kelleny. The only decent thing that had happened to him since he'd got out this last time.

He remembered her advice: don't do the little jobs, do one great big job. Okay, Mary Ann, I did one great big job, and it wasn't all that great, okay? Granted, it wasn't five million, but I can retire for a *while* anyway, on fifty-seven grand. Is that what you had in mind, Mary Ann?

Grinning at the idea of how the lady lawyer would react if she'd known how literally he was taking her advice, Frank put the rest of the money back into the suitcase, stacking it in rows. It took about half the space now as when it had been in all the different kinds of packages.

The old guy probably had grandchildren. He probably had candy in some of his other pockets.

Sure. At least he'd had a gun, there was that to say for him. No longer smiling, Frank put the gun in the suitcase with the money, and closed the suitcase, and put it on the floor in the doorless closet.

He wasn't sure why he was keeping the gun. He still didn't believe in violence, in fact more than ever he didn't believe in it, but now he'd been *in* violence, and somehow everything was changed. Of course he'd been around violence all his life, in the pen and on the streets, but never in that personal horrible way. It had been *around* him, but he'd never been in the middle of it, doing it and receiving it, feeling the bullets thud into a dead man's body, *using* a dead man's body like that. A simple burglar, slides in, slides out, like a raccoon in the attic; that's what he was, that's all he'd ever hoped to be. But now it was different. It was changed. He was in an altered landscape now, one he didn't know about yet, and the gun was his talisman.

The motel had cable, and cable had a semi-dirty movie about a kid comes home from college to his house in Beverly Hills and there's nobody there but the new Swedish maid. Sure. "I'll give you fifty-seven thousand dollars," Frank told the set, "for every time that happened in real life."

Somewhere in through there he fell asleep, and when the knock came at the motel door, waking him, there was a black-and-white war movie on instead. He switched it off, readjusted the towel around his middle, and let in a black kid carrying the pizza in a box and wearing a cap with the pizza store's name on it. He gave the kid a whole lot of money for one lousy pizza, and then when he opened it the smell was too strong. He shut the box and went back to bed and lay there awake, thinking.

The pattern had changed. That was what had happened today, he'd gone through the looking glass like Alice, he was on the other side now, and the pattern was completely different.

The lawyer lady had talked about the pattern, had talked about the rubber band attached to his back with the other end still in his cell, and all along he'd known she was right. He'd known it would happen again. He'd be out for a while and then he'd fuck up and then he'd be back in, the same old pattern, over and over, world without end, amen.

No more. World *with* end. The law would surely find some way to tie him to the robbery of the old man and the shooting of fat slob Joey. He didn't know exactly what it would be, fingerprints or saliva or threads from his coat or some damn thing, but *something* would lash him tight to that robbery-and-murder.

Frank had an almost religious respect for the forensic scientists who worked with the authorities. He believed they were omniscient and omnipotent and damn near omnipresent. And that meant, if the law ever got its hands on Frank Hillfen again, they would drape that robbery-and-murder around his neck, and he'd be *gone*.

I can't go back, he thought. Not this time. That's the change, that's what's different now. Now I *can't* go back.

I need Mary Ann Kelleny's five-mil job. The big one.

Hardly thinking about it, Frank got up and ate half the pizza, washing it down with cold water from the sink. The five-mil job. What would it look like?

Ananayel

Fantastic! He did all that on his own! I didn't influence the proceedings in any way, I haven't even had contact with Frank Hillfen since Mary Ann Kelleny gave him the ride to Omaha. (Isn't it touching how he saves that business card? There's something really very sweet and vulnerable about Frank. Hopelessly self-destructive, of course—of course! —but endearing, like a flea-ridden dog.)

And he surely remembered what Mary Ann Kelleny had to say to him, didn't he? And he made a mess of things absolutely on his own and without my help. He made himself ready so fast I don't even have the others in position yet.

Susan is still seeing Grigor Basmyonov sometimes, though less often than before. But she still phones him during the week when Andy Harbinger has monopolized her weekend. I'm afraid a vegetable love isn't enough to distract Susan completely from Grigor. I'm afraid we're going to have to become more deeply involved with one another.

But why should this affect me so strongly? When adrift, of course, when in my usual self, I still *am* my usual self, calm and obedient, but when in Andy's body I find myself increasingly nervous, expectant, apprehensive. As though there were things to be learned. Things to be learned? From Susan Carrigan?

21

There was a special on PBS that night about efforts being made to preserve the artistic heritage of civilization, the struggle against everything from acid rain to mindless looting, and a little puff piece in the paper mentioned that the International Society for Cultural Preservation would be prominently featured on the program. From the bank, that morning, Susan called Andy up at Columbia—he taught sociology up there—and left a message with the faculty secretary, as she had done before. He called back half an hour later, and she invited him to come watch the program with her. "The organization it's about is the one where I met Grigor, in Moscow. Remember the cocktail party I told you about?"

"Sure. What time's it on?"

"Nine o'clock. I'll make dinner, we can eat before."

"White or red?"

Meaning the color of the wine he should bring. "You decide," she said. "I'll make chicken."

• • •

Buying the chicken and the new potatoes and the baby green beans and the three kinds of lettuce on her way home from the bank, Susan found herself betting Andy would bring white wine, given that choice. Because it was bloodless.

Immediately she rejected that thought, angry at herself. She knew she shouldn't feel that way, so denigrating, knew she should be grateful she'd found a man happy to give her companionship without making demands, but then sometimes she couldn't help wondering why it was supposed to be such a big deal to be around a person who never made demands. Maybe she wanted demands. Maybe she should *demand* demands.

She grinned at herself over the lettuce bins, and a guy smirked at her and said, "You're beautiful when you smile," and she turned her back on him, heading for the cashier.

•   •   •

When Andy arrived, just after seven-thirty, he was carrying a brown paper bag up against his left side, and used his right arm to bring her close and kiss her cheek. How pretty he is, she thought yet again. He always surprised her with how good-looking he was, as though his appearance faded slightly every time they were apart.

"A treat tonight," he said, and reached into the bag, and brought out a bottle of French red wine; good stuff, from the look of it. "For dinner," he told her, as she took it.

So she'd been wrong. "Great," she said, looking at the label.

"And," he said, full of repressed excitement, "this is for *now*!" And out of the bag came a bottle of champagne.

"Why, Andy!" she said. "You surprise me!"

His smile bubbled over with delight. "I hope to," he said.

•   •   •

There's something about knowing you're going to, but you haven't yet, nobody's even made a move or a suggestion or a hint yet, and yet you both know it's going to happen, *this* time it's going to happen; there's something delicious in those last moments before you fall into one another's arms.

Susan couldn't remember when it was exactly that she'd *known*, whether it was when he'd brought out the red wine, or not until he'd shown her the champagne, but somewhere in there she'd understood that he'd made a decision. And that she agreed with it.

How will he do it? she wondered. He always seems so confident, but we've really known one another a while now with no moves at all, so what does that mean?

And how will *I* do? Will I be a klutz? One or two incidents in her life when she'd been a klutz came into her mind, keeping her edgy, but over the edginess was the knowledge that it was *going to happen*.

And tonight he didn't at all do that sort of fading-out thing that happened with him sometimes when they were watching a movie or TV. He would be there with her, and then a kind of glaze would come over him, his eyes became dull, his face less expressive. It was as though he were taking a nap, asleep with his eyes open, but somehow it was more than that. Once, in a movie theater, she'd touched the back of his hand when he was like that, and it was so cold it frightened her. But then he'd responded immediately to her touch—he always responded immediately from the fading-out thing, if his attention was called on—and when he'd used the same hand a minute later to pat the back of *her* hand it was no longer cold. Had she imagined the coldness? She didn't believe it; but she'd been reluctant to find out for sure. Since then, if she saw him fading out, she'd speak to him but not touch.

But tonight he didn't fade once. He was with her the whole time, admiring the dinner she'd thrown together (she was sorry now she hadn't paid it more attention) and even showing interest in her retelling of the story about the Moscow cocktail party, this time emphasizing the International Society for Cultural Preservation rather than the meeting with Grigor.

They sat on the sofa together to watch the program, and it seemed perfectly natural for him to put his arm around her and for her to nestle in against him, feeling the steady beat of his heart. They watched the program in silence for about twenty minutes, and then, during a boring bit—helicopters over imperiled green rain forest, portentous offscreen narration—he lifted her chin and kissed her lips. A great languor flowed into her from his mouth, a spreading softness and a heightened sense of her own physical self. His hand very gently stroked her body, and he whispered against her lips, ''You are so amazing to me.''

•   •   •

He filled her as though his body were all molten, soft and flowing, as though she were a small mountain lake, hidden and unknown, and his presence turned her to nectar. She moved in slow motion, her arms boneless ribbons around him as he nuzzled within her, her body holding and releasing in long easy swells of a great warm tide, physical sensations and yearning emotions all braided together, coiling around her, a close compelling spiral of flesh and she an electric dot in the very center. It all made her so sad she thought she must be dying, she thought this must be the great sad fulfillment of death, but she didn't care. She embraced the sadness, the salt of tears and birth and death, time contracting into that electric dot that was herself, everything contracting to that one infinitesimal point in the whole world, and she it, and then that point imploded and left nothing at all.

They smiled solemnly at one another, stretched out together on her bed, the warmth rising from their bodies. And he said two astonishing things. No, not astonishing things, but said in an astonishing way:

''I don't want to lose you.''

And, ''I didn't know about this.''

Ananayel

I didn't know about this.

I like being Andy Harbinger. I have made him healthy and attractive and reasonably strong. (I've tried a number of human types by now, and prefer comfort.) And he *is* human. I constructed him, from molecules of myself, so he is both me and human, and I am learning from him all the time, but I didn't know about *this*.

The experience of being with Susan was unlike anything I could have imagined. Not like that business with Pami at all, that brutal calisthenics. This was . . . this was like the best of the empyrean, distilled. How can humans spend their time doing anything *else*?

Of course, it was even more powerful for me, since I was in some general contact with Susan's feelings and reactions as well. Andy's and Susan's emotions, sensations, all mixing together in my semi-human brain; what an explosive cocktail!

I'm so happy I've had this chance to get to know and learn about humans, before the end.

22

Three-thirty in the morning. Pami'd only made two hundred twenty-five dollars tonight, but there wasn't any action left on the street at this hour. Most of the other whores were already gone. Three-thirty on a Tuesday morning, traffic up Eleventh Avenue for the Lincoln Tunnel was down to a couple tired dishwashers and accordion players; not customers.

Pami had to make a decision now: go home, or hope for just one more twenty-five-dollar hit. It was a tricky balancing act she had to do here. Rush didn't like her to come home much after three on weeknights—because he had to hear all about everything she did before they could go to sleep—but he could turn mean if she came home with less than four hundred dollars.

Well, it wasn't going to happen, not tonight. No more tricks tonight. So Pami Njoroge, the little twenty-five-dollar whore, left her Eleventh Avenue stroll and walked to 34th Street and Eighth Avenue to take the subway uptown. To *wait for* the subway uptown; sometimes you had to wait a long time at this hour in the morning.

And right there on the subway platform was one more trick for the night: a half-drunk Spanish man that first thought he'd just hassle her, but then grinned and got happy when she said, with her clipped, mechanical-sounding Kenyan accent, "You gimme twenty-five bucks, I give you blowjob. Else you go away."

Down at the far end of the platform was a five-foot-high orange metal box to put trash in. They went down to the other side of that, even though they were the only ones on the platform, and there she exchanged her service for his cash, and at the end of it she saw he was thinking about knocking her on the head and robbing her—Rush would *really* beat the shit out of her, that ever happen—so she showed him the little spring knife in her tiny shoulder bag, and said, "You want that was your last blowjob in the world?"

All of a sudden, he couldn't speak anything but Spanish. Backing away from her, brown eyes very round, he jabbered away about his innocence and how she was misunderstanding him, all in his New World Spanish—which she couldn't understand anyway, and didn't give a damn about—and then he hurried away to the middle of the platform, where he knew he could be seen by the person in the tollbooth.

About ten minutes later a bunch of drunk black teenage boys came in, loud and full of energy, and Pami tensed up, but they didn't pay her any attention and soon after that the train roared in. She boarded an almost empty car and sat there with her thoughts on the long ride uptown.

The apartment belonged to Rush, on 121st Street near Morningside Park. The big old building with its gray-stone facade didn't belong to anybody—maybe the city—and half the apartments were empty, all torn up, the sinks and toilets and wiring and wood molding all ripped out. Sometimes you'd see old mezuzahs on the floor—they looked like water beetles, only they didn't move—the parchment inside them gone, shredded to dust. The people who stripped the apartments were simple and superstitious, and they knew the mezuzahs were strong religious fetishes of the tribe who once lived here, so they pried the little metal containers off the doorposts with screwdrivers before carrying the wood away. They didn't want bad luck to follow them out of the building.

Nobody who lived in the building now knew the language or even the alphabet on the parchment papers folded into the mezuzahs. Nobody knew that the word *Shaddai* on the outside was one of the many names of God, or that the tiny writing on the inside was from the Hebrew Bible (also called, by others, the Old Testament), from Deuteronomy 6 and 11:

> Hear, O Israel: The Lord our God is one Lord: And thou shalt love the Lord thy God with all thine heart, and with all thy soul, and with all thy might. And these words, which I command thee this day, shall be in thine heart: And thou shalt teach them diligently unto thy children, and shalt talk of them when thou sittest in thine house, and when thou walkest by the way, and when thou liest down, and

when thou risest up. And thou shalt bind them for a sign upon thine hand, and they shall be as frontlets between thine eyes. And thou shalt write them upon the posts of thy house, and on thy gates.

And:

And it shall come to pass, if ye shall harken diligently unto my commandments which I command you this day, to love the Lord thy God, and to serve him with all your heart and with all your soul, That I will give you the rain of your land in his due season, the first rain and the latter rain, that thou mayest gather in thy corn, and thy wine, and thine oil. And I will send grass in thy fields for thy cattle, that thou mayest eat and be full. Take heed to yourselves, that your heart be not deceived, and ye turn aside, and serve other gods, and worship them; And then the Lord's wrath be kindled against you, and he shut up the heaven, that there be no rain, and that the land yield not her fruit; and lest ye perish quickly from off the good land which the Lord giveth you. Therefore shall ye lay up these my words in your heart and in your soul, and bind them for a sign upon your hand, that they may be as frontlets between your eyes. And ye shall teach them your children, speaking of them when thou sittest in thine house, and when thou walkest by the way, when thou liest down, and when thou risest up. And thou shalt write them upon the doorposts of thine house, and upon thy gates: That your days may be multiplied, and the days of your children, in the land which the Lord sware unto your father to give them, as the days of heaven upon the earth.

The people who'd tapped the little nails into the soft chestnut and oak and pine wood, holding the words in place at the doorposts of their houses as they'd been commanded, were long gone. The latter owners of the building, who also knew the law and the language but who had for the most part ignored or forgotten it, were also gone. There was no one in the building now to worry about the coming of the rains or the gathering of the corn, and it had been long since the grass here was for cattle. Nor was there anyone, in any language, to ponder the warning on those long-disintegrated scraps of paper: the kindling of wrath, the shutting of heaven, the quickness of the perishing.

Pami left the train at 125th Street and walked down through dark streets where people slept on the ground; but they were healthier than the people who slept on the ground in Nairobi. Sometimes more dangerous, too; Pami knew to keep walking quickly, keep the little spring knife in her hand, look only straight ahead. Her heels made nervous sharp sounds on the old cracked sidewalk.

The building where she lived with Brother Rush—he liked to call himself Brother sometimes, when he was trying to pull one of his political or religious scams—was in the middle of the block, with smaller brick tenements on one side and brick-strewn rubble where tenements had once stood on the other. The doorway was always open, the door itself long since gone. The still-occupied apartments were mostly in two vertical lines in the rear corners of the building, where the old chimneys and flues still existed and the water pipes hadn't frozen because of the heated occupied building on the next block which abutted this one at the back. There was water in the building—nobody was sure why—but of course no heat, so in winter the residents burned whatever they could find in the old shallow fireplaces originally meant for coal.

Pami and Rush used two rooms at the rear of a second-floor apartment, one with a mattress for sleeping and some cardboard cartons for storage and kerosene lamps for light and warmth, and the other with a table and some chairs and plastic milk boxes to sit on and actual electricity from an extension cord (a series of extensions cords, heavy-weight ones) snaking up an airshaft from another building, where a guy Rush knew had tapped into the incoming electric service, Rush paying him two bags for the service (both heavily cut).

It was in the room with the table and chairs that Rush mostly lived. He wasn't much of a dealer, but what little goods passed through his hands he sold at that table. All his schemes and scams with his druggie friends were talked out at that table (and came to nothing). He ate and drank at that table, and counted Pami's earnings there every night. And they sat there together for her to tell him everything that had happened since they'd seen each other last.

Pami didn't understand what that part was all about. She'd known men who got off by listening to their women talk about fucking other men, but this didn't seem to be like that. (Rush mostly didn't care about fucking anyway, which was a nice relief.) It was like he was listening for something, some special particular event, his narrow dark head cocked, his red-rimmed eyes brooding, his hands half-clenched on the scarred wood of the table. He never reacted to what she told him, never gave back anything more than a grunt when she was finished; and then they could go to bed.

He was waiting for her as usual tonight, seated at the table, alone in the room, illuminated by the light from one dirty-shaded table lamp on the floor over by the hot plate, an empty Kentucky Fried Chicken carton on the floor at his feet. He was waiting for her as usual, but *he* wasn't as usual, and she picked up on that right away. (She was always very aware of her environment, sharply aware of anything around her that might be a threat.)

"You late, baby," he said, that gruff hoarse voice as always sounding as though it was about to conk out completely, but there wasn't exactly the same menace in it as usual; something, whatever it was, had him distracted, kept him from turning the entire weight of his mean attention on her.

Still, she played her normal part: "Slow night, Rush,"

she said. "Very slow night. All I got's two-fifty, but there's nobody on the street an I didn't wanna come home too late."

She couldn't quite keep the wheedle out of the last part of that—when Rush was mean, he was very mean—but tonight he seemed hardly to notice at all. "Sit down," he said. "Tell me about it."

"Okay, Rush."

She sat across the table from him, putting her little shoulder bag on the wood in front of herself, and as she took out the wads of money and replaced the spring knife in the bag he sat and listened, his full lips moving sometimes, in and out, as though he was tasting some old meal. She told him about the johns, about the other hookers, about the people on the street, every encounter of the night, the Spanish man and the drunken teenagers and nobody much at all on the subway and nobody except sleeping people on the streets of the neighborhood.

He listened, smoothing out the money, counting it, stacking it, finally putting it away in his pants pocket. She finished her recital and sat up, ready for him to nod his permission for her to get up and go into the other room and get ready for bed, which was the way it always went, but tonight was different. Tonight, Rush fixed her with those dark eyes of his with the redness all around them, and sat there in silence for a long minute while she got increasingly nervous and scared, wondering what she'd done wrong. And then he said, "I'm gonna say a name to you. You tell me what that name means when you hear it."

Pami had no idea what this might be about. "Okay, Rush," she said.

Rush nodded. He seemed almost to go to sleep. Then he said, very slowly, enunciating much more carefully than he usually did, "Susan Carrigan."

Pami blinked slowly, thinking. Susan Carrigan.

Rush's horny fingers tapped on the table. "Well? Pami? Susan Carrigan. Well?"

"I don't know, Rush," she said. "It don't mean anything to me."

"It damn well better mean something to you," Rush said, "I'm *asking* you what it means."

Pami's fear and helplessness made her jittery at the table. Dark masses of shadow moved in the room, echoing every movement made by either of them. "I don't *know*, Rush. That's no kinda name I know. What is that? Some social worker? Somebody like that?" Then, thinking maybe she saw some corner of what this problem might be, she said, "Rush? Somebody say I talking against you to social workers? It's a *lie*. I don't talk to nobody but *you*, you know that."

Rush sat there, unmoved and unmoving. "There's gotta be a link," he said thoughtfully, as though to himself. "He's usin you. He's usin her. But what's he up to? If you don't know about each other . . ."

"Rush? Who? Nobody usin me, Rush. I just with *you*, man."

Rush paid no attention. He was deep in his own thoughts. "What if," he said, and then just sat there, brooding, rapping those fingertips on the table. He glanced at Pami as though he didn't recognize her, didn't know what she was doing there, wasn't even thinking about her. Then he roused himself, sat up straighter, took a deep breath, and frowned hard at her, as though he'd just had a thought and didn't like it. "What if," he said, "you aren't anythin at all? What if he finessed me with you, put me all over you while he's getting it together with *other people*?"

"Rush? I don't know what you're talkin about."

"And that's good for you, too," he told her. "It means you can go on livin."

"Rush?"

"A while, anyway. How's the sores?"

"About the same," she said, truculent, and looked down at the table. She didn't like it that he even mentioned those sores; she tried not to think about them herself.

The sores had started in the last few weeks, around her waist and in back under her shoulder blades; small but wet. She put drugstore greases on them, to keep them from showing through her clothes, but otherwise ignored them, or tried to. Hooking on Eleventh Avenue, she never had to take any clothes off anyway, so the johns didn't know.

"All right, baby," Rush said, sounding weary and, for him, almost kindly. "Go on to bed."

"Okay, Rush," she said, hiding her relief, keeping a cool surface. She got to her feet and went into the other room, and pulled off her clothing, being very careful where the material stuck to the sores.

Off this room was a small bathroom without fixtures. The cold water still ran, and they had a basin and a Scotch bottle to catch it in. The hole where the toilet had been removed smelled so bad they kept an old piece of Sheetrock over it, but they still used it, and Pami did now, holding her breath when she moved the Sheetrock out of the way, squatting over the hole, wiping herself with paper napkins from the Kentucky Fried Chicken, sliding the Sheetrock back into place when she was finished, and expelling the long-held breath with a *whoosh*. But the smell stayed in the air for ten or fifteen minutes; nothing to be done.

Pami was filling the Scotch bottle with water and pouring it into the basin when Rush came into the room, made a disgusted face, and said, "Shit. I got to steal some Clorox, pour it down in there."

"That's a good idea, Rush."

The basin full, Pami washed her face first, then her underarms, then squatted over it. Rush frowned at her sores. "You ain't gonna be workin much longer, girl," he said.

"I got time," Pami told him, trying not to know how scared she was. "I got plenty of time, Rush."

He ignored that. "I'm goin out for a while. Don't leave that light on, I don't know when I'll be back."

"Where you going, Rush?"

He gave her a look, as though to say she was lucky she didn't get a broken arm for a question like that, and left.

Pami heard the apartment door squeak. It never closed one hundred percent, but why would anybody break in here? Then a minute later she heard the door squeak again, so maybe Rush changed his mind.

She always used to sleep naked, but because of the sores, she now wore an outsize T-shirt, which she had to wash in the basin every morning. It was still slightly damp now when she put it on, but it would warm quickly against her body. She went out to the other room to turn off the light and there was a man there, standing beside the table.

Cop. It stood out all over him. Big and beefy and soreheaded, in a gray topcoat and dark suit and tie. He looked at her with disgust and said, "You want to go back to Africa with that T-shirt on?"

She stared at him in horror. Go back? It had never occurred to her—it had all been so *easy,* getting here, staying here. That a twenty-shilling whore in Nairobi did about as well as a twenty-five-dollar whore in New York only meant she wasn't doing *worse,* and in some ways life here was much easier. If she was arrested now, deported now, they'd be sure to find the sores, examine her, find out the truth. Lock her away somewhere, leave her to die. Trembling, afraid to speak because she would sound like a foreigner—I'm American! Black skin American!—she touched her shaking hands to the T-shirt, feeling her tight scared belly.

His look of disgust increased. "Go get dressed," he said. "And tell Rush to come out here."

He knew everything, this cop. But now she had to speak. Form the words with great care, she told herself, form the words the way they do in this neighborhood. "Sir, he isn't here."

"Oh, don't waste my time," he said. "He can't get out the back way, there's no place for him to go. Just send him out and get dressed."

"Sir—" Would an American even say "sir"? Oh, I'm destroyed, she thought, despair cold against her throat. "Sir, it's true. He isn't here."

The cop frowned at her, frowned at the doorway, lifted his head as though he was smelling for Rush. Like a dog. He seemed a little confused. He gestured for Pami to precede him, and they both went through the doorway into the dark second room, where there was just enough light-spill from the room they'd left behind to let Pami find her way around the cartons and mattress. But Pami knew the place.

The cop pointed. "What's that?"

"Kerosene lamp, sir."

"Light it."

Pami's fingers were awkward with fear. She struggled with the lamp, squatting beside it, small face furrowed all over with concentration. The light flared up at last, and she turned down the wick and lowered the glass chimney. The messy room came to amber life.

"Pick it up," the cop said, and Pami did, the shadows all moving together, like an orchestra. Again the cop pointed. "That the john?"

"Yes, sir."

There was no door to the bathroom, of course. The cop gestured for Pami to bring the lamp over and carry it into the little ruined room. He followed, standing in the doorway, wrinkling his nose. "How do you live like this?"

"I don't know, sir."

"Come back outside."

Still carrying the kerosene lamp, Pami followed the cop to the outer room, where he sat at the table—in her chair, not Rush's—and sprawled there, legs wide, thumbs hooked in belt. "Where'd *Brother* Rush go?"

"I truly don't know, sir." Pami had given up trying to sound like an American; whatever was going to happen would happen.

"You stupid little bitch," the cop said, but without any

heat, just weariness. "Don't you know I can help you, if I want?"

Pami's twisted jaw worked. He was offering her salvation—short-term salvation, it's true, but that's all she could hope for—he was showing her an open doorway, and she couldn't step through it. "I don't know!" she wailed. "I don't know where Rush is! I gotta go back to Africa because *that*? Rush don't tell me—nobody ever told me nothing my whole life! Why anybody like you be so stupid come ask *me* questions? I don't know *nothing*!"

The cop was unimpressed. With a jaundiced look, he said, "I bet you know what's gonna happen if you raise your voice to me again."

She blinked. The glass chimney rattled as she held the lamp. She kept quiet.

The cop nodded. "Put the lamp down on this table," he said. "Before you catch yourself on fire."

"Yes, sir." Putting the lamp down, growing calmer because of the calm in his voice, she began to think at last, and said, "Maybe . . . maybe he went to see that woman."

The cop raised an eyebrow. "Woman? You mean he got himself another whore?"

"No, sir. I don't know, sir. Not a name like that, sir."

"Not a *name* like that?" The cop glared at her, angry because she was confusing him. "What do you mean, not a name like that? What name?"

Panic leaped up in her again. She couldn't remember the name! Shaking both closed fists in front of herself, she tried desperately to think. "Oh! It's—it's—oh, please, oh, wait, it's—Susan!"

The cop's thumbs leaped out of his belt. He sat forward, meaty palms slapping on the table. "Susan? Susan what?"

"I don't know! He just said it, and then he went, and I don't know these names here!"

"All right, all right," the cop said, with less agitation, and raised a hand to make her stop. He stared at her very intently. "The last name. Was it Carrigan?"

That was it! "Yes, sir!" she cried, in great relief. "You know it, then! You know everything!"

"Do I?" The cop sat back. One hand flopped down limply into his lap, the other lifted to rub his chin. He was thinking it over. "Okay, Pami," he said at last. "Go in and get dressed."

She stared at him. "Why?"

"Because I'm taking you downtown, what else you think?"

"I helped you!"

"Not a lot, Pami." He shrugged. "Don't make it tough on yourself. Come on, get dressed."

She knew what she was going to do before she knew she was going to do it. She pointed at the lamp. "Can I take that in with me?"

"Sure."

He was sprawled again, across the table from her. She stepped forward, picked up the kerosene lamp, flung it in his face. His hands jolted up, but too late. Glass shattered, liquid fire splashed across the front of him, and Pami ran to the door and out.

Leaping down the stairs, in her mind's eye she saw him sitting there, not even moving, the kerosene burning all over his face and chest. Almost as though he knew she was going to do it. Knew it when she did. Knew it and didn't know it when she knew it and didn't know it.

Barefoot, dressed in the T-shirt, without her clothes and her shoulder bag and her money and her spring knife, Pami fled down 121st Street, as the fire spread behind her.

Ananayel

Susan!
As the fire burns this body, this table, this floor, I continue

to sit here, trying to decide what this means. I've been spending so much of my time near Susan, one of that creature's fellow demons must have found me and reported. And now he's gone to see what he can learn about my plans from Susan.

What will he do? He didn't hurt Pami, just stayed close to her, waiting for me to find her useful. Will he do the same with Susan? Or will he decide it's time to take action?

I must remind myself of the situation here. Susan is nothing to do with the plan. Susan was the bait only, to bring Grigor Basmyonov into play. If the bait is useful twice, how much better, of course. Of course. If Susan will now draw that devil off, distract him while I get on with my work, how much better. Of course.

I must remind myself of the situation here. At the *best* of circumstances, Susan Carrigan will survive no longer than one long inhalation of my life; and these, for Susan, are not the best of circumstances. Her life expectancy is now that of the planet: weeks, at most. What does it matter if her life is even briefer than that? What does it matter, between brevities?

I must remind myself of the situation here, as the fire burns through this floor and the living creatures in this fiery shell flee for their fleeting lives and this body falls with this chair and this table through the rotted smoldering boards through two levels of smoky heated air and the fire department sirens are heard in the night.

I must remind myself of the situation here.

She sleeps. I sit on her chest, almost weightless, scratching my upraised knees with my claws, and I smell the smells of her breath and her body. She has had sex, she is comfortable in her body and her bed and her mind. I touch her dreams with my thoughts, and she whimpers. She feels my touch, she feels my feather weight on her chest, and she is afraid.

This is no Pami. I'll tear this one into narrow strips and it will tell me everything in its mind. Everything. And that god-dung creature will never use it again.

I knead her chest with my toes. She opens her eyes. She sees me. She screams.

23

I should have stayed in New Jersey, Frank thought. The police car was still there in his rearview mirror, pacing him, not doing anything yet, just pacing him.

I shouldn't have driven into the city at five in the morning, Frank told himself. I should have waited and come in at rush hour, disappear in the crowd.

The damn thing of it was, he'd decided to *avoid* the rush hour. Here he was, still in the Chevy from Weir Cook Airport in Indianapolis, driving across New Jersey in the middle of the night, and he'd figured the hell with it, get the trip over with, drive on into New York and ditch the car tonight and get a hotel room and start fresh tomorrow.

So he'd pushed it across New Jersey, and then the tollbooth guy at the George Washington Bridge looked at him funny; he knew it, he felt it at the time. There was just something about Frank or the car or something that alerted the guy, Frank knew it. He'd spent a lifetime knowing things like that.

And then, on the Manhattan side, he was almost alone on the Henry Hudson Parkway as he drove down the west side, and at 158th Street a *police car* was just pulling up onto the highway. He slowed down to maybe three miles over the limit, and the blue and white police car tucked in at the same speed about six car lengths back, and here they both were.

The tollbooth guy turned me up, Frank thought. He knew there was something wrong, and he got the word to the NYPD, and right now those guys behind me are running this license plate through the computer at Motor Vehicle. Has it been reported stolen yet? Has the Indianapolan returned from his flight and taken the courtesy bus to the spot where his car used to be?

Even if not, *even* if not, if the cops back there decide anyway to just check out this guy in the Chevy on general principles and because it's a slow night tonight, Frank is without papers; not on himself and most especially not on the car. "Who is this car registered to?" "John Doe, Officer."

125th Street; the next exit. Driving smoothly, without fuss, even managing to *look* casual though no one in the world would be able to see his face at this moment, Frank steered for the exit, flowed smoothly down and around the curve, and the *police car followed*!

Damn! Damn damn damn! The first traffic light Frank came to was green and he went straight and the cops came right along in his wake, half a block back. The second light was just turning yellow; he pressed the accelerator and zipped through, then eased off again. Now would tell; either the police car stops, or its red and white flashers come on and start revolving and the cops come straight on through the intersection and right up Frank's tailpipe.

I'll have to try to outrun them, Frank thought, knowing how hopeless that would be but knowing also that he had no other choice. Take turns, cut back and forth in all these streets, try to lose them. He kept staring at the rearview mirror, not breathing, mouth open in fear, and back there the police car... *stopped*.

Green light ahead. Frank took the right turn, then the next left, then another right. Bobbing and weaving, losing them any way he could. He kept going, switching back and switching back, all on empty streets in that darkest time of night just before the dawn, no traffic, no pedestrians. Stay off the highway, that was the thing, find the direction to go downtown, get undercover some—

Sirens, off a ways. Looking for me!

A skinny little black girl in a huge bloodred T-shirt ran out of nowhere into the glare of his headlights, waving her arms at him, showing him her tear-streaked terrified face. She was barefoot, and at first he thought she was ten years old, some little kid, attacked, gang-raped, something, and he instinctively hit the brakes, but without completely stopping.

She grabbed the passenger door handle as it went by her at about five miles an hour, snatched it open, leaped headfirst into the car with the door banging against her legs, and Frank, startled, tromped the accelerator again. She pulled herself in and up, knees on the floor, arms on the seat, her pleading wide-eyed broken-jawed face staring up at him, the door imperfectly closed and rattling as he accelerated, fleetingly afraid of an ambush situation, and he saw she wasn't what he'd thought. She's a grown-up woman, he realized, staring down at her, ugliest thing I ever seen in my life.

"Mister, take me away from here!" she cried, with some kind of click-clack accent in her words; not like a spade at all; those mushmouth *brothers* on the inside. "I'll do anything you want," she begged, "but take me away from *here*!"

24

Susan woke from a nightmare to a worse nightmare, sitting on her chest, its claws puncturing her breasts, its red eyes gleaming at her as she screamed. It opened that hooked mustardy beak, and its breath was so foul that even in her terror she had to consciously try not to be sick.

"Susan," it said, in a husky croak, like a dog that had learned how to talk, and its narrow tongue, forked at the tip, flashed out and back, as though already tasting her blood.

I'm dreaming! But she knew she wasn't.

A forepaw reached out, one gray-green talon touched her nose as though in play, and fire seared through her body from the touch. She shrieked, her own breath as hot as sulphur in her lungs.

"Suuuu-san," it crooned, and increased its weight, suddenly and terribly; then was almost weightless again. "Who have you met recently, Suuuuu-san?" it asked, the red eyes sparkling as though it hoped she would refuse to answer. Would refuse at first to answer. Would refuse for as long as possible to answer. "Who have you met? What are you doing together?"

Andy! she thought, but didn't say, and thought again, *it's a dream*, and the thing suddenly looked up, as though startled, and bolts of white light shot out of its eyes.

No; *into* its eyes. From everywhere, from nowhere, the white light made two long thin cones, stilettos, two narrow blades plunging into the demon through its open eyes, filling it like milk, the white glow inside pulsing through the

scales and fur of its body, swelling it, the demon's mouth
yawping wide, dislocating its own jaw, the forked tongue
frantically flapping as though caught in a springe and trying
to escape desperately from that mouth, that body.

The white light seared the body of the demon from the
center, burning and charring, and the monster writhed in
furious pain, pressing down on Susan's body and then
leaping into the air. Great huge gray-black wings sprang
from it, filling the room, beating wildly, stripping the walls
of pictures and mirror—the mirror showing nothing—the
demon curling in on itself in the midst of its thumping
wings, trying to bite through itself to that tormenting light
that slashed and destroyed deep within.

Count Dracula sat quietly in the wooden chair beside the
window, right leg crossed over left, hands crossed calmly in
lap as he watched the battle proceed in the middle of the
room. Susan, battered by terror and pain, roused herself half
upward, blood seeping from the long claw-tears on her
breasts, and stared at this new horror.

Dracula turned his head, faint sparks of static electricity
springing from him as he moved, and smiled at Susan,
showing her his blood-smeared fangs. "So you are *that*
important to him," he said amiably, in no particular accent.
"You are the very linchpin of his plan."

The words made no sense, it was as though they were a
part of the torture. Susan stared at her tormentor in this new
guise, and he turned his attention back to the madness in the
air, where the fury of the wings had slowed, the struggle
had been decided. The demon sagged from its wings, which
fitfully shook, creaking like old leather.

No, not the demon; the husk of the demon. Susan
understood that all at once: the demon itself had fled from
that battlefield and now sat calmly watching from the
sidelines, amusing itself.

But so did the opponent understand, whoever or whatever
that might be. Abruptly, the chest of that ghoul-gryphon tore
open and light poured into the room, blinding Susan, who,

as she flung her hands to her face, saw the Count Dracula apparition cease to be. Gone.

In the semi-darkness behind her hands, eyes squeezed shut but nevertheless seeing through her lids and her hands, seeing the *bones* in her hands from the intensity of that light, Susan felt it all change. A great billowing tenderness enfolded her. The light lost its terrifying incandescence, became soft, soothed her, settled and calmed her in the bed, removed all pain and fear, caressed her brain, and she slept, dreamless and full.

The alarm sounded. Her eyes snapped open. What a horrible dream! But it was so real!

She sat up, unable to believe anything, neither that it had been real nor a dream. There were no wounds on her breasts. The pictures and mirror were in place on the walls. A faint scent, like burning tires, hung in the air.

25

Jurisdiction was the word they used. They talked over Li Kwan's head, or past his ears, as though he didn't speak English, or it didn't matter if he did. They used the word *jurisdiction,* and they smiled and smacked their lips and raised their jaws at one another, as though he were a juicy steak that only one of them could enjoy.

For four days they moved him around, from jurisdiction to jurisdiction. The *Star Voyager*'s crew had turned him over to uniformed men from the United States Immigration and Naturalization Service, who took him in a car across New York—so familiar, from all the photos, all the films, but so desperately foreign—to an office building and up-stairs to a large room with a mesh cage in it. They put him in the cage, and fed him one meal, and then New York City policemen came and took him away to a recognizable prison and put him in an isolation cell, and there he spent the night. Next morning the Federal Bureau of Investigation had a turn at him—and another cell, in another location—and then the Secret Service, and then the New York City police again. And back to Immigration. And occasional brief incomprehensible appearances before various judges, who muttered at the officials and paid him no attention at all. And so on.

For the first two days, Kwan kept trying to make his case, make it with somebody, anybody, but no one would listen, no one cared, not the judges, not the people in uniform who led him from place to place, not anybody. Men in shabby suits, carrying highly polished attaché cases, would occasionally appear and claim to be attorneys and say they had been assigned to "represent" him, and he tried to tell his story to *them*, but none of them was interested. That was the point, finally, if there was one: no one in the world was even interested.

One attorney, the most honest of them—the only one honest of them—said it straight out: "Never mind that, Kwan. You aren't political, so forget all that. You aren't political because it would be too goddamn awkward if you were political, so you're not. You're, let's see, you're"—studying the papers he'd taken from the gleaming attaché case—"you're a stowaway, an illegal immigrant, an accused thief—"

"Thief! Who says I'm a thief?"

"You'll have your day in court, Kwan. That's the name, right? Li Kwan? Your last name's Kwan?"

"My family name is Li," Kwan answered. "My given name is Kwan."

"Oh." The man frowned some more at the papers. "They got it backward here."

"Li Kwan. That's correct."

The man smiled in sudden understanding. "I get it! You *do* it backward! Is that a Chinese thing, or is it just you?"

"It is Chinese."

"So you're Mr. Li, is that it?"

"Yes."

"Like the guy does my shirts," the man said, and grinned in a sloppy friendly way and said, "I'm here to do what I can for you, Mr. Kwan. Mr. *Li*. I'll get it. And I'll do what I can." Kwan never saw him again.

But the worst was the women. Several of the functionaries who passed Kwan through their hands like worry beads were women, and Kwan simply didn't matter to them. They were in uniform or otherwise severely dressed, and their eyes were cold or indifferent or distracted. Most of them had muscle bunches beneath their mean mouths. They met Kwan in small bare rooms with hard metal furniture, they carried their attaché cases or manila folders, they clicked their ballpoint pens, they met him alone or they were accompanied by others, and at no time did he matter.

At first, he tried to attract their attention in the usual way, being a pleasant and interesting and unthreatening but sexually intriguing young male, and not once did they respond in any way at all.

It was not that he hoped for or expected a sex act atop one of these metal desks, but that he simply wanted interpersonal contact in a way he understood, an acknowledgment of their shared humanity, of the world of possibility outside and beyond the airless chambers in which they met. By not noticing him, they made him something less noticeable. By their refusal to have a gender, they refused him one as well; in desexing themselves, they desexed Kwan.

He didn't understand that specifically, only knew that to his natural outraged frustration at being silenced and stifled by these unemotional automatons, there was added a steadily deepening depression, a loss of self-assurance, a lessening belief that he could ever prevail. The governments robbed him of his high moral ground, the bureaucrats filched his rights and remedies, but the women emptied him of his natural self.

For eleven days they played him, as a cat plays with a mouse. No one listened, and no one ever would. He was simply the shuttlecock in their badminton game. He could not become a participant, so there was no way to win the game.

After eleven days, he decided to stop being nothing by becoming nothing. He took the full tube of toothpaste with which this most recent holding cell was furnished, removed the top, inserted the tube as deeply into his throat as he could, and squeezed as much of the toothpaste into his body as his trembling hands could press from the tube before the lights swirled around him, pain opened through his body, and he passed out.

If he hadn't made a clatter when falling, he might have died.

•　　•　　•

It was a black moment when he regained consciousness in the hospital. For the first day and night he took no interest in his surroundings, tried to pretend he'd died anyway. He couldn't speak, in any event, could in fact barely move. Tubes went into his nose and into a new hole in his throat. Needles pumped fluid into his arms. His wrists and legs were strapped down. White-clothed men and women passed through, ignoring his brain, caring only for his body; he ignored them as much as they ignored him. A bright window to his left showed the changing sky; he didn't care.

The second afternoon, a rumpled man in tweeds and a bow tie pulled a chair over next to the bed on the side away from the window and said, "I thought you Orientals were supposed to be patient."

This was so outrageous that it yanked Kwan immediately out of his lethargy, and he turned his head to glare at the man. Round face, round eyes behind round horn-rimmed spectacles, false-looking thick brown moustache. Stupid bow tie, dark blue with white snowflakes; what a stupid thing to wear. If only he could say that.

The man smiled at him. "You aren't particularly inscrutable either, Kwan," he said. "May I call you Kwan? Mr. Li seems so formal. If you could talk, you could call me Bob. As you've no doubt guessed, I'm a psychiatrist."

Kwan closed his eyes and turned his head away. Shame, disgust, boredom, rage. *Bob:* stupid name, like a sound a yeti might make.

Bob laughed and said, to Kwan's closed eyes, closed face, closed mind, "That's the true fate worse than death, isn't it? The trouble with suicide. If you fail, you have to talk to a psychiatrist."

Kwan deliberately opened his eyes and stared at the man, trying to make himself as cold and dead as possible. He knew what this psychiatrist was up to; he was so obvious, it was insulting. He wanted to become pals, become chums, force Kwan to accept this Bob as a caring fellow human being. If he were only to accept Bob's humanity, it would imply that Bob—and therefore mankind generally—accepted Kwan in the same way. Which was a lie.

Bob said, "Okay, Kwan, at the moment you just want the facts. Fine. You did a pretty good job on your insides, made enough of a mess that they had to bring you over here to NYU Medical Center, where they've got specialists and specialized equipment that can maybe put you back together again. So you aren't in any kind of jail any more, but there is a cop outside that door, twenty-four hours a day. They wanted to put him in here, sitting in the corner there, but several of us talked them out of that."

Smiling at the look of inquiry that crossed Kwan's face despite his best efforts to remain impassive, Bob said, "We felt a world full of cops is what drove you to this condition. We'd like you to know it doesn't have to be that way. Believe me, Kwan, if you'd waited just a little longer, all those faceless people *processing* you would have faded away and there would have been somebody to listen." He smiled, a coach full of positive reinforcement. "Well, fortunately, it isn't too late. In a week or two you'll have your voice back, and we can start figuring out what's best

for you. And we will. Kwan?'' The cheerful open face
above the stupid bow tie loomed toward him. ''Will you at
least give me the benefit of the doubt?''

No. And I don't want my voice back. I don't want
anything back.

He's Sam Mortimer, Kwan thought. He reminds me of
Sam Mortimer, the reporter in Hong Kong who betrayed
me. All heartiness and fellow feeling and honest concern;
and nothing underneath. Professional warmth. He gazed at
the professional and willed nothing to appear on his face.

Bob waited, then leaned back and shrugged. ''We have
time,'' he said, apparently unaware how chilling that statement was. ''You know, Kwan,'' he said, ''you don't have to
be strapped down like this. The only reason was to keep you
from hurting yourself, pulling the tubes out or whatever. I
mean, you know, you really and truly can't kill yourself in
this room, but you could probably do yourself some damage, and nobody wants that. Now, if I guarantee the doctors
and that cop out there that you won't do anything self-
destructive, I'm pretty sure I can get those straps taken off,
and then you could even sit up and look at the river outside
that window. Or I could get you something to read. Chinese
or English? Would you like some reading matter?''

Kwan closed his eyes. The tears on his cheeks felt like
acid. There was no way to win. They were legion, and they
had soldiers for every campaign. And here he lay, helpless.
Alone, helpless, hopeless, betrayed, despairing but not even
permitted to *stop*.

''Magazines? Chinese?''

Kwan, behind his closed eyes, nodded; another defeat.

•   •   •

Sitting up, his view to the left was of the East River and
some industrial part of Queens on the far side of the wide
water. River traffic was sparse and almost all commercial:
barges, tugs, the occasional small cargo boat. Every once in

a while, a small seaplane took off or landed. This side of the river, just barely visible at the bottom of the window, was the rushing busy traffic on the Franklin Delano Roosevelt Drive; all that barely glimpsed bustle on the roadway made the river seem even emptier, without at all suggesting that it might be serene. Looking out that way, watching the shifting shades of gray on the river, Kwan was reminded of his rowboat crossing from mainland China to Hong Kong. What a different person he had been then. With what hope he had pulled on the oars, and seen the lights of the city come closer.

His view to the right was of the door, through which the doctors and nurses and Bob from time to time came. Every time the door was opened, Kwan could look out and see a uniformed policeman, every shift a different one, seated on a metal-armed office chair against the opposite wall, usually reading a newspaper, sometimes just seated with arms folded and feet planted wide as he gazed away down the wide corridor, probably admiring some nurse's behind. Once it was a policewoman out there; she read a magazine.

So did Kwan. On the white metal table beside his bed were the magazines Bob had brought him, plus a pencil and notepad in case he wanted to ask for anything or make any kind of comment. He had nothing to say, no reason to use the pencil and notepad, but he did read the magazines, in Chinese and in English, and despite his efforts to keep it out, the world did crowd in on him, in its hopelessness and its faithlessness.

Other times, he slept. He took his medicines, submitted to the tests, underwent the physical therapies. Because of the damage he'd done to his throat and esophagus, he couldn't eat, or drink any liquids, or talk, but the intravenous-feeding needle fixed into the fleshy part of his left forearm dealt with the first two of those problems, and he had no need to deal with the last.

• • •

Because he slept so lightly, once they no longer needed to give him painkillers, he was aware of the door when it opened, and had turned to look that way while it was still swinging wide, so that the person coming into his dark room—venetian blinds closed over the night view of the river—was silhouetted against the lit corridor. Then the person swung the door shut and shuffled softly forward, and in Kwan's mind the afterimage showed the corridor, and the empty chair against the opposite wall.

The policeman? Coming in here for some reason?

No. The quick impression of that silhouette, the backlit border of it, had suggested the kind of long white coat worn by the doctors, not a policeman's uniform at all. But when medical staff came into the room at night, they always kicked down the little rubber-tipped metal foot attached to the door, to hold it open, so they would have the light from the corridor to help them see—plus their own little flashlights—and wouldn't have to disturb him by putting on the main lights.

Kwan, because he'd already been in here in the dark, could see faintly, could at least make out shapes. The other person in the room, who'd been in the brightly lighted corridor, was obviously having trouble finding his way across the blackness toward the bed; Kwan heard chair legs scrape when the person bumped into it.

And suddenly he knew. Trying to sit up, hampered by the board attached to his left arm that kept it rigid for the intravenous needle, and by the tubes still inserted in his nose and the new hole in his throat, Kwan gargled out hoarse ragged frightened noises, the first sounds he'd made since waking up in the hospital. These noises caused him extreme pain, but also caused that shuffling dark presence over there to stop, to become very still for a moment, and then to whisper, in smooth educated Cantonese, "So you're awake, are you, Li? I am here to help you." And he sidled forward again.

Kwan knew what sort of help this smooth bastard was here to provide. He had tried to kill himself, for his own reasons, to gain his own goals, but of course his desires had meshed wonderfully with theirs. How convenient of him to want to get *himself* out of their hair, eliminate all potential future embarrassment. But he had failed—as he had failed in everything, he now saw—and so they had decided to help him along the way, had sent this undersecretary or chauffeur or military attaché from their embassy or U.N. mission, to see to it that he didn't fail a second time.

Not this way! Kwan thought, instinctively resisting, clawing to retain life as automatically as he'd tried to throw it away. He made that hoarse croaking sound again, regardless of the pain, but it wasn't at all loud enough to be heard through that closed door.

And where was the policeman? The easy pleasant whisper answered him: "Relax, Li, no one will disturb us. We paid for one tiny mix-up in assignments—they believe, simple souls, they've gotten out of the way of a photographer from the *New York Post*—and so we're all alone. You want to sleep, Li, I know you do, and I am here to assure you of sleep. A long and dreamless sleep."

The figure was at the bed. Kwan, still struggling to rise, felt the man reach past him for one of the pillows. He dropped back, pressing his palm flat against the man's chest, pushing as hard as he could, but he was too weak, and the chest he pushed at rippled with hard muscles.

The pillow came down tight onto his face, wrenching the one tube from the hole in his throat, crushing the other inside his nose. The damage he'd already done to his throat was made worse, much worse. Kwan fought not for life but to make this pain go away. He flailed uselessly with his one good hand as the man bore down, his weight keeping the terrible pain inside.

Kwan's hand slid off the solid shoulder and upper arm of the man, waved out and back, flung wide, rapped his knuckles hard against the white metal table, scrabbled like a spider on that surface, found an object, stabbed upward with it.

"nn"

Good; a reaction. Kwan, planets and fiery satellites spinning against his eyelids, head and chest swelling with the need for air, stabbed again, and a third time, and a fourth, and the thing in his hand that he was stabbing with broke just as the weight on the pillow abruptly eased. Kwan pushed it away, gasping, to see that he held tightly gripped in his fist half of the pencil that had been placed with the notepad on the table, for which he had had no use.

And the figure was reeling backward, both hands clutched to his face. Kwan half leaped and half fell from the bed, the pain when the intravenous needle ripped from his arm almost unnoticeable in all the other pains clamoring at his body. He staggered across the room, good arm out, reaching for the door, finding the knob, pulling it open, so weak the door seemed to come toward him through water.

With a quick look back, he saw the man, Oriental, tall and sinewy, dressed like a doctor, wide-eyed with horror and rage, openmouthed, gripping with one palsied hand the pencil that jutted from his cheek, afraid to pull it out. He saw Kwan in the doorway, about to escape. He stared, then gave a little cry, and yanked the pencil free, flinging it across the room. Blood spurted from the attacker's cheeks, and Kwan fled.

Ananayel

They keep moving earlier than I anticipate. First Frank, and now Kwan.

I hadn't realized that some overreaching bureaucrat within the sprawling Chinese government would decide to order Kwan's execution. A close thing, that. Kwan saved himself, fortunately, or I would have had to begin all over again, abandoning this entire first group to work out their shortened destinies on their own.

I did arrive to help Kwan, though belatedly. When he let that room door close behind him and ran down the corridor on his tottering legs, his guardian angel was once more at his side. I permitted the assassin, back in the room, once again in the dark and going into shock, to fall over the chair I'd placed in his way, giving Kwan extra seconds to get to the double doors, and through, and find the stairwell.

Kwan's weakness would have ruined him, but I gave him of my own strength, enough to get him down the stairwell to the ground floor and through a door that was locked until one second before he touched it and locked again one second after he passed through. Various pedestrians—three nurses and one doctor—were shunted slightly from their original routes so that Kwan could pass by unseen. A closet he opened now contained—though it had not previously contained—a tattered topcoat that would fit him reasonably well and cover most of his hospital-issue pajamas. On their sides on the floor lay a pair of shin-high black rubber boots, only a bit too large for Kwan's feet. He tucked the pajama legs inside the boots and moved on.

A uniformed private security guard would have been at the side exit, except that he'd just been called away to a telephone call, only to find that his party had hung up. (More graceless and clumsy work on my part, but what was I to do with no time for preparation?)

Kwan emerged into a chilly and cloudless night. It was just after five in the morning. First Avenue was to his left, with very little traffic apart from the occasional cruising taxicab. FDR Drive was to his right, scattered with fast-moving cars, and the river lay beyond.

Kwan went to the right, found an on-ramp to the Drive, avoided it, followed a narrow street that ran between the Drive and the rear of various buildings in the hospital complex, found a group of three bundled-up people asleep on a warm-air grate against a high brick wall, and joined them. Lying down, immediately unconscious, the wounds in his neck and left forearm beginning to scab over, he became at once invisible, merely another of New York City's many thousand street sleepers.

I left him there, and went briefly back to Susan, only to assure myself the demon hadn't attacked her again—he had not, he was still off somewhere licking his wounds—and turned my attention to my other primary actors.

They're doing it on their own now. I don't have to do a thing. Particularly Maria Elena, and also Grigor. I started those tops spinning, but now it's all happening without any extra push from me. I don't even appear.

And they're moving so *fast*. It's as though they know, and are in a hurry to reach their end.

26

At ten-thirty the dryer buzzed, and Maria Elena carried the sheets upstairs. She looked out the bedroom window, and of course the gray Plymouth was still there, across Wilton Road, in front of the house two doors to the right. Yesterday it had been one house farther away, and the day before it had been on this side, down two houses to the left. Always facing in this direction.

Did they think she was a fool? Or were they showing themselves deliberately, trying to intimidate her? That would be ironic, wouldn't it? Having already given up her connection with the dissenters, to now be pressured by the government—the FBI, the state police, whoever that was out there—to do what she'd already despairingly done.

There were so few cars ever parked on the street along this curving suburban road at the edge of Stockbridge,

Massachusetts, that a strange vehicle would of necessity draw attention. Did they think, because the lone observer in the car was a woman—a chain-smoking woman—that Maria Elena wouldn't understand what was going on? The nondescript gray car, the vaguely progressive (but inoffensive) bumper stickers—I ♥ EARTH; SAVE THE WHALES—were hardly disguise enough, not in a neighborhood like this.

Making the beds—she and Jack slept in different rooms now—Maria Elena engaged in angry silent conversations with the woman in the car. But these fantasy speeches had lost their power to tranquilize. Her make-believe diatribes at the rich and powerful and greedy and cruel did nothing to solve actual problems, had never done anything but soothe her own brittle nervous melancholy. And now they didn't even do that much.

The worst of it all was, probably *she* was the one now who should go to the authorities, the one with the specific grievance, but she couldn't bring herself to do it. Although she was pretty sure by now that Andras had stolen her past.

Andras Herrmuil, the so-called record producer, the man who made all the promises, and who now, apparently, had disappeared. With her records, her posters, her photos, her clippings.

Not quite two months ago he'd phoned, this enthusiastic baritone voice on the telephone, saying, "Maria Elena? Is this *the* Maria Elena?"

Even here? she'd wondered, amazed, but even though the thought pleased her she automatically said, "No, I'm sorry, I don't know what you mean."

"You *are*! I can hear your voice!" And he dropped into natural native Brazilian Portuguese: "When you were singing I was still at home, I was young, I was one of your most rabid fans, I went *everywhere* you appeared."

"I'm sorry," she said, unconsciously answering him in Portuguese, "you're mistaking me for—"

"But I'm *not*. Do you know how many times you played Belém?"

A small city in the far north of Brazil. Maria Elena said, "What? No, I—"

"Three!" he announced triumphantly. "And I went to every one of them, even though I lived then in São Paulo. Maria Elena, do you remember the *Live in São Paulo* album? I'm on it! *Screaming* my head off!"

"Please, no, you've—"

"Forgive me," said that insistent voice, "I get so carried away. My name is Andras Herrmuil, I'm an 'A and R' man now with Hemispheric Records, and this is, believe it or not, a professional business telephone call."

"A and R" had been said in English; it caught at Maria Elena's attention. She said, "A what? A and R? I'm sorry, I don't know what that means."

Again in English, he said, "Artists and Repertory." Then, back to Portuguese, he said, "It means, I help select which records we put out. I don't know if you know Hemispheric—"

"No, I don't."

"We release in the United States," he said, "music from other parts of the Americas. Canadian, Mexican, Central and South American. To have *Maria Elena* on our list would be such a—"

"No, no, please, I—"

"You should *not* be forgotten! When you were singing, you were the best! You were the only one in a class with Elis Regina!"

One of the major superstars of Brazil, before she killed herself. "Oh, no," Maria Elena protested, feeling herself blush, "I was never, I could never have been—"

"Ah, you *admit* who you are! Maria Elena, may I come see you?"

How could she refuse? And so he'd come to see her, a darkly handsome man in his mid-thirties, who had flirted with her (but had not overstepped the bounds) and painted glowing pictures of her career reborn in this cold dry northern world. He had given her his card, and she had given him the two cartons that made up all that was left of her career.

Promising to phone soon, and to forward a contract, Andras had gone away, and for the next few weeks Maria Elena had moved in a happy daze, fantasizing her new career. Could it happen? Could she actually sing again? She was sorry she hadn't kept just one album, so she could hear afresh what she used to sound like. Could she do it now? Would the cold North Americans accept her?

But Andras didn't phone, and no contract came in the mail. Maria Elena fretted, she grew sleepless. She shouldn't call him, she should wait, businesses had delays.

But finally, yesterday, she had taken out his business card and called the number on it, in New York, and a recorded voice had told her that number was not in service. New York City information then told her there was no business in the city known as Hemispheric Records.

Oh, Andras. What have you done, and why? Were you just a fan, a cruel fan? Was *that* all you wanted, to steal my souvenirs for yourself?

One can get used to living without hope. But to have hope suddenly offered, to be tantalized with hope till one begins to believe in that bright specter once more, and *then* to have hope snatched away, that is unbearable. Maria Elena ground her teeth that night, alone and awake in her bed, thinking the darkest thoughts of her life.

And this morning, to hammer it home, there was the stakeout, the woman in the gray car.

Not yet eleven in the morning, and there was nothing more to do in this house, no other way to distract herself from her thoughts. This hateful place took care of itself with all of its "labor-saving devices." There was still labor, of course, it was actually time that was saved, but time for what?

Going downstairs, Maria Elena firmly turned her back on the living room and its television set. The daytime soap operas were too seductive, with their open-ended stories, in which great passion and great absurdity were at every instant inextricably mingled. The characters cared deeply, vitally, as Maria Elena had once cared and had always wanted to care and could no longer care, but what the characters in those daily stories cared so vividly *about* was invariably trash. Nothing that could possibly really matter to anybody ever arose in their invented lives, and that was why they were so seductive; become a regular watcher, a daily observer of these brightly colored puppets, let *them* experience your passion for you. All gain, no pain. A legal drug, as efficient as the illegal ones.

Maria Elena's pride would not let her give in to the release of drugs. Of any kind.

Turning her back on the living room, Maria Elena drifted purposelessly into the dining room. This elaborate neat house contained a separate dining room, perfectly waxed and preserved, never used for anything at all. When she and Jack took dinner together, which wasn't often, they ate at the breakfast table in the kitchen.

Maria Elena stopped in the dining room, not knowing where to go or what to do with herself. Her fingertips brushed the polished surface of the mahogany table. Seats twelve. What would she do with the rest of her day?

She thought of Grigor Basmyonov, but she'd been to see him again only the day before yesterday. And she'd told him—with such hope!—about Andras Herrmuil and Hemispheric Records and the sudden new career opening up before her. He'd been so happy and encouraging for her; how could she go to him with today's news?

But there was another reason to stay away. She was afraid of *using* Grigor, of turning him into a kind of flesh-and-blood soap opera of her very own, over whose dramatic problems she could wail without risk to herself, releasing her emotions in a safely ineffectual way.

But on the days when she didn't drive across western Massachusetts and into New York State to see Grigor, what was there to do? What purpose in life? She looked toward the plate-glass dining room window, with its view of Wilton Road, and saw the first slanted lines of rain sweep diagonally down it, as though God had shaken out his just-washed beard. Rain. So driving would be more difficult, staying at home even more claustrophobic.

Maria Elena stepped forward to look at the sky, to find out just how much of a storm this was going to be, and was astonished to see that gray Plymouth turning into the driveway of this house. Pulling up beside the house. Stopping.

Arrest! thought Maria Elena, and couldn't hide from herself the thrilled feeling, the sense that something of interest, something worthwhile, might at last be about to happen. Light-footed, suddenly lighthearted, she turned toward the front door.

The bell didn't ring for a long time, while Maria Elena stood in the front hall, one pace from the door, trying not to look eager, trying not to know just how eager she was. What was the woman in the Plymouth doing? What was the delay?

Ding-dong. Very loud, because the bell was set to be heard everywhere in this large house, and Maria Elena was standing directly beneath it. She started, even though she'd expected the sound, then stepped forward and opened the door. She would be calm, dignified, rigid, and silent.

At first she thought it was rain on the woman's face, but the rain was only a sprinkle, and the woman's cheeks were very wet, her makeup running, her expression twisted with emotion. Tears! Expecting arrest, Maria Elena was completely lost. Did the woman so hate her work for the government that it made her weep?

"Mrs. Auston?"

"Yes?"

"I'm Kate Monroe, I have to talk to you."

"About what?"

"About John."

The name meant nothing to her. Someone in the anti-nuclear group? "John?"

"Your husband!" the woman cried. "Don't you even remember you *have* a husband?"

"Oh, my God," Maria Elena said, and stepped back. "Come in, come in."

•   •   •

They sat in the living room, Maria Elena on the soft sofa, Kate Monroe on the uncomfortable wooden-armed decorative chair; her choice. She was about thirty, somewhat overweight, dressed in a distracted manner in bright colors in several layers of cloth, as though she were a fairy in a hippie production of *A Midsummer Night's Dream*. Her hair was ash blond, cut fairly short, at the moment tangled and unkempt. Her round face would be pretty if it weren't puffy red from emotion. Tears periodically poured down those round cheeks.

Kate Monroe, while they talked, used and shredded any number of tissues from the box Maria Elena had given her. "I love him, and he loves me! You can't hold a man who doesn't love you!"

"I know that."

"You have to let him go!"

Maria Elena spread her hands, at a loss. "Yes, if he wants. That is the American law."

"It's a mockery," Kate Monroe went on in her shrill voice, obviously not listening to a word Maria Elena said, "to hold on to him if he doesn't love you any more! We deserve our chance at happiness!"

Maria Elena lifted her head at that, suddenly incensed at this slobby ignorant person in her house. "Deserve? Why do you deserve happiness? What did you do that you *deserve* happiness?"

"You *must* let him go!"

But Maria Elena would not be sidetracked. "You said that you deserve happiness. But why? Why do you deserve anything? Why *you*?"

This time Kate Monroe heard the question. It made her blink, and look briefly evasive. "I said a *chance*," she decided, and became self-assured again, crying, "You *had* your chance!"

"Yes, I did," Maria Elena agreed.

Kate Monroe misunderstood: "If you and John lost what you—"

"Oh, not Jack," Maria Elena told her. "No. My chance at happiness was long before that."

Kate Monroe couldn't follow the conversation, and it was making her angry. She'd come into this house with a clear simple burning truth to express, but now it was all turning muddy and difficult. Maria Elena could understand what had happened there, could almost sympathize with the woman; this is the way it is when you try to act out your fantasies in the real world.

Trying to recapture the initiative, Kate Monroe said, loud and angry and vicious, "If that's the way you feel, if you *never* cared for John, if all you ever wanted was a ticket to the United States—"

"Yes, that's true."

Kate Monroe stared, thunderstruck. "You *admit* it?"

"Why not?"

"Then why won't you let him go?"

"Because he hasn't asked."

"That's a lie!"

"I've never heard of you, Miss Monroe," Maria Elena said. "Jack and I don't talk much. But of course he can go, if he wants."

"He did ask you," Kate Monroe insisted, clutching to the chair arms. "You refused."

Maria Elena got to her feet. "John will be home in six or seven hours. Why don't you look around the house, become familiar with it? When he comes home, you can discuss it all with him. You can tell him I will not stand in your way. That you yourself asked me if I would let him go, and I said yes."

Kate Monroe was getting frightened now. The solid base of her universe was sliding beneath her feet. Staring up at Maria Elena, she said, "Where are you going?"

"I have a friend to visit in the hospital. I will probably be several hours." Maria Elena pointed at the television set. "You could watch TV while you're waiting for Jack. There are several interesting dramas on in the daytime. I hope your car isn't blocking the garage."

"No, I put it on the— *Why?* Why won't you stay and talk with me?"

"Because it has all been said," Maria Elena told her. Imagining Kate Monroe's future, she couldn't hold back the smile. "You'll have your chance," she told the wretched woman. "At happiness."

27

More and more, in these latter days, Grigor couldn't get out of bed at all. He had a knob of controls handy beside the bed, and could raise himself to a sitting position, and there he'd stay all day, sometimes reading, but more often—when the books were too heavy to hold, even the paperbacks— watching television. There were many channels to watch, and almost always there was something of a news or non-fiction nature somewhere within range. Grigor watched such programs because he still thought of them as grist for the mill, the raw material for more jokes for Boris Boris. But the truth of the matter was, there were now weeks when he didn't fax even one miserable reject of a joke to the studio in Moscow.

He knew what the problem was, of course. It was obvious, and inevitable, and there was no way to counteract it; like the disease itself. The problem was that he'd been away too long. He no longer knew Russia as naturally as before, as automatically as he knew himself. What changes had taken place there, that Boris Boris should be commenting on? What was the *au courant* subject in Moscow this week? Grigor didn't know. He would never know.

Almost the only bright spot in his darkening and narrowing world was Maria Elena Auston, that strange lady they'd picked up at the demonstration. She wasn't exactly a cheerful person, not as *enjoyable* as for instance Susan, but Susan had her own life to live, had a man of her own now—not some bedridden shell of a man—and very seldom came all the way up from the city to visit. Maria Elena did visit, usually twice a week, and there was something about her very solemnity, that awareness that at all times she carried sorrow somewhere deep within her, that made her a comfortable companion for the person Grigor had become.

We have both been damaged by life, he thought. We understand each other in a way the undamaged can't know.

What a quality to share; he ought to make a joke about it.

* * *

When Maria Elena walked in, it was her third visit that week, a new record, and she was in better spirits than he'd ever seen her. "The plant is on strike!" she announced.

Grigor had just been brooding on how little of the world he recently understood, and here came Maria Elena to prove it. Unable to keep the impatience and irritation out of his voice, he said, "Plant? What plant?"

"Green Meadow! The nuclear plant!"

"Oh, yes. Where we first met. But you said you didn't go there any more."

"I drove by it."

Maria Elena pulled the green Naugahyde chair closer and sat down, her strong face transformed by what appeared to be happiness. She was actually a beautiful woman, in a dark and powerful way.

It's more than a nuclear plant being on strike, Grigor thought, but he didn't know enough about her private life to be able to guess at what had changed her. A new lover? Something.

Something to make her drift away from him, like Susan?

Maria Elena was saying, "It's the quickest route, so I sometimes drive by, and today there were many more pickets, and some had signs saying they were on strike! The workers are, because they know the experiments in there are too dangerous. A school bus was just going inside, with the pickets trying to stop it, so I had to wait, and one of the strikers told me the school bus was full of managers and supervisors!"

"But it's still operating?"

"Oh, yes. And they're still experimenting. But you know how they are, they don't care about the danger, the most important thing to them is that their authority not be questioned."

Grigor looked at the window. "That's very close to here."

"Eight miles."

"Too close." With a bitter smile, he asked, "Am I going to be assaulted by two nuclear plants in one lifetime?"

Maria Elena looked startled, then frightened, then disbelieving. "They wouldn't let that happen!"

"No, of course not." Grigor nodded. "No more than the officials at Chernobyl would let such an unthinkable thing happen." Again he brooded at the window, thinking of that structure eight miles away. "I'd like to get inside that place," he said. "Alone. Just for a little while."

Sounding breathless, Maria Elena said, "What would you do?"

Grigor turned his head to look at her. When he smiled, his gray gums showed, receding from the roots of his discolored teeth. "I would play a joke," he said.

X

What is he doing?

I prowl the earth, I tear furrows from the ground in my frustration, I sear the rocks and lash the gravestones. What is that silken slavey *up to*?

I can't attack him head-on, that's the most aggravating part of it. I have to acknowledge that now, after two encounters. He's too strong for me to meet in direct confrontation.

Well, what of it? Direct confrontation has never been *our* specialty. He has a back; eventually, I will find it, and I will drive a sword into it.

In the meantime, I watch the woman. Susan Carrigan. Dull as church, predictable as famine. She does nothing to even endanger *herself*, much less the species, the planet. God's alabaster moth hangs around her, sometimes in his enriched white-bread guise—Andy Harbinger! *that's* his idea of humor!—so I don't dare to make a move against her, not yet.

But what is his *plan*? What is this woman supposed to *do*? The aggravation is unbearable. Oh, the *revenge* I will take, once it's safe!

As for the other one, my little Pami, she's also disappeared. That's less important.

I dare not fail. I dare not even ask for extra help. *I dare not*. What would be done to me—

No. We don't even think about what would be done to me.

28

The doctor took Frank aside while Pami was getting dressed. "Have you had any sexual contact with that young woman?"

"Not me," Frank said. "I won't even shake her hand. I'm just here as a friend."

The doctor was a pleasant enough guy, skinny, balding, about forty. It was hard to tell if he was looking worried about Pami, or if he just looked worried all the time. Being a doctor with a specialty in AIDS, he might as well look worried all the time. He said, "I get the impression she's an illegal alien."

Frank gave him a careful look. He said, "The other doctor."

"Murphy. Who referred you."

"Yeah, him. He agreed, the deal was, medicine's the only thing we're talking about. Cause we don't want her to spread it, right?"

The doctor smiled thinly, but went on looking worried. "Don't worry, Mr. Smith, I'm not going to call the Immigration Service. The only point I want to make is that Pami will be needing hospitalization very soon, and I'm not so sure she'll qualify under any medical plan at all."

"So what happens? They leave her in the street?"

The doctor shrugged, looking uncomfortable. "They might."

"Nice people," Frank said. "How long's she got?"

"A month or two before she'll need to be in the hospital. After that . . . Less than a year, certainly. Less than a week, perhaps."

"And what can you do for her, between now and then?"

"You'll have those prescriptions filled," the doctor said. "The unguent will ease the chafing of the sores. The other things will help her symptomatically, make life a little more pleasant. That's all that can be done, short of hospitalization."

Pami came out, dressed again in the clothes Frank had bought her. She didn't quite know how to wear them yet, so they hung on her as though they didn't fit, but in fact they did. She smiled her crooked smile at the doctor. "Thank you."

"You're welcome," he said, and smiled back.

The doctor liked her; Frank could tell. The thing about Pami was, when she wasn't being tough she was like a sweet little kid. Like a pet that could talk. Frank was keeping her around because, as he told himself, she gave him an interest in life, now that he was in semi-retirement with the East St. Louis cash. Anyway, it's nice to know somebody that's worse off than you, somebody you can feel sorry for.

The doctor pointed to his receptionist, telling Frank, "You can pay Mrs. Rubinstein."

"Right."

Mrs. Rubinstein said, "How will you be paying today, Mr. Smith?"

"Cash," Frank said, bringing a wad of it out of his pants pocket.

The doctor, about to turn away, looked back and gave Frank a smile as crooked as Pami's. "You, Mr. Smith," he said, "are one of those enigmas that will keep me awake at night. I don't suppose you'd care to satisfy my curiosity just a bit."

"Nah," Frank said.

• • •

They came walking around to the back of the NYU Medical Center, where they'd left Frank's most recent car—a blue Toyota, stolen in New Jersey, now sporting altered New York plates—and some bum was lying on the ground against the curbside rear wheel. It looked as though he was drunk or something and fell off the curb, and now he couldn't get up again. The way the car in front was jammed up against the Toyota, Frank wouldn't be able to get clear without backing up, and he couldn't do that with this bum lying draped around the rear wheel, so he poked the guy with his toe, saying, "Come on, pal, rise and shine. Make love to some other tire, okay?"

The bum moved, in some kind of fitful and ineffectual way that did no good at all. Wiped out on cheap port wine, probably. Frank bent and grabbed the guy's arm through the sleeve of the ratty topcoat, but when he pulled, the guy just flopped over onto his back, the topcoat gaping open, showing striped pajamas underneath. "Jesus," Frank said, in disgust, "this turkey doesn't even have any clothes."

"Oh, look," Pami said, "look at his neck."

There was some sort of wound on the guy's neck, obscured by dried blood. There was more blood around his nose. He was Japanese or Chinese or something like that, and only half-conscious.

"Aw, crap," Frank said. "I don't even wanna touch him." And he thought, him, too. All round me, people I don't want to touch.

Pami hunkered beside the wounded drunken Jap, looking into his eyes. "He's from the hospital."

"You think so? Okay, lemme go get somebody, bring him back."

But that roused the Jap, who suddenly, fitfully, shook his head back and forth, massive woozy headshakes, as though he had a lobster stuck to his nose.

Frank frowned down at him. "You from the hospital? Why you don't wanna go back?"

The Jap was lying mostly on his back now on the asphalt, between the parked cars. He held his arms up toward Frank and pressed the insides of his wrists together, looking mutely past them at Frank.

"Handcuffs," Frank decided. "They'll arrest you?"

Now the Jap nodded, as vigorously and erratically as before.

Frank gazed upon him without love. "You got anything catching?"

Headshake.

Frank offered a sour grin. "Well, that'll make a change. Come on," he told Pami, "we'll throw him in the backseat and get the hell out of here."

•   •   •

While they packed he groused. "I don't see why we gotta keep the guy around at all," he muttered, putting his new all-cotton shirts in his new all-leather bag. "Some dumb Jap, can't even talk, probably a loony."

Pami paid him no attention. She didn't have a whole lot of clothing to pack, but she took a long time at it because she had to stroke and refold and grin at every damn piece.

"Can't even stay in one place on account of him," Frank griped.

The problem was, in New York City there was no hotel room anywhere that you could get to without going past the front desk, and there was no way Frank was going to carry that mute sick Jap in and by the front desk and up to a room, without getting stopped. What they needed was a roadside motel somewhere, that Frank could go into the office of and pay in advance and then drive right on down and park in front of the room. So nobody sees the Jap at all.

"I don't know how long we can carry him around, though," Frank said.

Pami said, "Maybe he'll get better." She shrugged, and looked more bitter than she had for several days. "Maybe *he'll* get better."

•   •   •

They'd left him in the backseat of the Toyota, lying there like a pile of wash on its way to the laundromat, and when they came back around the corner from the motor hotel they'd been staying in on Tenth Avenue he was still there. Either asleep or dead. He moved slightly, disturbed, when they climbed in, so he wasn't dead.

Frank made the light at the corner and turned right and they went up Tenth Avenue, north. He was still nervous about highways, after his experience when coming into this city, so he was going to avoid them. Drive city streets, and after that country roads. Just keep heading north, with no place special in mind. Stop where the country looks nice; with a motel.

The eyes that watched him all the time, judged him all the time, liked it that he was hanging out with these people.

29

Pami just couldn't figure out this guy Frank. He didn't want to fuck her, he didn't want to pimp her, he didn't seem to want to make *use* of her at all. Takes her to a doctor, gives her food and clothes, drives around with her, and doesn't want anything back.

Maybe I died, Pami thought sometimes. Maybe I died in that fire with the cop, and this is what it's like after you die, you have a nice dream to make up for all the bad things that went on before. She didn't really believe that, though. No dream would have that disgusting Jap in it. And if Pami couldn't figure out what Frank wanted with *her*, there wasn't a hope in hell to figure out what he wanted with the Jap.

But what difference did it make? Being with Frank was a lot better than being with Rush, that's all that mattered.

What did she care if things made sense or not? When had anything ever made any sense?

They drove and drove, up through the middle of Manhattan, spending most of their time stopped at traffic lights, and at one of them the Jap came to and struggled up into a seated position. He looked like hell, unwashed, caked with dried blood, a little scraggly Oriental beard starting to grow. He smiled and bowed, head bobbing in the backseat, thanking them for rescuing him, and Frank told him it was okay, looking in the mirror at him, saying they liked the company, and they were going to drive out of the city for a while. The Jap liked that idea.

Somebody behind them honked that the light was green. Frank jolted them forward and said, "Talk to him, Pami, for Chrissake. Find out if he's hungry."

What did she care if the Jap was hungry? But she twisted around and looked at him and said, "You hungry?"

The Jap gave a mournful nod.

Pami nodded back. She said to Frank, "He says yes. He's hungry."

"Maybe we'll stop and get a pizza," he said. "So we can eat on the way."

But the Jap was doing all kinds of gestures, pointing at his throat and shaking his head and making disgusted eating faces. Pami watched this for a few seconds and then said, "You got a hurt throat?"

Big nod.

"Can't eat?"

Sorrowing headshake.

Pami faced front again. "Says he can't eat," she said, and went back to looking at the people on the sidewalks. *There's* a hooker; that one right there.

"Liquids," Frank said.

They were way up at the top of Manhattan by then, where it's all Puerto Rican and Central American, so Frank stopped in front of a bodega and went inside, leaving Pami and the Jap in the car. The bums hanging out in front of the bodega, beer in their bandit moustaches, leered at her but didn't approach. "Like to give it to you all," she muttered under her breath.

Frank came back out and got into the car with a plastic bag full of small cans of apple juice, plus rolls and cheese and beer for himself and Pami. "Give him some juice," he said, "and make us a couple sandwiches."

So she did, and at the next red light the Jap cautiously took a sip of apple juice and made a horrible face as though it really hurt. But then he managed to swallow some—the rest dribbled down out of the corners of his mouth—and looked grateful.

Pami glanced back at him from time to time, interested to see how he was making out, and as they drove up through the Bronx and into Westchester County the Jap very slowly put away two of the little cans of juice, one agonizing sip at a time. Then he settled back against the seat, eyes glazing over, breathing with a raspy sound, his mouth hanging open.

Driving along behind a very slow pickup truck, waiting for a chance to pass, Frank said, "How is he?"

Pami twisted around to look back. "Better," she said. "He looks better." And she faced front again. Greenery up here, big houses. Like some of the hills north of Nairobi, the rich people's places, only greener.

Frank got around the pickup truck, then looked in the rearview mirror at the Jap. "Better, huh?" he said. "He looks like a dog that fell out of an airplane." He shook his head. "One halfway decent score in my life," he commented at the windshield, "and I turn into the welfare department."

Pami watched the fat men on the little tractors, mowing their lawns.

30

The reason the doctors had said it was all right for Grigor to have an overnight away from the hospital—his first since he'd arrived in the United States—was that nothing mattered any more, and everybody knew it, including Grigor, and including Maria Elena. But even though everything was now hopeless, there was still a great deal of awkward preparation to be made, medicines to carry, the foldaway wheelchair to be put into the trunk of the car, instructions for Maria Elena to write down and carry with her.

Grigor was in favor of the expedition simply because he wanted to go on seeing and experiencing the world for as long as possible, and he knew his time was growing very short. And Maria Elena wanted it because, in some angry uncomplicated way she herself didn't understand, she wanted Grigor to see her life, to *see* it, before his own life came to an end. To see what she'd done wrong.

They would drive to Stockbridge, to the house Jack had now vacated—sadly forgiving Maria Elena first for her heartless treatment of poor Kate Monroe, with whom he would *not* be moving in—and she would cook a dinner, tiptoeing as best she could through the mine field of Grigor's dietary restrictions. Tonight he would sleep on the living room sofa—the stairs would be impossible for him—and tomorrow they would drive back. Exhausting, futile, and more sorrowful than cheerful, but at least simple.

Until the blowout.

· · ·

"Now what?" Frank said, seeing the woman wave at him. Just beyond her, a car was pulled off the road, with somebody inside. The right rear of the car sagged down almost to the weedy ground. A few miles back they'd been delayed by some kind of demonstration in front of a nuclear power plant—with everybody in the car shielding their faces from the state troopers standing around—and now this.

"Stupid people," Pami said.

"By God, I'm gonna get to change another tire," Frank said, pulling into a stop behind the woman and the car.

Pami said, "Another?"

"It's just the way my life runs," Frank told her. Switching off the ignition, opening his door, he said, "Well, maybe this one will have good advice, too."

•   •   •

Maria Elena was too distraught to notice how odd the trio was in the car that had come to her rescue. She only knew this was a seldom-traveled road, far from the interstates and the Taconic Parkway, where all the traffic sped. She had Grigor as her responsibility, and she had no idea how to change the blown tire.

"I'm sorry to have to ask you," she said, when the rough-looking man approached her from the Toyota.

"That's okay," Frank said. He was feeling surly, because what was he going to get out of this? The hearty thanks of some broad he didn't know or give a damn about. Good-looking, in a kind of exotic too-strong way, but so what? Already loaded down with Pami and the Jap, he wasn't going to score on the roadside with some damsel in distress. He was just going to mess up his hands again and get all dirty, that's all. And Ms. Exotic here didn't look the practical type; she wasn't going to have any of those nice wet towelettes. "You wanna open the trunk?" he said.

"Oh, yes."

Pami got out of the car to stretch her legs. Also, she was

curious about the other person in that car. If he was a man, why didn't he change the tire himself? Why didn't he even get out of the car? She strolled forward.

Kwan had been napping. Now he sat up, sharply aware again of the nasty sting and burn in his throat. It had been so hard to get the apple juice down. He was very hungry, but how was he going to eat? These people he'd fallen among wouldn't be able to feed him intravenously. Should he just give up, return to his fate? Or try again to kill himself? He watched Frank open the trunk of the car and take out a wheelchair. Kwan closed his eyes. I don't think I can go on, he thought.

Frank put the wheelchair to one side and went back into the trunk for the spare, as Pami strolled by. Grigor, seated in the front passenger seat with the window open, watched the thin black girl in the outside mirror as she approached. He readied a small smile, not showing the interior of his ruined mouth, and looked up as she came parallel to him and glanced in. "Hello," he said.

"Yes, hello," Pami said, looking him over, understanding why he hadn't leaped out to change the tire. Merely curious, she said, "You got slim?"

"What?"

"No, that's not it," Pami corrected herself. "Here it's AIDS."

Grigor smiled again, remembering to keep his lips closed. "No, not me," he said. Then he looked at her more closely, the bone structure visible in her face, the darkness beneath her eyes, the boniness of her shoulders. "But that's what's got you, is it?"

"Oh, yeah," Pami said, with a shrug. "Anybody can see it now. No more work for me."

Grigor peered in the outside mirror again at Frank, just hunkering down by the rear wheel, pushing the jack in underneath. "Is that your doctor?"

Pami laughed. "You bet. Cure us all."

"Not me," Grigor said.

"Why? What you got?"

"Chernobyl."

"What's that?"

While Grigor explained to Pami what had happened to him, Maria Elena said to Frank, "I was feeling very lost before you came."

"Oh, yeah?"

"The tire breaking the way it did, it was as though everything I touched had to fail."

The lug nuts were giving Frank a hard time. He said, "I know the feeling."

"My husband has left me," she told him. "My friend in the car is dying. Everything I do has failed. I wanted to make things better, but I didn't."

Frank stopped his work to look up at her. A lid seemed to come off some boiling pot in his brain. He said, "I'm an ex-con, habitual loser, I jumped parole, did a million little burglaries. I never hurt anybody, but then I went in with another guy, and an old man died. That's the money I'm spending. I still dream about that old guy."

Maria Elena looked toward Kwan, barely visible in the backseat of the Toyota. She glanced back at Pami, talking with Grigor. She said to Frank, "Where are you all going?"

"To hell in a handbasket," Frank said, and pulled the ruined tire off its rim.

"That work will make your hands very dirty," Maria Elena said.

"Yeah, I know that."

"When you are finished," she said, "come to my house."

Ananayel

Now! my five triggers are together at last, and now all they have to do is find the path I have cleared for them, and the game is over.

I will miss them, I'm afraid, miss all of it, miss the Earth and the humans and even contesting my will against that fiend. The long doze of my life will be as comfortable in the future as it has always been, I know that, and the joy of doing His service will remain untarnished. But still, when I look back, from eons away, at this augenblick in my existence, this speck of time, this brief instant of vivid color and vivid emotion, I will remember it with fondness.

Susan Carrigan.

Well, yes. I have made a study of this problem, while my players have been ricocheting toward one another, and I have proved to my own satisfaction that Susan Carrigan is *nothing special.* There are millions of such young women scattered over the globe, unmarried as yet, doing small things with clean neat fingers, whether in banks like Susan, or in clothing mills, or in lawyer's offices, or in computer assembly plants, and they are *all the same.*

That's the point. Such minor differences as occur in the appearance of these young women is as momentous as, to a human, the differences between two collies. Such shadings and gradations of personality as they provide within their basic nature as wholehearted servants are of even less moment. There is nothing to distinguish one from the other.

The human males, of course, devote much of their lives to discovering the minutiae of whatever differences do exist in these young women, and make their lifetime choices on the basis of such highly emotional and transitory distinctions as they profess to find. But I am not a human male, though I have enjoyed playing at the part.

Susan Carrigan was the first of them I met, that's all. Nothing more.

I may drop in to see her again, once or twice, while the plotters work out the planet's destruction in the house in Stockbridge, Massachusetts, but that will mostly be because I enjoy being Andy. Oh, well, I'll miss it all, and her, too. I've said as much.

Regardless, it won't be long now.

SYNTHESIS

X

Pami!

I found it, didn't I? The center of the scheme, the very cockroach nest of that servile fog, the cluster of god's dunces all in one place. And what a crew!

We have kept him under observation, that blanched tool, that truckling toady. My winged allies, my fellow spirits of the air, they have viewed him unseen as he has to'd-and-fro'd on his lickspittle rounds. And why has he now caused a minor traffic incident to occur to an automobile on a side road in New York State? A blown-out tire, not very artfully arranged; but he is not an artist, is he, that bumble-fingered marplot? No, no, but no; truth doesn't *need* artistry, does it? (Thus the immemorial motto of the ham-handed.)

I had kept not far from Susan Carrigan, which is to say, I had been keeping not far from murderous boredom. But when the word came that heaven's stooge had made this upstate incursion into the quotidian, I fled from her—gratefully—and observed the two in the disabled car. They could give me aesthetic pleasure on their own, of course—what fortitude, in the face of what sorrow! hah!—but what did *he* want with them? Then the second car arrived, and *there was Pami!*

Oh, HA HA HA! I've got them now! I can destroy them at any instant, any instant at all. And once I discover Susan Carrigan's role in Armageddon, I *shall* destroy them. Not as lingeringly as they deserve, I'm afraid, but I'll do my best. I'll give them as much attention as I can spare.

But not yet. Susan Carrigan is somehow central, but is not present with this gallery of the agonized. Why not? What is her role? Until I understand her function, I will not understand that vaporous firefly's plot. I have to learn what he's scheming before I can be sure the scheme has been as permanently doused and trampled as a cookfire in dry timber country.

I told you you could trust me. I told you I would save you.

31

Frank carried Grigor into the house, seating him in a soft armchair in the living room, where his view ranged from the TV set on the left to the picture window and Wilton Road on the right. Kwan made his own way into the house, and collapsed onto the sofa, breathing with his mouth open.

Maria Elena took Pami to the kitchen to help put together some sort of dinner for everybody, but Pami knew nothing about kitchens and preparing food; it was embarrassing for them both. So Pami soon left and went back to the living room.

By the time Frank returned from the ground-floor half-bath, where he'd been washing the tire-changing grime off his hands, Pami and Grigor were deep in medical conversation and Kwan seemed to be asleep, so he went off to the kitchen, where he found a beer in the refrigerator, then sat at the kitchen table and watched Maria Elena work.

He had about forty thousand left, out of the East St. Louis money; almost a third gone already, on nothing at all. But it was an easy way to live, not nervous, not hustling all the time, not just barely scraping along. Frank hadn't broken into a house or a store for almost a month now, and he didn't miss the experience a bit.

Mary Ann Kelleny's advice came back to him: don't do constant little hits all the time, exposing yourself to risk over and over, but do it all at once, in one big major haul. The five-million-dollar hit. Well, fifty-seven grand wasn't exactly five million, but it showed the principle was sound.

Sitting there at the kitchen table, watching Maria Elena at her domestic work, Frank felt as though he was at some sort of watershed moment of his life. Already he could see that this was the place to turn himself back into a loner; Maria Elena would be happy to take Pami and Kwan off his hands. She *liked* worrying about fucked-up sick people, you could see that. Then from here, alone, Frank could maybe drive on up to Boston, hole in somewhere, try to think about that five-million-dollar hit.

People pulled jobs like that in the movies all the time, right? So what did they do, what kind of thing? Break into Fort Knox. Steal *The Love Boat* and hold it for ransom. All these make-believe capers pulled by *platoons* of good buddies, as well-drilled as the Green Berets.

Is that what the five-mil hit is supposed to look like? Then forget it, because it isn't realistic. Unless there's five million dollars lying in a room somewhere that *one man* can get into and grab and get out again, there's no such thing as the five-mil hit. No such thing.

So what was realistic? If a man got tired of exposing himself to the risks a hundred times a year for shit-poor returns, what could he do instead? Where was there even a fifty-seven-grand hit, three or four times a year? (Without any weak-hearted old man in it, please.) Money isn't cash any more, not usually, it's electronic impulses between banks, it's charge cards and pieces of paper and phone calls.

Frank would leave all that stuff to another generation to figure out how to loot; what he needed was tangibles. Money, or for second best, jewelry. And the greater the concentration of money or jewelry into one place, the tighter the security.

Maria Elena broke into Frank's thoughts when she put a bowl of carrots onto the table and said, "Excuse me. Would you do these carrots?"

Frank looked at them, overflowing the bowl, their long green fernlike tops still on, the carrots themselves large and thick and hairy. He had no idea what she wanted from him. "Do?"

She put a wooden chopping block on the table in front of him, with a small sharp knife and a scraper. "Cut the ends off each one," she said, "and scrape the skin off."

"Well, I'll try it," Frank said.

She was amused by him, but in a low-key way, as though she hadn't known she could be amused by anything. Moving back over toward the sink, she said, "Have you never had a wife to ask you to do these things?"

"Never," Frank told her. "And in diners they pretty much do it themselves."

"It is very easy to learn," she assured him.

"I'll give it a whack," Frank said, and did just that, decapitating one of the carrots. The knife was good and sharp. He nicked off the narrow end of the carrot, feeling pretty much on top of this job, and then had a hell of a time getting the scraper to work. It kept turning around on him, rubbing along the hairy skin of the carrot without accomplishing anything. "Bugs Bunny eats it with the hair still on," he pointed out, but she ignored him.

Once he got the hang of the scraper, Frank finished off the carrots with no trouble at all, and then Maria Elena gave him a bowl of potatoes to work the scraper magic on. "I gotta have another beer if it's gonna go on like this," he complained, and she brought him one.

Weird place to be. In the living room, Pami and Grigor had turned on the TV, and the sounds of music and voices came from there. The warm kitchen was beginning to smell very good. Frank sat at the table, sipping his beer and peeling the potatoes. The five-million-dollar hit, he thought. Where's the five-million-dollar hit?

• • •

The dining room table seated twelve; plenty of room to spread out. They ate roast lamb and two kinds of sausage and boiled potatoes and three kinds of vegetables and a salad.

All except Kwan, that is. Since he couldn't swallow any solid food, Maria Elena had made for him various drinks in the Cuisinart, giving him also a mixture of honey and warm water (known long ago as melicrate) to help soothe his throat between sips of the other liquids.

Since Kwan was sitting with the others, at their insistence, but couldn't eat, Maria Elena gave him a pen and yellow pad and pushed him to let them all know who and what he was. His despair was such (he was trying to figure out how to die without interference from all these unlikely do-gooders) that she had to press a lot, but finally he gave in and wrote as few words as possible, sketching his brief history.

That's how Frank learned he wasn't a Jap after all, but was a Chinese named Li Kwan. And Grigor, who was reading Kwan's notes aloud, suddenly recognized Kwan when Tiananmen Square was mentioned: "I saw your photo. With the, the . . ." Frustrated, Grigor held his cupped hand in front of his mouth.

"*Bullhorn*," Kwan wrote, and finished his biography, and went away to sit in the living room, where they couldn't question him any more.

They did come in with him later on, but not to pester him. There was a general desire to watch the eleven o'clock news. Maria Elena closed the sliding drapes over the living room's picture window and the possible eyes of neighbors, they all found places to sit, and the sound-bites of news started: little digestible chunks of events. A chunk from Russia, a chunk from Washington, a chunk from Alaska, a chunk from Berlin.

The first chunk after the first commercial break was about the strike and demonstration at the Green Meadow III Nuclear Power Plant. Pickets and police surged in a confused scrum, and a yellow school bus with some difficulty made the turn and drove through the gate. Within its windows could be seen embarrassed-looking middle-aged men and women. Then the neutral, the lobotomized, the castrated off-camera voice told the viewers that the plant was being kept on active status by managers and supervisors, who kept a skeleton staff in the mostly automated plant twenty-four hours a day. The disputed research continued, safely. Dutchess and Columbia county citizens were assured that power outages would not occur.

"Outage," Grigor said. "What a word that is."

"They are very good, officials," Maria Elena said, "at finding the words that put the people to sleep."

"The people want to sleep," Grigor said, and Kwan nodded emphatically at him.

"I don't care about that stuff," Frank said, unconsciously confirming Grigor's point. "I just wanna make it through *my* life."

Pami said, "So do I."

Repeating what he'd said to Maria Elena the other day, Grigor nodded at the television set, which was now showing an anti-racist demonstration in Brooklyn at which four pickpockets had been arrested, and said, "I'd like to get into that plant, for just one day."

Frank looked at him. "Why?"

"I'd play a joke," Grigor answered, with the same cold smile as when he'd said the same thing to Maria Elena.

"Big deal," Frank said, not really getting it. Nodding at the television set, as Grigor had, he said, "Easy to get in there, if that's what you want."

Grigor shook his head. "How could it be easy? They have such security. You saw it just now for yourself. Fences, and guards, and television monitors. And there must be other things as well."

Frank grinned; they were on his subject now. "Grigor," he said, "getting into places is what I *do*. That isn't security there, that's Swiss cheese."

Maria Elena said, "It doesn't seem that way to me."

"There's a dozen ways in," Frank said. "You saw the school bus?"

They'd all seen the school bus.

"On day number one," Frank explained, "you follow the school bus around. It's picking up all those managers and whatever they are at their houses, bringing them in. You take the night shift, midnight or whenever, and you follow it around. Day number two, you go to the last house on the route and you wait. When the school bus comes by, you climb aboard, you show everybody your MAC-11s, you—"

Maria Elena said, "I'm sorry, your what?"

"It's a gun," Frank told her. "Not my kinda thing, I don't use guns, but this is just a for-instance. So, for instance, you get on the bus, you show these guns, you say everybody just sit nice and quiet. You get to that plant there, the security guards wave you right through the gate. They *protect* your route into the place." Frank grinned. "My kinda security," he said. But then he shook his head and said to Grigor, "But what's the point? You're inside. *You* can play your joke, whatever that's supposed to mean. But what's in it for the rest of us? There's nothing in there."

"Plutonium," Grigor said.

"Yeah? What'll a fence give me for that?"

"Nothing, I'm afraid." Then Grigor smiled and said,

"And I must admit, even with a gun in my hand, I doubt I'd be very intimidating to all the people on that school bus."

"So there you are," Frank said. "Now, you find me a *jewelry store* where you wanna do a joke, could be we're in business."

•   •   •

Exhaustion settled on Grigor and Pami and Kwan after the news. Grigor would sleep on the living room sofa, as originally planned, with Kwan on the living room floor on a pallet made of cushions from the armchairs. Pami would sleep upstairs on the sofa in the den/sewing room. Maria Elena would sleep in her own bed, and Frank in the next room in Jack's bed.

But not yet. Neither Maria Elena nor Frank was tired yet; for different reasons, both felt keyed up, needed more time to unwind and relax. They went into the kitchen, closing the swing door, and did the cleanup together while Maria Elena told him about her background in Brazil, and he gave her a capsule summary of his own useless and repetitive life. He also gave her a more full account of the East St. Louis heist and the change it had made in his life. "Now I *can't* let myself get caught. No more little hits, little risks, three to five inside and back out again. This time, I go in, I'm done for."

"So you must reform," she said, as a kind of joke. She wasn't sure why she was taking his biography with such moral neutrality, but somehow it seemed to her that he was more a good man who did bad things than a bad man. He'd never, for instance, poisoned any children.

Frank was amazed at the things he was telling this woman, and finally said so: "I never shoot my mouth off like this. I don't know what's with me tonight, I just put my life in your hands and I don't even know you. One phone call, and you could blow me away."

"Why would I do that?"

"I dunno," Frank said. "Why do people do *any* of the shitty things they do?"

They had finished the kitchen work and were just standing there, she with her arms folded and her back against the sink, he leaning slouched against the refrigerator. Maria Elena said, "I would not do anything to hurt you, Frank."

He shrugged and grinned, in a joke's-on-me way: "I guess I must believe that," he said.

She unfolded her arms and spread them, saying, "You are the first person to talk to me in five years."

His grin widened. "Longer than that for me. Listen, you want to dance?"

Surprised, she said, "There isn't any music."

"You don't hear the music?"

She lifted her face, and at last returned his grin with her own rueful smile. "Now I do," she said.

He stepped away from the refrigerator, and she came into his arms. He was a miserable dancer, and knew it, so he just led them in a little slow-paced circular shuffle around the kitchen table. She felt heftier, more solid, than he'd guessed; but he liked that. She wasn't a girl, she was a woman. Her hair smelled clean, her throat was soft and musky. Holding her, moving in that slow jailhouse shuffle, he cleared his throat, geared up his courage, suffered a couple of false starts, and finally murmured, "Could we uh, uh . . ."

"Yes, Frank," she said, and patted his shoulder, and kissed the side of his neck.

32

In the morning, Kwan was weaker. He remained on the pallet on the living room floor, sitting up twice to force down small portions of purees Maria Elena had made for him. He was having trouble now even swallowing the melicrate (rhymes with consecrate, desecrate, execrate), and spent much of the day asleep.

But in the intervals when he was awake, Kwan burned with a new kind of desire. He had gone through the despair, and out the other side. He still wanted to die, he still wanted to throw away this failed self, but now, somehow, somehow, he wanted the world to know. The governments, the bureaucrats, the uncaring, unnoticing people who made it possible; he wanted them all to know.

Grigor also stayed mostly in the living room, seated on the sofa where he'd slept, looking out at the empty suburban road once Maria Elena had opened the drapes. He and Maria Elena were supposed to leave by ten-thirty, to get him back to the hospital before lunch, but when she came to tell him it was time, he admitted, awkward and hesitant, that he didn't want to go. "There's nothing for me there," he said, speaking softly because Kwan was asleep again across the room. "Not any more. There's nothing they can do for me. I want to be . . . somewhere. Maria Elena? May I stay?"

"I don't think the hospital will let you," she said carefully, sitting down beside him.

"If you don't want me—"

"Grigor, of course I want you!"

"It would only be for a few days."

He was trying so hard not to plead, to retain his dignity. She saw that and responded to it. "I could call the hospital, ask if it's—"

"No," Grigor said. Slyness did not come naturally to him, the expression sat oddly on his face. "Maria Elena, they don't know where you live. They don't even know what *state* you live in."

"But if you just disappear, they'll call the police, they'll worry . . ."

"Then let *me* telephone."

"Yes, that's a good idea," she said, thinking the doctors

would talk sense into him. She wouldn't at all mind having Grigor here, but what about his medicines? What about the entire hospital routine? Would he survive on his own, and for how long?

"Let me do it in private," he said. "There is a telephone in the kitchen?"

"Yes."

He walked there, with some help from Maria Elena, who saw to it he was more or less secure on the tall stool near the wall phone before she left the room, pulling the swing door closed.

In the front hall were Frank and Pami, getting ready to go out. At first, Maria Elena thought they intended to leave permanently, and something very like panic touched her, making her arms shiver with nervousness. "Frank?" she said, her voice trembling. "Are you going away?"

He grinned at her. "I'm not that easy to get rid of. Pami and me're gonna go get some groceries. We kinda used everything up last night, didn't we?"

It was true. The unexpected addition of three new people, and Grigor as well, had left Maria Elena with very little food in the house. "Oh, that's fine," she said, with a sudden rush of relief, knowing he didn't after all mean to go away, at least not now, not yet. "I'll make a list," she offered. "I'd go with you, but Grigor . . ."

"No, that's okay," Frank told her, "we can handle it. And that's good, you make a list. And tell us how to get to the store."

She did all that, and he kissed her goodbye without awkwardness in front of Pami, and they left. Maria Elena stood in the living room near the sleeping Kwan and watched out the window as Frank and Pami got into his Toyota and drove away.

How extraordinary to have this house full of strangers all at once. To go from the loneliness of life with Jack— without Jack, really—to absolute solitude, and then all at once to *this*. In place of Jack's aloof perfection, these imperfect people, sick, criminal, dying. But how much more alive to be among these dying than to be with Jack.

I don't ever want them to go away, she thought, though she knew that death would be taking some of them very soon, no matter what.

Faintly she heard Grigor's voice calling, and hurried out to the kitchen, half afraid he'd fallen, hurt himself, was in some sort of crisis she wouldn't be able to handle. But he was still perched on the stool, leaning on the counter. He held out the phone, saying, "They want to talk to you. I told them I refuse to go back for at least a week."

As she was taking the phone, he put his hand over the mouthpiece and whispered, "Don't give them your address or phone number or *anything*."

"All right." Into the phone she said, "Hello?"

It was Dr. Fitch, one of the staff she'd gotten to know; an older man, calm and professional, with an orange and gray beard. He said, "Mrs. Auston?"

"Yes, Dr. Fitch, hello."

"Are you a party to this, then?"

"Well, I guess I am."

"Is Grigor right there?"

"Yes, he is."

"All right, then," said his professional voice. "You needn't say anything, I'll talk. Except that we could keep him physically much more comfortable than you possibly can, Grigor's right about the hospital not being able to do him any good any more. Mrs. Auston, there's no particular reason why he isn't dead already. He may last a week, he may last a month. If he stays with you, the likelihood is he'll die with you. Will you be able to handle that?"

"I think so," she said, holding tight to the phone.

"I want you to write down some phone numbers," he said. "If you need help, any time, for anything, call."

"Thank you, I will."

She wrote down on the pad by the phone the telephone numbers he gave her, and the over-the-counter medicines that might be symptomatic help if Grigor began to break apart in this way or in that way. He then urged her to urge Grigor to rethink this idea, saying, "He might go as long as two days without serious difficulty, but certainly no longer. Very soon it will become extremely uncomfortable there for both of you."

"I understand."

Grigor sat smiling with closed lips as she finished her phone conversation, then said, "We will pretend you told me everything he said you should tell me."

"Good."

"This afternoon," he said, "we will go for a ride. You will show me things."

"I'd like to," Maria Elena said.

"And if there's a tomorrow," he said, with that compressed little smile, "we will do something else."

• • •

When Frank came back with groceries, he was bouncing and fidgety with some kind of excitement. Grigor was back in the living room by then, seated on the sofa, watching Maria Elena help Kwan down a small amount of broth. Frank appeared in the doorway holding full plastic bags in both hands. "Grigor," he said. "When we get this stuff put away, I want to talk to you."

"I'll stay right here," Grigor promised.

Frank and Pami put the groceries away, and then returned to the living room, where Kwan was still sitting up, trying to drink. Frank sat on the sofa beside Grigor. He kept snapping his fingers while he talked, apparently unconsciously. He said, "Pami and I were talking in the car. Did I tell you about the five-million-dollar hit?"

When Grigor said no, Frank told him—and Maria Elena and Kwan—the lady lawyer's advice. "She didn't know it, but she was right," he said. "The *only* way I'm gonna get out from under my own history is with the one big solid hit, and then quit. I've been going crazy trying to figure out what that hit is, and now I got it.''

Clearly, Grigor had no idea what Frank was talking about. Polite, nothing more, he said, ''And it's something you want to talk to *me* about?''

''You bet it is. You really want to get into that nuclear plant, like you said last night? No fooling?''

''No fooling,'' Grigor said, sitting up, becoming more alert.

''And you studied that stuff,'' Frank pressed him. ''How to run them and all that.''

''I have read about them,'' Grigor said. ''No one person can *run* such a place, but I do know how it's done. Some of the mathematics I wouldn't be able to do, that's all.''

Kwan clapped his hands to get their attention, and when they looked at him he grinned weakly and pointed at himself. Frank said, ''You're a math guy?''

Kwan nodded.

''And you want to be in on this?''

Kwan nodded, and waved an imaginary flag.

Grigor translated: ''For propaganda, like me.''

''I don't care what people's reasons are,'' Frank said, and asked Kwan, ''You could definitely help Grigor, if he needed it?''

Again Kwan nodded.

Grigor said, ''Frank, I don't understand what *your* reasons are. You *want* to invade that plant?''

''You bet,'' Frank told him. ''All I have to figure out is how to pick up the money.''

''What money, Frank?''

''The money they'll pay us,'' Frank said, ''to give them back their nuclear power plant, undamaged. You do your joke, whatever you want, just so *I* can do *my* thing.''

Pami, twisted mouth and scrawny voice, eyes full of leftover anger, said, ''Frank and me, we gonna kidnap the plant.''

''Hold it hostage,'' Frank said. ''For a five-mil ransom.''

Maria Elena had been sitting near Kwan. Now she stood up, looking and sounding scared, saying, "Frank, are you sure? That's so *public*, so dangerous. What if you're caught?"

"If I'm caught stealing a toothpick," Frank told her, "I'm still in forever. What difference does it make? I can't *do* anything that's more dangerous or less dangerous."

Maria Elena, terrified of the whole idea, floundered for something to reply, and could only come up with, "What if they won't pay?"

"They'll pay," Frank said, with calm assurance. "Just to be sure we don't accidentally hit the wrong switch. Or on purpose. This is the one, Maria, this is the only five—"

The doorbell rang. Grigor clutched the sofa arm: "They agreed! They said I could stay!"

Maria Elena left the living room, and the others sat silent, listening. They heard the door open, heard Maria Elena's question, heard a heavy dark-timbred male voice say, "I'm looking for Pami Njoroge. Saw her at the shopping mall, wanted to say hello, missed her there. Saw the car out front here, didn't want to leave town without I say hello to my old friend Pami."

He'd been approaching all through this speech, and now he appeared in the living room doorway: a big-boned, hard-looking black man with a cold smile and mean red-rimmed eyes. He glanced once, without interest, at the group in the room, then smiled more broadly and more meanly: "Hello, Pami."

They all saw the frightened look that came and went on Pami's face. They all heard the fatalism in her voice: "Hello, Rush," she said.

Ananayel

So Brother Rush is back.

Well, no matter. The process is under way now; he can't stop it. That strange quintet *will* get into Green Meadow III, I can count on Frank to make that happen. Each will go in for a different reason, but the reasons will unite them just long enough for my purposes.

Once inside the plant, the five will make their demands, and the demands will not be met. It won't be out of bravery or foolhardiness that officialdom will refuse to meet their conditions, but out of muddle and mess and ego and incompetence. Responsibility will be diluted among various private corporations, public and semi-public regulating authorities, even congressional committees. Those who are afraid to act will be counterbalanced by those who are afraid they will not get credit for whatever actions turn out to be successful. Publicity-hogging, buck-passing, all the common discourtesies of public life, will conspire to keep Frank from getting his money. And the usual spinelessness of the happy media will keep the various propaganda efforts from getting out of the plant and into the world's consciousness.

Gradually, but sooner rather than later, Frank and the others will begin to realize the enormity of what they've done and the hopelessness of their position.

And then my task will be finished.

33

No one knew exactly what to make of Pami's "friend," Brother Rush. Clearly, he wasn't her friend at all, but she seemed to feel powerless to deny him. There was at all times something cold and sly and insinuating about him, but the menace never quite broke the surface, never entirely solidified into anything you could call him on.

Frank felt the frustration of this the most, and took Pami aside to make her tell him what was going on: "What's with this guy? He your pimp? What do we want him around for?"

"I don't *want* him around," Pami said, "but Rush—he gets what he wants. But he won't bother nobody."

"He bothers *me*."

At which point, Rush came strolling into the room and said, "Hey, what's happnin," and that was the end of that.

That he would be staying for dinner was understood, somehow, though he never asked and no one invited him and in fact no one wanted him. But a sixth place was set at the table, Rush took his seat at the far side of Pami, and as the meal progressed he alternated between extravagant praise of what Maria Elena had accomplished in the kitchen and questions that confused them all.

He was pumping them, that was clear, or at least he was trying to, but about what? His questions were hard to answer because they were full of assumptions that weren't true. He said, "You just waitin here for somebody else gonna show up?"

Frank said, "Like who?"

"I dunno," Rush told him, shrugging as though it didn't

matter, trying to make that mean secret face look casual and innocent. "Somebody to tell you what to do next, where y'all gonna go from here."

Grigor smiled at Rush with closed lips, and said, "No one tells us where to go. We know where we are going. Some of us do. We are absolutely free."

"You know where you're going?" Rush looked interested. "Where's that, Gregor?" (He couldn't quite seem to get his mouth to twist the name all the way around to *Grigor*.)

This time Grigor permitted his lips to open when he smiled. "To the grave, brother," he said.

Rush looked merely interested: "You got what Pami got?"

"This," Maria Elena said firmly, "is not a thing to talk about at dinner."

"You're right, Maria," Rush said. "I love this sauce. You got some special spices in here, don'tcha?"

But soon he was at it again, saying, "Do you all have some special doctor you're gonna go see?"

Frank put down his fork. "Rush," he said, letting the exasperation show, "do I look like I need a doctor?"

"No, you don't," Rush agreed. "You truly don't." And he grew quiet again, if thoughtful.

The next time he spoke, it was something new; neither irrelevant questions nor extravagant praise. Lifting his head, sniffing the air, almost like a cat, he said, "You got somebody hangin around outside. This the guy you been waitin on?"

"Goddammit, Rush," Frank said, "I don't know what the hell is the matter with you, what Pami said to you or what—"

"I didn't say nothing to him!" Pami cried. "This is some idea all his own!"

"Whatever it is," Frank said. "Whatever gave you this wild hair up your ass, *Brother* Rush, let me tell you once and for all. We aren't waiting for anybody. We weren't waiting for you—"

"Absolutely," Grigor said.

"—and we aren't waiting for anybody else."

Rush nodded through this, smiling gently, and when Frank was finished he said, "Then you won't care if I go out and see to this fella outside."

"Be my guest," Frank said. "If you think there's somebody out there."

"Oh, somebody's there all right," Rush said.

Maria Elena, looking toward the curtained windows, said, "But who?"

"That's what I'll find out," Rush told her, and got to his feet. "Satisfy *all* our curiosity." Dropping his napkin beside his plate, smiling around at them all, he turned away and left the dining room. For a big man, he could move very silently.

Ananayel

They are in the air like bats, these creatures of the night, the lesser servants of Lucifer. He was the first schismatic, of course, Lucifer, that onetime angel and captain of angels, my former brother. Pride was his besetting sin, and darkness his punishment. He had been very nearly as immortal as God Himself, and remained so. It was not by a foreshortening of his life, his sensations, his awareness, that he was penalized, but instead by a near-eternity of darkness, a permanent exclusion from the Light. Yes, that's right: from the Light.

An odd judgment, when you stop to think of it. Lucifer was punished by being given his own kingdom, his own minions, his own realm and rule; and all for the sin of pride. Pride. So an angel can be proud. An angel can sin. An angel has free will.

We angels obey because we choose to obey. And so do

his creatures. They love their louche lord, their Prince of the Powers of the Air, they love the work they do for him, and now they swarm in the night air around me like moths, reporting my movements to that nameless demon, their immediate master, who struggles so hard to keep me from accomplishing the fulfillment of God's design. I take him, that demon, to be some minor baron in the Prince of Darkness's vassalage, some puffed-up satrap, arrogant beglerbeg of the middle mists, powerful, but, not, *deo volente,* so powerful as I.

(I would not be able to stand up to Lucifer himself, and I know it, but so does he, and so does He. The Prince of Darkness, even before the Fall, was a power and a might second only to God, which is what led him to his pride and his destruction in the first place. But if Lucifer were to confront me, it would no longer be me he was confronting. I would at once be retired, so that God Himself could take my place; and in *every* direct encounter between those two Masters it is Lucifer who has lost, it is he who has retired from the battle in shame and pain and degradation, forked tail between cloven-hoofed legs. Like the limited wars on other people's territories that the so-called Great Powers have indulged themselves in over the last half-century of Earth's little history, it is only through proxies that my Master and His Opponent can contend. Lucifer will surely try to cheat, will cast about for advantage, but he will not try to overwhelm me; that would bring into play a *truly* Great Power.)

No, it is only that nameless hospodar that I have to contend with, only he who has taken up arms against me. His master believes, or at least hopes, that this deputy devil will be enough to thwart me in doing God's work. But it is my firm belief that, with God's help, and in His gleaming Light, I will be enabled to perform His work, obey His commands, accomplish His desires, amen.

And for now, it is time to separate that avatar of the demon, Brother Rush (a name rich in association), from my quintet. Leaving Andy Harbinger seated quietly beside Susan Carrigan in Quad Theater #3 on West 13th Street, watching *Night Fall* (a film noir of current popularity), I made my way to Stockbridge and assumed corporate form in the darkness of a church parking lot not far from Maria Elena Auston's house.

The shape I had chosen to take was that of the man who had helped Kwan escape the police in Hong Kong, and who later rode the plane with Pami; an early version of Andy Harbinger, really. Two of my five people already have reason to trust me. It would be preferable to have their confidence, while I am ridding them of Rush. As Brad Wilson of U.S. Naval Intelligence, as the documents in my wallet testified, I would already have the presumption of authority, so it should be possible to perform the extraction of Rush from the group without the necessity of doing anything gaudy. Or at least I certainly hoped so.

I walked the two and a half blocks of curving suburban street—an early sign of sophistication in humans, I have noticed, is a distaste for straight lines—and as I approached the Auston house I saw that the drapes were open at the large dining room window, presenting my quintet at meal as though Hogarth had done a cover for some supermarket family magazine.

But where was Rush? The others sat and ate and talked and brooded—Kwan occasionally took tiny painful sips from a glass of pale orange liquid—and a partially eaten meal waited at a sixth place, but Rush was not to be seen.

I sought him with my mind, but couldn't find him. He had to be present, because of that meal in front of that empty chair. Had his rustling claque in the air above my head warned him of my presence?

I didn't want to declare myself to the others until I had fixed the position of Rush. I partially crossed the lawn, to its darkest segment, away from the light-spill out that dining room window and also clear of streetlamp illumination, and there I stood and watched, and waited.

Why were they so cheerful? By now, bitterness and sorrow should have made those five *much* more silent and introspective. It must be their companionship that was raising their spirits, but unfortunately I couldn't give them a properly disheartening solitude; they had to work together. Would they do the right thing when the time came? Yes, they would, they would, there was no real question. I would turn the screw until they *did* do what I wanted. Of their own free will, of course.

I was careless, I admit it. My attention had become too fixed on my five operatives, and insufficiently on my current metempsychosis, Brad Wilson of U.S. Naval Intelligence, *and* on the whereabouts of *Rush*! Before I knew it, the attack was well under way.

Damn him! I tried to take a step, to see another portion of the dining room, but my feet wouldn't move. Only then did I realize what he was up to. The Brad Wilson toes had become roots, digging down through his shoes into the soil of the lawn, burrowing down and down, clutching at rocks, entwining with the roots of other trees, luxuriating in the groundwater—

Other trees! Already the flesh of my ankles and shins was bark, already an irresistible pull drew my arms upward, already my joints were stiffening. In alarm, I tried to flee this body, but the chittering of the thousand thousand tiny counter-cherubs all around my leafing head imprisoned me. *They* couldn't hold me in, not by themselves, but with the power of Rush as well I *might* be defeated.

Defeated! This corporeal form was merely a temporary shape, but it was the permanent *me*, made up of my own atoms. (We do not inhabit and possess Earthly creatures, as the fiends do, as Rush was doing now, but make our shapes from ourselves.) If the demon and its million squeaking parasites could hold me, the essence of *me*, inside this terrestrial vessel until they completed the transformation, until they turned me into a vegetable, with a *vegetable's brain*, I would never break free, never be Ananayel again, never have power to be anything but what they would have made me: an inexplicable tree on a suburban lawn.

Failure was possible. And if I failed, what? There was no doubt, not the slightest doubt, that I would be abandoned to the effects of my failure. I would be encased here, lost here, shut up mindless inside this woody crypt for as long as it took Him to send another effectuator, a worthier deputy, to succeed where I had faltered, and at last to end this world.

And then? I would end with it, of course.

But now, *now*, what of now? Soon, in that theater in New York City, *Night Fall* would come to its expected end—the girl is innocent, it's obvious—and Susan would rise, but what would happen to Andy Harbinger? There isn't enough animation in him to get him on his feet and out of the theater, much less to take him through the complications of the rest of the evening. There would be confusion, then shock, then an ambulance. To the hospital Andy Harbinger's apparently living corpus would be taken, and I had not bothered to be meticulous about that corpus. It doesn't contain everything a human body would be expected to contain. Here and there, I did short circuits, took the easy way out. And now? Expose that body to emergency room staff? Confine myself to a severely abbreviated life span as a *tree*? Fail my God?

I still had teeth. I ground them as I forced this head to turn on its stiffening neck. Where was Rush? Where was Rush?

At the curb was parked Frank's Toyota. Its exterior left-side mirror was angled so that I could just get a glimpse into it. Among other things reflected in that mirror was not Rush but a Buick parked on a driveway down the block, on the other side of the street. Narrowing my focus, peering through the Toyota's exterior mirror into that Buick, into the interior rearview mirror of the Buick, my view included the plate-glass living room window of the house next door to the Auston house. The room behind that window was dark; the window was not a perfect mirror, but it would do, and in it was reflected the Toyota again. And from that angle, in the driver's window of the Toyota, very dimly, very darkly, hunched low in shrubbery around the side of the Auston house, *there* was Rush! Gibbering with glee.

My arms were almost vertical. My legs had been joined into one trunk, encased in bark. My sight was dimming, but I focused it, I focused it, and then I *opened my eyes*. The Toyota and Buick mirrors, the plate-glass window, the driver's window of the Toyota, all cracked with sounds like pistol shots. But as they went, the beam of my fury reached Rush where he hid, sliced into him like a harpoon, yanked him into the air, and flung him to the ground at my feet.

How they howled, that skyful of gnats! How their faint cries rose into the night, crackling like static electricity across the surface of high thin cloud layers. How they fled, fading into wisps of gas. And how their master squirmed inside his borrowed husk, trying to escape the agonized body of Rush.

Oh, no, not *this* time. I couldn't kill him, I knew that, not unless I was fast enough or lucky enough to convert *all* his matter to energy at once, which would be just about impossible, but I could give him a memory so searing he would never *dare* to confront me again. Pain so violent that the very thought of me, eons from now, would make him curl up like a shrimp. He was Rush now, he would feel what Rush felt, and he would *stay* Rush until I had taught him his lesson.

I boiled the blood within his veins. I turned his eyebrows to needles and embedded them in his eyes. I knotted his intestines, placed a living ferret in his stomach, turned his tongue into a piranha with its tail still attached to his pharynx.

He squirmed, that devil, he snarled, he shrieked in a range inaudible to any ear on Earth. He tried everything, tried to counterattack, to resist, to fight off the plagues I put upon him, strangling the ferret with his own guts, burning the piranha as it ate his mouth, but always and ever distracted by the pain I kept on inflicting and by the new horrors I thrust into his mouth and his nose and his ass and his eyes. Humans escape such torment by fainting or dying, but neither avenue was available to him. And he knew better than to beg for mercy. Mercy? To a foul fiend?

He first tried to escape as a worm, out Rush's ear, but I charred that worm to ash and less than ash, and he barely got back inside before I did for him completely. *Feel* my punishment, demon!

Then he tried, frantically, repeatedly, to kill Rush, to end the onslaught by robbing me of the field of play, but I resuscitated the body every time, and every time I blessed it with more plagues, more stabs, more clenchings, twistings, rippings, rendings.

Then I stopped. It cowered, still in the burning center of all the anguish of the Brother Rush persona, afraid to make another run for it, while I undid the damage it had done, severing the roots beyond my feet, reverting back to flesh, sap to blood, fiber to sinew.

When I could move I did so, stepping away from that thing that shivered and keened on the lawn. I looked into the dining room, where my five remained as before, and they had noticed nothing of the events outside. Good.

I directed my attention back to the former Rush. He would never be Rush again. He would never trouble *me* again. "I'm finished with you," I told him. "You may go."

At once, the body ceased to tremble, and grew slack. After a brief interval, a cockroach crept cautiously from its dead nostril. I broke one of the creature's legs, just as a reminder, but otherwise left it alone, and it hobbled away through the grass.

So there was no need for Brad Wilson here after all, no need to look in on my people. Rush was dealt with. I permitted Brad to discorporate, then carried the body of Brother Rush back with me to New York, leaving it in a neighborhood where it wouldn't excite particular comment, and made it back to Andy Harbinger just before the end of the movie.

"That was really good," Susan said, as we shuffled out of the theater with the rest of the audience.

"Yes, it was."

Oh, no, no, no, no more, no more . . .
  No more, no more, no more . . .
Hate hate hate hate hate hate—
No more!
No, no, not even *thoughts*, can't— Brain doesn't work, can't *think*, can't stop running, can't stop—
No more, no more . . .
Have to do it. *Have* to do it! But—
No more, no more . . .
But—
I must.

34

By the end of the newscast at eleven-thirty, it seemed pretty clear that Rush wouldn't be coming back, but no one wanted to go to bed just yet, in case something happened after all. Had Rush seen the police, and were they after him, and had he fled? Something like that, probably, which meant he still might come back when the coast was clear. In any event, everybody felt wide awake.

And besides, there was a program about to come on that interested at least two of the people in the house. Both Grigor and Maria Elena wanted to watch *Nightline*, on which Ted Koppel's guests would be a Dr. Marlon Philpott, the physicist who was conducting the experiments at Green Meadow III Nuclear Power Plant that had caused all the demonstrations and more recently the strike by better than two-thirds of the plant's workers, and in opposition to him another physicist, Dr. Robert Delantero.

"Our program might be considered somewhat strange tonight," Ted Koppel told his audience, with his small smile, "because the matter is strange. Our subject is a peculiar kind of thing known to physicists as strange matter. Some scientists, like Unitronic Laboratories' Dr. Marlon Philpott, believe that strange matter, once harnessed in the laboratory, can become the cleanest, safest, and cheapest power source in the history of the world. Other physicists of equal standing in the scientific world, such as Harvard's Dr. Robert Delantero, believe that strange matter, if found, and if carelessly handled, could be more destructive than anything we've ever imagined. Still other scientists believe that no such thing as strange matter exists at all. Dr. Philpott, have you ever *seen* strange matter? And could you describe it?"

Dr. Philpott was a heavy man with a spade goatee and dark-rimmed glasses. He looked more like a restaurant critic than a scientist, as though he'd be more interested in the ingredients of a French sauce than the contents of a Leyden jar. His manner was avuncular in a heavily condescending way. He said, "If we ever got enough strange matter together to *see* it, Ted, a chunk that big, why, we'd be in business right now. But I can describe it, all right, because we know it's there. It has to be there, the math says so."

"And what does this math say strange matter is?"

"A different way of combining the building blocks of

matter," Dr. Philpott told him, forgetting to call him "Ted." "As we now know, the basic building block of matter is the quark."

"Not the atom."

"No, Ted, the atom is composed of protons and neutrons. If you imagine protons and neutrons as little bags, what each bag contains is quarks, two up quarks and one down quark in each proton, two down and one up in each neutron. These bags are surrounded by a cloud of electrons, and the whole package goes to make up one atom."

"And what would be the difference in strange matter? Would there be such a thing as a strange atom?"

"That's precisely what we're looking for, Ted. And the difference would be, no bags. A strange atom consists of a cloud of electrons around a large collection of up quarks, down quarks, and some new quarks, known as strange quarks."

"I'm not surprised. Dr. Delantero, you agree these strange quarks, strange atoms, strange matter, exist?"

"I'm *afraid* they exist," Dr. Delantero snapped. He was a bony no-nonsense nearly bald man wearing a bright red bow tie. "The essential question," he said, staring sternly into the camera, "is which kind of matter is the most stable. There's every reason to believe that *we* are the more strange matter, and that matter composed of atoms containing strange quarks is more stable than the matter we know. If that's true, and if Dr. Philpott does manage to isolate strange matter, then God help us all."

"You'll have to forgive me, Dr. Delantero, but I'm afraid I didn't follow that. Dr. Philpott seems to think strange matter would make a fine energy source, safer and cheaper than conventional nuclear power. You don't think the stuff is safe at all, but I just can't seem to understand why."

Dr. Philpott horned in to say, "You're right not to understand, Ted, because it's nonsense. He's taking a worst-case-possible scenario and acting as though it's the *only* possible case."

"Yes, Doctor," Koppel said, "but let's just let Dr. Delantero try to clear this up. Dr. Delantero, assuming that you and Dr. Philpott are both right, and that strange matter does exist, or can be made to exist, why does he think it's safe and you think it's unsafe?"

Dr. Delantero looked more and more like a hanging judge. He said, "I can only presume Dr. Philpott turns a blind eye to the dangers here because he and Unitronic Laboratories see profit in it. That's why he's—"

"Profit for all mankind."

"Yes, Dr. Philpott, but let's give Dr. Delantero a chance."

"They threw his lab out of Grayling University," Dr. Delantero suddenly shouted, "because he kept blowing things up! So some *idiot* decided he'd be better off at a nuclear plant!"

"That's the most outrageous, most outrageous—" Dr. Philpott now looked like a restaurant critic who'd been served a bad shrimp; he was so offended he could barely speak.

Which gave his host an opportunity to say, "That is a question I'd been meaning to get to, thank you, Doctor. Dr. Philpott, would you like to reply to this rumor about explosions?"

"I certainly would." Dr. Philpott smoothed his shirt front with a shaking hand, stopped hyperventilating, and said, "Clearly, no one has been blowing up strange matter because we haven't *found* it yet. Nor, since my move to Green Meadow, not because I was *thrown out* of Grayling, I'm still tenured at Grayling, Dr. Delantero, thank you very much, but because the facilities at Green Meadow are better suited to my researchers, there has not been *one* incident, nor *shall* there be. Some very minor explosive incidents, causing no damage whatsoever, did take place in the early stages, when we were experimenting with various receptacles, pieces of equipment, gaseous elements for storage, but not one since, and I defy Dr. Delantero to dispute that."

Dr. Delantero too had grown somewhat calmer by now.

"All I'm saying," he replied, "is that we're babies with a loaded gun in this situation, and we shouldn't be taking the risks Dr. Philpott is taking up there at Green Meadow. The people out on strike are the sensible ones."

Koppel said, "As I understand it, and I freely admit I don't understand the entire matter all that well, but as I understand it, there are two distinct theories as to the effect of strange matter when it comes into contact with regular matter, and that's what the dispute is all about. Dr. Philpott, if I had a drop of strange matter here, and I spilled it onto the floor, what would happen?"

"Nothing. It would lie there, and slowly evaporate away into harmless alpha particles. But if we put it into a reactor, and fed it— The *point* with strange matter is, it's so much more dense than regular matter, it's the closest thing we can create on this planet to a black hole. A chunk the size of a BB would weigh more than five million tons. The energy in that dense mass—"

"Yes, thank you, Dr. Philpott, but we're running low on time here, and I'd like to ask the same question of Dr. Delantero. You subscribe to a different theory, and at this point there's no way to prove which theory is correct, but in the scientific world both theories are equally plausible, is that so?"

"It is."

"And each theory has its scientifically respectable supporters?"

"That is correct."

"So Dr. Philpott has just as much chance to be right as you have."

"He does. But so do I, and that's why we shouldn't take the risk."

"And what do *you* see happening, if I spill that drop of strange matter on the carpet?"

Dr. Delantero squared his bony shoulders. "As Dr. Philpott said, strange matter is much more dense than normal matter.

It is also likely to be more stable. That drop of yours would eat its way through the floor, through the ground—''

''Oh, really, there isn't the slightest—''

''Dr. Philpott, you'll have your chance. Dr. Delantero?''

''Combining with the matter around it,'' Dr. Delantero said, ''this extremely heavy, extremely dense drop of matter would burn its way to the molten center of the Earth, where it would get hot, and *really* go to work.''

''An explosion, you mean?''

''No, I do not. I mean that the one drop would, in a very short period of time, convert this entire planet, and everything on it, every tree, every person, the very atmosphere around us, into strange matter.''

''And what effect would that have?''

''The Earth would become,'' Dr. Delantero said, ''a featureless, smooth, glittering ball of incredible density, the same weight as it is now, but measuring less than a mile in diameter.''

With his small smile, Koppel said, ''And you and I would be part of that featureless ball.''

''We would.''

To the camera, Koppel said, ''As you can see, the difference of opinion is quite marked here, and the scientific stakes extremely high. On the one side, cheap safe fuel; on the other, the end of everything. Is Dr. Philpott actually close to resolving these opposed theories, and what safeguards is he employing to avoid the finish Dr. Delantero so vividly described. What would Dr. Delantero like science to do about the question of strange matter, if anything? We'll get into all that, when we return.''

During the commercials, Frank looked over at Grigor and grinned: ''Is that the joke you wanna pull? Drop the drop?''

''It has already been dropped, on me,'' Grigor said. He didn't sound amused.

Ananayel

I have rationalized Andy Harbinger. The close call at the Quad Cinema convinced me to take the time, to do this part without shortcuts. So Andy is now a complete human being, with all the usual and necessary parts, if in somewhat better condition than most.

And while I was at it, I gave him everything else a human being such as Andy Harbinger would have; which is to say, a job and a past. The sociology professorship—untenured assistant professor, actually—at Columbia has become real. Andy's co-members of the faculty have memories of him, mostly pleasant, extending back several years. His birth certificate will be found in the Bureau of Vital Statistics in Oak Park, Illinois. His school records, employment records, even dental and health records, are all in place. For the remainder of the time that life shall exist on Earth, Andy Harbinger is for me now fully functional, fully operative; what we might call my destination resort.

Oh, and yes, Dr. Delantero has described the end rather accurately. He will turn out—though the knowledge would not be likely to please him—to have been right about what will happen when that drop of strange matter is spilled on the floor at Green Meadow III Nuclear Power Plant. Or at least to be right when it counts.

After all, the universe is *His* creation. He can still tinker with it if He wishes, so long as He doesn't thereby change what is already known to be true. (Well, He can, naturally, and sometimes does, but those instances are called miracles. We're not considering a miracle here. In fact, miracles have been strictly enjoined in this case; deniability, you know.)

But there is still much of the real universe that is not known to human beings, not charted, not yet *proved*, and in that vast terra incognita God can do as He will, with no miracle involved. Human science, for instance, has reached the point with strange matter where two theories have been proposed, of more or less equal probability. The spilled drop of strange matter might result in Dr. Philpott's infinitesimal speck lying on the floor, quickly dissipated. Equally, it might result in Dr. Delantero's destruction of the planet by conversion of its entire mass to strange matter.

To prove either of those theories true would not, in Earth terms, constitute a miracle. Either theory could join the web of the already known without in any way rupturing the fabric of observed reality. Therefore, although I do not know which of those theories has been correct up till now, I know for certain which of them is correct as of this moment.

That is, after all, why I am here. To transmute the entire Earth, and everything on it, to a ball bearing.

35

In the end, it was easier to steal an empty school bus than try to board one of those carrying the Green Meadow cadre. The buses didn't pick up the supervisors and managers at home, to begin with, but only brought them from a well-guarded parking lot four miles away. Also, each bus carried its own armed private security guard. But the buses had been leased from a transportation company that serviced some of the public and most of the private schools in that part of New York State, and *its* large parking lot, usually at least half full of buses not at that moment in use, was barely guarded at all.

By this time, the demonstrations had been going on for months and the strike for weeks, and everybody was into the daily routine of it. There was a known role to be played by everyone who showed up at the plant gates: demonstrators, strikers, working cadre, police, private security force, media crews, and the large yellow buses saying things like *Istanfayle Consolidated School District* on their sides but always with the same company name—*Kelly Transit*, in green script within an outlined shamrock—on the door. Most of the drivers were women, most of the guards riding shotgun wore rent-a-cop dark blue uniforms. Sometimes the buses were nearly empty when they drove into the plant; they were never completely full.

*   *   *

"Are you sure you want to do this?" Grigor asked.

"Of course I am," Frank said. "It was my idea."

"But *I* have nothing to lose," Grigor pointed out. "If you are caught—"

"That's not gonna happen," Frank assured him. "Win or lose, they don't lay a hand on me. That's a little promise I made myself."

"But why? Why do you want to do it?"

"For money." Frank grinned. "I'm a simple guy, money's enough for me. You do your speeches, you warn the world, you get everybody's attention, that's all okay by me. But when they get their atom factory back is after I get mine. Or you'll *see* a joke."

*   *   *

Frank was the pro, he was the one who knew how to do all this stuff. He drove down into New York and rented a cop uniform from a theatrical costume supplier. Up in New Hampshire, he bought three pistols in three pawnshops; two of them would probably blow your hand off if you tried to fire them, but that was okay. They were just for show. The third one would have to be able to shoot, but not *at* anybody; just to attract attention.

Back in Stockbridge, he rooted through the worn old clothing Jack Auston had left behind and outfitted himself with old grease-stained dark green chinos and a dark red plaid shirt. He bought a clipboard and some standard inventory forms from a local stationer, skipped shaving one day, and went down to Kelly Transit. Walking into the big parking area, he strolled over to the dispatcher's window, consulted his clipboard, and said, "I'm here to pick up number 271."

It was four-thirty in the afternoon, and the dispatcher was almost at the end of his workday. More important, in half an hour there would be a shift change at Green Meadow; if things went well, Kelly Transit's bus number 271 would be the first to arrive with the replacement staff.

The dispatcher looked up from his crossword puzzle, frowned at Frank, and said, "Who says?"

"Hyatt Garage," Frank said, as though he didn't care what happened next, one way or the other.

"I'm not sure it's in."

It was; Frank had noted the number of the bus he wanted as he'd walked across the yard. But he shrugged and said, "That's okay, pal, I'll go back to the garage." And turned away.

"Hold it, hold it, I didn't say it *wasn't* here."

Frank stopped and looked at the guy. "Make up your mind, okay? I wanna go home tonight."

"We all do," the dispatcher said, and made a big show of looking at his dispatch sheets before he said, "Yeah, it's in. It'll be around here somewhere. Hold on."

Frank held on. The dispatcher reached around behind himself, took a set of keys from the many rows of hooks on the wall, finally got up from his stool, and came thumping around and out the door. "Let's see," he said, peering at the tag with the keys, then squinting out at his yard full of buses. "Should be right around here."

Frank didn't help, but still the dispatcher took only three minutes to find the bus standing in front of him. *271* was painted on the rear emergency door and like an eyebrow above the left side of the windshield. *Messenger of God Parish School* was painted on both sides, in block black letters, beneath the rows of windows.

"Looks like that might be it," the dispatcher said.

"If you say so."

The dispatcher had Frank sign a form—"George Washington," he scrawled—then gave him the keys, and Frank drove on out of there.

•   •   •

Maria Elena said, "Then *this* will do it." Do what? Accomplish what? She didn't care. She refused to even look at such questions. She had her answer: "Then *this* will do it."

She knew what she knew, and that was enough. She knew that movement was life, and stillness was death, and she'd been dead too long. She knew that a group with a goal was life and a solitary person without a goal was death, and she'd been dead too long. She knew that a singer was alive, and a person without a song (without, now, even the records and memories of the songs that had been) was dead, and that she'd been dead too long. She knew that death would come anyway, to all of them, some sooner than others, and that it was wrong for her to be dead before she was dead. That Frank made her feel alive, and Frank wanted to do this, and to *do* something was better, infinitely better, than the nothing she had been doing for so long.

•   •   •

Maria Elena drove the bus, wearing a chauffeur's cap and lightly tinted sunglasses, to help avoid accidental identification from any of her former acquaintances among the demonstrators milling as usual outside the gate. (As though there would be an "afterward" in which such things would matter.) Frank stood in the first step of the stairwell with the rent-a-cop uniform on, brazenly visible through the windshield. Kwan sat in the second row on the right, in suit and white shirt and tie; about a quarter of the scientific staff at Green Meadow was Oriental, so his presence added verisimilitude. Grigor, two rows behind Kwan, in open-necked plaid shirt, looked like the kind of unworldly blue-sky research guy who wouldn't know a necktie if he were hanged by one. Pami, seated on the other side, was got up in black sweater, one string of pearls, and horn-rimmed glasses, her usually explosive hair imprisoned in a neat bun; it was hard to say what image she projected, exactly, but it was at least respectable.

In any event, they didn't have to project any image at all for very long. The school buses never stopped when they made the turn to go through the just-opened gate into the plant grounds; it would make too tempting a target for the strikers and demonstrators. The state troopers and private security guards simply saw what they expected to see—a yellow school bus from Kelly Transit with a woman driver and a blue-uniformed guard and some egghead types aboard—at the time they expected to see it, and waved it on through.

The land within the perimeter fence had been carefully recontoured, to present to the public eye along the public road nothing but a gentle upslope in a parklike setting of specimen trees and well-pruned shrubs on a neatly mowed lawn, with taller trees, most of them firs of one kind or another, forming a dense year-round backdrop. The two-lane asphalt road meandered up this easy incline, and when it crested the ridge and started down the far side, the quintet in the bus could see what was really here, in among the trees.

Straight ahead was the dome-topped containment building, a featureless, windowless concrete box. Within the concrete would be a steel inner shell, and within that the reactor, with its core, control rods, steam generator, pressurizer, coolant pump, drain tank, valves, and sump. This was the heart of the power plant, the dangerous living essence of the thing, the part the quintet in the bus had to control if they were going to accomplish anything; if they were, in fact, to avoid being dragged right back off the property again, in handcuffs.

To the left of the containment building was its concrete baby brother, the auxiliary building, with its emergency core-cooling system pump, sump pump, borated-water storage tank, and radioactive-waste storage tank. A bit farther away on that side was the administrative building, brick and stone, three stories high, oddly matter-of-fact amid all the grotesqueries of nuclear architecture. It had the air of a faculty office building on a midwestern college campus.

To the right of the containment building was the turbine building, reassuringly like such structures from power plants of an earlier day. It held the turbine, generator, condenser, transformer, and all the other elements needed to turn the power emanating from the containment building into usable electricity. In the shadow of the turbine building was another smaller windowless concrete structure, containing Dr. Philpott's controversial laboratory. And behind them all, looming over them, were the twin cooling towers, salt and pepper shakers, huge concave edifices of pale gray concrete, like minimalist graven images of Baal.

But in front of the containment building, attached to it or thrust from it, was the squat structure of the control section. Here was where the servants of the machine fed it and cooled it and guided it through its life of bridled violence. And here was where the five people in the bus had to take command, or lose.

Maria Elena halted the bus in front of the control section. She pushed the long lever that opened the door. Frank looked back at his string, his four confederates. Jesus H. Christ, what a crew. Nodding, he said, "What have we got to lose?" and stepped down from the bus.

It was as good a battle cry as any.

36

"Professor! My God, look at this!"

Dr. Marlon Philpott, more rumpled yet somehow more serious in his laboratory than he had been on *Nightline,* turned reluctantly from the holding ring, in which, in the heavy swirl of liquid deuterium, *something* had been happening. Or about to happen. He squinted testily at Chang, jittering up and down over there in the doorway to the lounge: "What is it?"

"Something's happening on TV!"

Dr. Philpott was fairly sure he'd made a fool of himself, or been made a fool of, which amounted to the same thing, on that damn program, and so wasn't feeling particularly cordial about television at the moment. The damned Unitronic directors, with their worship of the great god Public Relations . . . "Something is happening in the deuterium," he said sternly, "something infinitely more important than television."

"No, no." Chang was really very disturbed, bobbing up and down over there as though he had to go to the bathroom. "It's something happening *here,* at the facility."

The demonstrators, the strikers: Philpott paid as little attention to *those* Luddites as possible. He was about to say so when Cindy, attracted by Chang's agitation, left her place at the auxiliary control console and crossed the lab toward the lounge, brushing blond hair out of her eyes in an unconscious habitual gesture as she did so, saying, "Chang? What is it?"

"I'm just not sure," the boy told her, his smooth face

expressing alarm by becoming even more round than usual behind his round light-reflecting spectacles. "They say it's been taken over."

Cindy shook her head, blond hair falling into her eyes again. "What's been taken over?"

"Us! The facility!"

Philpott, wanting nothing but to return his attention to what either was or was not beginning to come into existence in the liquid deuterium, spread his hands and said, "Taken over? By whom? I don't seem to see them."

"Not here, Professor. The control section!"

"Oh, my gosh!" Cindy said, and ran past Chang into the lounge.

The fact was, as Philpott well knew, graduate student assistants are vital to any coherent program of accomplishment in the scientific world. And graduate student assistants are the cheapest possible source of slave labor in the otherwise civilized world today. So it was necessary to let them have their heads every once in a while, to allow them their own little pursuits, their own enthusiasms, their own overreactions.

Moving at a measured tread, a condescending smile already on his lips, Philpott entered the lounge, turned to the television set, and saw on its screen what was clearly an even more turbulent scene than normal these days at the gates of Green Meadow. Vast groups of people milled about in the background, like battle scenes in Shakespeare films, while somebody's daughter, dressed approximately like a grown-up and looking very much like an older Cindy, jabbered into a microphone in the foreground.

"Well," Philpott said. "Reaching some sort of critical mass out there, are they?"

"No, wait, Professor," Chang said. "Listen."

Philpott didn't want to listen, but he did, and when he understood what he was hearing he even more emphatically didn't want to listen. Not to this:

"Who the terrorists are and what their demands will be

no one seems to know as yet. What is certain now is that they do include at least one expert in the operation of this type of plant. At their insistence, all plant personnel except the hostages have been evacuated, leaving the terrorists in charge of the reactor controls. The reactor is producing at its lowest possible rate. At this point, no electricity is being furnished by Green Meadow III. The slack is being taken up by other electric utilities in the Northeast and Canadian grids, and consumers are assured—"

"My God!" Philpott cried, at last accepting the unbelievable. "They're in *here*!"

"Yes, Professor!"

Philpott looked quickly around. "But they obviously don't know about us yet. They must not ever know. Quick, lock and bolt the doors. Switch over to our emergency generator, we don't want them to see us using power."

Chang and Cindy exchanged a glance. It was Cindy who dared the question: "Professor Philpott? You aren't going to go *on*, are you?"

"Of course I am. We're in the middle of— Shut down? Surrender to these mindless thugs?"

"But—" Chang floundered, almond eyes frightened behind those false-looking glasses. "The experiment, the risk . . ."

"There is no risk," Philpott snapped. "We've been autonomous in here anyway, absolutely self-contained. Do you want to be a *hostage* to these people, a bargaining chip in their absurd quarrel with authority, whatever that might be? I don't particularly relish the thought of being held for exchange of some political prisoner in someplace like Northern Ireland or Lebanon."

So. *That* part of the reality of the situation hadn't occurred to either of the young people. They stared at him, both frightened, both at a loss. Fortunately, he was not at a loss, nor was he frightened, though he was certainly concerned. "We're safer here than anywhere else," he told them. "We'll do nothing to attract the attention of those cretins out there. We'll stay within the lab building, locked in, until the authorities straighten out this mess. And as long as we're in here, there is absolutely no reason not to go on with the experiment. Agreed?''

They were both reluctant to answer, but he needed that answer. He bore his sternest gaze first on Chang, the more malleable of the two, and Chang fidgeted, awkward and uncomfortable, but unable to argue back. ''Yes, Professor,'' he finally said, low and mumbled. ''Agreed.''

''Cindy?''

Another hesitation, but her agreement was inevitable: ''I . . . suppose so. I suppose it's the only thing we can do.''

''Of course it is.'' He turned his glare toward the daughter on the TV screen, nattering on now about terrorist ''assurances.'' He muttered, as though at her, as though it were her fault, ''I will *not* be interrupted.'' Then he looked through the doorway toward the experiment in progress: ''Now, of all times.''

37

It was Frank's pistol, fired once, the bullet thudding into a wooden desk, that had focused the attention of the eight staffers in the control section, but it was Grigor who turned them from panic and disintegration into a cooperative and useful team. ''I was at Chernobyl,'' he told them, once Frank had assembled them and they stood frightened and demoralized in a little cluster in the middle of the main control room. ''I was a fireman there.''

He told them what had happened to him, and in their own technical jargon he told them why Chernobyl had gone wrong. ''I don't want to do to anyone else what was done to me," he told them, "I assure you of that. I am not here to cause a meltdown. With your help, we will do no harm at all. We are here only to force public awareness. That is all we want."

"And the money," Frank reminded him. "For the cause." Because they'd finally argued their way to an agreement that Frank's crass commercial motives would best be hidden within the social concerns of the others. The five million dollars—Frank's number, one he refused to change—would be for their *Committee for the Environment*. (The committee wasn't real, but the damn money better be.)

"Yes, the money," Grigor agreed, "but we'll get to that." And he went on explaining things, in his thin and non-threatening voice, seated at a desk facing them all, as though at his ease, successfully so far hiding from them the extreme weakness that had made it almost impossible for him to walk this far from the bus. (Kwan and Pami were also seated, necessarily, at the fringes of the group, leaving only Frank and Maria Elena to stand and wave guns around. But they were enough.)

Once the staffers began to engage Grigor in dialogue, Frank knew it was going to be all right. These weren't tough guys, no more than Frank himself. They were five women and three men, all of them technicians, none of them death-defying jocks. Because they were managers and supervisors, they were older than the workers who would normally have been on duty here. They would do what they were told.

And what they were told to do was simple. Do *not* shut down the reactor, but close down its output to the lowest possible minimum. Then make the phone call; the first phone call.

That was a job for the senior technician, a woman of about sixty, who might have looked a lot like Maria Elena in her younger days. She was the one who dialed the offices in the administrative building and delivered the message Frank gave her:

The control section has been taken over by armed and desperate individuals.

If everyone obeys the orders of the invading group, no harm will come to anyone.

The reactor is still being operated by the staff, but under the supervision of one of the invaders, who is himself an expert in nuclear-fission plants.

Everyone else within the Green Meadow perimeter fence is to evacuate; now.

Contact will be made with officials outside the gate once everyone has cleared the plant.

There is no reason for general panic, and in fact the invaders insist that the surrounding counties not *be evacuated.*

One hint that the general population is being moved, to make possible an assault on the plant, and the invaders will deliberately cause a meltdown, before the people to be affected can get clear; the invaders are absolutely prepared to die.

At this point, their only demands are that the plant be cleared and that a telephone contact be established outside the gate.

Once that is accomplished, and once it is generally seen and recognized that the invaders are both serious and responsible, a dialogue can begin.

X

Now what? A nuclear plant? These five misfits have blundered themselves into a nuclear plant? For what? How much damage could they do in *there*? I have come to save the world, only to find that truckling toady is content to destroy *New York State*? (It is true there are those who believe that New York—or at least the city of the same name, no relation—*is* the world, but surely the loathsome He is not among them.)

And what of *Susan Carrigan*? What is her part in the scheme, where does she fit, what is her *job*? He's driving me mad with that grimalkin, that heifer, that fur-farm. The other five are terrorizing the populace at Green Meadow, and *she's* in the arms of that smoky simulacrum, playing at love. Love! That's supposed to be *my* territory, you shameless bastard!

Shall I just kill her, and see what happens? Slowly, with boils and pus and scum from every pore? Or immediately, with a lightning stroke?

Come to me, my spies of the middle air, my northern apples of the twilight ether, extenders of my brain, my strength, my knowledge. What do they want? What do we know? What is his *advantage*, that bland mortician, that poisoned milk, that sterile tool?

Stable matter? *Stable matter! Stabat Mater,* what a vicious idea! So is *that* what the experiment in that plant is all about, the search for what the instable humans call *strange matter* (as though they weren't sufficiently strange themselves).

By Unholy Lucifer, he means to stabilize the Earth!

No, no, no. I have to get in there. I have to stop this, and at once.

And that's a pearl, that was my planet? No.

Ananayel

So he knows.

Well, he would, wouldn't he? And my little lesson in Connecticut didn't take, did it? But of course I should have realized that; intimidation is a cumbersome tool, as likely to stiffen resolve as to break spirit. Oddly enough, violence never *is* the answer. Things done in violence have to be done over again.

But what else is there, with as fallen and shameless a creature as this nameless slave of the Unholy? Reason? Persuasion? Argument? Emotional appeal? Bribery? He's an extension of his miserable master, nothing else, with no more free will than a moon.

All right, we'll stop him. Again.

In order to accomplish anything, this fetid fiend will have to take a corporeal form, which in his case of course means possessing a human's body rather than, as in mine, creating a pleasing person out of air. And his first idea—they're so predictable, so obvious, these tools of Satan—will be to take over one of the hostages in the plant, one of the staff members kept inside to run the machinery. But that's easily dealt with. I have my own assistants when necessary, my cherubim, swifter than thought, darting through space and time with arrowed precision. (How unthinking of human artists to portray them as fat!)

I have called upon them, these lean servants of the Lord. They hover now over the hostages, protecting, observing, prepared to alert me at the slightest hint of incursion. Until the end, each hostage shall have one of these, these, oh, let's call them guardian angels.

So he can't suddenly, all at once, *be* there, inside the plant. He'll have to start from the other side of the fence, take over some poor human somewhere out in the world, and try to scheme some way to move it through the maze of officialdom ringing the site. Impossible? I'm not sure; that diseased cur does seem to have a low cunning.

Outside, of course, his choice of host is wide. I can't give *everyone* a guardian angel. We'll simply have to keep a diligent watch.

38

These were the times that tried Joshua Hardwick's soul. To be public information director for a nuclear power plant less than a hundred miles from a major population center like New York City was no bed of roses even when things were going well. When the plant was under occupation by terrorists—nobody even knew for sure *which* terrorists, just to put the icing on the cake—the PID's life became, in a word, hell.

There were even times these days when he found himself thinking nostalgically of the advertising racket, that's how bad it was. (At least in the ad game, you could drink at lunch. And CNN wasn't training its cameras on you every time you blew your nose. And . . . Nah. There's no parenthesis big enough.)

Lately, Joshua hated to get out of bed in the morning, hated that first pre-breakfast phone call to the command post outside the Green Meadow gate—"Still there. No change." —hated sitting in his Honda for the twenty-minute bucolic (and so what?) drive from his once-happy home in Connect- icut to his once-cushy job. He hated the job, the reporters, the cops, the questions, the answers, and the fact that there actually weren't any answers, not really.

Possibly most of all—apart from the terrorists who were ultimately responsible for this mess—Joshua hated his bosses, and God knows there were enough of them for the hate to spread around. Green Meadow was a quasi-governmental, quasi-private corporation, run by three federal and two New York State agencies, plus a consortium of private companies led by Unitronic Laboratories, itself a subsidiary of Anglo Dutch Oil. Every one of those entities had its representatives here for the crisis, and the task of each and every one of those representatives, it had early become clear, was to see to it that some other entity got the blame when things ended badly.

That was kind of depressing already, knowing they all *expected* it to end badly. And that, rather than any of them trying to do something to change that gloomy prediction, they were all spending their time trying to scramble out of the way of falling debris. *Expected* falling debris.

Which meant they *all* wanted the ear—and the voice, and the heart, and the mind, and the soul—of the public information director. They all wanted to believe he was on *their* side, would present *their* waffling and cowardice in the best light while screwing everybody else. (The idea that everybody else should be screwed was as important to these businessmen and government officials as the idea that they themselves should be spared.)

As usual this morning Joshua had to show his two separate IDs—one wasn't enough for these people, because they were *very serious*—at the police barrier half a mile down the road from the plant entrance, and as usual it was a state trooper he never remembered seeing before, and who felt the same about him. Sitting at the wheel of his Honda with controlled impatience during the trooper's long slow inspection of his face, Joshua felt a sudden startling *clench* in his stomach, a sudden urgent need to throw up. "Oh, my God," he said. "I can't— You'll have to—"

Startled, the trooper backed away, hand whipping to his sidearm as Joshua came boiling out of the car, right hand clamped over mouth. Joshua managed two steps toward the far verge, all his muscles and joints lashing him with sudden excruciating pain, before he dropped to his knees and burst breakfast all over the westbound lane and slightly on his own trousers.

"Jesus Christ, fella!" the trooper cried, no longer

suspicious— nobody can fake that much vomit—"What's the matter with you?"

"I dun—I dunno." Kneeling there, head sagging, Joshua gasped, lungs searing with pain at every breath. He dropped back to sit on his heels, arms hanging at his sides, and felt the pain strike at him everywhere, as though a whole bag of cats at once were trying to claw their way out of his body.

"I'll call somebody," the trooper decided.

"Wai—" Joshua said, vaguely lifting an arm. "Wait."

Because the pain, as quickly as it had come over him, was now lessening, fading away. He was able to take deeper and deeper breaths, he could feel his strength steadily return, and he lifted a shaking hand to wipe his sweat-beaded and cold-feeling brow.

"What a hell of a thing," he said, his voice trembling. And now that the first attack was over, what he mostly felt was scared. What was this? Cancer? Leukemia? An early sign?

Oh, Christ, don't tell me I got something at the goddamn *plant*.

"Wait there," the trooper said, which Joshua was more than willing to do, sitting back on his heels in front of his breakfast like an extremely oddball worshipper, and the trooper went away to his impressive official Plymouth Fury II on the other side of the road, returning a minute later with a roll of paper towels and a Diet Pepsi. "Here you go," he said. "Try it, anyway."

Grateful, Joshua wiped his face and neck with the paper towels, then took a long swig of Diet Pepsi to clean out his mouth. It landed in his stomach without incident, seeming content to stay there, and Joshua struggled to his feet, the trooper giving him a hand. "Thanks," Joshua said. "Boy, I don't know what that was."

"You better check with your doctor," the trooper told him.

"I will."

"You're looking awfully red-eyed."

Terrific; a vampire for CNN. "I don't know," Joshua said, leaning one hand on the top of the Honda. "Maybe I ought to go home, call in. Maybe you could call in for me, the Press Office.''

''Sure,'' said the trooper.

But then Joshua felt a stiffening of the spine—he actually felt it, a surge of toughness through his body—and he stood up straighter, taking his hand off the Honda as he said, ''No, never mind, I'm all right now.''

''You sure?''

''Positive.''

Joshua got back behind the wheel, and glanced at himself in the rearview mirror, and by God his eyes *were* red-rimmed, as though he'd spent all last night in mad debauch. One of the secretaries would have Murine, Visine, one of those eyedrop things. He couldn't face a news camera like this; he could barely face a *print* reporter like this.

So why don't I go home? he asked himself, even as his body, following its own agenda, started the car, shifted into gear, and waved ''so long'' to the trooper, who called, ''Take care now.''

The last half mile between police barrier and plant entrance was the most peaceful ride in the world. There were no houses or farms along here, nothing but regrowth woods (containing shreds of stone wall, the faint pencil marks of failed settlements) and overgrown fields, not yet reclaimed by forest. The road was reasonably smooth and reasonably straight, and he was alone on it, his Honda a magic carpet through a world called Serenity. If only all of driving could be like this.

(The local newspaper's main news angle on the terrorist takeover at the nuclear plant was the fact of this road's being closed to normal traffic. They were editorially outraged, and brought out all the usual heart-tuggers: school buses diverted onto dangerous truck-ravaged highways, senior citizens facing an extra thirty agonized minutes to reach their life-giving medicines, all of that. They came as close as they dared to claiming that local dairy farmers' milk was curdling on its so-much-longer way to market, but if they followed that particular line much further the dairy farmers would surely rise up as one and burn the newspaper offices to the ground, so they were showing—some—restraint.)

Fortunately, the local weekly paper was not that high on the list of Joshua's media problems. He was distantly polite to their chubby girl reporter, gave her the same handouts he gave everybody else, and let it go at that. And enjoyed the half mile of sequestered road. It was one of the few things in his life these days he could enjoy at all.

By the time he got to the command post—a series of trailers scattered like a Canadian mining town all over the road in the vicinity of the main gate—Joshua's recent illness was completely gone, except for the red eyes. He left the Honda in its assigned space, walked to the Press Office trailer, and a steno there did have eyedrops for him. She paused in her endless work at the copying machine to root through her big horse-feeder-bag purse and find the little bottle, which he took to the men's room and used on both eyes, to no effect. The red fringe was just *there*, in his eyes, as though behind them his brain were on fire.

Out again in the bullpen, after returning the eyedrops with thanks, Joshua was about to look at the thick stack of message memos already making a leaning tower on his desk when the new Anglo Dutch press rep introduced herself. "Hi, Karen Levine," she said. She was thin, early thirties, ash-blond hair, clear level eyes, no-nonsense manner, hard bony handclasp. "I want you to know, from the get-go," she said, "you're the guy in charge. I'm just here to help out if I can, if any questions come up involving Anglo Dutch."

"Thanks, Karen," Joshua said, with his brightest and falsest smile, knowing he would have no more than two weeks of this one. "I appreciate all the help I can get," he told her, as he told them all. "Glad to have you aboard."

The fact was, Anglo Dutch had learned from Exxon's experience with the *Valdez*. Never keep your information officer around long enough to establish any kind of personal

rapport with the media; that way indiscretions and uncomfortable leakage lie. Every two weeks, whip into the slot
another trim slim thirty-four-year-old, bland and smooth and
bright, male or female (makes no difference), who will give
the company line a nearly human face; but before that face
becomes completely human get it out of there, and start
with a new one.

It had worked for Exxon in Alaska, and it was working
for Anglo Dutch at Green Meadow, and why not? Everybody likes to talk with a handsome person; so what if they
aren't saying anything?

Something about the encounter with A-D's latest clone
left Joshua too disheartened to look at his message mountain. "I'm going to walk the perimeter, Grace," he told his
secretary, a fiftyish civil service employee in whom the milk
of human kindness had curdled long before the closing of
any local roads.

She gave him a disapproving look. "What should I say to
callers?"

"Hello," Joshua suggested, and left the trailer.

The primary official presence was centered here at what
had been the main gate back when ingress and egress were
possibilities at Green Meadow, but guards of one sort or
another, mostly state troopers and national guardsmen, were
spotted all around the rim of what the more military among
them persisted in calling "the facility"; as though anything
about this were easy.

The citizen soldiers of the National Guard—mostly not
the accountants and supermarket managers of song and
story, but unskilled laborers who were grateful for the extra
money they got being guardsmen (but not thrilled at having
been called to active duty)—were positioned back in the
woods, in pairs and trios, within sight of every inch of
fence. Idiots of various kinds kept trying to climb that
fence—younger reporters, thrill-seekers, wannabe heroes,
drunks (after dark), and jerks generally—so it had to be
watched. There was no point having a group of nervous

terrorists destroy themselves and several hundred thousand worthier people simply because two dumb kids, for instance, were playing dare-ya.

Still, Joshua thought, as he walked away from the command post along the fence, it would be nice to get in there. Interesting. And almost his job, really, to know what was going on. Not that he would try to be a hero, rescue anybody or stop anything that was going on at the plant, nothing like that. Just observe.

Not far along the road from the command post the fence angled away into the woods, and Joshua strolled along with it. There was almost a path bordering the fence on the outside, the result of heavy traffic a few years ago by the construction crews that had built the thing. The path was now somewhat overgrown, with tree branches intruding into the space every twenty feet or so.

Joshua made his slow way along this path, ducking leafy limbs as necessary, and every time he looked around there were at least two olive-drab uniformed guardsmen in sight, rifles slung on backs. They paid no particular attention to Joshua, apart from marking his presence; the highly visible laminated ID clipped to his jacket lapel was bona fide enough, so long as he didn't do anything stupid like try to climb the fence.

A rock. On the ground, just to the left of the path; the fence was to his right. Joshua picked it up, and it was just hand size. His fist closed halfway around it, fingers splayed over the cool and fairly smooth rounded surface. It felt good in the hand, it felt good swinging at the end of his arm as he walked. Comforting; his pet rock.

He was a good twenty minutes from the road, maybe a third of the way around the outer boundary of the plant, when he saw, just ahead, partway up a clear slope, seated on the trunk of a fallen tree, a single guardsman; a young guy, maybe twenty-two, pale pimply skin and pale scraggly moustache tucked away beneath the helmet. Joshua veered away from the fence toward this person, who continued to sit there, watching him approach. Joshua noticed the guards-man's eyes take in the flapping laminated ID.

When he got close enough, Joshua grinned and said, "Hi. How you doin?"

"Fine," said the guardsman.

"I thought you guys were supposed to work in pairs," Joshua said. "Where's your partner?"

Gesturing over his shoulder, the guardsman said, "Way down by that stream back there, taking a crap. He's one of your self-conscious dudes."

"Well, that's fine," Joshua said, and smashed the kid in the face with the rock.

The kid went backward off the tree trunk and Joshua went after him, raising the rock high, bringing it down twice more before the kid stopped moving. Then it was the work of a moment to yank the rifle off the limp body, roll it over, peel off its wool jacket.

Leaving the rock behind, carrying the rifle and the jacket, Joshua moved quickly but without undue haste toward the fence. He tossed the rifle over, then swarmed up the chain-link, fingers and toes sure and fast. At the top were three spirals of razor wire. Joshua flipped the guardsman's uni-form jacket over these, then scrambled rapidly upward—the sharp razor wire sliced right through the wool cloth and into his knees and forearms, but he hardly noticed—and launched himself over the top and into the air. His stomach dropped first, and then he did, landing on all fours, jolted but unhurt.

(There were also electronic sensors in the fence, that would now tell the security people back at the command post—and whoever might be looking at the right instrument panel in the plant's control section as well—that it had been breached, but Joshua hardly cared. He was in; it was already done.)

Hands and knees smarted from the fall, and the razor cuts on his limbs stung, but he ignored all that. Leaping lightly to his feet, he picked up the rifle, held it at a loose port arms angled across his chest, and started to walk.

The land inside the fence was manicured, but cleverly, to give the illusion of unspoiled woodland glade. Joshua strode as though through a park, quickly out of sight of the fence, moving steadily up the gradual slope.

(Deep down inside, repressed, hardly noticeable, Joshua felt absolute terror. What am I doing? What have I done? What's happening to me? But these adrenaline flutters of fear were almost completely overpowered, like a weak radio signal buried beneath a more powerful one, overpowered by glorious feelings of pride and pleasure in his own quick sure competence, the skill and swiftness and determination with which he moved. But *why*? What am I doing? *Why?* Ah, but the why didn't matter; the dexterity, the adroitness, was all.)

His red-rimmed eyes surveyed the scene with satisfaction. What a beautiful world. Where else in the universe are there such greens? He strode up the gradual hill, feeling the young strength in his body, delighting in it, but before he reached the crest, from where he would surely be able to see the plant's buildings, a man stepped out from behind a quince bush ahead of him and said, "That's as far as you go."

"I don't think so," Joshua said, and swung the rifle down to fire from the hip, quickly, effortlessly, as though with the deftness of long practice, only to hear the *click* of emptiness.

The damn guardsmen! They patrol with *unloaded weapons*? What kind of stupidity is this? The *Boy Scouts* are better prepared!

(Who is that man? Why do I hate him so? Why am I so afraid? Why am I *not* afraid? How can I stop these arms, these legs, this brain? Oh, please, please, please, how can I *stop*?)

The man in Joshua's path was large and burly, with heavy shoulders and a narrow waist. He wore lace-up woodsman's boots, thick dark corduroy trousers, a dark flannel shirt. He seemed to be unarmed.

(How did he get in here, inside the fence? Is he one of the terrorists? What's happening? Why do I hate him? Oh, please, please, let me drop to my knees in front of him and beg for mercy. Heal me. Cure me. Save me.)

Joshua stepped quickly forward, reversing the rifle, grabbing it two-handed by the barrel, swinging it back and then around, fast and hard and vicious, aimed at the man's head. But the man ducked below the swing, his left hand coming up, fingers snapping like a bear trap onto the rifle butt, yanking it away as he crouched low, knees bent, and pivoted all the way around in a tight low circle, like a stunt dancer on ice.

The rifle was torn from Joshua's grip, the front sight gouging flesh from both palms, and now the man had it and was straightening, his jaw set, expression grim. Without a second's hesitation, Joshua spun to his right and ran, leaping over rocks and roots like a deer, ducking below tree branches, swiveling this way and that through the shrubbery like the finest running back in football history.

Was the creature following? Joshua didn't waste time looking back. He ran and ran, angling to his left, uphill, toward the plant.

A clearer section, the grass longer than the groundsmen normally kept it, the crest of the ridge just ahead. Joshua dashed toward that height, and a sudden blow in the middle of his back, a hard powerful hit as though from a battering ram, drove him forward and down, to skid painfully on the grassy ground, and lie there for an instant, breathless, stunned.

Many aches and pains crowded his body, demanding attention, but he had no time. Not for the racked wheezing of his lungs, not for the cuts and bruises, not for the grinding ache in his back as though bones had been broken, not for the sting of tears in his red-rimmed eyes. He rolled over, struggling upward, and saw *it*, the man, loping this way up the grade.

(What did he hit me with? What is he doing? What am *I* doing? Oh, let me out of this!)

"You won't stop me!" Joshua cried, his voice harsh and hoarse and rasping in his strained throat. "You can stop *this* thing, but you won't stop *me*!"

"A thousand times I'll stop you," the man said, coming to a stop, standing over Joshua, staring down at him with hate and contempt. "And a thousand times I'll give you a little lesson."

The worst pain of his life seared through Joshua, burning him, cauterizing him, arching his back, twisting his fingers into claws. He tried to scream, but *something* was scrambling up his esophagus, through his throat, across his trembling tongue, out past his stretched and grimacing lips. And out his straining ears, out his flaring nostrils, out his staring eyes.

Joshua dropped back onto the ground like a rag doll abandoned in mid-play. He was waking from a nightmare; or *into* a nightmare. His head lolled to the right, his bleary unfocused eyes saw the rabbit bounding away through the grass, saw it leap high and suddenly burst into flame, saw it fall to earth a charred lump, a smoking coal.

He forced his neck muscles to work, he turned his head till he stared upward. The man still stood there, huge and dark against the morning sky, head turning back and forth, looking for something more, something more.

"Help." His voice was a croak, it was scarcely a voice at all. "Help me."

The man looked down, as though surprised to see him there. "Yes, of course," he said, with great gentleness, and came down to one knee. He leaned forward, eyes soothing, arm outstretched. His large warm comforting hand moved downward over Joshua's face, and Joshua Hardwick exhaled his last breath.

39

Susan awoke again this morning in Andy's arms, and again this morning it was the most blissful possible way she could imagine to come awake. Especially this morning. Of all times, this morning.

This was the day after her FBI interview. Identification of only two of the band of insane terrorists who had taken over the Green Meadow Nuclear Power Plant upstate had so far been made, but one of them was Grigor! Susan hadn't been able to believe it at first—not humorous, sensible, calm, inoffensive Grigor—and even when she'd come to accept it she hadn't realized what it meant for *her*. She hadn't thought about the fact that she was, after all, the person who had brought Grigor to the United States.

Yesterday morning, she and Andy had been eating their minimal breakfasts together—coffee, orange juice, English muffins—and watching a special report on *Today* about the siege at the nuclear plant, when the doorbell rang. Well, no; Andy had been watching the report, with that intense interest he sometimes displayed and which she found so impressive, as though he were some incredibly vast energy system harnessed just for her, and she had been ignoring the television set to gaze around instead in quiet satisfaction at how pleasant and appropriate Andy's possessions looked in her apartment—they'd been living together less than a week, and she was not at all used to it yet—and that was when the doorbell rang.

They frowned at one another, in surprise; nobody *ever* rang the bell this early in the morning. She said, half whispered, "Who could it be?"

"I'll bet you," Andy said, nodding at the TV set, "it has something to do with Grigor."

So she was already half-prepared when she asked who it was through the intercom and the nasally distorted voice said, "FBI, Miss Carrigan."

Two of them came up, one white and one black, both male, both about thirty-five, both smooth and affectless, as though they'd perfected their characterizations by watching fictional FBI men on television. They showed identification, and asked both Susan and Andy to do the same, the black one copying down their driver's license numbers into a small notebook while the white one verified Andy's guess that the subject of their visit was Grigor Basmyonov.

Susan briefly described how she'd happened to meet Grigor, and how she'd happened to describe his case to her doctor cousin, and at first they seemed satisfied, but then they asked her if she could come down to the FBI office to make a statement. "But I have a job," she protested, feeling the first flutters of panic. "I should be leaving right now."

"That's all right," the black one said. "Any time today. How about four o'clock?"

So that was agreed, and they told her which office to go to in the building, which they said was at 26 Federal Plaza, an address that meant nothing at all to Susan (nor would it have to any other New Yorker). It turned out to be one of those made-up addresses, and to actually be a building on Broadway, downtown, between Thomas and Worth streets.

After they left, Susan said, "You don't think they think I'm one of them, do you? Andy?"

"Of course not," Andy assured her. "They just want to know everything they can find out about Grigor, that's all. Maybe something you tell them can help them negotiate with him."

"Poor Grigor," Susan said, thinking again how she'd abandoned him since meeting Andy. "And poor me."

"It won't be bad," he said, stroking her arm, encouraging her. "You'll just tell them the truth, and that'll be the end of it."

"I'll hate every second I'm down there."

"I'll be with you in spirit," he said, and grinned. "If that helps."

"It does," she told him.

•   •   •

And it did.

At work, Susan explained the situation—her co-workers already knew about her connection with the doomed Russian fire fighter, but hadn't made the link with the terrorist in the nuclear plant—and at four o'clock she kept her appointment.

Those two hours with the FBI agents—not the original pair but three new ones, two of them women, but all with that same impersonality—were grueling and frightening and bewildering, and left her with a terrible case of the shakes. It soon became obvious they didn't actually suspect her of anything, didn't believe she was part of some vast conspiracy to bring Grigor Basmyonov to America just so he could run a hijacked nuclear power plant, but they couldn't help their *manner,* which kept signaling Susan that she was guilty, she was in their power, her only hope was to confess all and throw herself on their non-existent mercy.

They asked a million questions, many of them repetitive, and when at last they were finished she was as drained and limp as vegetables that have been used for soup stock. She left 26 Federal Plaza like a shell-shock victim, and there was Andy! Waiting for her, on the sidewalk, on the real world's Broadway.

"How long have you *been* here?" she asked, delighted and unbelieving and warmed and restored by the sight of him.

He shrugged it off. "Not long." But he must have been there for a *long* time, to be sure he hadn't already missed her.

She let it go, accepting the gesture for the loving kindness it was, and let him lead her through a restorative evening of a good dinner out, a movie—a comedy this time, called *Mysterious Ways*—and lovely love back in the apartment.

The word "love" had not passed between them yet. Susan was afraid to say it, afraid it might scare him away, and maybe he too was uncertain how to move the relationship to a deeper level. But that was all right, they had time. All the time in the world.

Waking this morning when the radio alarm started playing its golden oldies—"All things must pass a-way"—finding herself still in his arms, she smiled as she snuggled closer to his chest, their combined warmth in her nose like the aroma of the nest: home. Her eyes closed again. She floated with him in warm space.

He stirred. Sleepily, he mumbled, "Time to get up."

Oh, well; yes. Moving around, freeing herself from the covers, she rose up onto one elbow and smiled at his grizzly face. His eyes were still half-closed. "Still here, I see," she said.

His smile was as lazy as she felt. "I don't disappear that easily," he said, and tousled her hair.

Ananayel

"I don't disappear that easily," I said, and tousled her hair.

But I do, don't I? Or I will. Or she will, in fact. I'll still be around, but she'll disappear very easily indeed.

Per our agreement, she got up first, since she takes longer in the bathroom, and I lay a bit longer in bed, brooding. (Already we are working out these fine points of cohabitation.) But what am I going to do with her, what am I going to do with Susan? It's absurd, I know it's absurd, but I want to go on pleasing her, watching her reactions. I have never felt so enjoyably at *service* before.

I even want to go on inhabiting this body, which, for all its oafish awkwardness, has been serving me well. And the fact is, the way the humans have structured their civilizations, their bodies aren't even that much of a liability. Chairs, automobiles, restaurants; they have worked out fairly ingenious and even enjoyable ways of overcoming their limitations.

But what am I to do about *Susan*? I've thought and thought, and there's simply no way to take her with me, to pluck her off the Earth before it transmogrifies. How would I do it? Where and how would she live? In a bubble of air and soil from her former planet? First she would lose her mind—I mean, *immediately* she would lose her mind—and then she would pine and die.

Susan is of this place. More, she is of this place and *time*. There would be no life for her in the deep spaces of the real, alone, the last of her kind, with no companion but an amorphism she's expected to call *Andy*. If I'm going to think about this, I at least have to think realistically.

But I don't want to lose her. I don't want to stop knowing her, that's the long and the short of it. I don't want to stop being Andy, and I don't want to stop being in love with Susan. (We haven't said the word, humans are often wary of that word, but we both know.)

I have choice, I know that, I have free will, but on what could I bend that will? Where is the alternative? If Susan stays on this Earth, she will be snuffed at the same instant as every other creature, every plant, every molecule of air. But where could she go instead? Nowhere. So where is the choice?

40

"I'm sorry, Congressman," Reed Stockton said, "but I just can't go along with it."

Congressman Stephen Schlurn leaned forward, his reddened eyes burning into Reed's. "Do you know who you're talking to, young man?"

Yes, he did, Reed Stockton knew exactly who he was talking to, worse luck. A hell of a way to start a new job; first day, first *morning*, and he has to stand up and say no to a hotshot congressman, in fact the congressman in whose district Green Meadow III Nuclear Power Plant festered, and who had a sudden urge to be a . . . a what? A hero? A media star?

A headache and a jerk, in Reed Stockton's opinion. "I know who you are, sir," he said, being both firm and respectful, "and I have to tell you, it wouldn't matter if you were the president, I'd still have to say the same thing."

The congressman shook his head, showing how exasperated he'd been made by Reed's stupidity. "It's not as though," he said, "I'm talking about going in there *alone*. I want you with me, that's the whole point."

"Congressman," Reed said, "I have to tell you this is my first day as PID, and I'm not really prepared to put my job on the line on any one person's say-so. My predecessor, a fellow named Hardwick—"

"I heard about him," Schlurn said. Hardwick's shocking bewildering finish was being downplayed in public as much as possible, but of course Congressman Schlurn would have his sources, he would know all about it. "Went crazy, didn't he?"

"Yes, sir. Killed a national guardsman with a rock, went over the fence with the man's rifle, and apparently killed himself inside. The helicopters have seen what's almost certainly his body."

"I fail to understand," Schlurn said, "what that garish adventure has to do with you and me. I want *us*, representing the people and the media, to walk openly and boldly straight through that main gate and down to the plant and *talk* to these people, one on one. All these telephone negotiations aren't doing a damn thing, and I don't care if you only got the job ten minutes ago, you still have to know I'm right about that."

Give me strength, Lord, Reed Stockton prayed, and he meant it. He was a religious person, raised a Methodist by devout parents, married to a devout girl himself, the two of them raising their first child—with more to come, God willing—the same way. When troubled or harassed, Reed prayed for help, for guidance, for strength, and it seemed to him his prayers were always answered.

And they would be again this time. *Knowing* that God was giving him eloquence, Reed said, "Sir, you may be absolutely right about everything you say. You're an intelligent man, and a very persuasive man, and I wouldn't doubt for a second that *if* you could get into a face-to-face discussion with the unfortunate people sitting in at the plant right now you would very eloquently—"

"Sitting in?" Schlurn stared at him with revulsion. "Did you say sitting in?"

"Yes, sir, Congressman Schlurn, I did." Reed permitted himself a small pleased smile. "And frankly, sir, I'm proud of it. That was my idea."

"Your idea."

"Yes, sir. When I took over this morning, there was a briefing session with General Bloodmore and the other people in charge, and I made that suggestion and they accepted it at once. And thanked me, sir."

"Sitting in," repeated Schlurn.

"It's a much less emotive word than anything else that has been used," Reed explained. "Talking about hostages, and terrorists, and invasions, and captures, and threats and all that, it simply serves to escalate the danger quotient. Sir, I was a poli sci major at Cal Tech, with a minor in communications history, and I like to think that I understand what words do in public discourse. I think of that as my specialty. And to say that what we have to deal with here is a sit-in suggests the possibility for reason and discussion on both sides of the issue. It suggests a situation that isn't *really* dangerous."

"But," Schlurn said, "it is really dangerous."

"Sir, we don't want to emphasize that with the folk outside. Particularly those within one hundred and twenty-five miles of the plant. Which includes, as you know, New York City."

Schlurn considered. He and Reed were standing on opposite sides of Reed's desk—formerly poor Hardwick's desk—in the Press Office trailer, surrounded by activity they'd both been ignoring: secretaries typing, telephoning, making copies. Now Schlurn, with those painful-looking red eyes as though he hadn't slept for a week—dreaming up this insane scheme, no doubt—looked around the trailer, looked back at Reed, and in a new low voice, calmer than before, said, "I'm not going to persuade you, am I?"

"To let you on-site, sir? And to go with you? No, sir, you aren't."

"The idea of yourself becoming a media figure has no appeal to you."

Reed smiled thinly. He *used* the media, he didn't subscribe to it. "No, sir," he said.

"No, I can see that. Is there a men's room?"

"Of course, sir."

Reed, magnanimous in victory, was solicitous in pointing the way, and beamed at the congressman's back as Schlurn stumped off.

Eloquence, that's all it ever took. Eloquence and calm.

Reed, pleased and relieved at having survived his first crisis in the new job, sat at the desk and went back to sorting through the vast collection of messages left unreturned by poor Hardwick, who hadn't survived his last crisis at all, whatever it had been.

Five minutes later the congressman was back, looking better than before, calmer and more in control of himself. Even his eyes were clearer. He said, "Reed, I want to thank you."

Reed jumped to his feet, scattering message memos. "Yes, sir!"

"That was a dumb idea I had," Schlurn said. "I woke up with it this morning, and it just seemed great, and I couldn't get it out of my head all day. What I needed was a calm rational person to look at me and say you're crazy, and I'm grateful to you for doing it."

"Oh, Congressman," Reed stammered, "I never meant to suggest, uh, suggest . . ."

"Don't worry about it, Reed, you were right," Schlurn told him, and grinned in a friendly reassuring way, and slowly shook his head. "I don't know what got into me," he said.

How do I get in there? *How?*

With all the temporal and heavenly powers *both* blocking my way, with them *all* united against me, guards and angels and fences and force fields all opposed to my will, how do I get my hands on that miserable quintet, those hopeless pawns? *How?*

HOW? HOOOOOOWWWW!!!

And how much time have I left, to get there?

41

Frank didn't want any chummy relationships developing between his group and the hostages, the eight staff members kept here to run the plant under the eye of Grigor, but what could he do? Human beings interact. It's easier to be friendly, or at least courteous, than impersonal and aloof.

So it wasn't long before Grigor was saying, "Rosie, would you bring me that printout, please?" or "Mark, it's time to check the pressure gauges," or even, "Fran, I'm thirsty, could you get me a glass of water? Thank you."

Frank wasted a little breath arguing against this fraternization at first, but gave up when he saw he wasn't getting anywhere. And in any case it was easier for him, too, to address the hostages by name, to say "please" and "thank you," to act as though this was just some kind of stupid boat ride they were all taking together, instead of what it was.

So they knew the hostages' first names, and after a while even some of their backgrounds and personal lives. And the hostages knew Grigor's and Kwan's names, because the whole world knew their names. Early in the negotiations with the people outside, Grigor had announced both of their names and histories, to demonstrate the seriousness and capability of the people who'd taken over, and to start to get their stories out. And to show, as well, that they believed they had nothing to lose.

The hostages—and the world—didn't know Frank's name, or Maria Elena's, because on that he insisted, firmly believing they were going to pull this caper off somehow. And they didn't know Pami's name because they didn't need to

know it. Pami had gone all boneless and weak the minute
they'd established control of this place, as though that's all
she'd been holding herself together for, and she spent most
of her time now either asleep in the dayroom or slumped in
a chair, glowering at the world around her with sunken eyes.
There was no making human contact with Pami, not by the
hostages and not even by her companions.

Frank had expected Grigor also to have collapsed by now,
to be of little more than symbolic use once they'd got
themselves inside the plant, but that emaciated body seemed
to find sustenance and fresh vigor here in the control
section. Dealing with the plant and the hostages, negotiating
with the thickheaded officials outside, it all gave him a wiry
energy that made him move as though he were plugged into
his own electric source.

Kwan was the one losing vigor, particularly after the
television announced he was simply a common crook after
all, and not a revolutionary, not a hero of Tiananmen Square.
This was two days after Grigor had given the names to the
media. Apparently there was no way for them to smear the
hero fireman of Chernobyl, but the Chinese government was
happy to announce that Li Kwan was no more than a
garden-variety criminal, lying about his past in an effort to
gain political sanctuary. And the American State Department, for reasons of its own—no doubt solid hardheaded
realistic mature reasons—was happy to announce it had
studied the documents the Chinese government had provided
as "proof" and to pronounce them genuine.

"That's all right, Kwan," Frank said, trying to cheer him
up, "the lie comes apart, don't worry about it. You already
had a lotta ink, right? A lotta stuff in the newspapers about
who you really are."

Kwan shrugged, silent little face bitter, not caring.

"You'll get your story out," Frank told him, and then
made a mistake. "You'll have plenty of time after this is all
over," he said.

Kwan looked at him, with painted-on eyes. Frank cleared

his throat, and blinked, and patted Kwan on the shoulder, and left him there.

Despite the weirdness of the situation, despite its unprecedented craziness, life soon settled into a kind of routine, which was something else Frank didn't want or need. What he wanted and needed was steady forward movement, negotiation and then planning out the final details of the endgame and then doing it and home free. Stasis was his enemy. Being stuck here in stalemate could only help the people outside, who didn't have this fragile cat's cradle to hold together.

Meanwhile, nothing was getting accomplished. Their grip on the plant was secure, but somehow that didn't mean as much as it should. The propaganda effect, for Grigor and Kwan, was just about non-existent, buried within the media's overriding interest in the caper. Maria Elena's more general ecologic point couldn't seem to get made at all. And Frank wasn't getting his money.

The way that part was supposed to work, at the final moment Frank was to split off from the rest of them. The others all had their propaganda objectives, so were willing to let themselves be captured to accomplish their agenda. So, assuming the goddamn stumble-minded officials finally did come around to agree on the five-mil ransom, Grigor would tell them to put it in suitcases in a car just outside the gate, and that a member of the group would go out and drive the car away.

The story was, if the driver wasn't arrested or followed, and if he was permitted to get clear away, he would telephone the plant six hours later and tell his partners still inside that everything was okay. No phone call, the partners would destroy the plant. (In reality, Frank would just clear out, and then the others would surrender. He'd like to take Maria along, if she'd go, but that didn't seem likely.)

First, though, the morons outside had to get the idea into their thick heads that they had to come up with the five mil. *Had* to come up with it, or they could kiss their goddamn nuclear power plant goodbye.

And time was getting short.

• • •

Pami did the most sleeping, and even when she was awake she was listless and cranky, like a colicky child. Frank slept the least, driven by nervous energy, but they all, invaders and hostages alike, took their turns on the sofas in the dayroom, covered by the thin cotton blankets normally kept in a supply closet in case an emergency ever arose in which staffers would have to remain at the plant for an extended period of time. (Societal breakdown outside the perimeter had been the emergency the planners had been thinking of, not the standoff that now existed.)

The only television set was also in the dayroom. They kept it on all the time, to see how the world was perceiving their situation, but turned the volume low, since there were always sleepers in the room. It was the afternoon of the fifth day of the siege that Dr. Philpott was first mentioned on that set.

Frank and two female staffers were watching at the moment, sitting close to the set in order to hear it, with Maria Elena and Pami and two other staffers asleep across the room, and Grigor and Kwan and the remaining four staff members out in the main control room. "To this point, nothing has been heard of the situation of Dr. Marlon Philpott, the eminent scientist whose controversial experiments with anti-gravity led to the strike at Green Meadow, which in turn—"

Frank looked away from the set. The two women watching the program with him looked scared. You could see them praying he wouldn't ask any questions. But their prayers were not to be answered.

• • •

Dr. Philpott stared at the TV set in the lounge. "Antigravity? What the *hell* are they talking about?"

"Professor," Cindy said, sounding frightened and looking

wide-eyed as she brushed the hair out of her eyes, "they *told*. They weren't supposed to tell."

And of course that was true. The level of lay ignorance demonstrated by that anti-gravity reference had distracted him from the even more egregious error in that announcement: they weren't supposed to tell.

The media knew he was hidden in here, of course. He was the closest thing to a celebrity connected with Green Meadow, so naturally the media would have sought him out at the very beginning of the crisis, for statements and comments and interviews and all that, and God knows the authorities had initially *wanted* him out of here. But he'd convinced them, finally, after a number of phone calls— fortunately, the phones in here didn't have to go through any switching system that the terrorists would see—that both he and the lab were safer, that the whole plant would be safer, if he stayed right here. (He didn't tell them he was continuing his experiment, merely that he was "safeguarding" it; a white lie, that's all, a venial sin of omission.)

But the media wasn't supposed to tell. As one of the officials he'd talked to on the phone had said, there would be a "news blackout" on the whereabouts of the eminent Dr. Marlon Philpott until this emergency was over. (And why were all scientists "eminent," anyway?)

But, as ever in human affairs, there's always someone who didn't get the message, some temporary assistant sub-editor in precisely the wrong place at the wrong time. "All we can hope," Philpott said, "is that the terrorists are too busy to watch television." And he went back into the lab to see how Chang and the infinitely minute speck of *something* in the deuterium was coming along.

•   •   •

"This raises the ante," Frank said. "I'll go in that lab there and get him and bring him here and put him on the phone with those assholes, and maybe we'll start to get somewhere."

"I should come with you," Grigor said. "We're not sure what's happening in that lab."

"I must come, too," Maria Elena said. "I want to see this laboratory. I want to see what this man is doing."

"You don't leave *me* in here with these people," Pami said. She'd had trouble waking up just now, and was more irritable than ever.

"Well, somebody's gotta keep an eye on the store," Frank said.

"You know," Grigor told him, "most of this is automated, it's merely a matter of watching the gauges. We could lock the staff in the dayroom while we're gone, five or ten minutes. We would bring Philpott here, and let them out again."

"But who looks at the gauges?"

"Kwan."

Frank looked over at Kwan, huddled in a chair in the corner, lost in his own helpless despairing rage. "We'll see," Frank said, and went over to him. "Kwan? You get the idea?"

Kwan looked at him without response.

Frank said, "We'll lock these people up, go over and get the mad scientist, and bring him back. You sit at the controls there, keep an eye on things. If it looks like something's gonna blow, you fix it, right?"

Kwan's head lifted slightly. A faint gleam came into those dead eyes.

Frank touched his shoulder, feeling its bony hardness, tense as a bridge cable. "You don't wreck it, okay? Not yet. I tell you what: if the time comes to say screw it, let er rip, you'll be the guy to do it. Okay?"

A faint smile touched those gray lips.

Frank grinned at him. "You'd like to blow the whole thing, wouldn't you? China and everybody."

With those eyes, and that smile, on that fleshless face, Kwan looked like a death's head.

•   •   •

No one was in the lounge to watch the television set three minutes later, when a scared-looking newsreader tried to shut the barn door, now that the horse was out and off and running. "From his vacation home in East Hampton, Long Island, the eminent scientist Dr. Marlon Philpott today broke his silence on . . ."

In the lab, Dr. Philpott broke a long tense silence to whisper, "It's there." He sounded as though he'd seen God. "Chang? Cindy? It's in there."

It was. This time it was. The radiation monitor showed definite gamma ray activity in the holding ring. Somewhere within the swirling deuterium something now existed that hadn't been there before. It had been trying to be born for some time, for weeks, as high-speed streams of heavy ions had been directed into collision courses inside the holding ring. But to get a specific result out of these collisions was as chancy and difficult as getting a specific result out of *any* collision; like smashing two Hondas together and coming out with one Cadillac. Or like throwing a deck of cards into the air and having them land, all faceup, in exact sequence by suit and number.

Well, this time they had it. And they would keep it. While Philpott and Cindy watched, barely breathing, Chang operated the switching circuit that would transfer the—*thing*—from the holding ring to the storage bottle. "Gamma radiation has stopped in the holding ring," Chang announced.

"Then it's in the bottle."

Chang looked stricken. "There's no gamma activity from the bottle!"

"Strange matter," Philpott reminded him, "only gives off radiation while it's being fed, that's one of the reasons it's so safe. Shoot deuterium across the center of the bottle.''

"A reaction!" Chang's round face beamed with delight.

"So it's real," Philpott said, as though he *still* hadn't really believed it, not even one minute ago. His mouth was dry. Knowing that something was real was in no way the same thing as experiencing it; the difference between being out in a blizzard and looking at a snowscape on a Christmas card.

Held poised in the storage bottle was a piece of strange matter, known as an S-drop. The storage bottle itself was a simple glass vacuum jug on a table, containing one positive and one negative hemispherical electrode, with the S-drop suspended by electric current between them. Facing the bottle, a video camera was lined up with an ordinary bare light bulb on the other side, the S-drop centered midway between the two. The camera informed the computer at which Chang sat, and the computer directed the power supply in maintaining the equilibrium of the S-drop. To make the S-drop fall—to the terror of alarmists such as Dr. Delantero—all one had to do was wave a hand in front of the video camera. Dr. Philpott would do it himself, simply to prove Dr. Delantero wrong in the presence of these two graduate student witnesses, but it would ruin the experiment, and who knew how long it would be before he could produce another such beneficial collision?

Chang broke into the self-satisfaction of Philpott's thoughts, saying, "Professor, it's getting larger and a whole lot heavier."

"What? Are you still feeding it?"

"Well, yes, sir."

"Turn it off," Philpott told him. "Turn off the deuterium. If that drop gets much larger, I won't be able to use it. In fact, we won't be able to *hold* it."

Leaning close to the bottle, vision hampered by the guidance light to his left, Philpott peered into the center of that enclosed airless space. Could he see it, actually see it? A speck? Or was that wishful thinking?

* * *

Once Frank had convinced the staffers he really would shoot the locks off the lab doors, no matter how much that might startle Dr. Philpott or louse up his experiments, it seemed they had keys to that building after all. "I'll tell him you fought like hell," he promised, as he locked them into the dayroom.

Then it turned out Grigor couldn't walk, not more than a dozen steps. "I'm sorry, Frank," he said, with a shamed smile. "I think I hid this from the staff people—"

"You hid it from us all."

"But I cannot possibly walk from here to another building."

"No problem," Frank said. "I'll carry you."

He did, and Maria Elena damn near had to carry Pami, too. She was also a lot weaker than anybody had known, staggering like a crackhead forced to walk in the middle of the high. Maria Elena took her arm and helped her steer a straight line.

It was the first they'd been outside since they'd taken over the plant, the first they'd *seen* the outside. It was a bright day, but not sunny, with very high white clouds and low humidity, so that the whole world had a look of flat clarity. The air wasn't really cold, but there was still a touch of oncoming winter in its crispness, a sharp sensation in the nose, too faint to be called a smell. The deciduous trees and shrubs were far along in their seasonal color display, so that the conifers looked an even darker green.

The concrete paths curving between the buildings were clean and neat and empty, as though these four were the last people on Earth, the slope-shouldered man carrying the feather-light bundle of the second man, the sturdily built woman leading the skinny little black girl who tottered and reeled as though about to fall at every step. The four made their slow and uneven way along the paths toward the lab, moving as though to the tinny sound of a toy piano that only they could hear.

The lab beyond the turbine building was the smallest of the structures within the plant perimeter. A separate windowless concrete-block rectangle two stories high, it had entrances on three sides. The main front entrance, a pair of black metal doors that faced a neat curving concrete path flanked by low tasteful plantings, had been dead-bolted on the inside, in addition to the locks, so they couldn't get in that way.

"Wait," Frank told his group, and walked around to the left, to the single door, also black metal, that opened onto a path directly to the nearby turbine building. This too had been bolted on the inside.

"They're beginning to piss me off," Frank informed the others, as he walked by on his way to the right side entrance, another pair of black metal doors, this one on a higher level, opening onto a loading dock over a blacktop driveway. A dozen black plastic trash cans were lined up on the loading dock, along the wall beside the doors. This was where deliveries were made and unwanted materials taken out, and the construction of the loading dock and doors had made dead bolts impractical here. Frank opened the two locks, and then the right-hand door. "More like it," he said, and went back to get the others.

•   •   •

Seated on a lab stool, leaning on a metal table, Philpott was dictating, and Cindy was taking it down in her private shorthand:

"The S-drop is stable. It is not, as many of my fellow scientists feared or hoped, or at least theorized, quasistable. It has not decayed into a different form. The radiation monitor shows gamma ray activity where we know the S-drop to be. It stops when we stop feeding the drop, and begins again when the drop is fed. At this point, its mass is still below the lowest limits of human vision, but when the current disturbance here at the facility has come to an end, it is my intention to feed the drop further, until it is large enough to be seen by the naked eye. To make it any larger than that, however—''

''Professor.''

There was something so strange in Chang's voice that Philpott didn't even think to protest at the interruption. He looked over at the boy, and saw him staring toward the corridor door. Pretending the fear he felt was only irritation, Philpott swiveled around on the stool.

42

The four people who stepped into the lab room were not at all what Philpott had expected the invaders of the plant to be. Of the four, only the man waving the pistol with such easy familiarity looked at all like Philpott's idea of a terrorist. And only the rather exotic-looking woman had anything of the manner of a fanatic. The other man and woman were both very obviously sick; horribly sick, both of them.

Yes, of course. The man would be the Russian, the spokesman for the group, the fireman who'd been poisoned at Chernobyl. Could the black woman also have been there? That seemed so unlikely, and yet she was clearly as sick as the Russian. In fact, there was such an air of hopelessness and dejection and desperation about this entire quartet that Philpott's first immediate reaction was pity.

A reaction that didn't last. Quasistable, it immediately decayed into irritation and outrage. ''I suppose we must obey your orders now,'' he said, speaking to the man with the pistol, the obvious leader. "But I would ask you please not to disturb anything in this room. You can gain nothing by it, and I could lose a great deal."

"I saw you on television," the man said.

Of course. If this is fame, Philpott thought, I'd prefer to do without it. "I have been on television," he agreed.

"You're gonna be on television again," the man said, with a faint tough-guy smile that didn't fool Philpott for a second. "When you explain how you yourself, all by yourself, made the breakthrough that got us all out of this place and let everybody get back to normal."

Philpott's smile now was pitying; but sardonically and deliberately so. "Is that what you think?" he said. "That *I* will make any difference?"

"Sure you will." The man gestured with the pistol. "They want their power plant back, but they don't think we're serious about that. They'll want *you* back even more, and you can talk. You can let them know we really are serious."

Philpott had only a few seconds to decide how to handle this. Go along with them, keep quiet, agree to their fantasies? Or disabuse them of the notion they would ever under any circumstances successfully complete whatever childish scheme they were acting out here?

Marlon Philpott was, first and foremost, a scientist, a rational man. His strong tendency would have been to come down on the side of reality versus fantasy in any case, but this time there was an even more cogent reason to be realistic from the outset with these people: their fantasies were keeping a lot of men and women from getting on with their normal lives. Including, now, himself.

If this unfortunate incident were to end without bloodshed, it seemed to Philpott, it would only happen *after* the invaders had accepted the hopelessness of their position. Therefore, he said, "I'm sorry, but you know, it really won't work. I'll do what you say, of course—you have the gun—but please, when it fails, don't put the blame on me.''

There was such calm conviction in his words that they had no choice but to hear them, to at least think about what he was saying. The Russian, who had crossed to sit on the nearest stool while Philpott was speaking, and who leaned his back now wearily—weakly—against the wall, said, ''Why must we fail?''

He sounds reasonable, Philpott thought, surprised and saddened by the realization. With unexpected empathy, he suddenly saw the route—like tracking a molecule through its invisible journey—whereby an ordinary small-town fireman could be transformed by something like Chernobyl not merely into a person subsumed by his terminal illness but into *this* person, blundering into this totally untenable position in one last doomed effort to make his life have meant something.

Concentration on his specialty had made Philpott narrow and cold in his dealings with other human beings, but he was an intelligent man, and he was capable of sympathetic and emotional responses to other individuals when his attention had been caught. At this moment, his attention was caught.

Basmyonov, Philpott suddenly remembered, glad to have retained the name from the television reports. ''Mr. Basmyonov,'' he said, with passable Russian inflection, the accent on the penultimate syllable, ''the world is a rather well organized place, all in all. The damage you can do here is, at its worst, infinitesimal in comparison with the planet, with all the hundreds of nuclear power plants producing electricity around the globe, with the *thousands* of power plants of other types. In human terms, more people are being *conceived* at this moment than you and this plant could possibly kill. I'm sorry, I don't mean to make light of your situation, but what you people are doing is a very small blip on the screen. They can afford to outwait you. Stall, talk, negotiate, never come to any conclusion. And meantime, your food is running low. It certainly is in here. We've eaten just about every bit of junk food we had in the lounge.''

The thin black woman slid slowly down the wall behind her and sat on the floor, head lolling, like a doll left behind when the family moved. The other woman stooped as though to help her, but there was nothing to be done, so she straightened again. The black woman's eyes were glazed, mouth slack. She seemed to take no interest in anything that was being said.

The Russian said, "But why isn't it easier for them to negotiate?''

It was the exotic-looking woman who answered before Philpott could, turning her attention away from the woman seated on the floor. "*Authority,*" she said, with such disgust it was as though the word were a dead mouse she had found on her tongue. "Their authority must be unquestioned. They must be permitted to do what *they* want with *their* world. In Brazil, they killed entire valleys, killed the people, the trees, the waters, the ground, and no one was permitted to question their right to do so.''

So that's *your* bugbear, Philpott thought, and said, "I wouldn't phrase it quite the same way, but yes, that's essentially it. All of this was thought out, worked out, in the capitals of the world, years ago. I was on some of the preliminary working panels myself, and I know the decisions, and I know the thinking behind it. No nation can afford to give in even once to nuclear blackmail. It can *never* be seen to be a paying proposition, or it will proliferate, and the carnage would be unbelievable.''

The man with the gun said, scornfully, "They'd let us wreck this place?''

"If you're that mindless, yes. Listen, there are five billion human beings on this Earth. How many do you think you could kill with this plant? I mean, if every circumstance went exactly your way. Thirty thousand? This lady mentioned dead valleys in Brazil. How many more dead valleys could the human race create, and still survive on the planet? Hundreds." To the Russian, he said, "Your nation has managed to destroy an entire sea, the Aral. A huge inland salt sea, mismanaged to a brackish puddle the size of this room. The salt floats in the air. Infants are dying there, because there's salt in their mothers' milk and they can't eat. A vast expanse of your own nation destroyed, with everybody and everything on it, but the Soviet Union goes on. The planet goes on. The human race goes on."

The Russian said, "We're too unimportant, you mean."

"All of us are," Philpott agreed. "You, I, the negotiators, all of us."

The man with the gun said, "What if we start shooting hostages?"

Philpott frowned at him. "I don't think you will," he said, "but you might. If you do, communication will stop. They would write us all off, and just wait."

"For us to wreck the plant." That false scorn was there again, the man trying to convince himself of his potency; but of course failing.

Philpott said, "I'll tell you what I think is happening out there right now. I believe the area in front of the gate is full of fire trucks and other emergency equipment. I believe there are hundreds, perhaps even more than a thousand, people in radiation suits, poised and ready. The instant you give any indication that you are damaging the plant, they will pour in here to contain that damage as best they can. As the weather reports on television have been telling us, civilization has been getting a lucky break and you an unlucky one—"

"Civilization," the exotic woman spat, and *her* scorn was no affectation.

Philpott looked at her. "I can see civilization has harmed you," he said. "It does that. I can't feel your pain, of course, but I still believe human civilization is worth the price we pay."

"The price you pay, or the price I pay?"

Philpott spread his hands. "We all make that decision for ourselves." Turning back to the armed man, he said, "What I was saying about the weather. There are neither high winds nor rain anywhere in the forecast, and those are the two weather modes that would spread radiation and destruction the farthest. Given the current weather, and given the emergency teams no doubt waiting outside the perimeter, there's a very good chance they can contain the damage to this immediate area only."

"*You'll* die," the armed man pointed out, "along with the rest of us."

Philpott sighed. "I know that. But what am I to do? It frightens me, naturally, and it saddens me, just when I've—" He glanced toward the storage bottle with its invisible S-drop. His triumph; too late?

Suddenly he realized he shouldn't draw their attention to it. "That's why I hope," he said, more loudly, looking at the armed man, "I can convince you to give this up. So far, I believe you've harmed no one. Two of your partners here are in desperate need of hospitalization, and—"

The thin black woman on the floor roused herself, from what had seemed like a drugged sleep, to say, "No hospital help me. Nothing help me. I'm dead meat."

Philpott pushed forward, concentrating on the armed man. "If you're willing, I could try to negotiate your surrender, terms, lawyers—"

The armed man pointed the gun at Philpott, but not as a threat. It was as though he were pointing a finger. He said, "I'm not going back. I already promised myself that."

The exotic woman wrapped her arms around herself. She looked cold, and utterly bitter. "It's no good," she said. "Nothing ever works. They always win. You can't fight them. It's *their* world."

"I'm not going back," the armed man repeated.

Philpott wasn't sure exactly what he meant—back to a madhouse?—but he could see that *this* was no bluff or braggadocio. He said, "I'm sure we could negotiate some sort of press conference as part of the surrender. You *could* get your story out, we could at least make sure of that much."

The exotic woman said, "That's what they told Li Kwan."

"That's what I'm remembering, too," the armed man said. He looked meaner, colder. He's made a decision, Philpott realized, and I'm not going to like it.

The Russian suddenly said, "Is *that* the experiment you were talking about on television?"

He saw me look that way, Philpott thought. The Russian was pointing directly at the storage bottle on the table on the other side of the room. Philpott's mouth was very dry, his palms wet. He said, "We're still trying to find the particle."

"Are you?" The Russian kept peering at the storage bottle. "Then what is the camera looking at?"

"Nothing."

"Then why is that light bulb on?"

Philpott had no immediate answer, which was wrong. The hesitation gave the game away, even though Chang tried to salvage the situation by blurting out, "We were testing it when you came in."

"You weren't."

The armed man said, "Grigor? What's up?"

The Russian looked at him, and pointed a bony finger toward the storage bottle. "That's the thing they were talking about on television. Him, and the other scientist. The thing that, if it fell down, either nothing would happen or the world would come to an end. The whole world."

The armed man smiled for the first time, a faint smile but an honest one. He said to Philpott, "You're the guy says it's safe."

All at once, Philpott understood the dangerous depths they were in. The back of his neck felt cold, as though some wind from eternity were blowing on him. Choosing his words with great care, he said, "I say I *believe* it is safe. No one yet knows. Dr. Delantero, some others, they might possibly be correct, after all. Nothing is *proved* yet. I would be, of course, extremely cautious with the material until we had tested it a thousand different ways. I would bring Dr. Delantero himself here to—"

The Russian said, "We could test the theory for you, Doctor." To the armed man, he said, "We just go knock that table over."

Philpott could hardly breathe. He hadn't known it was possible to be this afraid. In a choked hoarse voice he said, "Man, why would you do that?"

The Russian's eyes were sunk into his head, as though his brain looked directly out from the center of his skull. He said, "I'm leaving very soon, Doctor. I don't mind the idea of taking everybody with me. I *like* that idea. The best joke I ever thought of." He turned that fleshless head. "Pami? Should we bring them all with us when we go?"

"*Yes!*" You wouldn't have guessed the woman could speak so forcefully, or that she could rise up so powerfully, onto one knee, foot on the floor, before she had to reach out and clutch at the other woman's leg for support.

The Russian shrugged. "And we know how Kwan votes."

They couldn't *all* feel that way. But the exotic woman, holding to the black woman's wrist with one hand, took the armed man's free hand with her other and said, "There's nothing for us here, nothing anywhere. We can't win. Why should it be *their* world?"

"I'm not going back, that's all I know." The armed man showed that chilling smile to Philpott again. "It's a crapshoot, right? Fifty-fifty. Either nothing happens, and we'll figure out what to do next, or our troubles are over. Even money, right?"

"Please," Philpott whispered. "Please don't."

"Fuck you," the armed man said, "and the horse you rode in on." He freed his hand from the woman's, and walked toward the storage bottle.

Please. But Philpott couldn't even speak any more. What have I done?

The armed man approached the table. He reached out for the storage bottle, and the phone rang.

Everybody stopped. The armed man looked over his shoulder at the Russian. The phone rang a second time. "The last phone call in history," the armed man said. "Should we answer it?"

"I will," Cindy said, stumbling in her hurry as she ran to the desk where the phone sat. They all watched her pick up the receiver. "Yes?" A little pause, and she looked around. "Is somebody here named Frank?"

The armed man frowned, thunderously. "Who knows my name? What's going on? Who is it?"

Cindy held the phone out to him. "She says her name is Mary Ann Kelleny."

Ananayel

I just couldn't. When the moment came, when the time came, I couldn't. I saw my future, the high far calm reaches of my future, the long ages of emptiness, the occasional Call, the endless time remembering, and I could not. I could not obey.

It is not only Susan. It is the whole existence of which she is a part, the existence that makes it possible for two humans to be so selflessly bound together, to elevate their mutual caring so far beyond their petty selves, for each of them to attain such an intensity of altruism toward one other person that all of eternity *does* exist in the space of one shared thought.

He should have sent someone with more experience of the humans, someone who had already grown as bored with them as He. I tried to remain aloof, but I could not. What at first seemed to me human squalor has become human vibrancy. The cumbersomeness I first thought of as pathetically comic, I now see as endearing; and with what ingenuity they struggle to overcome their physical helplessness. And the violence of their emotions, once repugnant to me, is now elixir to my pallid soul.

Pallid no more. We all have free will, but we all must be prepared to take the consequences when we exercise it. I know what my consequence shall be: ejection. Like Lucifer before me—but at a much more frivolous level of rebellion—I shall be cast out. But not to join that greatest of dissenters in *his* dark sphere. No; the punishment for my defection will be suited to my crime. Do I love the humans so much? Then I will become one of them.

But first, I must save them.

43

Frank took the phone from the little blonde girl as though it was hot. Two seconds ago, he'd been ready to risk everything on one throw of the dice—if he got snuffed, that was okay; and if he was still around after he dumped over the professor's experiment he'd probably be so happy to be alive he might even *stand* the joint for one more tour—and now he was scared. *Now* he was scared; not before.

Into the phone, cautiously, as though the damn thing might bite him, he said, "Who's this?"

"Hello, Frank. Not doing too well, huh?"

It was her voice, all right, he remembered it clearly, and it evoked the picture of her the first time he'd ever seen her, getting out of her car after the blowout, standing there shaking with after-the-event jitters. The lady Nebraska lawyer, maybe thirty-five, tall and slender, with straight brown hair. The one that put the five-million-dollar-job idea in his head in the first place.

He said, "How in Christ's name did you know I was here?"

"Frank," she said, "I blame myself. When I said all that to you about the one big job, I didn't expect you to do anything like *this*."

"Am I blown?" he demanded. "Do they have a make on me out there?" Not that it really mattered any more; he just wanted to know.

Surprisingly, she said, "No. I'm the only one who knows it's you, Frank, and I want to—"

"How?"

"Oh, come on, Frank, what difference does it make? I know you people must be about ready to give up in there—"

Frank looked over at the experiment on the table, and grinned a little. "You could say that."

"You don't have to," she said. "Will you trust me, Frank?"

Why should he? On the other hand, why should he not? She'd treated him decently back in Nebraska, when he changed the tire for her, even tried to give him three hundred dollars to keep him from a life of crime. And if she was really the only one on the outside who knew a guy named Frank Hillfen was among the hijackers, then maybe she *was* trustworthy as far as he was concerned.

But, still. *Why* should she be reliable? What was in it for her? Frank said, "That depends. You want me to walk out there and give myself up?"

"No! That's the last thing I want you to do, Frank. Well; the next to the last thing."

"So what do you want?"

"I want you to convince Maria Elena to go on living, that's the first thing."

Frank was astonished all over again. "You know about *her*? *How?*"

"Frank," she said, sounding hurried and impatient, "I'm not going to answer any of those questions, so just stop asking them. I want you to convince her to live, Frank. Then you can leave Grigor in charge—"

"Leave?"

"The others are going to die anyway," she said, brisk and callous. "You and Maria Elena can live."

"In jail," he said bitterly.

"No. Listen to me, Frank. If you go outside and pass around the right cooling tower on the outside—not between the towers—you're going to see a radio mast on a mountain way ahead of you. If you walk straight toward that, when you come to the perimeter fence you'll find a small hole at the base of it, dug by animals."

"The fence is wired. They'll know when we go through."

"The switches are in the control section," she said. "Grigor can turn off the rear security area twenty minutes after you leave, then turn it back on ten minutes later. You'll have plenty of time to get through. Then you keep walking straight, and when you get to the county road there'll be a car parked there. No keys in it, but you can jump-start a car, can't you, Frank?"

"I don't get this," Frank said. His mind was swimming; this was James Bond time. How did she *know* all this stuff, if nobody else knew any of it? The only thing certain was that she wouldn't answer that question.

"I'm trying to make it up to you, Frank," Mary Ann Kelleny was saying, "for steering you wrong in the first place. Now, listen. If you can convince Maria Elena to come with you, then when you get clear away you'll find out that something happened two days ago that will see to it you never have to work again. You did like retirement, didn't you, Frank?"

Frank couldn't help it; his mouth twisted with sardonic disbelief: "Another five-mil hit?"

"Oh, you don't need that much, Frank," she said, as though they were just kidding around here together. "You do want to retire, don't you? With Maria Elena."

Frank looked over again at the funny-looking glass jug on the table; the professor's experiment. There's something truly weird going on here, he thought. *Truly* weird. His voice barely audible, he said, "You know a lot of stuff, don't you, Ms. Kelleny? You know what's happening here."

"Some," she said.

"And that thing's loaded, isn't it? It really *is* loaded."

There was a little silence. Then, "Don't bump into anything, Frank," Mary Ann Kelleny said. "On your way out." And she hung up.

44

The half of the telephone conversation that Grigor could hear made no sense. All he knew was, the exertion of the last hour had worn him down to only the smallest spark of self. But at the same time, this delay was taking from his resolve.

The idea of ending it with *everybody else;* how's that for the ultimate joke? No longer would I be an object of pity, of study, of embarrassment, of condescension. We're all in the same boat together, and the boat's at the bottom of the ocean. Yes, that was a good way to think of it: the ultimate joke on the human race.

But the phone call, the delay, the incomprehensibility of what Frank was saying, all served to confuse the issue in Grigor's mind. He found himself remembering Boris Boris, that aggressive comic bear, the only other man in the world who was entitled, the man who had appreciated and nurtured

Grigor's small talent, given him something to think about beyond his own imminent end. What would Boris Boris think of Grigor Basmyonov's last joke?

"Not funny, Grigor. You owe me some good jokes, or what the hell are you doing in my office?"

The doctors at the Bone Disease Research Clinic in Moscow; the doctors at the hospital just a few miles from here. Is this the way to settle their bills?

That's the problem with getting rid of everybody: there's nobody left.

What a group we are, he thought. Not one of us has any close living relative, nor anyone who deeply loves us. (A rueful thought of Susan crossed his mind.) And then we had this perfect meeting with the scientist, the coldly rational man who explained to us our own futility and shameful inadequacy, so that even we could see it.

A momentum was there, a readiness to *do* it, to risk the destruction of everything simply because we ourselves had already been destroyed. And who could blame us afterward? (Another joke.)

The phone call has broken that momentum. I am not the man I was three minutes ago. My revulsion from the human race does not include revulsion from certain humans. Boris Boris. Susan.

I don't think I can go through with it.

But what about Frank? Grigor watched him, trying to make sense of the phone call, and when it finished and Frank hung up the receiver and turned around, Grigor saw from his face that he too had changed. But in what direction?

Frank looked at the scientist. "It isn't fifty-fifty," he said.

The scientist's face was softer, more pliable, than when they'd first invaded his domain. His emotions now were more readily decoded there. And at this moment, Grigor saw, the scientist was torn, wasn't sure what to do. He strongly wanted to defend his beliefs, but not if doing so would lead to violence or destruction. And he'd lost some of his earlier assurance in his own theories. He stammered a little, under Frank's steady look, and then said, "Whatever the odds, I beg you not to do it."

So it really *is* the end of the world, Grigor thought, looking again at that bottle in the bright light. That's what's in there. It contains nothing that we can see, but it's a nothing that could make nothing of us all.

Frank was saying, "Maria, why don't we live to fight another day?"

Maria Elena responded with a haughty, angry look, stepping away from him, putting her hand on the crouched Pami's shoulder. "You *want* to live? In *this* world?"

"It's the only one we've got."

"We don't have it! *They* have it!"

"Maria," Frank said, "I think we just got a chance to pull ourselves out of this."

Grigor, pressing his palms onto his thighs to give himself the strength to speak, said, "*I* don't have a chance, you know. Neither does Pami."

Frank turned to him. His eyes looked very sure. He said, "Grigor, I could die twenty times, it wouldn't change what's gonna happen to you. You know that."

Grigor's eyes half closed as he considered, as he tried to find his place in this. He said, "But I am better testimony if I am here, in this plant. Alive or dead. There's no point in my making an escape."

"You're right about that," Frank agreed. "But staying behind, you could help Maria and me get clear."

Maria Elena said, "Frank? You've really changed your mind?"

He reached out for her hand, but she wouldn't let him have it yet. He said, "That thing over there, that's not suicide, that's killing everything forever, ending the whole story. Maria? You don't want to kill *everybody*."

"BUT I DO!"

The voice was Pami's, a terrible amplified crow-squawk. She lunged forward, away from Maria Elena's hand. She couldn't walk, but she could scramble on all fours, as quick as a crippled cat, scuttling toward the experiment on the table.

The Chinese kid, the lab assistant, launched himself at her, grabbing her arm and shoulder, pulling her back. Her head snapped around, teeth flashing.

Grigor stretched out a useless hand: "She has AIDS!"

The Chinese boy recoiled from that snarling, biting mouth. Pami lunged again for the table, but this time she'd pushed her body too far. Her torso arched, her bones jutted out against her clothes, and her mouth stretched wide as she curved impossibly backward. She managed one short scream, blocked by a gush of blood, and dropped to the floor, a thrown-away rag. A red halo of corrupt blood circled her head.

HAAA HA HA HA HA!

HA HAAAAAAAAAA! Oh, HA HA HA HA HA HA HA!

Come into my arms! Come into my arms! Come into my arms! I have *saved* you, my darlings, come into my arms, let us dance!

How we'll dance.

45

They walked through the parkland, silent at first, separate at first, just happening to walk more or less together in the same direction. They went for five minutes up the long gradual slope, past ornamental shrubs, specimen trees, small neat groves. A slight breeze rustled through leaves and pine needles above their heads. Birdsong established territory, called like to like, praised insects and worms.

They reached the top of a long ridge, and started down the other side, just as gradual, just as neatly cared for. After a minute, Maria Elena stopped and looked back and said, "You can't see it any more."

Frank turned and it was true; the slope blocked all view of the plant. "Good," he said. "Ugly thing anyway."

Turning in a slow circle, Maria Elena said, "You can't see anything from here, except that radio tower. Nothing else human. No buildings, nothing."

"Pretty good," Frank agreed. The air smelled sweet, like fresh corn you bring home from a farmstand.

"It's like the beginning of the world," Maria Elena said.

Suddenly remembering, Frank said, "Listen, Maria, it'll be the *end* of the world for us if we don't get to that fence pretty soon."

"Yes, of course."

She reached out her hand, and he took it, and they started walking again, picking up the pace. Soon, Maria Elena began to sing, in a clear strong voice, to the rhythm of their walking, the melody rising up into the trees, spreading out over the shaggy park all around them.

"Nice," Frank said, as she smiled at him and went on singing. He didn't understand the words, they were in some foreign language, but he understood the song.

Ahead, the fence.

Andy Harbinger

The car was not there when Frank and Maria Elena reached the county road. My powers had been removed from me by then. But I'd already distracted the national guardsmen, so they made their escape anyway, in the five hours before Grigor collapsed in the control section and Philpott phoned for assistance.

Frank's and Maria Elena's fingerprints were not found among those brought up by the police technicians in the control section and the lab. The various witnesses' descriptions of the two missing terrorists were so confused, with so many uncertainties and contradictions, as to be useless. When Kwan died in the hospital the day after the siege ended, and Grigor followed two days later, neither having given a statement, the last link to the missing terrorists was broken.

At home in Stockbridge, once she and Frank had made their way there, Maria Elena found on her answering machine a message from the local police. Fearing the worst, and with Frank already packing, she telephoned and was told that her husband, John, had been fatally shot two days before by a distraught woman named Kate Monroe, with whom he had apparently at one time had a relationship, but which he had recently ended. (I didn't do that; it was Kate's idea.) John's two-hundred-thousand-dollar insurance policy paid double indemnity; not the five-mil hit, but enough to keep Frank out of trouble.

Frank did spend one long frustrating day trying to find Mary Ann Kelleny's business card, which seemed to have disappeared from his wallet. (While he was talking to her on the phone, in fact.) Then he tried to find a lawyer named Mary Ann Kelleny through Omaha directory assistance. Then he gave it up. (You must understand, by then I had neither the time nor the inclination to try to cover my tracks. I simply had to get the job undone, and fast.)

Susan and I hurtle through our days. It doesn't seem to her that time literally flies, but I *know* it does.

Ah, but how I'm enjoying this brief life! And how bittersweet that paradox: the more you enjoy it, the faster it's gone.

I don't know what's happening otherwise; I mean with *His* plan. I might as well have always been human; except for the trailing tendrils of my scheme as it unraveled, I have no access at all, no link to that other sphere except my memories.

I wonder sometimes if my defection might have piqued His interest, might have made Him a little less bored with this particular Lego set, so that He will decide to keep it around a little longer. If not, there is undoubtedly another of my former fellows afoot in the land right now, gathering his people, planning his strategy. One chosen more carefully, one less sentimental and susceptible than I.

Is that messenger, that effectuator, unlikely to find another group who can stand in for us all—*us* all!—and who can be brought to believe that the end of everyone is the best solution to their own problems? Are there no disaffected people in this world?

And will the new holy one not find another catalyst, something perhaps to reduce the globe not to a ball bearing but to a burned-out clinker, endlessly revolving around the sun? Are there not yet great destructive forces to be found?

I don't know. I cannot say for sure what will happen, or what might happen, or when. I only know this: He doesn't give up easily.

PRIME CRIME
from
DONALD E. WESTLAKE

Multi-talented and award-winning Donald E. Westlake is acclaimed for his comic crime capers and tough hard-boiled fiction, as well as some very criminous science fiction. Hailed the *Los Angeles Times*, "He is a writer of uncommon talent, imagination, flair and unpredictability." Here are some of his best works.

- ☐ **TOMORROW'S CRIMES** 0-445-40917-7/$4.95 ($5.95 in Canada)
- ☐ **SACRED MONSTER** 0-445-40886-3/$4.95 ($5.95 in Canada)
- ☐ **TRUST ME ON THIS** 0-445 40807 3/$4.50 ($5.50 in Canada)
- ☐ **NOBODY'S PERFECT** 0-445-40715-8/$3.95 ($4.95 in Canada)
- ☐ **JIMMY THE KID** 0-445-40747-6/$3.95 ($4.95 in Canada)
- ☐ **DANCING AZTECS** 0-445-40717-4/$4.95 ($5.95 in Canada)
- ☐ *HELP!* **I AM BEING HELD PRISONER**
  0-445-40344-6/$4.50 ($5.50 in Canada)
- ☐ **TWO MUCH!** 0-445-40719-0/$4.95 ($5.95 in Canada)

The Mysterious Press name and logo are trademarks of Warner Books, Inc.

**Warner Books P.O. Box 690
New York, NY 10019**

Please send me the books I have checked. I enclose a check or money order (not cash), plus 95¢ per order and 95¢ per copy to cover postage and handling,* or bill my ☐ American Express ☐ VISA ☐ MasterCard. (Allow 4-6 weeks for delivery.)

___Please send me your free mail order catalog. (If ordering only the catalog, include a large self-addressed, stamped envelope.)

Card # _____

Signature _____ Exp. Date _____

Name _____

Address _____

City _____ State _____ Zip _____

*New York and California residents add applicable sales tax.   505